FOR THOSE WHO COM

Gary Raymond

FOR THOSE WHO COME AFTER

Gary Raymond

Parthian, Cardigan SA43 1ED
www.parthianbooks.com
© Gary Raymond 2015
ISBN 978-1-910409-93-0
Cover design by Dean Lewis
Typeset by Elaine Sharples
Printed and bound by lightningsource.com
Published with the financial support of the Welsh Books Council
British Library Cataloguing in Publication Data
A cataloguing record for this book is available from the British Library.

To Grandad

PROLOGUE

June, 1999

Claus Julius was my lifeline. He didn't sound like the great emancipator down the phone, and he looked far from it in person, tall and grave on the doorstep; but he was all I had. I could feel the paycheque slipping away as each day passed until I took his call. I had been hired to write a biography of Ki Monroe – poet, visionary, satirist, enigma. *Enigma*, by God: there were chasmal holes in his story! Dead ends and misted decades the like of which I had not previously encountered. He was a man of whom the myth heavily outweighed the facts. I had always assumed that's why his estate had hired a journalist to write the book rather than an academic, a poetry professor from deep in the dusty halls. There was legwork to be done. They weren't to know the legwork would count for little as well.

I was at the edge of reason. Monroe did *this*, Monroe did *that*; there was a minor scandal or two, forgotten poetry, times past. He was a Bloomsbury outcast; was in Spain during the war; retired to a fishing village in Portugal when barely into middle age to farm and cast his net; died in nineteen fifty. The advance was handsome, the story was not.

Claus Julius caught me in my office on a typically moribund day. I was tired, snappy, preparing to face the reality of my predicament more as every day went by. Our first conversation went something like this:

"You're an American?"

"Canadian," I said. "What can I do for you, Mr Julius?"

"I understand," he said. "I am Austrian. People assume I am a German always."

1

"I was just on my way out," I said.

"Mr Buren used to say that sooner or later you realise everybody is from somewhere else."

"Is that right?" I said.

"He used to say everybody is looking for adoption. What brings *you* to London?"

"It was *you* who called *me*, Mr Julius; and I don't have much time."

I could hear him sucking his teeth.

"You are writing a biography of Ki Monroe, are you not?"

"I am," I said. "And how can I be of help?"

"Are you finding it a difficult task? Frustrating?"

"It's all part of the process, Mr Julius."

This was my fifth biography: two movies stars, an aeronautical pioneer, a race car driver and now a poet.

"As I thought. Then you may be interested to see something that I have. My former employer, Mr Harold Buren, wrote a memoir. He knew Mr Monroe well."

"That name is not familiar to me," I said.

I looked across my study at the wall I had papered with little sticky notes; names, dates, events, in tasselled patterns of disjointed yellow shadow – a sight that had come to look more and more like a final curtain.

"It is not a name familiar to many. My former employer was a very private man."

"This Mr Buren is no longer with us, I take it? No longer able to speak with me personally?"

"Sadly Mr Buren passed away some years ago."

"And I don't know anything about this memoir, Mr Julius. I have read everything ever written on Monroe, twice over."

"Oh, dear; you misunderstand. It has not been published. I have the only manuscript under lock and key."

I opened the browser on my laptop.

"So how did your employer and Monroe know each other?" I said.

"They first met, so I understand, in the mid-nineteen thirties."

I typed Harold Buren's name into the search engine.

"So he was part of the Soho crowd?"

"He knew them," said Julius.

What came up on the browser was a surprising and suspicious lack of information. But there was a photograph. Harold Buren. A serious face, handsome, clean, long; his eyes were conspicuously blank, unsympathetic, but bold; it seemed to be a close-up from a group photo. Buren was a South African, like Monroe. His father died young and his mother brought the family to London. It seemed as if the cause of his wealth was, essentially, war; some speculative investment or other by his father in American armament firms and they hit the jackpot in nineteen fourteen. Harold Buren inherited these investments, had an astute mind for business and slowly added to his portfolio with gold and more arms. He never married. Never had children. Died in nineteen eighty four and left his money to an educational trust in Spain. There was nothing else.

"It seems your Mr Buren would be an even more difficult subject to write about than my Mr Monroe," I said.

"Not if you read the manuscript I have," said Julius.

I thought for a moment. There is a point in these things when going deeper is the only way on offer.

"Why was this memoir never published?" I said.

"Mr Buren did not write it for publication. He wrote it as testament."

"Testament to whom?"

"Mr Buren was the last person to see Mr Monroe alive."

That had my attention: Monroe's death. As enigmatic an exit as you might expect. His body never found.

3

"What do you mean he was the last person to see Monroe alive?" I said.

There was a pause; Julius sucked his teeth once more.

"It is not for me to say," said Julius. "You need to read the manuscript."

It got me to the house. Claypole: an enormous white Georgian building in central London. Julius was a tall man, old but fit, straight, but – and so confident was he around the halls of the house it was not immediately obvious – he was almost completely blind. I knew that his myopia was not absolute as he knew where to put his hand when I held out mine, but he held his head high, tilted back, and his pupils were a wintry grey. He explained his blindness as being only a slight concern at birth, and that it crept over him, through him, as the decades went on. His final blindness, he said, would be at the moment of death. He had been closing down since the day he was born, he said.

He was aging, now perhaps in his mid-seventies. Harold Buren had left him a small fortune (a pinprick into Buren's actual worth), as well as the house in which we stood, and as he felt it difficult to work for anyone else in the same capacity after Buren had died, he retired on his money and indulged in his hobby of restoring old books. I asked how a man with his particular impairment could carry out such delicate work. He said that he had steady hands and all the time in the world.

His study, on the ground floor, was lined with glowing old spines of forgotten tomes on every subject, from seventeenth century botany, to census documents, novels, journals, science manuals and ornithological sketch books, even Kama Sutras.

Julius had a steadiness to him that suggested he was more than able at his tasks – more able than a seeing man. Every movement was considered, a method that almost amounted to a sixth sense. Within the walls of the house that entombed him was a world of its own rules. There was a professional spirit, I figured, hanging over from his days as a valet, always having to be at hand, a man machine attuned to the atmosphere of the room. He had modified the design for this peacefulness into an artful attention to detail, to restoration – he could never fully appreciate the work he did on these books, and yet he didn't seem to have anyone else in mind.

He presented me with the Buren manuscript as if it was a sacred text and, at first inspection, inside was an example of delicate penmanship. The script was hand-written, hundreds and hundreds of pages without so much as a single alteration or blemish.

"This is the final draft?" I said.

"It is the *only* draft," said Julius. "Mr Buren was painstaking in its composition. It had to be a pure truth, you see."

"Could I take it?" I said.

"No," said Julius, softly. "But I will permit you to read it and make hand written notes. Here."

I'll admit, as I looked down at it, cast my eyes across several passages, it did not strike me as a breezy read.

"It may take some time," I said.

"There are plenty of rooms. You are welcome to be my guest."

A cavernous fatigue prevented me from negotiating the script out of Julius' possession, and I'm not sure I would have got anywhere even on top form.

I was still looking at Julius with a sideways glance. The whole encounter seemed from another era – he was dressed in a pin-striped three-piece suit with a fob chain, and yet, by his own admission, he spent most of his days alone in his big old house leaning over dilapidated manuscripts, carefully bringing them back from the dead, feeling his way through their scars.

He motioned for me to follow him and led me to a room up several flights of stairs and, placing his hand on the doorknob looked over his shoulder in my direction, his grey eyes like those of a snake, and he said, "This was Mr Buren's study for much of his later years."

We entered. Julius moved easily about the room lighting it by switching on the various and many lamps. The room was large, the walls of a deep, regal burgundy; towering columnal curtains hid tall narrow windows – it was like a gallery of a long lost era, an era of empires and ball gowns, but in place of young sharply dressed soldiers and beautiful debutantes were mismatched sofas and armchairs, all piled with loose papers and books and magazines. And in the centre of the room was a desk.

"There is no disputing Mr Buren's wealth," said Julius; "though some may have questioned his sanity toward the end. But I was the only one to be with him for those times. I protected him from intrusions. Toward the end, you see, Mr Buren was plagued by ideas of truth and recompense. He wrote his memoir to try and clear his head. He was a good man; but I always thought he carried a great weight. He spoke to me about these things. He felt he failed his brother. He felt he had wronged Mr Monroe. He felt that all his life he misplaced his energies. He was gifted with the most valuable commodity in human existence: time. He outlived everyone who meant anything to him. He was rich beyond reason. And yet he felt he had failed in everything because he had wasted his time."

It was a well-prepared, if odd, speech which Julius delivered with a round chest and a certain oratorical gravity.

On Buren's desk was a stack of charcoal drawings – a young woman's face, over and over again, from slightly different angles, but the same expression.

"Who is this?" I asked.

"I would imagine it is his brother's wife if you mean the drawings?" said Julius.

I looked through them all. A beautiful woman, she looked relaxed but serious, a labyrinthine glint to her eye, a downturn to the mouth, she was held up in a deeply-dug charcoal background.

Julius' intentions were grander and more central than he had first let on, I figured. Harold Buren was not just a former employer; Julius lived in his master's house, and had kept his study as a shrine even fifteen years after the old billionaire had died.

"This all seems a little like another project," I said.

"You don't know what that book is going to tell you about Mr Monroe," said Julius. "I took employment with Mr Buren in nineteen sixty five. I was the only staff member. He spent much of his time in this study. Toward the end I often came in at the sound of him talking, as if to someone, but I knew there was nobody with him. He talked to me often about his brother, and about Mr Monroe.

"One day, he returned home from a business trip – it would turn out to be his last trip, in fact; he stayed very much within these four walls after that – he told me that he was going to write a memoir, and that I must take each page and keep it safe, and safe from *him* so that he had no way of revising his memories and his thoughts. I always believed that he trusted me entirely, but that it was my blindness that he trusted, rather than my character. He wrote this for the sake of committing it to paper, I believe. It is there to explain and to teach lessons."

"Lessons? To whom?"

"That I do not know," said Julius. "He was careful to be vague about such notions."

"So why do you want me to see it now?"

Julius seemed to soften, his mouth gave up its punctiliousness, and he even allowed his hands to loosen from their dutiful tensions.

"I am old," he said. "Part of me also would like to know what is in it. Part of me would like to know the truth of the man I dedicated myself to. I suppose we all have these moments of redress late in life."

We came to an arrangement, Julius and I; and I returned to the house to spend my time examining the manuscript, to spend my time with the careful and strangely fresh hand-written memoirs of Harold Buren.

The words and testament of Harold Buren

FOR THOSE WHO COME AFTER

THE VELDT

When I was a child I talked to dragons, and they told me all about the future.

There was a time when they wandered the countryside, graceful and prodigious, but by the time I was around they spent most of the time in the mountains across the veldt, only coming down when they had something to say, or I had something ask.

"You will have to keep an eye on things," they said.

They circled me. I was dust to them, with a muss of dirty blonde hair and my grey short-trousers.

"Don't worry about the great battles to come," said one of them.

"You just worry about the great silences between," said another.

I didn't know what they meant. But one does not answer back to dragons; that much my father told me. The creatures of myth are older than us all, he said. Before I was born he hung around my mother's neck a pendant, known as The Dragon's Eye, made from the first diamond he ever dug out of the ground. It was to remind us where we were from – from the earth, our wealth and our souls. It was to remind us of the importance of that thing we are all born from: *truth*.

I am here now at the other end of my life. And I'll tell you what I know about *truth*; and what I know about myth also. I will do it because, even though I have never known you, I love you. I want to tell you the things that I know; the things you should know.

I saw my century as something best forgotten. I worked hard to forget. As somebody once wrote, I concentrated on "inviting quicker the inevitable inconspicuousness of yesteryear". But, it seems, at the point of this welcomed oblivion I had to fight it off in order to remember once again. And the first thing I remembered was the dragons of my distant childhood. And then the pendant. Games and trinkets. Monsters and trinkets. Perhaps as good a title for a memoir as any.

What sparks this? The *great occasion*. Everybody who is lucky enough to experience one should take the time to document it. My great occasion was long awaited. And now I am here in my home – back from Spain and all those circles squared – I will make my document.

Remembering must involve unlearning what I know to be right. Forgetting, when intended, is the most difficult of tasks. A life of knowing, watching, listening to the birds of every colour sing; and I gave it up for the good of all. But now I need to remember. I need to remember for you. I need to remember for good. You are my redemption and my final punishment. But I bow to the knowledge that I must tell the story for those who come after. You are my centre point, my audience, my apostle-if-you-wish. It is you who are the meaning of it all.

* * *

The Childe Harold Buren. *Formed or fabled at the minstrel's will!*

I was a bright child, I think. I was forced to indulge myself because nobody else would. I played the knight in armour in the furthest stretches of the veldt, like Don Quixote, far at the other reach of life's bookends of senility. It is not senility in a toddler. *Imagination*, perhaps. *Play*. I can tell you all about *play*, too. When I told my father I had encountered dragons in the scrubland he told me to treat them with respect, to not interrupt them, and he returned to hammering at the fence post. I might have told him I'd spoken to devils, or witches, and he would have said the same thing. A modest, tight, condensed existence – the veldt was my world for those first six years. I see it, all those decades ago, no different to captions of film. I see myself as a character in a frame.

I have spent much of my life blowing dust over my footprints. You will find very little written about me anywhere. There are some people of extreme wealth who float about above it all like undetected gods. I was one of them to an extent. I had my interests in walking amongst the hedgerows, though.

I am not trying to impress you; I am trying to save you time. You will not find me in any annals or encyclopaedias. You will find words that amount to little more than gossip, words that begin unsure and taper off to nothing. I have always dealt in silence as the most powerful currency. You will find many estimations of my wealth – but you already know about that. Its substantiveness is not in dispute.

You will find out I was born in South Africa, on a farm some miles from Durban. You may be able to find a date of birth. Nineteen hundred and eight. (I forget the exact day; I have not celebrated a birthday since I was a boy). You will find I grew up and was educated in London and that I have called England my home ever since I was six years old. I still live in the house I grew up in.

Claypole is a grand Georgian town house built for the richest of merchants in the early part of the nineteenth century. In the 1860s it was home to a famous botanist who named it, and turned the top floor into a museum of dried exotic fauna and taxidermic birds and rodents (his *sideways* hobby, according to his biography, which I read when very young). The doctor went on many foreign expeditions culminating in several years at sea investigating antipodean climes. His early life was dogged by his naive claims to have discovered the carcass of a phoenix, and the egg of a griffin. He grew to learn to keep his mouth closed tight about such things. He rescued his reputation in inches over time, a testament to hard graft and the supercilious forgetfulness of his peers, and he eventually experienced minor success as an expert in birds' nests. But Claypole had proved too large for his progeny and they gave it up whilst leaving *his* mark – the stagnant zoo. I remember the peculiar glass cases in the attic, creatures frozen in natural poses, death trapped in life.

Claypole has high ceilings and expensive tiles and ornate bannisters that curl up and out of the hallway. The rooms are solid and square, and have the capaciousness of Regency apartments. The library on the first floor is full and grand. Claypole pines with the ages of elegance; that is one reason why I could never let it go.

I write now in the dark fire-lit room that used to be my mother's study. I can picture her in her finest days, looking out the window, or writing at this desk. I hunch over it. I scratch at the paper with my pen, like a short-sighted engraver of tombs. Matilda, my mother, was never so ungraceful. She was tough – the veldt would not allow you to be anything else – but she was forcefully exquisite. She spent quite some energy on her poise; she was practiced and pointed. She had strong edges like a coastline, embattled and aged in the aeons. What was beyond those edges was a little more difficult to discover. She grew tougher when my father died, closed in, compressed like the collapsed mouth of a cave. Claypole, dark now, warren-like, groans with her floating image. And the images of many others.

It is these ghosts who remind me I am Harold Buren first and foremost, and it is neither important nor irrelevant that I exist. I am midway. I am clean *and* defiled. But now maybe, in the most unlikely chapters of my life, I can do some good by telling you my story. Explain my cold, luxurious deficiencies in the hope that you may learn something of yourself. The story will be done with the writing of the thing and I will give what life I can to those who are gone, those who I wish you could have known. My brother Piers, Matilda, and of course, most importantly, Bess. And I will tell the truth about Ki Monroe. It is time that I put it all down and missed nothing, and no-one, out. It is time that I gave them all their space. I will give the past its due.

And I can see now how this must be done: I must begin at the beginning.

* * *

I am six years old, round-faced, I have long but reluctant arms and an inelegant lurching walk. I am tall for my age but able to be invisible. I would have been a difficult child for any mother to love, as the saying goes. My hair is always thick with dust and my skin is a deep burnt yellow. I speak very little. I make barely any noise at all these first few years. I regurgitate words during my spelling tests and that is that. I am spectral, inconsequential, lumpen yet ephemeral, a graceless ghost about the whispering deathlessness of the veldt.

I used to play on the porch as the sun ducked down; the courtyard in front of the house would turn a deep orange, as if the sun was swallowing the farm. Father had made me a model biplane out of leftover strands of timber, painted, I remember with the blue and red emblems of the Royal Air Force, and I was making figure eights in the air with it when my eye caught the kick of dust in the far distance, way away in the flat sandy dirt fields.

This kick of dust, like a snag in a carpet, moved through the enormous wide silence of the veldt. I knew what the image meant; it meant someone was riding quickly toward the farm. My father, John Buren, often rode slowly, carefully; he cared for the feet of his horses, and for the price of shoeing them. My arm stopped the swirls. Something about the scene was not right, and I moved to the edge of the veranda. I could see that it was Belky, the foreman of the farm, a big wide-shouldered Indian, riding with his crop high, toward the house. I put the plane on the floor, went inside and stood facing the doorway from the shadow of a corner by the stairs. I waited for the sound of the horse's hooves as they bit down onto the hard dry courtyard floor and I heard Belky hurriedly dismount and his big boots clamber onto the hollow wood of the porch. Belky stood tall before me, the whites of his eyes, glistening, horrible and burning, his figure steady and filling the doorway, behind him the dust and the wilderness.

"Where is your mother?" he said.

I made no sound.

Belky was young and powerful, a muscular inverted pyramid of a man. He liked to smile at me with his yellowed teeth when he knew no other adults were watching – he liked to maintain his burly presence in their company. But he was a playful giant who spent his long hard days far away from his own children. This time he did not smile down at me. He went off into the house. I didn't know what was wrong but Belky rarely came into our home, and he never looked frightened. There was not a sound, I remember; even the chattering dusk creatures were on hold.

Within moments Belky had found Matilda and in a pale panic she was out of the door and away on horseback, Belky catching up with her on his horse. I moved back out of the shadow and watched them shrink into the distance from the porch.

The silence shuddered and withered and my baby brother began to wail from his cot in the parlour. I went and stood just inside the room, my feet cold on the wood. Baby Piers cried and screamed, but it soon exhausted him. He sighed, spluttered and began chirping, chatting gurgled nonsense to himself.

It occurred to me then that Piers and I were alone in the house for the first time. Matilda did not like me being around the baby. I took a few steps closer, softly, and peered over the cot and baby Piers saw me immediately.

He had large brown eyes, glassy like our father's; his brow was old and creased. I slowly put my hand into the cot and my little brother took my finger and pushed it and pulled it like a lever. He felt cool, and the skin of his tiny hand crumpled around me like crepe paper. I examined his form; this featureless, shrunken person, who was yet to grow into his sagging skin. He was just four months old, and seemed to have a happy, secretive existence at Matilda's chest. I had been watching them communicate with their cooing and chirping ever since he came into the house. They had their own language, and I had none at all. Matilda had no time for me; she addressed me very much as one of the servants, in short declarative sentences. She approached me with sturdy steps, and she gazed at me with a cold curious glare. And our father was a silence as wide as the veldt. *As quiet as God*. One of Matilda's sayings.

He sat at the dinner table with a blank expression, a weathered face. He would occasionally run his hand over my head, through my thick unkempt hair, but would withdraw his hand quickly as if remembering the disease of touch, the guilt of contact.

Our father was a cut-out, an avatar for his absent intent. I did not know until many years later that he had fought at the bloody mess of the Spion Kop. I did not know that the world was made up of days that sat upon mounds of human corpses. I did not know that then. I did not know that my father had fought in wars. I did not even know he had been a soldier. He was a gunner, an aficionado of armaments, in fact. But I do not know anything else about him. I don't know if he loved me, or Piers, or even if he loved Matilda. I do not know if he would have been proud or ashamed by what his country became. Had he lived he would have been an old man by the time Verwoerd was elected, that grizzled scrofulous professor of hatred. Perhaps my father would have been a Nazi just like Verwoerd had been. But perhaps it was not his way to favour one race over another. I remember John Buren being as curt and detached with the blacks who worked our farm as he was with anybody else. No special treatment for anybody. We were all down low at the end of my father's regards.

I think a person needs to know certain things about their father. You need to know your father's politics; about what sways him. My lack of politics, my distrust of the devout and the cynics alike, perhaps comes from this void. To not know one's father is a void, an imperishable silence, and the void pushes up and out of you all your life. I did not know this – I did not know that this shadow of mine was cast by an absence. It is natural to wonder how life might have turned out had my father not died that day. We would have remained a family in the veldt, for sure; I would have grown up in the nooks and crannies of the farmhouse that I already knew so well and maybe something more useful would have come of me.

Belky and Matilda were gone for hours. Matilda walked slowly, her face blank but used-up, and she came into the parlour where I was sitting rocking baby Piers to sleep in his cot. She came close and placed her hand on the rail next to mine, looked down at Piers and smiled sadly. Then she looked down at me and I saw her face straighten.

"You go off to bed now," she said.

I hopped down from the chair and trotted out of the room into the hallway. Belky was motionless by the scullery door. We looked at each other in silence as Matilda slowly closed the parlour door, shutting herself in there with Piers who had begun to cry again.

"Why don't you come in the kitchen with me, Master Harold," said Belky. "Let's see if Cook has left you milk and biscuits."

I followed Belky's gesture. He went to the pantry, poured a glass of milk and put it on the table with some of Cook's freshly baked buttery biscuits and sat next to me.

"I need to tell you something," he said. "I have some bad news. I'm afraid your father has died."

I said nothing. I don't think I felt anything. I didn't realise, perhaps, that this meant little would ever be the same again.

"Do you know what that means, Master Harold?"

I looked into Belky's large lucent eyes.

"It means he won't be coming home," he said.

There was a long pause between us before Belky, looking to the ceiling, licking his lips, and then looking back to me, said, "Do you have any questions?"

I shook my head.

"Then I suppose you should get off to bed."

I nodded, jumped down off the chair and went to my room leaving Belky alone in the kitchen with the silence and the darkness.

The next day that silence around the farm was broken by visitors coming to pay their respects to Matilda the widow. I watched them come and go from my bedroom window, and later, when the heat was at its height, I watched them from the spot by the pigpen, where I could see everything and nothing looked back.

* * *

Time, after my father's death, lost its function, lost its form. Matilda did not sleep, and she did not expect her sons to keep regular hours either. She was often in white, great folds of lace; she was never without the Dragon's Eye pendant that hung around her neck.

This pendant, she would whisper to Piers in the ochre light and red darkness of the farmhouse, this first diamond John Buren lifted from the earth, this was the family soul, the spirit of our blood. It was forged to remind the us that everything we had came from the dirt. It was as much a part of her as the veins beneath her skin; swaying, catching even the dullest of light in a sparkle of phantasmagoria. She said it is what made us African, but she meant it was what made us *Boers*; that we took from the earth without a spiritual bone in our bodies, and it is what gave us eternity, an umbra of soul and spirit. We ingested from the mother soil. The blacks had a connection to the ground us Boers, at best, were suspicious of. Mainly they were hated for it, mocked for it. *Never underestimate the affairs of other races*, is what the lesson boiled down to. We will all be won over by the craving for explanations in the end. We will find our own faiths, our own mythologies. The Dragon's Eye pendant dangled from her neck like a crucifix, like a vial of the Saviour's blood.

Matilda was awash with strange declarations like this in the period after my father's passing. Awash with the habits of a lunatic awaiting the moon.

Each morning Belky would ride up to the farm and address the gathered farmhands, handing out their duties for the day, just as father had done when he was alive. I thought this was to be life. I did not even know I would one day grow up to be a man. Nobody had ever explained this to me. I thought

23

nothing, but if I had done it would have been that creatures maintain their form, and that everything else was witchcraft.

I was left to live, or to die if that is what God wanted for me. Matilda walked around me as if I was draught of air. Cook would feed me. Belky would make sure I was out of bed and I was clean – clean of a *sort*, anyway. Indeed, Belky was coming into the house every day now. Matilda, who never had anything good to say about the coloureds, and certainly not the blacks, had no objection. Most of her time was spent sitting in the parlour with Piers in her arms, rocking back and forth, whispering to him in thick grey Afrikaans.

A month or so after our father had been buried – Matilda had not allowed me to attend the funeral – a man came to the farm. Short, balding, his fob watch chain kept catching the deep orange light of the setting sun and sparking into my line of vision. I was unnoticed, drawing with crayons – my dragons most likely; I must have sketched thousands in my childhood – on the sill of the small corner window of the parlour. I heard the man introduce himself as Viktor Rasmussen senior, and he clipped his heels and bowed his head as he said it. Matilda, in her white lace dress and gloves had shown him into the parlour and offered him a seat with his back to the window.

"You say you have news about my late husband's accounts," she said with a stern face, and took the seat opposite him. They both sat in the centre of the room, oddly positioned, formal, presentational.

"There are some complications with a few of his investments," said Rasmussen.

"I don't understand," said Matilda.

"How much did you know about your husband's business affairs?"

Rasmussen dipped into his briefcase and took out a paper

file bound with red ribbon. Matilda watched carefully as he undid the tie and opened the file on his lap.

"Could we get to the point, Mr Rasmussen?" she said.

Rasmussen took a pencil from his breast pocket and dabbed the nib on his tongue.

"Your husband had made considerable investments in Shukor, Davenport and Sinden."

Matilda began to blink, her hands held tightly to her knees.

"I don't know who that is," she said.

"*Them*," said Rasmussen. "They are three of the largest engineering firms in the United States."

"So what does that mean? What did John know about engineering?"

"Well, I don't know about that," said Rasmussen, "but he had a keen eye for *war*, it seems. These three companies have recently secured armament contracts with the British government. Initial forecasts project an increase in profits of around a hundred and fifty per cent. Expect that to increase several fold if, as expected, there is war in Europe. After all, why would the British need these contractors if it wasn't all but certain?"

Matilda leaned forward.

"You knew nothing about these investments?" Rasmussen said.

"How much?" Matilda said.

"Well, it's difficult to tell," said Rasmussen, flicking through the yellow sheaves of the file. "Two million dollars. Expect that to be twenty in times of war. Sixty if the war lasts five years. More if America gets involved. Your husband invested in prototypes, Mrs Buren. Their time has come."

Matilda stood – she was tall, straight, an Elgin marble with erratically-pinned hair. She walked around the room, and then she put her hand to her mouth. She spun and faced the little bald Rasmussen.

"You said there was a complication," she said.

"Yes," said Rasmussen. "Obviously, your husband expected to live to a grand old age, with you at his side in sickness and in health."

Matilda glided toward him and stood over him in the darkness of the room. Rasmussen said, "The shares in these three companies pass on to your son, Harold. The child."

And that was when, as if drawn by an unseen force, Matilda's eyes set on me for the first time, tucked into the shadows on the sill, as if she had known I was there all along. I remember that look even now, her eyes as sharp as if she had shot bullets at me.

It was barely six months later that Matilda announced the family would be moving to London.

***

London brayed with congestion.

I had never seen a true city before. Durban was flat, splayed, and I had only ever equated it with the promise of a city – my mind had always envisioned Troy and Thebes and Mycenae from the books I had read, and Durban was none of these places. London, however, disregarded such ideas, and was like a giant termite mound, crawling, rumbling with other lives, hissing with the wider mind. I had not known the world could be like this. Reading books, and even looking at the cities on the shore as we made our way to Southampton from South Africa, could not have prepared me for being in the midst of it. I must have been open-mouthed for a month.

We were met at the harbour by Mr Algernon Radnor, a distant associate of my father's, who had offered to find Matilda a house in the city. He was an uneven man, not without charm, who had a textiles business somewhere in the north of England where he lived most of the year with his family. My mother instructed early on that I should call him Uncle Algie, but I continued to call him nothing at all. He curved to look down to me and he smiled with a crooked, smooth-cheeked alacrity that I just did not trust.

Algie Radnor – Uncle Algie – took us to the house. Claypole was momentous then. If I had imagined civilisation to be an ancient palace, Claypole could be the House of Atreus – the curses yet to come.

"I thought you'd like this, Harold; seeing as you're the Lord of the Manor," said Algie.

I took no notice; but Matilda did not find the joke funny.

Inside the house was chasmic, with deep hallways, high arching ceilings in bright white, colonnades and heavy sheened tiles. The staircase opposite the door stretched up and out like

27

dragon's wings. The furniture was covered in white sheets. It was to be my palace, I thought, innocently. It was large enough to be a world for me all of its own. And so it proved.

"You have done a good job, Mr Radnor; this will do us fine," said Matilda.

Algie Radnor had also organised staff for the house. A cook, a butler and a maid. They arrived the next day and stationed themselves around the house much in the same way furniture was. The butler, Mr Champion, was an aging, half-deaf, snap-toothed man who walked with a dignified stoop. The cook, like Cook at the farmhouse, was large, rolly, but white, jolly but preoccupied. The maid, Clara, was a pale, sad-faced young girl of sixteen who curtsied softly at every opportunity. She spoke to me often, asked me about the games I played. I had never had a friend before.

"Are you shy or has the cat got your tongue?" she would say.

But I was, in truth, ashamed of my accent. I had not heard its like since leaving South Africa. As the weeks went on, and school term approached, I spent hours in front of the mirror trying to shape my mouth like the English did – I spent much time examining the lips of the servants as they spoke. I think Mr Champion thought I was of simple mind, because I was always staring at him as he gave out instructions. Matilda told me that I needed to wear eye glasses. I was not immediately sure what she meant, and when she explained, snapping impatiently at my blankness, I was confused as to why I would need them. My eyesight was perfect, I thought. Matilda was adamant that I would need them for school. And I was given large, cumbersome, black-framed spectacles. My ears ached from their weight, and I stopped mouthing my vowels in the mirror. I avoided mirrors altogether for a time.

Clara began to act as nanny to me and to baby Piers. She

would take me for walks in the park; but only when Piers needed fresh air would Matilda accompany us, walking at the side of the perambulator, her big hand draped over the side. She was tall, Matilda; almost top-heavy. Clara once giggled in confidence to me that, "She walks like she was a fete attraction being pushed along on a float". I thought she looked like a Holy Mother icon, carried through a festival, unsteady and sacred. And people – strangers – would wave to her, come up and take her hand, kiss it as if she were royalty. Walking in the park became a chore, a bore, stopping all the time for Matilda's tributes. Those armament contracts had made real money for the Buren family – none of this diamond fakery; no more digging wealth from the dirt. War had brought heavy money.

It was decided we would cut back on the walks and play mainly in the cavernous adventureland of Claypole. The rooms were all square and under-furnished, except for Matilda's parlour on the second floor – later to be the study in which I now write these pages. This room was cluttered with furnishings attached to her memory; items she had brought from the farm, items that tied her to the past.

I watched a lot as a child, and I went largely unnoticed. And don't think for a moment this was not how I liked it – it had advantages that suited both my character and my position within the house.

I watched visitors – they all looked like smaller versions of Matilda in their lace and large hats. I watched the servants. I often watched Matilda sitting near the window with Piers in her lap – just as on the farm, only this was well-lighted now, and the noises of the London bustle came in through an open window. She reading aloud, Piers – hardly a person yet – dribbling and pulling gently at the corner of the page with his chubby fingers.

"Harold, what are you doing loitering? That is an awful habit. Off with you to your studies."

Clara would come and gather me up as if she had been looking for me, the little troublemaker, all this time. She would curse under her breath as she led me away by the hand along those high-ceilinged corridors and through the sweet damp air of the never-used rooms.

Claypole has always been a quiet house, full of the silence of loneliness, the song of poetry often subdued by the long heavy hours of nothingness. I think of it now, in my old age, in my halted decline, as a time trap. I wonder if Claypole is the thing that has kept me alive; long enough to outlive everyone I ever loved, but long enough to perhaps give you guidance and emotional riches. I can look over to that window from my desk, mottled by the memory of Matilda's figure, her wide shoulders and strong jaw, her mousy hair tightly bound; my brother – the whirlwind of my quiet plains – in her arms. How can I reach out to a ghost if we are all ghosts of different times, each of us lurching away from our present? I realise now, hopefully before it is too late, that we should be reaching forward.

But I only know, like the common man that I am beneath this wealth, how to affect the future by drawing on the past. So I will get on with the story. The beginning of the end of Matilda comes about now, as does the seed of the union that set everything in motion.

I was sitting on the floor of my bedroom, drawing crayoned scenes from the *Iliad* on large sheets of coarse paper, Clara kneeling opposite, her pretty neck curved toward my work, watching, both of us in silence but for breath. Matilda appeared at the doorway. Clara, her face quickly hardening and her eyes draining of light, clambered ungainly to her feet and stood to attention. I turned and looked up at my mother;

she was like an alabaster golem, enormous to me in the frame of the door. Matilda looked at Clara, about to castigate her for laziness or some such, and then she looked at me on the floor. She put one hand on her hip, her large fingers crawling around the bulb of her joint.

"Pack some things," she said. "For you and him. We're going away for a few weeks."

And she was gone, back into the shadow of the hallway.

Clara slowly, incrementally relaxed, her shoulders unknotted. She looked down at me and smiled with a forced warmth.

We had been invited to holiday with Algie Radnor.

* * *

The Radnors enjoyed a comfortable middle-class life.

Every summer they spent a few months at their cottage in the Black Mountains of mid-Wales, and this year, as an act of something disguised as charitable outreach, although we wanted for nothing materially, and Matilda largely detested company of any sort apart from that of baby Piers, we had been invited to visit them.

The weather there was as warm as back in Durban, but it was light, a pleasant breeze carried gentle clicking, a twirping country sound.

As the car pulled up to the cottage – a snug, portly stone building with a thatched roof like an ill-fitting wig – I wound down the stiff window and sucked in the cut-grass air, the warm pollen and distant light whiff of fresh manure.

The Radnors were stood on the doorstep waiting for our arrival, waving: Algie Radnor and his wife Sarah holding her new-born little girl, and the two boys, Michael and Matthew, smart and clean and high-nosed; the dog, Shiner, a collie, sitting obediently at Algie's feet.

Algie ruffled my untidy mop of hair.

"How's my boy?" he said, and I scrunched my nose in protest at his attention.

Matilda pressed me on the shoulder.

"Assist Clara by taking one of the bags inside," she said.

I picked up the smallest bag that the chauffeur, with his hefty brown gauntlets, had unloaded from the car, and struggled with it to the house, past the Radnors, who paid me no attention. Sarah Radnor looked on with her pale pink eyes and boyish sombre plainness.

I walked into the musty dankness of the cottage and thumped the luggage at the foot of the stairs. It reminded me of the old farmhouse a little; the lighting, the softness of the wood, the corners and the dust. The others came in behind, Piers wide-eyed and bird-like in Matilda's arms.

"I'm so glad you accepted our invitation," Algie was saying.

Sarah Radnor walked obediently behind her husband and his guest. She was a sullen presence, much younger than Algie, and I remember her as having the air of someone who had given herself up meekly to a functional existence.

"I was quite glad to receive your letter," said Matilda.

"And how is London?" said Algie.

"It will do," said Matilda.

I moved into the kitchen, and Clara, who had been taking the rest of the luggage up to the guest rooms, came in and stood in the doorway as if awaiting instruction, trying her utmost to conceal her shortness of breath.

"You brought your maid?" said Algie, as if Clara was an object to be commented upon, like a drab painting in a gallery.

"That boy needs watching," Matilda said dismissively waving a hand in my general direction.

"Sarah," Algie called out of the kitchen to his wife. "Bring the baby in."

He turned to Matilda, who stood over him, and gave her a mischievous grin. He looked at Piers and pinched his cheek gently between his forefinger and thumb. "We should get these two acquainted, don't you think?"

Sarah came into the kitchen where the soft, wooden floor became cold stone, her face was turned down, the baby in her arms. She walked up to Matilda, a flower to a tree, and held her baby daughter forward.

"Piers," said Algie; "meet baby Elisabeth."

"We have taken to calling her Bess," said Sarah.

Bess was glassy-eyed, tiny bubbles coming from her tiny lips, a little tuft of dark Mohawk hair on her head. Piers, agile,

33

keen, gazed at her – the first person he had seen smaller than himself. He examined her and began to laugh a haughty child's laugh. Sarah, glowing in the reflected light of her beautiful baby, smiled. Algie began to laugh and his shoulders went up and down. And even Matilda smiled, I saw. That was how Piers and Bess met; in a room of conventional happiness.

But it was a cameo of normalcy in a set-up of wickedness.

It would have been a peculiar scenario had I known any different at that age. You have to watch out for things. If something feels rotten, it most likely is, whether you can put your finger on it or not. And I could feel the rot, it was soft in the air, and gave a taste to the back of the throat.

That first summer at the Radnors', the inhabitants of the cottage would only meet for the evening meal. The Radnor boys were off playing in the countryside for most of the day. Sarah Radnor would walk the gardens with baby Bess. Matilda and Algie would play cards, or go walking, or take trips into town. Baby Piers and Clara and I would stay in the cottage, in the safety of the stone walls. Clara was chatty, bright, childish in many ways. Piers enjoyed her company, it seemed; she was keen to embrace him whenever his arms went up, and she would play the unending repetitious games of children with as much verve as the children. Whenever the adults returned she was still, like a lamp or a bureau, expressionless, untouchable, like a drip trapped in a moment of time. I liked her very much.

These trips to the Radnor cottage were to become annual. They would last between several weeks and several months. I remember them as long drawn out days, and everything happened slowly and as if seen through a thick plate window. Sarah Radnor would spend much time walking the modest gardens, or along the trail to the ridge that oversaw the village nearby. I watched her sometimes from the window of the bedroom I shared with the two Radnor boys. I had seen Mrs Radnor sitting near the duck pond at the far end of the small orchard patch on more than one occasion. She had a book closed in her hand. It was there to be opened if anyone was seen coming. She was staring out to the slowly gliding ducks, those serious, dreary little birds.

"What are you looking at?" said one of the Radnor boys to me. He had come back to the room to fetch a fire truck from his toy box.

I said nothing, did not even turn to look at him.

It was Michael. He came and peered out of the window next to me, his breath making a smudge on the pane.

"My mother," he said. "She's always sitting and staring into space. She's no different at home. She just likes to be on her own. Are you coming to play?"

Neither of the boys had asked me to play before.

Michael climbed down from the windowsill.

"Please yourself," he said.

Matthew and Michael were aged a year either side of me, if I remember rightly.

"Wait," I said. "What is the game?"

Michael turned at the door.

"We're going to go up to the ridge and start a fire," he said.

"Start a fire?"

"Not a real one," Michael whispered. He held up the toy truck. "We don't have a real fire engine."

The cottage was empty. Sarah Radnor was in the orchard. Algie and Matilda were out, presumably with the babies.

The walk to the ridge was a long one. Michael and Matthew, the elder, walked ahead of me. I lagged behind, whipping at my heels with a stick. Shiner, his big pink tongue flapping stupidly from the side of his mouth, ran circles around us the whole way. Michael was running the fire truck through the air like a bird. Matthew marched. The grass was long and our knees came up high as we reached the ridge, waving our arms through a cloud of midges as we did so.

Up on the ridge the Radnor boys seemed to forget about plans for faux fire-building and instead set about tormenting their collie. It seemed a regular pastime; both Michael and Matthew knew the drill.

"Come on, Harold," called Matthew. "Get stuck in." And he whipped a long thin stick across the dog's hind legs. The dog spun and snarled, yelped, at which point Michael whipped the poor animal's legs from a different spot.

"Is kicking at your heels and poking at wasps' nests all that branch is good for?" Michael said.

I looked down at the stick in my hand, a battered wand from a weeping willow.

"The first one to get a bite out of him wins," Michael said.

"I don't know why you have that dog," I said.

"He's ours to do with as we please," said Matthew and slapped his stick across Shiner's hind quarters. Shiner let out a yelp and tried to sidle off with his tail between his legs, but Michael blocked his path and again swiped down at him. Shiner snarled, showed his back teeth, but then whimpered and tried to escape, a moment of debasement from a miserable animal.

I wanted nothing to do with it. I chucked my whip onto the floor and walked down the far end of the ridge. The Radnor boys laughed and carried on with their game. I watched them from the lakeside, a silhouetted dance of torment on the horizon. They tired; the dog found a gap in their line and ran away. Michael and Matthew found other things to occupy them and Shiner eventually came back and they began playing fetch. I sat in silence, without moving, watching the boys go through their games and we remained this way until the sun began to set behind them, and I saw them gesture over that it was time to head back.

For the next three days the same thing happened. By mid-morning the cottage was deserted but for Sarah Radnor sitting in the orchard looking out to the ducks with the closed book in her lap. I would follow the boys up to the ridge and I would sit by the lake most of the day and watch them torment Shiner, climb trees and run the fire truck through the air as if it were a bird. And then we would head back.

On the fourth evening we returned to a cottage of uncommon ongoing activity.

Algie and Matilda were playing whist; Sarah Radnor was nowhere to be seen. Baby Piers – a small two year old now – was playing with building blocks on the floor at his mother's feet. It had been a dismal day, warm but wet, and the three of us brought clumps of dank clay mud into the parlour on the bottoms of our shoes. Matilda stood sharply at the sight.

"Look at all the mud, you silly, careless boys," she said.

Algie stood also and took Matilda by the elbow. Matilda shouted even louder at us. It was not unusual for her to do so.

"Matilda; I'll sort the boys," Algie said, and called for Sarah at the top of his voice.

I looked down at my shoes and at the shoes of Michael and Matthew. They were not so filthy.

Sarah Radnor came in – she looked as though she had been crying – and she grabbed Matthew tightly by the wrist. He screeched and Michael grabbed his brother's other wrist and a tug-of-war ensued. Algie shouted at them to stop.

"Do you want them clean or not?" Sarah Radnor shouted back.

"Sarah," said Matilda; "there is no need…"

"Michael, stop pulling at your brother's arm," shouted Algie, moving forward and in turn grabbing him. There was now a line of screeching, shouting adult-child-child-adult, twisting like a wounded snake. And added to this Shiner was barking, jumping and barking.

And that was when I noticed that little baby Piers was not crying in order to add to the chaos as children are want to do, but there was blood on his hand. I went to him – he was crying, screaming, his face erupting into a gap-toothed gummy flytrap, tears bubbling from his clenched eyes. He looked so beautiful.

As the Radnors and Matilda screamed at each other above us, I held my little baby brother's tiny bleeding hand and said, "Don't cry, little Piers. It's nothing to cry about, little Piers. I won't let this pain win over us."

I examined the hand. There was a cut along the thumb, quite deep. I lifted it to my face and kissed it gently, and then I blew on it calmly as I had seen others do to wounds. Piers' crying juddered but did not stop and he looked directly into my eyes. And I could smell wet dog on my baby brother's hand, the fur of a wet dog.

I stood and looked at the ridiculous scene, which now had Sarah Radnor on one side shouting at the two boys, Algie and Matilda on the other; those four shouting back at her. I went up to Matilda and tugged at her sleeve.

"What?" she snapped down at me.

"Piers has hurt himself," I said.

The room went silent and everybody looked at the baby who was crying.

Matilda gasped. "What have you done to your brother?" she shouted and dashed for Piers, lifting him and dotting his face with kisses.

I said nothing.

Matilda glared down at me.

She swiftly handed Piers to Algie and grabbed me strongly

by the arm. She fell back into her seat and threw me over her knee, and pulled down my short trousers. I could feel the pleasant feeling of the cool air upon my naked skin. And I knew what came next. I looked at the floor, at the few specks of mud the Radnor boys and I had brought in. I knew everybody was silently watching me, and so, even though I was now too big for Matilda's blows to really hurt, I forced myself to cry. I did not want to embarrass her.

The next day, with Piers' little thumb disinfected and bound, all seemed forgotten. Sarah Radnor was quiet – but she was quiet more often than not – and Matilda and Algie went for a walk up to the woods. I had had a sleepless night – every time I closed my eyes I could see baby Piers' smooth twisted face. I waited patiently for Matthew and Michael to come into the parlour and tell their mother they were going to play up on the ridge.

"Take Harold with you," she said, staring out of the window toward the woods on the horizon.

The walk was quite steep, and we three boys were quiet, and Shiner sniffed in zig zags through the grass in front. Matthew picked up a stick and began swatting at the tips of the tall grass. As we reached the top of the ridge Michael ran on ahead to a tree he liked to climb. Shiner chased, barked, and when Michael went up the tree the dog bounced on his back legs, putting his forelegs against the trunk. He looked back at Matthew and I who had now also reached the top of the ridge, and he came bounding toward us, barking, jumping. I watched the patterned movements of the dog. I watched the calm, cruel forgetfulness of the Radnor boys. Nobody seemed to care that Piers had been attacked the way he had. Bitten at for trying to pet their stupid, servile mutt.

Why didn't the dog run away from them, from the whole damned family? They beat him, whipped him, and still he came back.

I could feel my throat go dry. Shiner ran past Matthew, who was concentrating on stripping his branch bare, and on to my direction, bounding, bounding. And as he reached me, I crouched down and lifted a stake that I had been kicking along with me for some hundred yards or so – it looked like one of the very sticks the Radnor boys had been tormenting Shiner with the day before – and, using the pace of the oncoming dog, I held it sturdy from the turf and allowed Shiner to drive his own throat onto it, the stick piercing the middle of the dog's neck and coming out of the top. Shiner yelped and gurgled and sputtered to a muffled silence all in one swift second. There was no blood, I remember; at least there was none on me. I winced and held the stake firm, crouched on my knees, and Shiner tumbled down the side of the ridge through the long grass and toward the unkempt reeds of the lakeside. I had ended up on my back, my arms outstretched, my legs out long, looking into the clear blue of the summer sky. It all happened very fast. I could hear Matthew's voice, unsure, concerned, quite a way away, calling to Shiner and to me. It skipped along the dense summer air, that little voice. I looked up at the sky, a deep cloudless blue, and the silence came back.

It may have been minutes, but to me I was in that long grass for an endless moment of happiness. Not elation. But a flat, level happiness.

Matthew's voice eventually grew louder. He called his brother. He called Shiner. I sat up.

"Where's Shiner?" said Matthew, with a hollow, concerned look to his face. "I heard him yelp."

"I've been looking at the sky," I said.

I continued to sit in the grass as Matthew and Michael began searching for their dog, calling his name – the only sound.

It took quite some time to find Shiner. It seemed he had

crawled some way to die, to a hiding of shrubs at the far foot of the ridge. The boys cried, cried for days, and never once did either of them accuse me of anything.

We buried the dog at the end of the garden at the cottage.

"He loved it here," said Algie in his short improvised eulogy.

The boys cried; Matilda rolled her eyes.

Sarah rocked Bess in her arms a few feet back from the rest of the congregation. I stood next to Matilda, quite close. I looked at the dog's corpse wrapped in swathing in the shallow hole. The dog should not have bit my brother.

* * *

To take a life is no small consideration.

But if my century can teach anything, it is that taking life as a form of punishment is a facile endeavour, it forms only a puerile recompense to the feeble minded. There is no more punishment in death than there is darkness in light. We have always believed men fear death, just as children fear the dark, but that fear does not translate into some coarse understanding of the afterlife. Did I punish the Radnor dog? Revenge is a wild justice. It is all very well that Solomon could say *it is the glory of man to pass it by*, but he had an army to protect his kith and kin. I was a child. I did not think in terms of moral balance. What child does? I knew right from wrong, I would not lay down an excuse of that sort. But I also knew the best way to achieve three things: to protect my brother, to hurt those cruel Radnor boys, and to release that tormented animal from this world. We must make our decisions in the best way we know at the time. The child Harold Buren killed the dog.

After this, the summer trips continued year after year, although the mood of them seemed to change, seemed to soften, warm, as if someone had stoked the fire in the cottage and a dampness drew back.

Sarah Radnor returned the following year with some colour to her cheeks. Bess was a bright and handsome baby, inquisitive and happy, with that defiant surety in her ignorance which is one of the few characteristics most people hold on to from infancy, refreshingly absent from her features. She seemed to give Sarah a distraction from her apparent miseries, the nature of which I continued to remain blind.

And my relationship with Matthew and Michael had changed – although nothing was ever mentioned of Shiner. I thought nothing of the dog. When I was a child on the farm, I had played a game where I pretended I was a bush spirit bestowed upon the family for protection. Whenever I saw a dog in the street I thought of this game. I felt solid, like I had not done before, like my veins were filled with liquid concrete. In this world and future ones, the child Harold Buren moved among spirits and creatures that many others could not see.

Great monsters hung in the sky. I had seen a Zeppelin one spring. It moved slowly over the London rooftops like a whale. It was alone in the sky, and low, a dirty brown, as if it was lost, cut off from the herd. I had told the Radnor boys about it that summer and they had reacted like wild apes. The Radnor boys did not know anything about the world beyond their garden. Whereas, to them, I had come from afar, I was already versed in the vastness of the human world, and the curiousness of the creatures of children's minds; I had sailed the seas, from the furthest tip of Africa to the cold mists of the great magical city of London.

When Piers was older, a toddler, and I was home from boarding school for the holidays, Piers would sit up in bed and ask about the veldt. It was a mysterious place to him, a place that Matilda would mention but not talk about – "This would never happen in the veldt!" she would say of some trivial London annoyance.

I would have to make up most of what I told him. I would tell him of the dragons and he would listen, agog. They are great graceful creatures, I would say; but they rarely come near the veldt now, they stay in the hills.

I remembered the heat, the dust, Belky in the doorway with the news that my father had collapsed from his horse. Little else. I would mix the stories of Homer with the landscape of the veldt as I remembered it. It was *our* mythology. Some nights there would be more veldt, some nights there would be palaces like that of Alcinous, and feasts like those of Menelaus. And Piers would sit up in bed wide-eyed and bewildered. The veldt was not that much different to the plains of ancient Greece, after all.

Piers was old enough by that point to know that war was something as important to man as family – that is, he was old enough to believe it was the main topic of conversation in every household. Piers did not know that war was an unusual state for a country to be in; an unusual thing, at least, for a common Englishman to be threatened by. Algie Radnor, his asthma chronic enough to keep him from the trenches, talked often of the fighting going on in Europe and the Dardanelles. I listened from shaded corners, from the undergrowth of the unmanned garden. I was twelve when I heard the war was over. The Hun had been defeated in the mud. It was the fifth year we had spent the summer at the Radnor cottage.

The landscape of those summers did not seem to change though, even as I grew older, entered my teens, and everything bent and the order of things changed. Matilda stopped celebrating my birthday from the age of twelve. I was never sure if there was logic to this in her mind or whether she simply began to forget.

Bess Radnor was a playful child; she had brought a new light to the holidays with her innocence, her enquiry, her ability to turn those silences into something natural. Piers, a somewhat wan specimen himself, avoided her with suspicion. Her cotton blonde hair turned a thick brunette by about the age of four, like a swan to a raven, and her temperament seemed to change with it. She was not a morose child, but she could give a glare that belied her inexperience of the world. She played with dolls, roughly pulled combs through their knotted hair, and Piers drew pictures, and tugged at my cuffs, pressing books into my hand urging me to read them to him.

"Read to me again, brother," he would say. And I would stop what I was doing and read more fairy tales, more adventures, more myths.

He was not a child engaged with the world. Children should live in dreams, of course; harmless dramas and tragedies. But I suppose I had suspicions of the man he was to become. He had no interest in anything other than stories, and whereas stories prepare us for much, life has no such narrative continuity. And it was to be Piers' own story, which is my own story, entwined, that was to teach me the evils of trying to imprint such patterns upon the natural world of things.

＊ ＊ ＊

I was sent to Montclare when I turned eleven.

It was a small, expensive boarding school in the lush Kent countryside, an old manor house built adjacent to a ruined monastery. There were some eight hundred pupils there, from eleven to sixteen, and the schooling was rigorously classical, tinged with that solemn form of Jesuit bravado. If you can imagine such a place your mind is inevitably drawn to English drama, the English novel, or the biographies of our English heroes. It was, in many ways, a "good" school, even though it subjected me, academically, to unremarkable things. But it is important to my story for what it gave me emotionally; it is integral to my coming of age. I'm sure you have a canvas too, by way of which you can transmit your fruition. Montclare gave me steel, gave me flesh, and gave me that first taste of non-familial affection.

Very little was asked of me at this school. It was no secret I would be a millionaire at eighteen. Cracking out of my pupae with dollar bills for wings. I suppose it was deemed enough for the institution that I was there at all.

The teachers at Montclare saw little reason to push the efforts of a distracted, silent child who appeared diligently average in every way. I knew what I was. They treated me kindly, bearing in mind the potential for reciprocated fiscal generosity in later life (something I gave them).

My fellow pupils treated me less so, but I did not take to heart the comments about my race, my alien accent, my thick black-rimmed spectacles, my mop of unkempt hair. I felt for my bullies. They were abandoned to the halls of Montclare just as I was.

Although, I was not entirely sad to be away from Claypole. I was evolving into character, as people do when the puppy fat is shed. The sadness of my mother's house was oppressive; at least at Montclare I could breathe as loudly as I liked – indeed, I was encouraged to exhale with generosity and courage.

I was fourteen when I met Douglass Karlchild, a young Irish swashbuckler with a cut-glass English accent. His parents had brought him over from the manor house of his birth after the outbreak of the civil war in nineteen sixteen. Karlchild was *dashing* – that was the word – a cool slip of blonde hair, sharp cobalt-blue eyes, a long slender nose and vulpine mouth. I had not known being in the presence of another human could be such a chaotic wonder. I had never seen anything so beautiful, so assured; in his presence *my thoughts became like children grown too headstrong for their mother.*

He was Captain Blood as played by Huckleberry Finn. He was Achilles *and* Odysseus. I watched him often from afar, as being close to him made me weak, it made me vulnerable to the curtain down. He could have destroyed everything in a glorious whimper. Whenever I saw him about the grounds of the school I would find myself staring, digging into a corner and watching him for as long as I could.

One clear summer afternoon I was reclining on the curved hammock-like first branch of an oak tree near the ravine at the farthest end of the school grounds, reading Virgil.

"You have quite the perch," came a voice from below.

I looked down to see Karlchild there, his halcyon face peering up, with that smart lop-sided smile on his lips.

"Yes," I said. "I don't know why nobody else ever uses it."

"You wouldn't give it up if they did, would you?" he said.

I turned back to my book. I felt tense, nervous; I was blushing.

"I hadn't thought about it," I said, as calmly as I could.

There was a silence and I was putting all of my effort into not looking back down at him. Instead I focussed hard on one line of Virgil's verse. I did not read it but I stuck to the marks of ink, the curves and the sharp ends like it was a charm to fend off sickness. As I stared, a burn coming up through my centre, my throat drying, I heard the scuffle of shoes on bark, a few puffed breaths, and before I realised what was happening, Karlchild was up on the branch next to me and shoving me over to one side with a thrust of his hip.

"Shift up," he said.

I was shocked, rigid almost with an incomprehensible stiffness that began in my midriff and moved down and out, a mixture of pain and elation, and indeed I "shifted" over. Karlchild breathed out a satisfied sigh and looked out over the school grounds, the yellowing grass, toward the playing fields and the main building across the ravine, the midges dancing around in the warm light. We sat shoulder to shoulder. I held my book with white knuckles.

"It's as good up here as I thought it'd be," he said, smiling to the view and then to me. We were so close that I could feel his breath on my mouth, and that burn in my centre became the most wonderful warmth, and the dryness of my throat became wet with a metallic saliva.

"What are you reading?" he said.

"*The Aeneid*," I said, looking down at the book in my lap.

"Ah, I love it when he goes to the underworld. That's when it gets good."

"I'm not at that part yet," I said. "He's about to go."

Karlchild suddenly burst into animation.

"*Dido, unhappy spirit, was the news that came to me of your death true then, taking your life with a blade? Alas, was I the cause of your dying? I swear by the stars, by the gods above, by whatever truth may be in the depths of the earth, I left your shores unwillingly, my queen. I was commanded by gods, who drove me by their decrees, that now force me to go among the shades, through places thorny with neglect, and deepest night: nor did I think my leaving there would ever bring such grief to you.*" He threw his head back and laughed loudly, hungrily. "You'll love it."

We sat in silence for a while; Karlchild reclined and closed his eyes to the warmth of the sun; that smile remaining on his face. I looked at him, the smoothness of his skin, his long eyelashes, his strong jaw. Life was how it should have been, sitting up in the tree with Douglass Karlchild.

After a while of watching my new companion, I turned back to the book, but I could not concentrate. I kept looking at him, who soon had slipped into a doze, his hands behind his head, his face turned up to the sun, dappled with the shadows of oak leaves.

Douglass Karlchild and I quickly became good friends. Every book I was about to read, he had already read, and he would tell me the best parts to jump right to. The other pupils began to treat me as one of their own, infused as I was with the charm of my new companion who was admired by all for his looks, his charm, his wit, his intellectual acumen and his athletic prowess on the sports field; as if I had turned up anew the same morning Douglass had entered the gates for the first time.

I began to play the part of the thoughtful intellectual, the exoticism of my origins outreaching even Karlchild's tales of the Irish wars. Karlchild would easily gather a crowd and relay the recent history of his troubled nation as if he was writing his own Homeric poem, and I would sit at his side as strong, silent adjutant.

"I've been thinking about our friendship," Karlchild said to me one dusky evening as we walked the gritted path that circled the playing fields.

I don't think I had really had a friend up until that question was asked me. There had been Clara, who had gone to nanny for a family in Brighton six or seven years earlier. And there was Piers, six years my junior. So I had not experienced the friendship of peerage before, parity, where things – even age – are shared. I had not thought of Douglass as my friend, as such; my leader, my idol, perhaps. I felt lonely when Douglass was not with me, I felt bleak. I had interpreted this as a rudderlessness; as a platoon without a captain, an army without its hero.

"What have you been thinking about?" I said.

"You told me how you detest your summers."

I scratched my neck and tried to remember having said such a thing.

"We have a tradition," I said. "I suppose you could call it that; of spending some weeks at the cottage of another family. I don't enjoy it."

"So, I think you should spend the summer with me."

Karlchild said things of importance always with a smattering of indifference, a casual approach to heavy reality.

"I don't know what you mean?" I said.

"My parents will be delighted to have a guest. In fact, they won't even be there."

"I can't come and spend the summer with you, Douglass; especially if you're parents are not going to be there. Matilda would not allow it."

Karlchild stopped and held me at the shoulder.

"Are you for real?"

I knew what Douglass was getting at. What I had told my friend of Matilda gave no suggestion that she would object. No evidence that she would care at all.

Karlchild said, "I'll write your mother a letter and pretend to be my father."

"Will that work?"

"Hal, you'll learn that most people spend most of their lives wrapped up in a fraud of some kind. It's how things get done."

And so Douglass wrote Matilda a letter saying how I would be most welcome to spend the summer with the Karlchilds at their country home in Norfolk. He added, in his father's hand, for added spice, how the family were extremely wealthy Anglo-Irish gentry that could boast an ancestor who sat atop a horse a few feet from William at the Boyne. Matilda wrote back, her prose awakened by Douglass' spices (it turned out that these elaborate claims were true, in so far as the family actually did profess them). And so I went with Douglass at the end of term.

We took the train and were picked up from the station by a driver – Douglass referred to him as Jones.

The Karlchild mansion, Hamilton Hall, was enormous, like a town of its own, and indeed, Douglass' parents were not there; nobody was there. Jones informed us Lord and Lady Karlchild were travelling around Europe. Douglass had the option to follow them and meet up in Corsica, Jones said.

"From whence hailed Napoleon," said Douglass grandly, swishing his arm around like a swordsman. "I don't think so. Not this year." And he smiled that half-smile.

"Very well, sir," said Jones. "I will send them word you'll be staying at Hamilton Hall."

The first afternoon Douglass and I walked around the grounds of the manor; a wood, and some large hills, a brook, and a rose garden. We discussed Tennyson and Wordsworth and how London still had some catching up to do. I recited Wordsworth, but Douglass could always outdo me with Tennyson.

We dined together in the main hall, a delicious, bountiful meal, prepared by an unseen cook and presented by Jones in evening dress. I felt a need to be nervous in this strange, empty environment, but I was in fact unable to prevent feeling a broad sense of happiness with Douglass – something stronger than happiness; it was contentment. It is impossible to overstate how grateful I was to him for giving me his friendship after a young life of emotional solitude. At that table, dining, I felt as if my life had finally begun.

That evening Douglass led me up the long wide staircase.

"I thought it would be much more fun if we shared a bedroom," he said. "This is such a large old house. It seems silly to sleep so far away from one another."

"That seems quite sensible," I said.

But I could sense something around Douglass, something perilous, something absolutely part of him since the day we first met. I was no longer nervous, but I was curious; my heart was grievously fluttering, my mouth was dry just like that afternoon when we had first spoken on the oak branch.

The room Douglass had chosen for us was dimly lit with candlelight and an open fire.

"There is just the one bed," I said and turned to see Douglass closing the door, turning the large iron key in the lock, and beginning to unbutton his shirt. The half-smile that permanently shaped Douglass' mouth had gone, his lips were glisteningly moist and his eyes were skipping in light. He stepped slowly toward me. His hands came up and took my spectacles from my face.

"I like to see your face, Hal," he said.

He stepped forward and kissed me on the mouth. I pulled back at first. It was shock. The shock at being touched at all, I think. He tasted salty, and of the food we had just eaten. And his skin was not as soft as it looked. It was hot to touch.

It seems half-comical to think all those years back now at that first clumsy night with Douglass. The usual sensations of intercourse were actually subdued by the sensations of human contact. It was not his mouth that fascinated me, nor his genitals that aroused me, but it was his breath, his chest as it rose and dropped, the creases in his palms, the down across his jaw. This night, as common as it became, was an ingredient of that summer that was entirely made up of every second we spent together. And we walked the grounds of the house, reading to each other, telling each other stories, and whenever I spoke of Matilda, I spoke of how petite, loving, careful she was, and I made up brothers and sisters for myself, painting a picture of a large happy carnival of familial joy. I did not want to think of the reality, my poor brother, trapped with the Radnors summer after summer.

What did I feel about lying to Douglass about these things? I don't think it mattered to either of us what truths were. Not at that moment.

It was Douglass who put a pen in my hand, you see. I had never written anything before, but Douglass had this idea that we were blessed, blessed with riches and love and life, and he and I would write the great poetry of our age. We wrote through the day, and read each other our work. Douglass played jokes on Byron's metre, and I wrote a new heroic saga with a towering queen of ice who marched through cities striking fear into the hearts of gods. We wrote so much. We were going to be *the* great poets.

Was there anything that survived? Within me, there was whatever turned me to poetry. It was always there. I can only tell you my story, and you can decide what corruption and corrosion can do to the spirit of the soil.

But I tell you this now because you must understand that the fictions I told Douglass were just a part of this wider exuberance.

I gave myself a clan, and Matilda was the queen. It seemed fitting that I left behind a tribe, it seemed noble. Does it mean

I loved him less because I could not really be honest with him? I have read extensively about love. It is purported to be the most powerful of motives for some of the most illogical of deeds. If I have experienced it, I would never defile it by using it as an excuse for my puerile missteps.

My story goes like this: I met a boy when I was at school – he was my age – and we became at one with each other, a single entity moving in two vessels, our bodies and minds melded and immersed. We were best friends first and foremost, but with some men it can become beyond just that, the purest form of comradeship. He introduced me to poets, to rugby – my first foray into physical excellence was from joining him in Montclare's first fifteen. And we remained entwined in each other for many years, until his father called him away to serve family financial interests in the United States. We were eighteen by then. We had never once been cross at each other, never once grown tired of each other's company. And when he left it was sudden and cruel. We held each other and I cried and Douglass told me to "get a hold of myself" as he held back his own tears, and we made promises I'm sure we both felt we could keep. After all, we had the poetry we had drawn out of one another.

But we had also both learned to understand the nature of such connections; that they are impermanent. And I hold Douglass now in these pages, a glow on the parchment, ageless in his long ago perfection, a spark the likes of which makes the great globe of fire of this universe a human one.

* * *

I was preparing to leave Montclare for the final time; Oxford beckoned.

It was 1926, and I received a letter from Matilda; a further, more urgent beckoning for which I was not prepared. We had had little contact the preceding few years. We had become what I always felt she had wanted us to become: irrelevant to each other. By this age I visited London frequently without telling her, without thinking of telling her; and I knew little of her pastimes. But the letter informed me in her scrawled, deep hand that I would be expected at the Radnors that summer.

I had no plans, other than to wander aimlessly and read. Douglass had left for the United States immediately after school ended. I was in a stupor of loneliness and meaninglessness. I packed my things, making sure I carefully stored the copy of Virgil's *Aeneid* Douglass had given me as a parting gift.

"Think of me like this as I sail away," he said. "And try not to kill yourself." And he smiled widely. He knew he had to leave me with that most profound sense of melancholic joy.

We had read it together several times, to each other. And I had copied out great portions of the poetry in letters to Piers. It made me feel as though I was with him. And it also made me feel as though I was introducing Douglass to Piers. I could not ever speak of him to my family. My eyes, often noted for their expressionlessness, I am sure would have given away the true nature of our relationship.

As time went on in these years I began to value the nature of Aeneas' duty in Virgil's great poem. It first helped me understand Douglass' leaving. And soon after it helped me understand other things, too. The leaving of Dido in the chasmal chambers of her Carthaginian palace. Loneliness must have seemed all the darker in all that space, looking out from the royal veranda at Aeneas' ship sailing away in the frame of the burning sun. I felt the hearts of them both as I grew older. I felt her loneliness – as if anyone would have more cognizance of loneliness than a queen! Aeneas, the hero, came to her, he loved her, and she realised that she was a *woman*, not simply a queen; that she had blood and the quivering desire to be vulnerable. And Aeneas remembered his duty – to go to the banks of the Tiber and settle; to settle the foundations of Rome, no less. He gave up her love for the glory of the future, for the understanding of those who come after.

In this Douglass had given me two things: an understanding of humanness and an ambition in poetry. The two of course are connected irrefutably. Douglass gave me Virgil, gave me hope, gave me destiny, gave me the many colours of love.

I now see Virgil knew that the true understanding of a person can only be achieved in the aftermath, when the entire story is known. His fiction was *only* in that he created a character that understood (although often with strange, lurid, proto-Messianic doubts) the nature of his own aftermath. In these pages, for you, I am not such a character. But you are at will to understand the truth from where you are.

That summer, then.

It was to be the alignment of many lives. I held Matilda's scratchy-looking letter in my hand the whole of the train journey to Wales, looking often with suspicion at her signature. It had grown crooked, perverse, etched.

I remembered the Radnor cottage unwelcomingly. Sarah Radnor wandering the grounds like the ghost of her own story, sitting at the pond, longing, it seemed, to be nothing at all. Now with my understanding of poetry, I feared she was destined one day to take the Socratic route, and sacrifice herself for the young. I feared some bleak end to her of some kind, anyhow. I remembered – and still do – her pale skin and long princely neck, those sad glacial eyes. I remembered the body of that dog buried in the shallow grave at the bottom of the garden. Dead at my hand. A boy's first murder.

Matilda came through that cottage in great waves, Algie bobbing on her crest. Ludicrous little man. The cold, damp building was a suffocating droning, whispered prose.

I felt for the sanity of Piers in such an environment, every summer in that strange place, although in our letters he never spoke of misery. He spoke of a friendship with Bess Radnor, that peculiar young girl of theirs. No longer the suspicion of the sullen dark-haired, bare-footed young girl creature, he spoke now of a reciprocated kindness and warmth, and mutual a love of poetry, a love of walking, wandering, and that she possessed a *symphonic* laugh – *Stravinsky*, he wrote, *a laugh of light melodious all-devouring passion*. He wrote that they would play in the fields, and he would mock her affectionately, and she would hiss at him – *kksssssss*, was how he wrote it – and she would bend her knees and curl her fingers like cat claws. He said she liked the French. She read Baudelaire and Stendhal and Flaubert; *the greatest essayists on the theme of boredom*, he wrote – *which is something I never am when in her company. I could never be.*

Apparently she talked about boredom often to Piers. *She is bored, she says, when she is at home, in the house on the outskirts of the linen factory. And she is equally bored when at this cottage every summer. But she does not talk about the summer in the same tone as she does the linen factory. I think she is toying with me, and I think she values my friendship as much as I do hers.*

I remember these words well because it was the first time Piers had really written about her in any detail. I do not recall my reply.

Looking out to the green-grey blur of the countryside passing the window of the train, I wondered about this young Bess. I had not seen her since she was a toddler. Now she would be thirteen – the age of Shakespeare's Juliet. Piers was fourteen. The age I was when I first encountered Douglass. I must have realised that theirs was not a simple friendship between two children flung together by the odd confluences of their parents' commitments to each other. But I remember the scene on the platform.

I alighted; it was a bright and clear day, pure. And, to my surprise I could see Piers and a girl, who I assumed correctly to be Bess, making their way toward me from the far end of the station. Bess was light, almost gliding, her skin dappled blue it was so pale. I remember she had wide hips for such a young girl, and her hair was thick and unkempt like black straw. Her glide became a trot, like a child playing at being a horse; she was a fashionable mixture of innocent girl and knowing young woman – but that is where her fashionableness came to an abrupt end. She had full red lips with no rouge applied, and round cheeks on a full but bonny face. Her eyes glistened somewhere between golden and hazel, a constant altering miasmic pool in the pitches of sunlight and dusk. She moved smoothly but was never still, when there was nothing for her to engage in her shoulders would sway, or her head would sway, or she would pull her hair fully behind her shoulders and arrange it into a loose plat that would become undone the moment she let go of it, or she would form a bun on the top of her head, revealing her fine jaw and her marble neckline, a bun that would unfurl and collapse the second her hands would fall restlessly to her sides. Some of these youthful, energised ticks she would never lose.

Piers, in contrast was quite still; but now I noticed in him an infected energy, as if Bess electrified him. No longer at

Matilda's hip, he was sometimes bouncing on the balls of his feet. He looked at Bess always as if he was learning. I could sometimes see the embarrassment fill his face for a second as she left his company, and he realised how he must have looked to others. And then, once she was gone, he would become himself, stained with her soul. I realised I would likely never know Piers again without his Bess.

"Hal, I have to tell you something," he said, his grin from ear to ear.

He was a strong lad, I thought; still with some growing to do, but his shoulders were widening and his waist narrowing his shape into an imposing triangle. His eagerness now, youthful and crude, I knew would soon become a mature reticence and resolve. He was intelligent; I knew that from the way he wrote to me about Bess. He had never written anything at length about the passages of the *Aeneid* I sent him; only to say that he liked Aeneas. That was enough for me, I suppose. *And Bess is becoming quite fond of Dido*, he wrote.

"Wait a minute," I said. "Where is my greeting? Where is my shake of the hand?"

Piers laughed, straightened, and held out his hand to me. I returned the laugh and grasped him in a tight embrace.

"Don't tell me you didn't realise it was I who wrote the letter," said Piers, and he laughed again and turned to Bess who laughed along with him, bending at the waist as she did so, a little out of puff from the sprint up the platform.

"You *see*," she said to Piers. "I told you he wouldn't guess it."

I could see at that moment that they were closer than childhood friends, although I still felt foolish for not seeing it in the letters.

"Why would you sign the letter with Matilda's name?" I said.

I suppose I had suspected mischievousness on Piers' part. There was surely something in the many letters I had read from Piers over the recent years to be found in this fakery. I could see immediately the barely concealed satire in the fake Matilda's tone. But I could not see it when I read it. Piers moved across my vision so often like a magician, where so many others were like beggars. I so often did not see his hands move, while with others I could see the beads of sweat first emerge on the brow.

"Enough, enough," said Piers. "That's not important now. The important thing is that you are here."

"Okay, okay; what is it?" I said.

Piers smiled, as did Bess.

"We are in love," he said.

I stopped, looked Piers up and down, and began to laugh again.

"What's so damned funny?" said Piers.

"You shouldn't curse, Piers," I said through my laughter. "It is ungentlemanly. And what would your love think?"

"Why are you laughing?" said Piers, boyishly annoyed.

I gathered myself.

"I am sorry, Piers. I did not mean to laugh. Bess, please accept my apologies."

Piers and Bess looked at each other, vexed, embarrassed, and then looked back at me.

"You think we're foolish," said Piers.

I did not find this quite so funny. I had offended my dear little brother, and furthermore I realised how hurt I would have been had he, with all of his younger years, has laughed at Douglass the way I had just laughed at Bess. But as I was about to make amends and straighten the situation, I gazed past Piers to the lonely pale figure of Sarah Radnor at the far end of the platform.

"I do not think you foolish," I said, and I put my arms around them both. "I think it is beautiful that a Buren and a Radnor can be happy at the same time."

I turned them and began to walk them down the platform. All three of us grinned warmly, as part of me tried to figure out exactly what dreadfulness I had detected in Sarah's demeanour.

"So, tell me how this all came about," I said.

"We were picnicking near the lake – all of us – it was the perfect day," said Piers. "*Even* mother was in a pleasant mood. Bess was picking flowers down on the bank and I went up to her – she was the vision of an angel knelt near the reeds – and I went up to her and said, 'I wanted to tell you, Elisabeth,' – I thought it appropriate, given the nature of what I was about to say, to use her full name – 'I wanted to tell you, Elisabeth, that I am in love with you and that I cannot ever envisage a time when that will not be the case; and I want you to know that, should you want it, you have my heart, but that my soul is yours whether you want it or not'. Well, halfway through my speech she dipped her head into a blush and I couldn't help smiling and it finished with the both of us laughing. O, Hal; *my heart leaps up when I behold a rainbow in the sky: So was it when my life began; so is it now I am a man.*"

"And you announced your love to the family immediately, I suppose?" I said.

"Of course," said Bess, beaming, bouncing on the balls of her toes.

"We marched up the bank hand in hand and told them that we loved each other," said Piers.

I knew the difficulties of this, and now I understood a little of Sarah's look. I knew that what was to come would not be reverie, even if the young lovers were blind to it.

Sarah Radnor – who now looked twenty years older than her age – greeted me with a slow and hollow kiss on the cheek, with hard uneasy eyes. It was the only time I ever remember Sarah looking at me, or even touching me.

"I'm glad you're here," she said.

Sarah Radnor did not say why she felt that way and the drive to the cottage was silent from her corner. Piers and Bess flitted questions at me like chirping birds.

"Are you excited about going to Oxford?"

"Have you visited the city yet?"

"Aren't you happy for us?"

I smiled, nodded; but really I was concerned. I was concerned on the outer rim of my soul as to whether I had looked this foolish when I had first discovered Douglass. Could I have acted so excitable? But beneath that, in the immediate, I was concerned with the grim silence of Sarah.

The cottage had changed very little. The Radnor boys had grown tall, but were weedy, Michael with myopia, spectacles like bottle bottoms, Matthew with a nervous tick and translucent skin – the same translucence that made his sister angelic made him look on death's door. They looked intimidated by me, by my height, my athletic physique, my smart dress. It all suggested I had been away and become a man, whereas they had withered in their father's business.

Matilda looked grave. She looked lessened, an eroding rock. Algie, edgy, weasel-like now, shook me by the hand with downcast eyes, and took me to one side, walking me out from the kitchen where everybody was congregated for my arrival, to the hallway and through to the sitting room.

"Son," he called me, and I tried not to correct him. "Son, I am glad you're here."

He stood at the fireplace and affected an unsuitable dominant pose.

"I'm getting the feeling there is something causing everyone concern here," I said.

"You need to talk to your brother."

"About what?" I said.

"About my Bess."

Algie was now forced to look up to me and I could see clearer than day just what a weasel of a man he really was; his skin was unclean, perfumed not washed, his eyes flickered with the bare dullness of low-schemes. He was irritated, fidgety.

"I don't understand what you're asking of me," I said.

Algie blinked, tried to widen his back and stand up to me. It was no good – the rugby had made a hefty shape of my frame, and I had good suits cut to emphasise my definition also.

"You can't think the union of my daughter and your brother is a good idea can you?" Algie said in his wiry voice.

I said nothing, just looked down into Algie's face.

"I mean, Piers is a good lad; I think of him as a son."

"Well, there's no need," I said.

"You know what I mean, Harold; I could not love the boy more. But he is not right for Bess."

"Not right?"

Algie huffed and took a step back, looked down at the floor and put his hands on his hips.

"I understand you don't see much of your family nowadays," he said.

"I see plenty of them," I said.

"Well, I trust your mother and she's having none of it."

"Is that right?" I said.

"The boy talks of being a *poet*. I mean, have you ever heard of such a thing?"

"Does he indeed?" I said.

"There; I knew you would be my ally on this, Harold. A man of sense, a man of business. I cannot allow my daughter a life of destitution."

"Destitution?"

Algie looked confident now, for the first time his chest puffed out. And I realised that I was being lied to. I had often suspected that a union with the Buren family was Algie's only real goal in life, to put his hands into our pot. He was wealthy, but not in the way that the Burens were.

"She cannot marry a *poet*. She is a woman of means."

"We are a family of means, Algie. Considerably so," I said.

I had never used his given name before.

Algie spluttered, sucked in his stomach.

"*You* have wealth, Harold. Your mother has made it quite clear that *that* money is not there to support Bess. So she is to marry a *poet*. You would not let *your* daughter marry a poet," he said.

I said nothing.

"So, you see my point," said Algie. "We have to put a stop to this before it becomes problematic. You know how young girls can be. And poets, no doubt."

"How do you mean *put a stop to it*?"

"Well, tell them it just is not on."

I stood tall, pushed my jacket behind my wrists and planted my large hands into the pockets of my trousers.

"But I think it *is* on; I cannot think of a finer pairing," I said.

Algie was silent for a moment. He squinted one reddening eye at me, almost waiting for the punch-line, almost sizing me up.

"If they are in love then I suggest we encourage it," I said. Algie's face was turning a deep pink. "And the Buren family fortune will see no poet go hungry and no poet's wife either."

Algie gave in to his anger.

"You're not too old to be lectured too, young Harold," he spat, his eyelids flickering.

I stepped forward and I clasped Algie Radnor by one lapel and lifted him back onto the desk of a bureau, lifted him with one hand as if he was a doll, and I leaned into his face, and I said:

"You have had your fill of my mother these last years; I will not allow you to dirty my brother with your filthy instructions. And so I advise you to keep your nose out."

Algie squirmed, his face pink to pop. I let him go and stepped purposefully along the floorboards, my boots clomping, into the kitchen.

Bess and Piers were sitting at the table, Sarah and Matilda were either side of them, and the Radnor boys were behind leaning on the kitchen unit.

It had been a long time since I had stood in that kitchen and I must have looked enormous against the rustic wood, my neck bent under the beams amidst the hanging pots and china dishes. In comparison Michael and Matthew looked anaemic, dwarfish, as if they were still those stupid children whose dog I killed, trapped in the memory as well as in the family.

"Did you bring me back for this?" I said, looking at Piers. My blood was rising and I could not hide the anger from my voice.

Piers did not know what to say.

My eyes met with the unusually quiet gaze of Matilda. She looked exhausted, as if riddled with something unclean. She looked small. She looked drawn-out, under her own shadow. Something had gone on here. One battle too far, perhaps.

Algie came in.

"This bastard just threatened me," he said with bluster.

I waved a dismissive hand, did not even look at him.

"Boys, help your father run this hoodlum out of our home," he said.

Michael and Matthew went to take one reluctant step

65

forward, but I looked at them strongly, I looked at them straight, and my feet took firm positions, ready to take them both on – and I knew that they knew I had run Shiner through, and they had always known, and although I had never noticed it before, they had always been afraid of me.

I looked at Algie, furious in his impotence. I looked at my family. Piers and Bess glared at me. Matilda said nothing, her back was straight but her eyes were down to the table top.

"Are we going?" I said.

Piers stood up.

"I will not be apart from Bess," he said.

"Then if she wishes the same Bess will have to come with us to London," I said.

Matilda looked up sharply, submissively almost.

"I do wish that," said Bess.

"It is not going to happen," said Algie.

I turned to him sharply and said in a calm steady voice of gravel: "Do not think I will not hurt you."

And Algie shuddered and took a step back.

I looked over the room. Sarah Radnor was silent, almost elsewhere; the Radnor boys were rooted to their spots. Bess stood and looked into Piers' eyes. They whispered something to each other and kissed gently, consolingly.

"This is not the end of this," said Algie.

I did not look at him, I paused, looked past him.

"Yes; yes, it is," I said.

And within the hour the Burens and Bess Radnor were on the train back to London.

Bess and Piers were quiet – there was an air of relief to the cabin. Matilda looked from the window, her head against the head rest. I sat opposite her glancing at her at regular intervals. I could imagine the whirlwinds going through her mind; how life twists and scolds on its journey.

She had been having an affair with Algie Radnor. I had known this for some time – perhaps I had known from the first day at the cottage all those years ago. It seemed Sarah Radnor had finally, after more than a decade or so, called her husband to heel. A conjugal connection between the families via offspring was a twisting of the knife, and unacceptable.

As I sat opposite my mother in that carriage I went over the questions I wanted to ask. How could she give herself up to such a man? How could she allow herself to be drawn in to such an ugly scene? Look at what it had done to her: she looked a poor cartoon of her towering strength.

"Can I get you anything, mother?" I said.

Matilda did not look at me, her gaze continued to the fast-passing greys and solemn yellows of the countryside, and only her lips moved when she said in her most growled, masculine Afrikaans, "There is nothing *you* can do for me."

I was beginning to understand some things about love. I was beginning to understand that love is not an excuse to do whatever the hell it is you like. If anything it is the opposite: it should inspire a duty to respect and to restraint, and the ability, the desire, to suffer in silence.

* * *

Algie Radnor wrote letters.

He wrote that no daughter of his would marry a poet. He wrote sometimes, with little cryptic skill, that the Radnors and the Burens were destined to be together, but not like this. It was I who had written to Algie in response – I had snatched the letter from Piers.

"This calls for a steady hand, not poetics," I said to Piers and Bess, who sat slightly nervous opposite me at our weekly dinner.

That had made Piers laugh. Even in dire times – and Algie had wanted to send his precious daughter to a nunnery – Piers could laugh. A second was more important than an eternity, and Piers responded to each second on its own merit. Bess was there, close to tears, frightened for their love, she had said.

The Bible is a fine book, I wrote to Algie, *but should not be used as a legal document*. I knew this would break the back of the thing one way or the other. Algie, a Lancastrian Presbyterian, which may or may not have accounted for his short temper, would have tossed tables at the thought of a young man – a *foreigner*, at that – lecturing him so sardonically on perceived limitations of the Good Book. But it was all façade, anyhow. Sarah Radnor, for all her greyness, had apparently offered her husband an ultimatum: his fortune or that of the Burens'. I talked about it with some Oxonian associates who had business near his textiles firm. The rumours were simply ill-kept secrets up north.

Piers and Bess seemed happily alone and free in a wildly adventurous place. Claypole was a playground for young lovers, just as it had been a playground for innocent observant children, and just as it was a dreamscape of memories for us as we all grew old. Though Piers and Bess had separate rooms in distant spots, they could go days without seeing another soul.

I would take them out for something to eat on Saturday evenings. They would dress for dinner, and Bess would beam with excitement, she would put all her efforts into not bouncing along through the restaurant to the table. I would sit quietly opposite them both – children in the midst of adult-games – ask them the occasional question. I was keeping tighter watch over them than either could imagine – and I wanted them to feel free.

I was curious as to how such emotional freedom worked in others, I suppose. What if their love *was* real and it was pure? It could have been a remarkable thing to have seen. I had certainly not seen its like before. They were one creature, living through two machines. They understood the essences of each extremity, and it was *all* they understood: the world was nothing to them; not then. They grew to look outward, dangerously so. But for now they brought a small but comforting heat to my centre. Just to be with them each Saturday for a few hours propelled me through the week.

This was an arid time for me, you see? It was not just I was alone without Douglass – whose letters were becoming less frequent – but I was an attraction to many people, my fortune sounded a solid bugle call. It was as loud as it was unwelcome. Piers and Bess were soothing to be around. But in truth everything about me was complex during this time. I was a vortex of possibilities and damnations.

I was soon to become the sole controller of the family fortune, and I was being educated in the ways of money by various solicitors who were salivating at their legal and professional attachment to the bequeathment. They were like Alexander's generals, loyal but waiting for the king to die to grab the empire. It was greying. It was hollowing. But in my loneliness it was occupying. So I became good at it; the schooling made something of my average skillset even though the intricacies of business deadened my spirit. I wrote poetry and mailed it to Douglass in the hope that every line of verse was a shot of pure oxygen for a drowning soul. And every week, looking at Piers and Bess from across the dining table I saw real life, shot through with electricity like Frankenstein's monster.

Bess looked at me sometimes from across the table, an unfathomable, unearthly depth to the gold of her eyes, her mouth would curve so slightly it was almost imperceptible, and I would wonder if she wasn't inviting me into a secret, just the two of us, and a secret that involved the reasons for her love for my brother. She was older than time when she did this, her knowledge and understanding of this love was an ancient thing, and she could see my feral curiosity in my emotional stasis from across the table. It was, no matter how untrue, my first conspiracy.

As for conspiracies in general, I entered into them with myself quite frequently. I suggested to Piers and Bess that they think about marriage. They received the idea with a mixture of awe and nervousness, as if they had not considered these things available to them.

Bess asked me why I had suggested it. It was partially to secure their happiness, I said. Partially to end the tiresome correspondence with her father – a correspondence that was not solely now done via letter, but had begun to include lightweight solicitors turning up at Claypole and being met by a Matilda, angry and sightless in a whirlwind of enraged depression.

Back to our old ignorance of each other, I saw nothing of Matilda in these days. I would ask Piers every time we met how *his* mother was. He would roll his shoulders and look at anything but me and offer a half smile and say she was fine.

"She's maybe a little lost in some sense," he would say.

"In what sense?"

"She could maybe do with something to pass the time."

And so the marriage of Piers and Bess was also my way of taking Piers from Matilda and giving him to someone else. He had become a remarkable young man, for all the mollycoddling and the claustrophobic maternalism – he grew up wearing a suit of armour made from the hard skin of his Boer mother.

But I could not bring myself to go see her. I would stand in the street opposite Claypole and see her silhouette move smoothly past the upper window. She would not have wanted to see me. She was frozen in the moment when I did the right thing and simultaneously deprived her of her one breeze of human affection. I cast Algie Radnor and all that business out of our lives forever. She learned that I was not to be trifled with, and that I would do what needed to be done. She did not like either of the things she learned. I think that is why Matilda would always hate me.

Life, in all its courage, settled into a routine. Mine of two halves still; living the bachelor life whilst living every moment for news from Douglass. Part of me functioned, part of me hung in stasis, cocooned in a crisp transparent loneliness. I could not talk to any member of my family about my thoughts, my desires, my ambitions.

What were they? You have every right to ask. Long forgotten. Scars cover them now. And these things change over time. Ambition is one of life's most dishonest characteristics, morphing and mutating as the circumstances dictate. Never trust ambition.

How does *ambition* start out? As tadpoles of thought, mistimed, poorly judged, and they become amphibious and belong neither in the water nor on land. Eventually some realise their place on the earth. I am a believer in a supersymmetry that has no regard for our feelings, just a preoccupation with keeping chaos at the door. This was interpreted as God very early on. We, as a human race, are getting over that now. You are lucky to be of the first exodus from the shadow of that dangerous misinterpretation of the universe. My generation was grappling with that. Had I been an eminent Victorian I would have had so few problems of this kind. Believer or faithless, everybody seemed so sure of themselves back then. Douglass would say to me, "Would you rather be Lord Byron or John Donne?" "Byron," I would say hesitantly. "You?" "It wouldn't matter to me which," he would say. "Donne only gave himself to God when he had something to talk to God about. A sinless life is a quiet one."

I spent months in this netherworld, operating only by half in each. Douglass' letters had stopped altogether. I wrote and mailed more poetry. I received nothing back. I was screaming into the face of the darkness.

I never saw Douglass Karlchild again.

Douglass broke his neck playing rugby in the United States – it appeared the Yanks had no finesse when it came to it, and a high tackle did for him. He spent several months recuperating in hospital, and he was told he would not walk again, but when his parents summoned his return to England to live in the family home, Douglass pushed a knife into his own heart – a beautifully romantic gesture; I thought that even then. He was discovered in his hospital bed one morning. He had expected, quite understandably, the lonely life of a mansion recluse. Jones, the valet, had written the letter. *I felt it right that you were informed*, he wrote.

I do not know the darkness that subsumed me, but I know some of it has always remained. The world will never change this element of its nature for people. Happiness is fleeting; a good meal, a fine tobacco, an orgasm. But despair, true despair, never leaves. What had made Douglass end his own life? The darkness offers many painful responses, and to a thousand other questions. For me; I never wrote another word of poetry. Not another word of meaning until I opened this memoir.

THE POETS

∗ ∗ ∗

Piers met Ki Monroe in the winter of 1932.

At sixteen my brother was beginning to carry himself surely, already taking on what Emerson called *the serious occupation of manhood*. He had not learned to do so from the rod of public school education, as I had done. Piers had been reading Hemingway and Fitzgerald, but also Maupassant and Tolstoy, Verlaine and Rimbaud. And he had also been reading Eliot, Pound, the novels of Charlotte Latimer and the verse of Ki Monroe. And whereas Paris, it seemed, was for the dead and the Yanks, he had heard he could find some of these other writers if he just stayed up late enough in his own city. He feared I would disapprove, and I may have done. Piers occasionally projected onto me, unjustly, the role of paternal disciplinarian. He had little to go on other than my authority over him. That was my age, a trick of biology. But I did not dissuade him (or Bess) from that perception. It seemed to provide a strand of stability for them.

I still spent my time in London at my apartment in Kilburn and not at Claypole. But much of the time I was abroad. I was being guided by Alexander's generals to be the young athletic figurehead of the Buren fortune, which now took in gold as well as diamonds and armaments.

I was in Germany several times during this period, being fed and entertained by industrialists who could perhaps smell something I could not; it is a businessman's job to sense the coming storm, after all. My sense of smell improved.

My problem was that I liked the Jews. I admired their duty to family. I had little interest in anything else – I already judged by my own ears and eyes, if I had ever been any different. So I cut off my dealings with the Germans. The money I let go, and the world was a large place filled with opportunity. My generals shrugged, frustrated but still loyal, and turned once again to face America. It was a complex time for the investment business and one that I will not bore you with. You will never learn anything from the narratives of the accumulation of money.

Suffice it to say, I was preoccupied. Piers and Bess, who I believed to be strong, continued in their formula of unity in a small series of London tributaries that twisted amidst galleries and coffee houses and museums and dens.

I could not have known what Piers crossing paths with Ki Monroe would mean in the long run. Nobody could have known. Piers had found where his destiny lie. He could have crossed the path of Dylan Thomas and become a drunk, T.S. Eliot and become a genius. But it was Monroe and he became what he became: a searcher for tragic human truth.

Many years later, in her maudlin period, Bess told me the story of how they first met with Monroe.

At breakfast one morning, in the parlour at Claypole, Piers said to Bess: "I've found out the name of the coffee house they all go to in Soho. It's called Sedgemoor's."

He said it casually and without looking up from the newspaper.

Bess stopped spreading butter on her toast. Matilda poured tea for the three of them.

"Just like that?" said Bess.

Piers looked up.

"Why, of course," he said, and gave her a short sharp smile.

"And what will you say to these great writers?" said Bess.

"It doesn't matter what *I* say; it matters what *they* say."

"But you have to introduce yourself," said Bess.

Piers looked back down at the newspaper.

"Piers will be fine," said Matilda through dry lips. She spoke often now, forgetfully, in Afrikaans – it had become thicker in her solitude – and Piers would translate for Bess from behind his hand. "These are the kind of people he should be getting to know."

Bess pulled her robe tighter around her neck and resumed the buttering of her toast.

The rest of breakfast was taken in silence, apart from the rustling of newspaper and the dainty clinking of bone china and sterling silver.

Later that morning, as Piers read by the window of the parlour and Bess awaited her tutor, she said, "My love, I didn't want you to think I was being negative about your intentions earlier at breakfast."

"Of course not," said Piers, not looking up from his book.

Bess, her hands folded in her lap, began to twist her thumbs.

"I have never read your poetry," she said. "I mean you have never showed it to me."

Piers looked up slowly, and then began to gaze out of the window.

"No," he said. "It's not ready."

Bess did not take it any further.

Piers kept his notebooks in a locked wooden box. She would not have dared try to look into it. But, as she explained to me, Piers had spoken of them as being as one creature, and this exclusion had a physical, surgical effect on her. If they were to understand each other in their entirety, then his writing was vital to this. It was a hurtful way, at a young age, to learn that nothing can be wholly known.

And now she looked at Piers gazing down on to the street from the parlour window – although his thoughts were not on the commotion of the street-scene; she knew that – and wondered what she could do for him, how she could bring them closer together.

She stood up.

"We shall go to this Sedgemoor's; I shall take you," she said.

Piers looked over to her. His eyes looked tired; his face was soft and relaxed. He smiled at her gratefully.

"Okay," he said and nodded sleepily.

"I shall take you and if you don't know what to say then I will introduce you; I will introduce you as the greatest poet nobody has ever read."

And she walked over to him, her arms swinging, and kissed him hard on the mouth. He looked at her, at the bones of her round cheeks, the golden swirl to her eyes, and the curl to her dark hair.

"I love you," he said.

"And I you," said Bess.

Sedgemoor's was quiet – a low ceiling, scattered booths, anterooms, autumnal colourings and smoke in the air. Nobody turned when Piers, in a great coat and trilby, and Bess, in a straight dress and made-up, entered. Piers recognised no-one and his heart felt a little cheated at first. Bess noticed his disappointment; he was depleted by the time they found a seat. Unsure exactly of the protocol Bess waited, then stood, then sat and a waitress came over. They ordered a pot of tea, and Piers began to examine the clientele closer, a second burst of hope and a dismissive wave to the puerile heart.

"Do you recognise anyone?" said Bess.

"Can we not just *be*?" he said, annoyed, and he made a point of not looking around.

Bess looked on his behalf. A man with a bowed head, he was examining a newspaper, his brow in his palm, a cigarette pushing a twirl of smoke away from his head. He looked sad, stuck with sadness, tied to it. He could be a writer, thought Bess. On the next table was a couple, young but older than she and Piers. The woman was wrapped up tight, smiling, touching the man often on the forearm; they spoke but looked past each other, looked into some distant philosophical notion of love, no doubt. The man looked European and so did the woman, but they did not look alike, not like they came from the same corners of abroad. She laughed, he smiled, they moved in slow-motion, lethargically, her head tilted back, the man, with his pencil-thin moustache, tipped forward. Writers?

Another woman, middle-aged, sat rigid in the corner, sipping tea and reading a book, held the recommended distance from her eyes. Further on, before the first ante-room, a man made notes into a tattered book not bigger than a pack of playing cards. Bess felt energised by these slight exotic moments of the lives of others.

She told me how I should not underestimate this moment in my understanding of her then. *People*! She had never observed other people before. She had never before understood an existence through a glimpse. It is the building of narrative; an ocean built from the confluence of droplets. That is how the past presents itself to us, and Bess understood the past to be a part of the present, like eyes are a part of the seeing.

Bess looked back at the dejected, sullen Piers.

"Perhaps not today," she said.

Piers looked around once more. His face changed, it relaxed, he puffed.

"I do like it here," he said, unconvincingly, for Bess.

And he smiled.

"I do to," said Bess.

The waitress brought the tea and Piers heaped three mounds of sugar into each cup and stirred gently. Bess copied, but just the one sugar. And they spent a few minutes in silence, breathing in the smoke, breathing in the warm golden coffee-stained air.

The door opened, a gust came in followed by a substantial

figure, a man who unfolded into the place, unfurled from his wrapped-up collar and his large-brimmed hat. He stepped heavily with concrete steps, shook his chops from the cold and straightened tall and broad. Piers recognised him immediately as Ki Monroe – he did not recognise the three men who followed him in. Monroe was a big South African – Durbanese, no less – a bushman, a brawler poet, a swashbuckler. His reputation, in the right circles, was mythological. To see him in the flesh, to be in the presence of his physical shape, brought a reality to an idea, flesh to imagination; his large handsome head had keen eyes, his teeth always bit down on a three inch quellazaire; his thinning hair, rather than making him look old or unattractive, made him look monolithic, a Christmas Island mystery coming straight down the centre of the room. In his bone, in his bulk, were the ages and the wisdom that was ploughed out of them.

Monroe had a collection, *The Master of the River*, which Piers knew well enough to recite. The verse ticked over through him as he went about his days. Monroe's nature work put soil under the feet, even in these hard cityscapes. He wrote poetry with rough hands, he dug out images with iron forks and turned them with hoes. Monroe's idea was to find a meaning deep down in the depths of whence we came. A Monroe poem was craggy and robust, earthen, burned, it could burst a room open. Much like their author.

Piers' throat went dry but he did not let on, he fought the widening of his eyes, the elongating of the mouth. And he looked down to his cup. Bess noticed nothing until she noticed the change in Piers.

Monroe and his friends took a table near the back and the waitress brought out four short ink black coffees before any order was made. Piers kept one eye on them – he was interested in the behaviour of the *poet*, how did a *poet* drink coffee, how did he sit, cross his legs? How closely did a *poet* shave? Maude Gonne had written in her diary the day she met William Butler Yeats that the great Irishman was "every inch the poet", and that he was unkempt, distracted, intense, serious. Piers could not be all of these things all of the time. And he was sure that Yeats was not. And now there, in front of him, was Ki Monroe, dashing, athletic, powerful, a man's man but a mind also. Yeats had seemed other-worldly to Piers; Eliot was a banker, Pound an incantatory druid. Monroe's poetry was earthy, dusty, mossy, every line the verse of Piers' world, and there he was now sitting just a few yards away, a real flesh and blood man.

"Ki Monroe is here," Piers said calmly to Bess.

Bess knew the name, obviously; she had read the poets' book.

"So this is the place where the great take their coffee," she said, and looked around. "Which one is he?"

Piers patted her forearm and ducked his head as Monroe looked over to their table.

"Bess," Piers reprimanded in a hush.

Monroe continued to look at them both as the others of his group arranged their smoking paraphernalia and sugared their coffees.

"Go and introduce yourself," said Bess.

"I will not," said Piers.

"Then *I* will," said Bess and made to stand, but Piers held onto her sleeve and prevented her.

"*I* will do it," he said. They were not being particularly quiet and he stood with some purpose.

"What shall I say?" said Piers.

Bess looked up to him.

"Tell him simply that you admire him," she said.

"Wait," said Piers and his hand felt into his breast pocket.

"I have a copy of his book. I'll ask him to sign it. He will be impressed that I have it and even more impressed with how obviously well-thumbed it is."

Bess smiled and nodded. Piers nodded back and stretched his shoulders.

Monroe was watching them now, leaning back in his chair, his arm draped over the back, his other holding his cigarette. The others in Monroe's party had followed his attention and were now watching the young man approach the table. Bess admired his progress nervously.

"Mr Monroe?" said Piers before he had quite reached the table.

Monroe held very still.

"Yes," said the poet.

"My name is Piers Buren, and I am a great admirer of your work, and I was hoping you could put your signature to this copy of your book that I have here?"

Piers pulled the small volume from his breast pocket and held it out. He felt small in front of the big man and his friends, serious-looking men.

Monroe hitched forward on his chair and thick clouds of smoke came out of his mouth and nose. He took the book from Piers and took a pen from the inside of his jacket.

"Are you sure you want me to sign this?" said Monroe.

"Well, sir; of course. I feel you are a great poet and I know everything you have written."

Monroe looked at the young man wryly and held the book up for the whole table to see. It was a copy of *The Love Song of Alfred J. Prufrock* and immediately Piers remembered it was Eliot he had been reading that day, not Monroe. He felt his face burn from the neck up.

"I could sign Thomas' name if you'd prefer?" said Monroe. "Or I could take it to him. I see him often."

Those around the table began to laugh. Before Piers could gather himself Bess was at his arm. She looked at the book, snatched it from Monroe's large hand and said, "Well, *how* rude; Piers just wanted to tell you how much your work means to him and you ridicule him in front of your friends. A poet maybe, but the behaviour of a sailor."

"Miss, I beg your pardon," said Monroe with a slight smirk. "I meant nothing by it."

He seemed genuinely sorry, but still lightly amused. He said sternly, "It is not right of me to mock a reader of any poetry, certainly not a reader of my own. Please, accept my apology."

Monroe's friends hushed and began to look anywhere but at Monroe, Piers and Bess.

"In my naivety, I always imagined poets to be a sacrosanct fraternity. I don't think we *will* accept it," said Bess.

"Please yourself," said Monroe and leaned back in his chair, biting onto the stem of his quellazaire.

"Rude," said Bess, and she tugged at Piers' sleeve and began leading him away from the table.

"Hey," said Monroe. Bess and Piers turned. "You're a poet?"

Piers, finding it difficult to hide his dejection, said, "Hardly, in your company, sir."

Monroe laughed.

"Yes, you look like a poet," he said. "Come and join us, let me action my apology."

Piers immediately forgot the mockery, the show of which he had just been a part – for at least it *was* a show, wasn't it, and Piers was just an actor in it? He heard the words of Monroe's: "you look like a poet," and his chest puffed up. He didn't even look at Bess, but just walked toward the table, pulling her along with him.

They talked for a while, Monroe and Piers. Bess sitting a

little at an angle to them – invited to the table but not the group, she said. Monroe asked what he wrote. Piers was vague, blushing. He reluctantly agreed to allow Monroe to see his work sometime. Conversation drifted back amongst the group, and Piers became a satisfied onlooker; the group of four men around the table seemed to enjoy their young audience.

Bess' first impressions of Monroe? She said, "It is difficult to speak ill of him. I thought he was arrogant, but it was a hard-fought position. And who was *not* arrogant in that place? Later you learn about his life, you learn about his loves and his prejudices, and you find he is a lover of nature and a socialist and a family man, and a farmer and a peasant-at-heart, a poet of the earth and the soul, and it is difficult to speak ill of him. If it had just been that afternoon, I would have said he was a bully, a braggart and a brawler – and I would not have been wrong; he was all those things too. But it was not just that afternoon. And so I ended up thinking a great deal of the man."

* * *

I decided I was going to spend more time in London.

My experiences of the world had been narrow but complex – the world of business was as it is now: tethered to the ignorance and solitude of money – but I *had* learned that it is quite a thing to emerge unbroken. Individuals had fallen, as well as nations, in the short time I had spent as an adult. In the time since I have seen even soaring peoples get belly-sick with rotting corruption. America is a virus now, and Great Britain was forever thus. My adopted homeland fought Germany twice for the world rights to despotic exploitation. The further I went out into the world as the figurehead of the Buren Company, the quicker I wanted to be done with it. There was no reason for money to be the reason we worked. No matter how wealthy I was, I could still only wear one suit, drink from one cup, eat from one bowl. By the mid-thirties I was ready to allow the generals to have their way, answering to me in my hermitage. It was they who had the compulsion, not me.

And it was around this time that Bess and Piers decided to marry. It was Bess who told me, coming to my apartment alone. It was unusual for her to do that. But she said that she hoped the marriage would mean that she and Piers would get to see more of *me*.

"You are important to us both," she said.

"I have been thinking over my business commitments," I said. "And much seems to be in place. I hope I can be in London more often."

This seemed to please her. And it was this relieved smile that contrasted with what I could understand as concern in her first question. She was worried about something, something to do with Piers, something I had not been around enough to register for myself.

Bess was eighteen, Piers nineteen by now and preparing to go to Oxford to study literature a year later than was originally planned. When I spoke to him about the wedding he forced out the enthusiasm.

"Is there something wrong?" I said.

"Of course not," he said. "How could there be?"

"You want to marry her, don't you?"

His smile drooped and he looked very stern.

"Who wouldn't want to marry Bess?" he said.

The wedding was brief, functionary, attended by a few friends and Matilda and myself, on a warm day, and they spent a few months travelling around the edges of the Mediterranean as a honeymoon. It was I who suggested Piers take Bess to South Africa for a time, so he could see the land of his birth, learn something about himself and his family, see his father's grave. But it was Italy and France and Spain he wanted to see, or so he professed. His fuller story, told from where I am now, suggests his plans were more complex. But for now his interests lay in Europe.

I asked Bess, privately, as an aside, why he was so determined about this. She sighed and, looking out across the restaurant, said, "He has heard great things about these places."

He admired Mussolini as well as Largo Caballero – the bravura of the former and the studiousness of the latter – despite their opposing politics. He discovered that he had no time for the wheezing windbag Lebrun, but that the French villages had stolen his heart. His opinions of the politicians were naïve, but it was a new interest, a new angle of view on the world outside of Claypole and Sedgemoor's. He began to talk in long rambling sentences when it came to politics, he adopted clawed histrionics and I noticed the language of the clothcap Left begin to infest his vernacular. His worry at my disapproval seemed to have subsided.

I was fully settled back in Kilburn, dealing with my generals mainly from a telephone I had installed at the desk by the window. I soon became suspicious that Bess was making moves to have me as close to the two of them as possible. For a long time I thought she had simply grown worried at what she clearly thought of as Piers' jejune political poses. But then I could see he was becoming distracted from his hitherto preoccupation of love, and perhaps it was that Bess did not like the competition for his intellectual stamina. So I humoured this cute insecurity. I regret that I did not take the issue more seriously. Of course I do.

We went out the first night they were back from honeymooning in Europe, and we went out most nights after. They both seemed very happy. The trip appeared to have satiated Piers' political interests, at least I had half-expected him to return with grand ideas, with attitudes that only a tourist who thinks he has had a worldly education can have. But he was quiet about such matters, circumspect, and for the most part was not the one to begin conversations around current affairs. His interests returned to poetry, to the role of poetry, and to Bess.

Here, if I am guilty of some things in my brother's fate, then I am guilty of misunderstanding him. He was honing the parameters of a philosophical quest, not moving from one phase to another. I did not see it because I did not know him well enough; I did not involve myself fully in his life whilst at the same time I convinced myself that I was his steward and his better. I had a superficial literary idea of my position in his life. We were two characters, and I believed my duty was done by filling the shoes of my assigned character. This, let me tell you, is the period when I could have done most good, and instead I spent my time believing in the peripheries of grand themes – loss, tragedy, solitude, mortality – but the truth is my poetry had gone, and so therefore so had my depth and, shamefully, my interest. Not just for my brother, but for everything.

Bess would call me every day and make arrangements for our evenings out. She would find parties, restaurants, drinking establishments that were as close to my apartment as I wished them to be, judging by the enthusiasm in my tone. I was flattered when I should have been alerted.

And then Bess had a friend, Madeleine Disidion, and Madeleine was more and more in attendance whenever we went out. We became a foursome. It was a further attempt by Bess to keep me with them. I had no romantic interest in Madeleine, and I'm sure her interest in me was purely superficial. But still, I was told that Miss Disidion had made it known to Bess that she was in love with me. We had barely passed a sentence between us when alone.

Madeleine, who talked often of Hollywood movie actors, liked tall, dark and handsome men; of which I was all three, to a degree – and I'd suggest her attraction to me was only intensified by my reticence to indulge in small talk. *Do not speak unless you have something to say*, was a favourite catchphrase of Matilda, *and even then give it some serious consideration.* I could keep silent – unless spoken to – for entire evenings if it suited me. This did not put off Madeleine Disidion. It had the opposite effect.

Madeleine was very beautiful – blonde, tall, slimmer than Bess, who had retained something of the country girl about her. But Madeleine was exact, tense, rigid as bone china. She might have had something going for her had she been classless – alluring, deceptive, forbidden, spoilable. But there was nothing to really interest me in her clean, somewhat entitled femininity. Madeleine was the daughter of a Lord, albeit a rather forgettable one who spent much of his time in India when not dozing through debates in the Second House.

Madeleine, beyond her wan beauty, was paper-thin. She fluctuated in the breeze of conversation like a shed feather. She sat awkwardly amidst my careful silences. She never once offered an opinion on any affair that I had not already read in the editorial pages of that morning's *Times*. Often her gaze would turn to the ceiling under the searching pressures of her brain as she tried to remember what she had read. She was condescending to waiting staff, and loathsomely malleable to me, and to Piers. She was called a friend by Bess, and yet Madeleine's face never did stop from turning sour at the sound of Bess' light northern cadences that would slip from her mouth when she became particularly animated. They were not easy to pair as friends anyway. Bess floated and bobbed like a weightless bubble; Madeleine was stiff and angular, she moved like a yacht in barely choppy waters – (she would never be so bold as to move through anything rougher than 'barely' choppy). I was at pains for some time, trying to figure out the connection between the two. How did they meet? Through mutual friends in Soho, Bess said. They *immediately hit it off*. Neither looked convinced when Bess said this across the dinner table. I realised what Madeleine in fact was: the idea of what Bess thought was good for me. A pretty and harmless socialite. It is always a surprise to see yourself how others see you, no matter how inoffensive the portrait.

Madeleine would have taken little convincing of our suitability, I'm sure. She felt our pairing was the ultimate triumph of the moneyed advance. *Her* titles and *my* wealth. The future of the Empire depended upon unions like that. Her father would have almost certainly approved.

Was I ever tempted to indulge in Madeleine as a symbol of propriety? To see how my adoptive class progressed from one unhappy generation to the next? Perhaps I was. I don't remember. But I never did. She was too comical in her weak and unearned trust. And she was virginal, despite the bitterness that lived beneath the surface of her skin. Bitter because of her virgin state perhaps. But bitter most likely because her father paid her no attention. If she loved me because I was older, mature, stern, it had only a little to do with her father. How had the conversations between Madeleine Disidion and myself sounded?

"So, you are a businessman?"

"I have several business interests."

"That sounds exciting."

"Well, the world is made of a diverse crowd."

"Do you go to the movies?"

"I don't."

"Do people tell you that you look like William Powell?"

"I don't know who that is."

So perhaps it is important for me to make it known to you that I am not an animal, and did not go about taking whatever was on offer (and *everything* is on offer to a man of money). I could have married Madeleine and spent the next few decades crushing her, as she would have wanted, and as her family would have expected. But I did not. I avoided dim moments of intimacy with her. We were never alone, despite the efforts of my brother and Bess. And so parties were the best option.

Amidst all this, Piers was my least concern. I prowled about the cage of Madeliene's interest in me – it was not beyond comprehension that a slip up on my part would have ended with the two of us married – I had to be on guard when with her. And I believed that Bess' concern was something that my mere presence would rescue her from. I was sorrowfully arrogant. And I didn't see Piers' quietness for what it was: preparation. And then he was gone.

* * *

It was late 1933 when Piers went back to the farm.

He told me of his plan during lunch, and how he wanted to keep it from Bess and Matilda – he would write them from the ship that would take him to South Africa. This was something he had *to do alone*. He was a man now. He had a powerful gaze, a straight mouth, and a fiercely intelligent sense of humour – not something our family was ever marked out with. He was sure of things, but, it must be said, I saw in him a remarkable naivety, a bold lack of circumspection in his ideas. He was, in a word, a *Romantic*. And *they* never lasted long. They're all gone now.

He promised me, and to Bess in his letter, that he would be gone a month. After three months, Bess came to me and pleaded that I go get him.

"I have not had a letter from him in two weeks," she said.

"It is a long way, Bess. Anything could be happening to the mail."

And then she showed me the last letter she had received from him – erratic, formless and written in a slashed hand, it said, *Bess, I do not know if I will write again for a while, because, you see, my father is here, he has come and I must spend time with him while I still can.*

Of course I had to go. He had cracked; what other explanation could there have been? His quest had proved too much for him. My poor brother, I thought – I had let him down by allowing him go in the first place.

So I went to the old farmhouse – still owned by the Buren Company, and found my brother Piers strong but delirious in a derelict version of our birth home. But I will not pull everything down to that moment when I found him. No. Instead I will give you a glimpse into the work he was

93

attempting, the kernel *and* the husk of his quest. What else can I say other than he was trying to give meaning to his life, and to the lives of us all.

This is much of what he told me during those days in the farmhouse once I had arrived and rescued him from his solitude. It took time, this journey back to reality. He went through a fever, and I fed him fresh food and cleaned him up. Lord knows when he had last slept. He cried and slept for two days. And then, with the fire lit, the sun setting, and the wine poured, he sat across from me and, with his voice steady, careful, methodically recalling the most real of his days, he told me this:

Piers disembarked the *SS Danmark*, a merchant schooner, the beard he had grown on the journey shaved clean that morning, his greying shirts washed and crisp, his shoes shined – he was ready for land.

He waved farewell to the sailors he had made his friends on the journey as they threw ropes and hauled beams; the sky was a clear lost blue. The sailors, he had discovered, had ocean all around them in their work, above and below. They lived in an amniosis. He had taken no interest in the mechanics of their profession in the weeks at sea, but he had been curious of their stories. The seafaring life is a magical one. It is somewhere between life and death. A beautiful, deathly existence where everything is held in stillness. He found stillness there, something utterly detached from the world. It was as if he and his fellow passengers were in purgatory, and this ship was delivering them to the afterlife.

The other passengers constituted, if I remember rightly, a middle-aged German doctor and his family, all of them clad in black, on their way to Burundi to fight exotic diseases in the Christian missions. There was a young female school teacher, and a young man, around Piers' age, who was returning to the family home after studying in Amsterdam.

They dined together with the Captain and the officer crew – a ragtag brotherhood who had to be reminded every evening to take off their caps at the dinner table. Piers admitted to me there were nights when he drank gutsily. It seemed right somehow – the company, the atmosphere.

The Captain was a handsome but raw Dane – there was something troubled about him just below the surface, a man caught between the savagery of the sea and the civility of dining with passengers. If he was the deliverer he himself would never be delivered. Piers imagined he would be unhappy in either world, fully living or fully dead. Life at sea is not a happy one, despite its magic.

Piers decided this Captain might make a character in a poem. Captain Svensson was hardly the Ancient Mariner, but he was perhaps the updated version, the modern avatar. He spoke about James Cook often when into the second carafe of wine.

"Yorkshireman – are you from Yorkshire, Mr Buren?" he said.

Piers said he wasn't even English.

He looked at my brother suspiciously.

"That is a shame. I hope to visit his home one day. A great man."

Piers could see that the other passengers around the table did not take the Captain all that seriously. He would overstep the mark on his drinking, he would appear childish in his adoration of the explorer Cook, and Piers felt they did not trust him. It did not help when Svensson said that he hated 'The Rime of the Ancient Mariner', that it was false, that it was cruel, that it "made us all seem like ghost-chasers, spooks ourselves."

"Coleridge and Cook did have a connection," said the German doctor one evening.

"What kind of connection?" said Captain Svensson, leaning on his elbow, steadying himself, his eyes heavy with the grape.

"His mentor was William Wales," said Piers. "Cook's astronomer on his second circumnavigation of the globe."

Svensson nodded, drank more wine. He looked unhappy at the revelation. Poetry and science are not *things* – this is how people like Svensson thought. The only *thing* is the direction of the bow, and the sea it ploughs through.

The young teacher, pretty and pale, dainty and polite, blipped a laugh and Svensson looked embarrassed.

"I don't like literature," he said, angrily. "I was schooled well but I discovered I wanted to touch things rather than read about them. What is the point of literature, anyway?"

"To make sense," said Piers.

"I do not need things explained: I understand," said Svensson, and Piers stood down.

The Captain seemed happy with this kind of victory.

The German Doctor stayed silent – he was a rigorously humourless man.

"I bet our good doctor does not need literature to explain the workings of the human body," said the Captain, getting blood to his cheeks.

The Doctor, after asking the permission of the women at the table, lit a long thin cigar and replied, "I am from the land of Goethe, Captain; I see no difference between art and science. We are all trying to understand."

The conversation had stuck with Piers, he told it to me with the glassy eyes of nostalgia. To Piers it was the first important moment of his journey.

As he walked the streets of Durban, his luggage just one heavy sack of clothes, books and writing equipment, he ran over the implications in his mind. Captain Svensson was neither a poet nor a scientist, surely; unless the German Doctor had meant by *scientist* anybody who runs mechanical method in their work, one who shuns inspiration for strategy. But Svensson had James Cook. What Svensson meant was to travel and see the world, to witness the same sun lower over many different horizons; he was beyond both these things.

What was Piers *doing* in Durban? If you think he was a young man who lived a doubtless life you would be wrong. He was doubtful immediately.

The German Doctor spoke often of Goethe on that ship.

Goethe wrote that he feared the modern world would become one big hospital; everybody would be sick. Goethe understood more than Freud, it seems. Piers felt remiss for not asking the German Doctor who his hero had been. Had he become a doctor in order to work against Goethe's prophecy? Or did he think he could cash in at the Goethian hospital? Goethe was not *wrong*, was he?

Svensson was tied only to his own miseries, it seemed; shackled to a sickness of the mind. The school teacher did not seem happy; she was simple but sad. The young ex-student from Amsterdam; he was dreading a return to Africa, leaving behind Rembrandt and silk and Van Gogh and rosy cheeks and bright enlightened Europe.

Goethe's *sickness* was the shrinking of the globe. Home is not where you are *from*, it is where feels *correct*. Modernity was intent on breeding discomfort. Yeats was shouting about this. Piers' head was awash with these brilliant, shining ideas. The hero will be crushed by the machine; the veldt will be sprayed with dull thudding concrete. So, was Piers here to see it all before it was swallowed up by the Beast? He would write a poem about this, he thought; it was the cycle he was born to write.

The ground beneath his feet felt hard, thoughtless and hard – he had been too long walking the soft wood of the rocking ship deck. He should write a poem about his arrival in his homeland, Piers thought to himself. There is much to be said. The unfamiliarity of the earth. Was it usually this hard, or was it his sea legs joking with him? The sun was heavy; it came up from the ground as well as bored down upon it.

As he rode out to the farm – a four hour buggy ride – he worked over ideas for poetry about the countryside, about the dirt and the yellow grass and the distant mountains and the dryness and peculiar lizards and, at one point, far in the flat distance a grazing herd of antelope, languorous and meaty.

He thought of a poem about creation, written in blank verse, perhaps undercutting the Biblical, origin-story formula with a swishing modern brush. And then he thought about the antelope as a symbol of the old world, of the age of myth and fawns and nymphs; the antelope a talker, a wise beast being outside of the trivial conjectures of man. The king antelope would be a creature of great glory with his long head and thick feminine eyelashes. And he thought about a buggy carrying a young traveller who would never reach the farm to which he headed, instead he would just travel for all time through this dry hot wilderness, always toward a mountain-range that never altered in size. How we are all travelling, thought Piers, and never arriving. The whole veldt could end up being a metaphor for death anxiety – a different kind of desperation altogether, Piers decided. That is a creeping undermining of life. Vast; a bowl with mountain sides. Piers began to imagine beings floating down from heaven and landing gently upon the dry earth of the veldt; angels, Martians – whatever – this is where they would arrive.

His hired cab reached the farmhouse. It was large, white, wooden, sprayed with clay-coloured dust from a recent dry storm. It was standing, worthy, but abandoned, inside like a ghost ship. Belky had lived there after his wife had died, but in his dotage he had since moved to Pretoria to be near his grandchildren. The farm had been forgotten.

But Piers felt he could remember it – perhaps the smell, the dry air, the cool whooping sound of the wind as it swirled around the front yard. He looked over to the filled-in well at the far end, the pigpen, the enormous barn, like a sleeping giant bug.

Piers examined the farmhouse as if it were a palace, his gaze running up the walls, along the furniture, the staircase, the fireplace; his cot was still in the corner of the parlour and he placed his hand on the side of it, rocked it gently, wondered how he would have judged such a face looking down to him when he was a baby. The new born; so sick-free. Or is that just a myth of perspective? Who knows what babies think and to where those thoughts dissipate?

A wind picked up and a tumbleweed blew across the dust-top of the yard. Piers grinned with satisfaction. This was the beginning-world he had been promised, the land of the burgeoning hero of which Homer spoke, of which I spoke. Of course, he knew now there were no palaces or Minotaur or Cyclops, as I had told him when he was little – how mischievous I had been – but he could imagine one of any of these creatures walking around the corner at any moment. What was it Monroe had said about myth? Piers recited the quote, and my god, if it wasn't the first time I had been introduced to Monroe's place in my brother's life.

"Myth is not un-fact; it is a place where we begin, and our dramatizing of these origins is where we will end up. You need to find that myth, Piers. Find your own mythology. Have you ever walked about the veldt?"

"I have not," said Piers. "I have not even been there since I was a baby."

Monroe feigned a dropping of the jaw.

"You must go," he said. "You must go and find your origins in order to find where you are to go. That'll get you writing, if nothing else."

Piers told me of that exchange and I could see the moisture in his eyes, I could see the power this Monroe had over him even at this point.

Piers set up a camp, as it were, in one room of the house – he wouldn't have known it, but it was our father's study. One room, a fire and a table and a fold down bed, some chairs, a stove he brought in from the shed.

The first night there was quiet. Piers lit a fire and ate with one hand whilst making sketches for the myriad poems that had come to him that day. The German Doctor would have to be a character, a voice. He should give the poem about Goethe's hospital a rigid, perhaps Germanic metre. Who was it who wrote the libretti for Wagner? That could work. Knead the ideas into this pulsating rhythm. *No* – it had to be rigid, just as the Doctor had been.

And then there was the poem about Captain Svensson. It could be a pastiche of Coleridge. But Svensson deserved better than a lyrical game, didn't he? It seemed to Piers that the man was placeless, and so sailed the world looking for an end, looking for an abyss. He could not trust science and he could not trust art; he could only trust his own eyes and tongue and fingertips. It would be a tragedy.

And then, on that first night, it came to him: perhaps Piers was not here to write a book of poems at all, but a verse play about the tragic schooner Captain and his troublesome passengers.

Svensson was a despot, a tragic figure who would send his charge to their watery grave if he found his abyss, and his passengers laughed at him behind their hands. Svensson becomes drunk one night at dinner and challenges his passengers to prove the worth of the material world, to prove the worthiness of art and to prove the worthiness of science. *Yes*; that is a good opening for the play, thought Piers. The German Doctor, stiff and thoughtful, gives up examples of human endeavour; of Faraday and Pythagoras and Da Vinci. The school teacher, a far simpler creature, says that the children she teaches are proof of a central unifying force, for they come to conclusions about profound topics that have already been reached by genius. They can be guided but they understand the workings of the universe because science and art make the universe the way it is. And the young poet talks of Dante and Shakespeare and Keats and Yeats and explains that a raindrop in their hand is like a dragon's tear, like a silver flame. But the whole time they have been pleading their case in the dining cabin of the ship, the Captain has been sailing toward a secret island, the island where God died.

And they go onto the land and Svensson takes them to the crater where God's body lies, frozen in its final moment of supine air-gasping all-humble mortality. Each of them has a different reaction. The German Doctor refuses to believe that the giant corpse is God. The school teacher falls to her knees and immediately becomes a devout Christian, crying her devotion into her lace gloves. The poet runs to the hills to a cabin and begins to write the story as a verse play.

But this was a parable, was it not? Piers wrote sketches over sketches and the next day Piers wrote more, tried to break the poetry from its parabolic egg. He wrote and wrote and soon lost the ideas of day and night, lost the ideas of hours and minutes.

In that farmhouse time evaporated. He wrote to Bess every day – told her how he was becoming a poet; some days he wrote exactly what he had written the day before – and he wrote to Matilda and to me sometimes, too.

It was now Piers had strange waking dreams of long walks along a cliff top looking out to the ocean, the black-tipped waves curling greyly upon one another. His verse play was stretching – would God have a voice? He looked up to the sky and shouted it – "Do you have a voice?" and bushes rustled and the waves crashed.

And was it to be an elaborate hoax – like a Hans Christen Andersen story? Or was it really the corpse of God? How was the play to end? The longer he worked at it, the further the end got from him. His shouting at the sky became conversations with shadows cast by the flickering candlelight against the wall. And on the night when he decided that God should have the same voice as his mute father a figure came to the door, dark and dripping from the rain.

Piers, who had been scribbling obsessively his idea of a Latin speech for the school teacher as she professes to know nothing of classicism, slowly raised his head from the page. He had not shaven since the SS Danmark had docked – several months ago now although he did not recognise that – and his clothes were fading and filthy with sweat and dirt.

"I seek shelter from the rain," said the figure.

The rain gently hitting the roof and the crackle of the fire were the only noises between them.

"I have game and wine," said the figure, taking another step in. "This lodge is usually uninhabited."

Piers stood cautiously. He could not see the man's face – he was past his prime, the outline suggested, but he was still built-to-work.

"I have some stew on the stove, friend," said Piers, and waved him in to a seat.

The man stepped in to the light. He was handsome, a triangular jaw beneath the soft triangle of his mouth, and his eyes were the brightest blue, like shots of lightening through the dark. Piers stared at him as he took a seat at the table, strewn as it was with loose pages of his play. Piers knew about visitors like this – he had read about angels, about spirits who wander the earth.

"You are a writer," said the man.

"I am."

"Not a hunter?"

"No."

Piers put a healthy amount of stew into a bowl and placed it in front of the man who took off his wet overcoat and brushed his hair back from his forehead. Yes, it could be his father, Piers thought; it could be that man.

"What are you writing?" he said, spooning some stew into his mouth.

"I am trying to decide if God has a voice," said Piers.

The man smiled wryly and ladled another mouthful of stew into him.

"You have never heard God's voice?" he said.

"I have not," said Piers. "Have you?"

"I have not either," said the man. "But I don't think it's something you hear. I think it is something you see. I see it in the veldt. I see it in those birds I shot."

He pointed to the birds tied together by the feet piled against the door.

Piers picked up his pen, dipped it in the ink and began to write.

"I'm glad you came," he said.

Piers remembered nothing from that moment to seeing me. Whatever his story – and I feel it is integral to what happened in the years after I got him back to England – I found not a drop of ink on a single sheath of paper in that farmhouse. He told me he had taken to burning the pages once they were done, but I wasn't convinced. I don't think Piers knew what had happened to the work, and he could not allow himself to believe he had not written anything. Burning it? Poetical insanity was preferable to *sheer* insanity.

I as good as nursed him on the voyage back. A luxury liner, first class. I remember stepping up to him just a few feet from the gangway and, from behind, placing a reassuring hand on his shoulder.

"I always felt like you would come for me, Hal," Piers said. "Somehow I've always felt you would come for me."

And then I remember Piers turned to me at the gangway and said, "Please Hal, let them think it was I who came to you?"

His breakdown was to be kept a secret, then. I obliged. My mistakes, you might notice, are accumulating.

Of course, Piers was showered with tribute, like a returning general. I stood just inside the doorway as Matilda fell at his feet. She cried and cried, pressed him to her. It was close to hysteria. The butler picked up the cases and sheepishly made his way up the stairs, out of the way of such unseemly behaviour. I just stood by the door and waited to see if the anguish would to turn to joy. I seem to remember leaving quietly, Bess awkward at their side, waiting for access to her beloved husband.

* * *

It is time I tried to draw for you the scene of the occasion of my first meeting with Ki Monroe. It is the logical place in this story. You have to know the man to understand the story as a whole. And he was not an easy man to know. Piers found him easy to know like wood knows fire. There must be ecstasy in the burning. There has always been ecstasy in the burning.

The night that I stepped in to Piers' world was very much like any other at the outset. Dinner. Myself, Piers, Bess and Madeleine, all in good form, all relaxed and well-fed, well-watered.

"You have to admit she is a work of art," Piers said.

I said nothing, but watched Bess moving across the edges of the dance floor, swaying between the large round tables of drinkers and diners, her gown, golden, glistening in the chandelier light, straight and brittle, hanging like chainmail from her small shoulders. Her head was bowed, watching her own footsteps, her hair falling about her face.

"And yet Madeleine is not good enough for you? You know you are the envy of all London having her on your arm. She's like a movie star," said Piers.

"She is most certainly good enough for me, Piers; if not better," I said, still admiring Bess' dainty, gliding walk. "But Madeleine is not *on my arm*."

"Are you really so settled in your life? A twenty-five year old bachelor? You won't come across anything finer than Madeleine, my man."

I shuffled a little in my seat.

He spoke to me like this often now with a few brandies inside him. He would lightly punch my shoulder and lean back in his chair, hooking his thumbs into his waistcoat pockets. He puffed out cigar smoke and grinned widely, a confident if unconvincing totem of life-satisfaction. I knew he was mimicking something. Or someone.

There was still something about Piers that wanted to prove to me that he was on track. He had worked hard to prove to me that his visit to the farmhouse had *gotten something out of his system*. If I believed that entirely it was because I chose to. But he could not hold up the charade even for an entire evening. He would flit between conversations, and he would try and quicken my mood also.

"Madeleine loves you," he said.

"This infatuation will pass," I said. "And then where does that leave us? Trapped in a rather unattractive pose while the whole of London gazes on?"

I could feel my brother's incredulous stare.

"Are you so incapable of light thoughts?" he said, waving his hand dismissively. "Unbutton your shirt a little, Hal, for Christ's sake," this tailed off just as Bess reached the table.

She placed herself next to Piers, kissed him on the cheek, and asked what all the laughter was over. We brothers were very quick to act dismissively at these moments.

Bess and Piers danced for a while, a little off tempo. They were too energetic for the place.

"Is there somewhere we can go and really let our hair down?" Bess said when they returned to the table.

"I like it here," said Madeleine. "The food was excellent."

"But we're done eating, Maddy," said Bess. "You know a party is going nowhere when the Billboroughs are the main attraction." And she waved over to the old couple across the way.

The Billboroughs: Roger and Hetty. Serious old money. Roger had spent many years trying to get me to part with mine, to put some of it into Guinean mining. *I am all about the overground now*, I would say to him. *My father dug our first wealth out of the dirt and he had no desire to see me get back down into it*. But the truth was I just didn't like Billborough. His face was sallow and graceless, plump and dusty. He flitted about me like an old fat moth and it made me feel like a carcass. That's what I hated most about those early days of my adulthood: those who gathered at my side prepared to loot, or just graze; the Germans with their dark dens and sordid peacocking, the Spanish with their open vistas and family myths. All the while my father's investments were beginning to arm the Russians.

"Piers, you know where all the good parties are," I said, ushering them on.

"Well, I know *of* a party – should be getting interesting right about now – a place called Sedgemoor's in Soho," said Piers, looking at his pocket watch.

"Isn't Soho a little far at this time?" I said.

"Nonsense," said Piers. "And you can meet some of my friends."

"Will Monroe be there?" said Bess, and I caught the sharp glance she received from Piers in return.

"He may be," said Piers.

"Monroe?" I said.

Bess leaned forward with an incredulous smile on her face.

"You haven't told your brother about your friendship with Ki Monroe?"

Piers scoffed.

"I wouldn't call it a friendship," he said.

Bess frowned.

"How else would you term it?" she said. She turned her face to me. "Ki Monroe is a great encourager of Hal's poetry."

"Ki Monroe, eh?" I said.

I had heard of the poet. He had caused a stir with a satire around about that time and he had made the news in some quarters.

"And when he is in the country Piers cannot be wrenched from his side," Bess said.

Piers waved a dismissive paw.

"Nonsense," he said.

"Perhaps you two could go on and Hal could take me home," said Madeleine.

I glanced at her tired and expectant face, forcing with every inch of the muscles around her eyes a continuous prolonging of the game we seemed to be playing with each other.

"And pass up an opportunity to meet some of Piers' friends?" I said. "I won't hear of it."

If I had the mind to prejudge a place like Sedgemoor's, I would not have been inaccurate. A house of misfits, pulsating with the energy such incongruities encourage. There was a bar serving wine and spirits, and a band setting up in the corner. Piers nervously dotted around me, expecting me to turn my nose up. I was in my suit of darkest blue, the businessman amongst artisans, undertaker amongst choristers. I was introduced to several writers. I pretended to not know who they were.

I moved through the party, glided, pushing my shoulders forward into the gaps of the throng, cigarette and drink held level at all times. I gave a cursory examination of every face I passed; shallow, etched with the destitution of choice, all of them players. I remember feeling a little disgust; disgust at the dirt, disgust at the pretences of revolutionary spirit, the stench of middle class pontificators. I didn't like their idea of what made a good person, and I did not even have to ask what that was.

The place was too discursive, too tied up with the grammar of the hive – the hierarchy was dishonest, I could see. There were leaders and followers, but they all wore the same uniform in an attempt at communist charades. There was energy, but there was waste. Everywhere *waste*! Conversations rattled on, Piers came and went from my side like a bird. Bess seemed to know everyone, and Madeleine – I had left her in one corner being wowed by a painter or sculptor or some such – had no trouble attracting men toward her and her iron-clad small talk.

I was on the lookout for the fabled Ki Monroe, but I could see no-one who matched his description – a hero's portrait on most counts – and when I asked Piers about him he replied with suspicion, "I don't think he's coming."

I had been, I suppose, on the lookout for some time for the central element that brought together my vague suspicions regarding Bess' recent behaviour toward me. It might have been another woman, but I always suspected Piers was capable of many things, but clichés were not a part of his language. Once the name of Monroe was given to me, it became obvious. She was frightened of him, frightened of some influence he had over my brother, and she was recruiting my help, in reserve, should I be needed.

I spoke with Piers; we both looked out over the party. I could read something in his eyes now when he said Monroe's name; it was a childish coyness, a protectiveness, but also an invention of seclusion for the poet-class. *Tread carefully on my grassland with your boots*, my brother's eyes said; *do not lumber into the veldt with your accumulated dreariness*. Monroe was a bushman, a South African, a warrior-poet. I did not even have the accent anymore.

Piers told me to try not to look so bored and make some friends and he went to get some drinks.

I recognised Charlotte Latimer from her solemn photograph in *The Times*. Charlotte Latimer, author of the *unreadable novel of unfathomable genius*, as I recall the review – more people had an opinion on *Banderbay* than had actually read it.

She herself was lean, equine, her features noble and uneven, her eyes were oval and pleading while her face was anything but; her clothes hung from her like a nomad's caravan; her voice was low, steady and judicious, it had the melody of the stage, as if spoken through a hollow, dusty pipe. Of course, everybody knows the name now. She is a giant of the age. But at that time the age was not done, and she was still years away from her legendary madness. But I could see the *otherness* of the woman even then. She was uncomfortable with herself and her surroundings, as if her mind would have preferred to have just left her body to it and retired back to the writing shed.

The crowd worshipped her from a position of chronic reverence – the type that leaves the subject isolated with monarchical duty. *Loneliness*: it is a price as well as a disease. Latimer was standing alone on the steps to a raised veranda, watching over the proceedings. I introduced myself.

"Buren?" she said. "Why does that name sound familiar?"

"You may know my brother Piers."

"I see; you're Piers Buren's older brother, are you? How delightful."

It sounded anything *but* delightful to her.

"It's an honour to meet you, Mrs Latimer."

"An honour? You've read my book?"

"No."

I smiled wryly into my drink.

"Then why would it be an honour?"

"It's always an honour to meet someone who has had their picture in the newspapers," I said.

And there was the trace of a smile on that large sinking face.

We are, all of us, displaced throughout our lives. If we see a visitor, we may wonder, in a moment of unusual comfort in our own surroundings, why they would ever want to leave us. But our comfort is not theirs. And we know this because we are often visitors ourselves. We force a smile where the native's comes with genuine warmth. And then there are the places where we are all visitors. Is this part of the search for ourselves? Do you have these lusts and longings? To be in a place where you will never be the visitor? Have the walls around you always felt so familiar? I clutch on to Claypole; I have known this place for longer than I did not know it.

Did I understand this transient nature of people back then, at Sedgemoor's? I know that I understood something of Charlotte Latimer. She did not invite me into that understanding – and that barrier is all a part of the stance, isn't it? I hope you don't come to be as familiar with this antechamber of the human condition as I have been. But also I would not want you to be ignorant of it.

I saw in Latimer a depth to her glacial detachment that most took for superiority, a defiant sadness. Her features had not always been so morose, I thought. All those years later, when I began to sketch, I attempted her, in retrospect of her tragic demise – an inevitable demise. It was impossible to draw her because her face was made up of etchings itself. Who can draw a drawing, and more importantly, what is the point? A replica of a replica. She wore the face in order to confront the visitors to her life.

"Is Mr Monroe here tonight?" I said.

Latimer's long arm pointed across the room to a figure standing alone. The man was half in shadow, wide-shouldered, his suit heavy-looking; he wore a Stetson – it was a bush hat, in fact; like the one my father used to wear.

"What is your interest in Monroe?" said Latimer.

"I understand he has become quite close to my brother," I said.

Latimer dragged long on her cigarette and offered the slightest of shrugs.

"You *are* protective, aren't you?" she said.

I could sense a duplicitous tone. She seemed preoccupied with her own boredom – a common trait in people with afflictions like hers. People like that often become players of games, winging from intrigue to intrigue. She wrote novels, but between them I could see the things she got up to written all over that curious drowsy face.

"No more protective than any other brother," I said. "I was just interested in meeting him."

I had not quite expected anything of the man – I think I had regarded him as a notion rather than a man; but he was a striking figure and that was difficult to shake. It was a room of striking figures, and even then there were Olympians that rose above the smoke.

Monroe seemed elsewhere. People passed him by as he smoked in the half-shadow as if he was a picture on the wall, an ancestral portrait that commanded authority but little attention. And yet he looked as if he could raise a hand and the room would stop, the band would hush and they would all turn to him for his wisdom. He was the concentration of a man rather than the physical entity – he stood there like an idea waiting to be expressed.

"I'm surprised he's here, actually," said Latimer.

And as if a spotlight hit, Monroe gazed slowly across to us, his pink eyes showing no sense of recognition or awareness that we were looking back at him. He raised a slow hand of greeting to Latimer, and she returned it, and then he looked at me, and his gaze lingered. He sucked on his cigarette and then his eyes returned to the party.

"Last time he was here he threw Jacob Epstein over a table," Latimer went on. "I thought he'd be keeping a low profile."

"He threw him over a table?" I said without inflection.

"Epstein is a gossip. Which would not be so bad were his tales not so tall."

I sipped my drink and turned at the waist to flick the ash from my cigarette and when I turned back Monroe was gone.

I looked around for sign of Piers, who had succeeded in his quest to find Bess amidst the ever-increasing melee that was rising and falling in time to the small swing band playing in the far corner. Bess was in hysterics of laughter, her drink spilling in tiny waves around her glass, her hand over her mouth. Piers was in front of her, smiling coolly, placing his hand on her shoulder. Madeleine bounded up to them both to share in the joke – she lost much of her grace when the booze took hold.

Piers caught my gaze and the laughter upon his mouth subsided. I realised what a bored, superior couple Latimer and I must have made up on those steps by the veranda. With a scratch of the back of his neck Piers made his way over to us, handing Latimer a fresh drink as he did so.

"So, you've met Charlotte," he said.

Latimer did not respond, dipped her head half an inch in thanks for the drink and continued to look over the party.

"She's been kind enough to give me an overview of things," I said.

Latimer looked at me side-on, a new look of curiosity in her eyes.

Piers took me to one side, leading me by the elbow.

"You don't have to look so out of place," he said.

"I am perfectly fine," I said.

"Really? Because you look bored to devastation."

"I'm not much of a party person," I said.

Piers sipped his drink and looked back over the throng.

"I'm sorry if my life does not interest you," he said.

Piers was on edge – the opposite of the figure laughing with Bess moments ago. I went to say something – *of course it interests me – why would you say such a thing?* But I did not.

"And where is Madeleine?" he said. "You could at least stop leaving her places."

I ignored the comment.

"Mrs Latimer tells me that Ki Monroe holds you in very high regard," I said.

Piers seemed to soften, but he did not look me in the eye.

"She flatters me greatly," he said, flatly.

Modesty was not a usual pose for Piers.

"Do you know who he is?" he said fidgeting on the spot.

"I'm not a complete philistine, you know."

"But a neophyte; yes," said Piers, and he laughed – it fell out of his tense mouth.

I smiled along with him. It seemed the easiest thing to do.

Had Piers forgotten our childhood together? I often wondered this? Was he entrenched in the person I presented now, with no memory of the books I gave him and the poetry I passed down to him? We are all of us shackled to the immediacy of time. It is a shame.

Within an hour or so the party had loosened, as if a lasso had slackened from around the room, and jackets came off, the band played "Mood Indigo", ties unfurled, ladies' hats soon were being pressed on with one hand, the drink being steadied in the other, as if drunkenness was a mischievous gust of wind.

"Don't you just love these people?" said Bess to me, falling into a pile of coats atop a stool.

I took the gibson from her in one smooth motion – she drank gibsons all her life, and this was the first time I remember seeing her with one – and placed it on a shelf behind us as she straightened herself. She didn't seem to notice. She had no need for any more.

"They certainly know how to have a good time," I said, leaning in to be heard.

"You know, Piers adores you," she said through a long winding grin, her head swaying in rhythm to her voice.

"And he adores you," I said, looking down into my scotch.

People act this way sometimes. They have a primal need to have conversations that don't need to be had, in order to touch the void of human meaning. And then she said:

"Do *you* adore me, Hal?"

She said my name deliberately.

I looked at her. I was more surprised at the question than she had envisaged me being. I thought about not answering. Her eyes were glistening, they were moist, and her mouth, the wet lips, the smile fell into something else, something she had not expected. And with the band stepping up a gear into a sweaty version of "Moon Glow" there was something quite theatrical about the whole encounter.

"How could I not?" I said, softly.

There was a heavy silent pause between us, and we were examining each other. And then I became aware of a presence over my shoulder.

Bess looked up past me. I turned. It was Ki Monroe.

The poet's hand was large and rough and I stood to take it. Bess patted down her dress, swallowed deeply, pressed her palms into her hair. She stood and, as if a switch had been flicked, she jumped up to Monroe and kissed him on the cheek.

"Oh, Mr Monroe – I'm so glad you're here. And that you get to meet Hal Buren: the *man* of the family," she laughed. "Have you seen Piers? I'll go and find him."

And she was gone.

Monroe grabbed a bottle from the table near and topped up both our drinks.

"Everybody seems to be having a good time," I said, stepping closer to Monroe so as to not raise my voice.

"This is just a Friday night," said Monroe.

"I thought it was the launch of someone's book? A poetry reading of some kind, I think somebody said."

"Not that I know of. Although there's a great deal I don't know. I've been in Spain; I'm quite out of touch with all this."

Monroe pushed a cigarette into the end of the holder.

"Someone will end up reciting something or other at some point, no doubt," he said.

"Piers?"

"Your brother doesn't go in for exhibitions," said Monroe. "He is a very promising poet, however."

"You've read his work?"

Monroe looked me up and down. His head was large, like rock, and his eyes sunken.

"I understand why we've heard more about you than we've seen," he said.

He sucked on his cigarette and looked at me from down the end of it, the smoke swimming around his pink marble eyes. He smiled a short, lean smile. I had given no response.

"I'm just saying you look a bit from the other side of the street," he said.

His voice was a cutting Durbanese, but the lyrical sort, not full of grit and dust like Matilda's.

I thought again about his hands. Not like mine, not like Piers'. Like my father's, I suppose. A poet digging into the earth. I found out later that Monroe was renting a farm from Charlotte Latimer for his family while he was in England. He spent much of his time when away from London tending to the land himself, chopping wood and growing vegetables in the gutsy English earth.

"Did you not win the Hawthornden a few years ago, Mr Monroe?" I said.

"And your point?"

"That perhaps *our* streets are narrower than you thought," I said.

"Touché, Mr Buren," said Monroe.

It was the moment Monroe put aside his suspicion of me. He was not a man to hold prizes in high esteem. Monroe told me that WB Yeats had one question when his editor called him to inform he had won the Nobel Prize: how much money is it worth? *Prizes are for publishers*, Monroe said; *and they mean I can feed my daughters for a year without writing book reviews.*

He told me that he saw whiteness besieged by blackness in everything he did. He purged himself with his work, but his intellect deserved a better life for his family. He said the world was in a grim economic hell of its own making, but that war would come soon, and the death and destruction would see them all put right. He talked about Spain, where he and his family had recently been. Spain is where the whiteness and the blackness collide, he said. The past and the future of governance are come together in a volcanic state. Oil and water. Iron and rust. He spoke as both poet and peasant.

Piers joined us, left to dance, returned red-faced, grinning. Bess, also. Many, many others; all of them drunk, tardy, sloppy. Madeleine had gotten very drunk and was taken home by "one of the finest young novelists in the country" according to Piers. I was relaxed by now. Monroe had made me feel as though we were separate from the party. Even separate from the table we were at.

We talked like this:

"Man is the only creature that pauses before it inflicts pain," Monroe said.

"Do you think that is a pause of conscience?" I said.

"I think it is the mark of a being of reason."

"And if there is no reticence?"

"Then you are an animal."

"Or Divine," I said.

"Ha! You got it. And which are you?"

"I am neither," I said.

"Then you have your own special category," said Monroe and erupted into laughter, banging the table and rocking back; I was feeling drunk at this point. I had lost track of the number of drinks I had had.

The party began to thin-out; couples left, those around our table admitted honourable defeat and began to make their excuses. Monroe patted me firmly on the shoulder and said, "I think it's the end of the night; we live to fight another day."

"I need to find my brother," I said.

"Piers left a while ago with his girl," said another of the group, struggling to find the sleeve of his coat with a blindly searching crooked arm.

"I see," I said, stubbing out a half-smoked cigarette in the ashtray on the table.

"Whiskey at my place," Monroe stood and called out to the company. "Millie will be so pleased to see you all."

He spoke mischievously, childishly, and ducked his forehead as if the mere mention of a house party would have him punished. I made it clear I'd had enough – I'd realised it the moment I got to my feet.

"Nonsense," said Monroe, and wrapped an arm around my shoulder.

Monroe and his family had been in London a few days, at a hotel, waiting to move to Latimer's farm. I'd heard that it was the city that corrupted men like Monroe, and it was the countryside where they replenished and became the people that their wives loved. Had I been sober I would certainly not have gone back to the hotel. But I did. We numbered ten or so, all drunk, all tip-toeing loudly like harlequins down the corridor toward the room. Monroe put his finger to his lips as we entered and he searched for the light switch. But when the room was lighted Millie Monroe, who had apparently fallen asleep on the sofa with her new born baby draped across her chest, awoke and sat up, her eyes reaching for some sense.

Ki Monroe straightened on seeing her, his face became serious and the rest of the group stopped in the doorway as one. The baby stirred and began to cry.

"Ki, what is going on?" his wife said sleepily, standing and rocking the baby which subdued the wailing only slightly.

"I thought we'd come back for a drink but I can see it was a bad idea," he said.

At this point, from the embarrassed group in the doorway stepped forth the young man Quimby, a painter or some such, and one whom I had noticed early over-estimated his own ability to charm.

"My dear, my dear," he said drunkenly, "we are the light and the word, and we have come to bestow our greatness upon you."

He laughed to himself and planted his behind on the sofa, pouring himself a whisky from the decanter on the sofa-side table into what was presumably Millie's glass from earlier in the night.

Monroe's face changed shape, subtly, but the edges grew harder, he lost age, his creases filled.

"Now you go put baby in the other room and come back in and join the party," said Quimby, concentrating heavily on sipping his whiskey.

The rest of the group, who were trying to leave discretely it seemed to me, saw the rescue of their night in the arrogance of Quimby, and the slow shuffle toward the door – the group moving as one like Roman soldiers in turtle-shell formation – halted for a moment in anticipation. But I had sobered slightly.

I stood away from the turtle-shell, by the fireplace. I was interested in the change I had detected in Monroe's posture. I stepped forward and stood over Quimby.

"I think we should leave," I said. It was the first time I had spoken to Quimby all night. He looked up at me.

"And *you* are?"

The baby cried, the air in the room had changed – the baby could sense it – and the turtle-shell resumed its shuffle to the door.

"I am the man asking you to come with us and to let this nice lady rock her baby back off to sleep."

Quimby stood, his half-closed eyes and bad breath close to my face.

"I am a guest of the poet Ki Monroe," he said. "Do you even *know* who he is?"

"I do," I said.

"Then you should be aware that not you, and not this baby is going…"

I could only predict the ugliness of the remaining sentence, but from behind me came a large arm, swinging like a tree-trunk battering ram, and the fist at its hilt connected with Quimby's head with a terrible crunch, and Quimby flew across the back of the sofa as if a torrent of bullets had torn into him. I had never seen such power, or such capitulation in the face of power, such utter relinquishment of physical custody. The sofa fell onto its back, the sofa-side table crashed with the decanter and a standing lamp toppled over. There were gasps and the baby even stopped crying. Millie rolled her eyes and I'm sure she almost began to laugh.

Monroe turned to the group.

"Get him out," he said, lowly.

Two of the group picked up Quimby by the arms and walked him out – he didn't know what day it was, his head was wobbling, his jaw was not straight and was already going a shade of blue.

I went to follow them.

"Wait, Buren; stay," said Monroe, and he walked across the room to the ice bucket, wrapped some napkins around a handful of ice cubes and pressed them to the knuckles of his punching hand.

I said nothing; just stood in the spot I had retreated to when Monroe hit Quimby.

Mille Monroe was paying no attention to either of us, just rocking the baby and smiling into her, making baby-noises, moving from one foot to the other.

Monroe lifted the sofa back upright and sat on it with a hefty thump. He let out a sigh. And as if nothing had happened he pointed gently at me with his hitting hand and said, "This is Piers' big brother."

"Very nice to meet you," Millie whispered, not interrupting her rhythm.

Monroe did not whisper.

"Piers and Bess are coming to stay out at the farm this summer," he said.

This was news to me.

"You should come," whispered Millie. "Do you have a wife or a lady friend?"

Ki Monroe wryly half-smiled to himself.

"No, he doesn't," he said.

"Well, come as you are," said Millie.

I, against my better judgement, began to relax again.

"That is a very kind offer," I said. "But I simply couldn't take the time."

"What is it you do, Mr Buren?" said Millie.

"Please: call me Hal."

"Hal is a rich man," said Monroe. "That is what he does."

121

Millie's face lit with interest.

"Really?" she said, still whispering.

I was not sure how to take that response. Millie was small, dark, extremely beautiful, wild, perhaps even more beautiful for her unkempt drowsiness. She was slurring slightly – I had spotted the empty whiskey glass. She had bright glaring eyes, even when sleepy and misty, and she was wearing a baggy blouse and trousers – in those days I don't think I had ever seen a woman in trousers before. She had thick dark hair, pouty lips and a firm-but-feminine jawline, like a Romany.

"Let me go and put Carmella down in the other room and you can tell me all about yourself," she said. "Your brother and Bess are simply adorable."

And she was gone into the other room.

"I would offer you a drink but I seem to have wasted all the whiskey," said Monroe gesturing toward the smashed decanter on the floor.

"No, thank you; not to worry," I said. "I think I've had enough."

"Thank you for that," said Monroe, pointing over his shoulder with his thumb to the spot where Quimby had landed.

"Does that sort of thing happen very often?" I said.

Monroe just shrugged. His eyes had lost their pinkness.

"I must be going," I said. "Can you apologise to your wife. I'm sure we'll get the chance to see each other again."

Monroe nodded, said nothing, and pressed the ice to the knuckles of his hand.

***

I did not see the Monroes again that summer, although I did receive a letter from Millie reiterating her invitation to the farm.

My reasons for not going were genuine. There were some important contract negotiations coming up, ones with some German manufacturers that I wanted to ensure we stayed away from. It would not be easy to avoid involvement without putting politics on the table, but I had my perceived eccentricities to utilise. *He makes these strange decisions*, my generals could say, exasperated, once I had left the room. The coming war, which they could sense but did not discuss, would one day have a victor, and I did not want to be remembered as an enemy of either side. *That* was a decision about survival.

But also to be the fifth peg at that farm would have meant the poisoning of the atmosphere. I know that Bess would have wanted me there, and possibly Monroe and Millie, too. But Piers would not. I knew that to be the case.

Bess explained that summer to me many years later, when everything was different.

The Monroe farm, she said, was less the country home she had rightly or wrongly been looking forward to, but was more "a consolidation of withdrawal," as she put it: "a condensing of the energies of the city into small tasks, small rooms, small gestures."

Piers and Bess arrived just a few weeks after the Monroes had moved in, giving them time to dust off the rustic furnishings and add some fresh flower colour and replace the must with tobacco smoke and candle wax. It was a calm place, a rested place, and it coughed up dust like an old man being woken from the dead.

The cottage, as I mentioned, was owned by Charlotte

Latimer who lived in the country house on the other side of the valley with her husband, Marshall, the reclusive publisher. The cottage was small, but had enough nooks and crannies to make something of itself, and the vegetable patch in the front garden gave the place the feel of a boat made of earth floating above the green sea of the valley below.

The Monroes were keeping some sheep in a field off to the west, and Ki tended them every afternoon, and there was a goat and a bull. Piers could not fathom its working, it was hardly like a farm at all, more a self-sustaining neighbourhood of one leaning on the kindly earth to give up some food, and looking to the kindly sky for some light and cover.

Piers had always wondered how the Greek heroes had lived when not at war. Bess said he mused about these things when the Monroes were not around. The heroes must have had small farmhouses like this, he thought, on hillsides, with a bull and a small flock, and some cabbages and cucumbers and radishes in the black soil. They must have spent their time on their hands and knees playing with the dirt, becoming acquainted with the thing that was to claim them, inevitably. It was, after all, ground dirt – be it soil or sand or dust – that would be the last thing they ever encountered, if the gods were just. It was the aim of all heroes to die that way, in the dirt, a sword in their ribcage. And so, outside of battle they must have placated it, gently tossed it between their fingers. Achilles must have – *simply must have* – spent some time rubbing the dirt of his farmland to his cheek, becoming known to it and allowing him to spend time with the inevitable final sensation. As the blood escaped the dirt would find its way into all the places it could know. That was how all the real heroes would die.

Was he thinking of Monroe when he talked this way? That was how Bess took it. She could not get away from the idea.

The way Piers moved and looked when he talked of the Greeks, it was the same way he talked when talking about Monroe. She said it was not adulation, it was sorrowful, coming from the back of the throat, resentful, jealous, but full of tragic love. He was like a child trying to understand a game, she said. Curious and frustrated, as if he believed his mind did not have the maturity to work something out.

Days were long and often lonesome – everyone had to do their bit – but at sunset there was Monroe glowering, glassy from his afternoon cider, bare chested and powerful, the smell of Millie's excellent cooking drifting out into the woods.

Everything turned a dirty golden as the sun set. Greens became grey, reds became holy light, and each of them – Ki, Millie, Piers and Bess – gained dips and weaves as the shadows fought it out with the candle flames across their skin and clothes.

They would often eat on the back porch if the weather was warm enough, or in the kitchen if not, a dank, beautifully busy and cluttered workspace for the energies of Millie. And her energies were abundant.

As well as the new-born there were the two Monroe girls, Katherine and Petunia. They were quiet, watchful – Katherine never let her cat out from her arms – they had large eyes; and they had both Millie's darkness and the potential for their father's broad shoulders. They were four and six, daughters of the pre-Spanish experiment; something Piers tried to ask about on more than one occasion as he searched for earthy conversations of tangible philosophies at the dinner table.

As bread was broken and stew dished out, Ki Monroe was keenest to talk about poetry, about the acts of God that drove men to verse, and then about Kant, and then onto Dostoevsky – always it turned to Dostoevsky, and occasionally to the naïve intellectual patriarchy of Tolstoy – and then onto Lenin,

Zinoviev and the new naivety of being caught with your pants down when the catcher has guns and tanks.

The world – the world away from this farm – was going to *Hell*. Monroe had no doubt about any of this. It was time to love – the human race had been building up to this point of utopic transcendentalism for millennia and when the moment came it was pressed between the fists of bullies the world over. And he saw bullies not only in parliament and the Reichstag and the White House, but in Bloomsbury and Russell Square and in the quadrangles of Oxford and the lazy fens of Cambridge. The pulpit? What harm could a preacher do? He would say. Bess noted Monroe's own naivety in this. Piers seemed to lap it up.

Monroe would go from Dostoevsky, from mocking Tolstoy, to Emerson and the Oversoul, to the unreliable ideal of the American Dream – "They haven't finished chasing the definition yet, Buren; never mind chasing the *actual* dream." Whitman had it right, said Monroe, or he was headed in the right direction, but he would have had to have lived to three hundred to *actually* get it. Monroe had time for Whitman the wanderer, they were kindred spirits in that sense; he said it often, but it was obvious to anyone who cared to look – it was in Monroe's walk.

Sometimes Millie would lean forward and say something like, "But at least Tolstoy had beauty on his side." And Monroe would wave his hand in the air, take a bite of a piece of bread and say, "She thinks she can see something of the Karenins in us." And he would erupt into coarse bitty laughter, like a geyser.

Bess was sometimes amused by Monroe, sometimes tiresome of him, and just when Piers began to think that she may be on the verge of wanting to leave and return to Claypole, the following night she would be in the thick of the action. The time on the farm had driven her to read *Anna Karenina*, and she would read until the light died in bed at night, and then she would come down on Millie's side when the discussion of genius arose.

"But Tolstoy was *valse profeet*." Monroe spat when he slipped into Afrikaans. "How do I know this? The *real thing* doesn't die in a train station waiting for someone to free up the washroom. The *real thing* gets martyred, or ascends to the heavens in a beam of piss-coloured celestial light."

"So what are you, Monroe?" Bess said.

"What am I? I'm a vaudevillian, my girl; a song and dance man. I've always struggled to understand why so many people take such offence to me."

Millie did not find this attitude at all amusing. They had gone to Spain as pariahs off the back of a verse satire Monroe had published where he ridiculed the pretensions of the whole London literary establishment. They had been ostracised by their friends, mocked, even worse: *ignored!* To the point where they decided to leave. It happened to fit with the pattern of their lives as city dwellers-rustic folk. The Monroes were indeed split half and half.

The four of them and the children would go for long walks around the Sussex countryside and Monroe would often begin talking about all those they had left behind in the coffee shops of Soho and Bloomsbury. And when in London he would often talk of shark fishing off Capri, hunting in the Pyrenees, chopping wood – *Nothing builds the muscles like cutting down trees and cleaving them up for firewood with a great axe, and you need those muscles to compose poems, by God you do*.

On these long walks he would talk about the benign claustrophobia of the city, the low-hanging mist and the red bulbous noses of the policemen with their helmets pulled tightly down to their eyes. But even when Monroe was on a downer he would always speak brightly of London.

"Paris – oh how much do we *not* get on with Paris, Mills?" he said.

Millie and Bess often walked just a couple of yards behind the men talking their own topics, keeping one eye in four on the children.

"Paris smells," Monroe went on. "That is not a myth. I met Hemingway there. He is a cliché despite his genius. But compared to London it is where the excreters go to lay eggs. Everyone is high. We *all* like a drink, Piers; but in Paris it comes first. In London things get done. Look what Thomas Stearns has achieved from his seat in the bank-master's office. A money-man; like your brother."

"My brother? What has my brother ever achieved?"

Monroe looked surprised at Piers' response, his dismissiveness.

"Don't underestimate your brother, Piers," said Monroe, and the conversation moved on quite swiftly, as all the conversations did.

It was Bess who first noticed the change in things at the cottage.

On the walks they would go down the valley and then turn west away from the Latimer house. Sometimes Bess could see the dark, tall figure that could have only been the famous writer, standing in the window; perhaps looking down at them, perhaps not.

During the days Bess would read, or pick veg, or tend to laundry, but always Millie would go away at lunch time. And by the time Piers came looking for her one afternoon for his daily dose of afternoon cider – he had been mending a fence on the far side of the valley – Millie had been gone for some five hours. Neither of them thought it suspicious, but both avoided making any reference to it in Monroe's company.

Monroe himself was becoming short-tempered, particularly with Millie. And the one evening when dinner was not prepared by the end of the day Monroe made the comment, "Well, if you spent a little less time at the Latimer place…" and he slammed his open fist into the door and walked out. Nothing was mentioned again. After a few days Millie continued her daytime flits.

And the spring began to burn into summer like the edges of green crepe paper.

Some nights they would walk to the local pub, drink from pewter tankards with other farmers. Monroe would pinch Piers on the arm if ever he tried to talk about literature or philosophy or tried to tell the clientele that they were in the presence of a great poet. That would annoy Monroe in particular.

They would get drunk every night, stay up until the early hours. Bess would stay awake and listen to them talking about Spanish politics and Russian kulaks and more Tolstoy and Dostoevsky. And still Monroe would be up at sunrise to attend his land. Piers, still a youth, was far more hazy.

When it was time to leave and return to London, Bess said to Piers: "You could do with some of the tedium and dirty air of Matilda's house, I think."

And she was only being slightly mischievous.

✳ ✳ ✳

This was the summer of 1936.

It seemed most of the country could not and would not understand the inevitability of war. Hitler's aims were to build a mechanised army. And in Spain an army of disaffected soldiers was making its way up from Moroccan outposts to create a civil war. People did not want to know, and the news outlets were loath to turn away their readers with stories of war. It was twenty years since the last one, you understand; a repeat was inconceivable.

So I do not criticise the ignorance via fear, nor the ignorance caused by incredulity. And we were no different. I knew the nature of the oceans' waves, but I did not warn anybody or frighten anybody. In fact it was a subject that bored me.

By the time I saw Bess and Piers again Spain was at war – the army of Franco and Mola had turned on its socialist parliament. It was to change everything for us, and yet we never spoke of it. It did not come up that next time we met, and yet looking back that war in Spain was like a black hole, sucking all matter toward it.

It was a brief lunch in Kilburn – without Madeleine – which seemed designed to let me know what a significant experience they had both had on the Monroe farm. Being close to nature, being close to poetry, being close to things that matter.

"So, you're writing?" I said.

"Monroe thinks Piers could be very important," said Bess.

"You're going back there?" I said.

"Perhaps toward the end of the summer," said Bess. "It can get quite intense."

"Hardly," scoffed Piers.

"You wouldn't notice," said Bess.

"What do you mean by that?"

Bess rolled her eyes and slumped back in her chair.

Despite this lack of confidence in Piers' faith, Bess appeared otherwise light and happy, leaning in to him throughout lunch, clasping onto his elbow; and Piers looked well, too. The farm work meant he was finally adding some muscles to those bones. I had no reason to be worried about either of them on the face of that meeting. Bess, she said, had found something of a soul-mate in Monroe's wife. She spoke of her with a feminine enthusiasm, as a little sister might her elder.

When we parted on the pavement outside the restaurant, I asked Piers once more, "You plan to go back to the Monroe farm?"

"You should come," said Piers.

I gave my brother a conciliatory smile.

"You know where I am should you need me," I said.

A few days later Piers turned up unexpectedly at my apartment. He was excitable, talking about a new arts exhibition.

"You simply *have* to come. I simply *have* to go. And I won't go without you," he was saying. Piers took my hat from the stand by the front door and put it in my hands. "We *have* to go."

We walked for an hour or so.

"What is so important about this exhibition?" I said.

"They're going to change the world, these artists. They've come from all around. France, Spain. And nothing will be the same again."

"And why is it so important I come with you?"

Piers, walking fast, smiled.

"Is it so unusual I want to share these things with my brother?"

"A little," I said. But Piers laughed loudly and walked even faster.

It was a warm day, the grey walls of London shining silver.

We stood outside the New Burlington Gallery; Piers jittery with cool energy.

"Your tendency to believe in the spiralling fate of things is biblical in nature, Hal," Piers said.

"Biblical?" I said, arching an eyebrow.

"You know; everything in its right place, the river rolls unto the sea. Bess says it is why you stand so straight."

Piers laughed.

"I stand too straight?" I said.

"She never said *too* straight," said Piers.

The banner across the frontispiece of the gallery read simply, cleanly, *The Surrealist Exhibition, London, 1936*. We walked up the steps and through the open doors into the algid tiled gallery.

There was an energy to the room. It was large, but still cluttered with strange sculptures and huge vibrant canvasses. There was something unorganised, gritty, grubby about the place, the white sheen of the room invaded by a party of carnival folk.

We stood in front of a great canvass, startling in its colours, a painting unlike anything I had seen before of a twisted bleak mutant on a desolate landscape.

"And what is a *surrealist*?" I said, leaning back on my heels.

"It is a new artistic movement," said Piers. He gestured vaguely with his hand. "From Paris."

"To be *sur*-real?" I said. "To be *built upon the grounds* of the real? Is that the etymology? Or the Latin? *Sur*? What is that? *Sur-sum Corda*? To lift one's heart up to God. Have you brought me to see an exhibition of new wave iconographers?"

Piers rolled on the balls of his feet, hands in pockets, his bottom lip curled over the top one.

"I wanted to see what you think," he said.

"Yes."

"It is kinetic expression."

"Messy," I said.

"It's more to do with disorder," said Piers. "*Unreality.*"

I said nothing. We continued looking at the painting.

Piers looked up at me after a moment or two. He frowned slightly, pensively.

"You don't like us," he said, "because you think we too easily trust others."

By *us* he meant *creative souls*, I knew.

"Whoever said I don't like you?"

"You don't like us because you think we are incapable of love," said Piers.

"That's probably quite accurate," I said.

"You think we're frivolous," said Piers.

"I don't think you're done for, if that's what you mean."

"You think I'll flower into an ant."

"I think you'll settle down."

We continued to look over the painting in silence.

"Well, what do you think of this one?" said Piers, his nose creasing.

"You can certainly see the craft in some of it," I said, my hands firmly pressed into my trouser pockets.

"It seems lacking in narrative, a lot of it," said Piers.

"*Sur*-real." I rolled the term around my mouth.

"Narrative is important," said Piers.

I looked the painting up and down a further time. Monstrous, I thought, but not ugly. An enormous, towering, dismembered troll-like figure, a wood-dweller, an arm holding up the leg that stamped down. Twisting clouds, an arid, clawing landscape. The colours were arresting; the browns, the greys, the ash and the oak, made bright, grabbing.

"It is downright ugly," said Piers.

"I don't think so," I said, almost whispering. I bent down to read the card at the side of the canvass that had the artist's name and details on. "It is a comment on the coming revolution in Spain."

The artist was a Salvador Dali.

"Do you know him?" I asked Piers.

"No – I've heard *of* him," said Piers. "He's quite the showman, apparently. He gave a lecture here the other day dressed in a diver's outfit. Apparently David Gascoyne had to rush on stage with a spanner to save his life when the oxygen flow stopped. Quite the showman."

"Does everything *really* need a narrative?" I said.

"In art? Of course."

"Does your poetry never get lost in your own musings?"

"*My* poetry is not important," said Piers. "And anyway; poetry that gets lost – that loses its discipline – is just juvenilia."

I looked at my young brother, handsome, bright.

"Is everything okay?" I said.

Piers looked back to me, and the two of us stood small and lean before Dali's painting.

"Everything is very fine, my brother," said Piers. But his head was still, his eyes moist, his tone unconvincing.

His head dipped.

"I think perhaps I have been foolish," said Piers.

"Foolish?"

"You must have thought it. Me trying to become a poet."

"I do not think you foolish."

"I don't believe you," he said.

"Perhaps I think you over-excitable. But no-one can demand to stymie that in someone like you."

"Someone like *me*?" Piers turned back to the painting. "A fool."

"Where is your poetry, Piers?" I said. "It seems that, perhaps, you may not be the best judge of your own work."

"I have nothing, Hal. I burn it. Once it is written I burn it. Just as at the farmhouse. There is nothing for me to write about other than my own curiosities and my own concerns. And what are they? I need the rules of profundity and I am not a profound person, Hal."

I said nothing. Piers' shoulders dropped.

I do not know if he really burned his work; he was certainly capable of such catholic gestures of self-punishment. I wonder often what this aspect of him would have become had he reached old age. Darker? Lighter? Priestly? Likely it would have been supressed or come out of him in shades of cruelty. Kings, the thoughtful ones, often hate themselves before they send their subjects to war.

"Should art not offer hope?" Piers said.

"I do not know," I said.

"This hideous great creature," – he pointed softly at the Dali painting – "with his torso over there and his head in agony and his arms and legs reaching out – it does not offer me hope."

What could I say? That hope meant very little to me? That hope was for the hopeless?

"Art should be a conversation with God," said Piers.

I looked at the grey twisted head of the troll-figure, long grey hair – like Beethoven, I thought – the head bent back, muscles taught, veins creasing outwards – agony, such as a soldier's agony, perhaps; the agony of the bereaved. Was that face not pleading upwards to the heavens?

"I think maybe this is," I said.

Piers looked at me curiously and let out a short sharp bolt of laughter.

"You know, Bess thinks we're two halves of the same person," he said.

"She does?"

"She thinks we should have been one – one great genius."

"So both of us fall a bit short, is that it?" I said.

"She thinks with your seriousness, your attitude – your money – your outlook, your calmness, your silence; and with my passion, my eagerness, my poetry, that we really are two halves."

"I'll take those things as compliments," I said.

Piers looked back at the painting.

"If anything were to happen to me, Hal," he said. "You would protect Bess for me, wouldn't you?"

I looked at my brother, the nervousness in his face, the moisture in his eyes.

"Of course."

It was the only thing to say.

"I mean, she is the world to me; as my brother, I am asking you that if anything happened to me then nothing would be too much to protect her."

"What are you talking about, Piers?" I said, pulling back, making light. "What could possibly happen to you?"

"I'm serious", Piers said, his tone becoming frayed. "Promise me."

"I promise you," I said.

He looked relieved. His shoulders squared up again, he swallowed, looked down at his shoes. Then, rebuilt, he turned back to the painting. I followed his gaze, and after a moment of silence, Piers said:

"You know, if this is the future then I think I'll continue to fight for the past."

And he walked off, slowly, his hands in his pockets, his gaze easy, flowing around the room. I watched him go. And I stayed for a little while longer looking at Dali's painting – *Soft Construction with Boiled Beans;* I reread the card next to it – and I stayed and looked at the white and grey twisting clouds above the broken limbs.

★ ★ ★

Bess and Piers did return to the Monroe farm.

And the next time I saw them was back in London – my presence was requested via telegram. They wanted me to come to a party. They couldn't wait to see me. But I was on a list of such people, apparently, and the others would be there *en masse*. The Monroes were going back to Spain for the winter and they had decided to say goodbye in lavishly dowdy bohemian style.HalHa

It was in Soho, at Sedgemoor's – it was loud, wild, but the booze and the dancing had made the party one huge cumbersome beast by midnight and the gaslights were dimming, conversation was lowering, and the gramophone jazz – mainly the stodgy French parping that Monroe was passionate about – was becoming smokier and smokier.

Monroe's friends and enemies alike had congregated. It was humid at night and city folk sought a midnight breeze as a nomad searches for water.

Much of my night had been spent with Bess on the small veranda; a vine-festooned portico with a few fold-down chairs and candles dotted around sills and on railings.

Piers was very excitable, flitting between groups of conversations. Bess was unenthused, unresponsive, quiet, she seemed beaten down. Whenever I asked her if everything was okay she would *shoo* me away with a barely-friendly flick of the wrist. Tired, she would say.

I noticed Monroe had spent some time in heated conversation with Charlotte Latimer on the sofa. An incongruous pair – she was so rigid, her nose so high – and Monroe, with his hefty shoulders and his hunter's glare, waved his arms in gesture as if he was going to swallow her up at any moment. Bess watched them out of the corner of her eye. I watched Bess.

Piers came up to the veranda and dumped himself into one of the fold-down chairs at our table.

"You wouldn't believe what is going on in Spain," Piers said.

"Civil unrest – yes; I heard," I said coldly.

"Unrest?" said Piers. "It is *war*."

Bess patted his arm down.

"Don't be so silly," she said. "Europe won't put up with any more of those."

I watched Bess examine with regret the current in Piers' face diminish. Her calculated superficiality had dented his vulgar enthusiasm.

"Is that Millie Monroe?" I gestured to the small attractive woman standing over Monroe. She looked pale, deathly; I hardly recognised her. Charlotte Latimer, sitting on a sofa next to Monroe, stood to leave. Millie held her arm out to her; Monroe stood also now and put his arm across Millie. Words were exchanged and Monroe walked his wife away.

"Ignore them," said Piers. "A disagreement on poetic metre, no doubt."

"A lover's tiff more like," said Bess morosely.

"Nonsense," said Piers.

"What do you mean?" I said.

"Monroe's farm belongs to the Latimers. They were renting it," said Bess.

"And so my dear Elisabeth has drawn some wild conclusions from that seed of fact," said Piers.

The three of us looked at each other in silence, each waiting for another to speak. I could see from Piers' gaze that he did not believe his own defence and from Bess' that she was speaking the truth.

"I will not indulge in gossip," said Piers, annoyed, and he went to get another drink.

I said nothing.

"Piers is blind when it comes to that man," Bess said eventually.

"I must say I don't really have much taste for gossip, either," I said.

"Piers does not want to be part of Monroe's shame, part of his humiliation. Gossip doesn't even come into it."

I sipped my drink.

"Millie was having an affair with Charlotte," Bess said, almost laughing. "That is why they're going; Monroe is picking up his belongings and running away to Spain."

There was a silence between us.

"Have you no response to that?" said Bess.

"What kind of response were you expecting?" I said.

"At the very least it's rather scandalous," said Bess.

I stubbed out my cigarette in the ashtray.

"I'm more concerned about you," I said.

Bess looked at me. Her gaze softened, something like that night at the party.

"Everything'll be fine once they're gone. Piers is not his own man when Monroe is around," she said solidly. "It has been a difficult summer when it should have been the most wonderful. I have this overwhelming terror within me, Hal. It is like a weight in the pit of my stomach. I feel like something is all going to go wrong."

I told Bess not to worry. I told her a lie; that she was feeling dread for a war that would not come. But I knew war was inevitable, and that Spain was the opening rally. But this was not what she was talking about anyway. She felt something else, something that had grown in her like a cancer. And I could feel its first black twinge that night, too. From the veranda I could see my brother in deep conversation with Ki Monroe.

✱ ✱ ✱

It was several weeks after that party when Bess came knocking on the door of my apartment. It was early, and I answered the door in my robe.

"Have you heard from Piers?" Bess said. She was on edge, wrapped up in unseasonal clothes, as if she was incognito; her hat was pulled down, her shoulders hunched.

I looked her up and down.

"Hello Bess," I said.

"Have you heard from Piers?" she repeated.

"Would you like to come in?"

Bess' lips moved as if to speak, her face was narrow, but she said nothing, downed her eyes and moved swiftly passed me and into the airy light of the apartment.

"Would you like some tea?" I said putting the morning paper I had been carrying on the corner of the table by the window where the breakfast paraphernalia was stationed.

Bess walked restlessly around the sitting room. She looked uneasily out of the window down to the busy street.

"I don't know where Piers is," she said, exhaling.

"I had assumed you had gone back to the Monroe farm."

Bess looked at me sharply at the mention of the name.

"The Monroes have gone. You know that," she said.

"I just hadn't heard from either of you."

Bess' face sunk once more, as if the energy of her nerves came in tides. She took a seat by the window and continued to look out onto the street.

"He's been gone since Wednesday morning," she said.

I poured tea and handed a cup and saucer to Bess.

"Is that unusual?" I said.

Bess gave me a hard look, one that seemed unwilling to engage in frippery.

"I don't know the minutiae of my brother's comings and goings," I excused myself.

"It is not so unusual," admitted Bess. "But I know where he is when he doesn't come home."

"And you have checked those places?"

Bess' voice softened.

"He is always with Monroe. He loses track of time, you see, when he's with that man."

"Of course, now Monroe is not around."

"Precisely," said Bess with a timid, forced half smile.

"And you have no idea where he could be?"

"I cannot find him."

A silence fell between us.

"I've been thinking about all the things you've ever done for us," said Bess.

I sipped my tea, looked at her expressionlessly.

"I have done nothing," I said.

"You have protected us both."

"I have done what a brother would do."

Bess stared up at me, her face beginning to tremble with frustration and disappointment. She was wanting to say something bold, to let something free.

"I think he has gone to Spain," she said.

I considered this for a moment, and as I did so it seemed undeniable.

"What evidence do you have to believe that?"

"I just know he has followed Monroe."

"But what evidence?"

Bess squeezed her eyes shut and pressed out from behind clenched teeth, "I just know."

She was angry and sorrowful.

She closed her face, retained tears by sheer will, and began to gently press the back of her hand up to her cheeks. Softly she said, "I came here for help."

I looked at her, her pink cheeks, her soft moist eyes; her elsewhere demeanour, her chaotic, rumbling mind.

"What if I made some enquiries for you?" I said.

She looked up to me plaintively where I stood.

"What kind of enquiries?"

"You shouldn't worry about that. He is my brother, Bess; I want to know where he is, too."

"Matilda said you wouldn't help."

Bess knew how to raise the hairs on the back of my neck. I didn't know just how wily she was at the time, but I grew to understand this, and admire it.

"She did?" I said.

"She said you were too ensconced in your wicked little ways now to go chasing Piers."

I said nothing.

"You love Piers. I know you can find him."

She stood and put her untouched teacup onto the table.

"Go make your enquiries," she said. "But then I need you to go to Spain and find my Piers." She seemed to straighten as she said this, to call up a distant reserve of steel.

I sat in the chair by the window after she left and smoked cigarette after cigarette. I thought of Piers, and of Monroe. I thought of Matilda and how I could confound her opinions of me by going and finding my brother. But why should I do this? Was my life to be a languorous joust between my own deficiencies and the policing of my brother's pizzazz? And Bess comes to *me*. Protect *your* brother, she screams from her desperation. Never once had I suggested to Piers that life was not precious, and that he should not hold on to it. Why was it my responsibility to protect, come hell or high water?

And I had to think over the fact that maybe Monroe was right anyway. Monroe and Piers had known each other some years, after all. It was not for me to come between that sort of mutual experience. Love can be accumulated, I thought. Such stock cannot be burned with a single flame. A second cannot be traded for a lifetime. And Monroe was a powerful force, perhaps one worth pursuing.

Whatever I may have become, I still remembered the short time I had the honour of knowing Douglass Karlchild, you see. Perhaps I was still numb to it on the outside then, with Piers gone and Bess pleading, but that is what it boiled down to. The answers were in our conversation with God, I thought. Everything is in the art, is in the poetry. Piers had done well to hide the extent of his obsession from me on this matter. Perhaps he did not hide it from Monroe as I did not hide things from Douglass. What freedom he must have felt with that man. A corpulent release, a geyser of relinquishment, it must have been how he defined himself, the thing that he understood to be his essence.

How could I reclaim him from that?

I did what now all these years later seems a strange thing to have done. That afternoon I drove to the Latimer house, overlooking the valley where the Monroes and Piers and Bess had spent so much of the summer. I stood at the hilt of the valley-side and looked over the lush carpets of green and off to the small stone farmhouse on the far side. The wind blew hard and my greatcoat flurried around me like a burial flag.

I knocked on the door of the house. It was pretty, somewhere between a grand cottage and a modest manor; it was rustic and lived-in. A man opened the door – he was lean, worn, distracted, his spectacles rested lightly on the very end of his nose, and he was digging at something with a small iron rod, trying to dislodge something from a cog. This was Marshall Latimer, Charlotte's famously reclusive husband. His reputation was one of pleasant eccentricities, a mild manner, but of a nervous disposition, occasional break-downs, and a peculiar way of interacting with people. He looked harmless enough.

"I've come to see Mrs Latimer," I said.

With deep-yellow fingers Marshall Latimer pushed a cigarette between his thick lips and sucked hard. His eyes squinted, and he looked me up and down as the smoke twisted around his head.

"She's not seeing anyone," he said. "Unless you're the doctor?"

I looked over Marshall's shoulder at a corridor stacked high with books and bundles of newspapers, coatings of dust as thick as the lush carpets of turf all around their valley.

"I am the doctor," I said.

"Young for a doctor. Called you herself, did she?"

I took off my hat and held it to my chest as I imagined a doctor might do at the doorstep of the needy.

Marshall sucked another deep drag, the lines in his face smoothing out whenever he did so.

"A mutual friend asked that I might pay her a visit," I said.

"Who?"

I smiled sympathetically.

"I'm afraid the mutual friend asked that their identity remain a secret."

Marshall looked down at the floor and began to nod.

"Quite sensible," he said. "You'd better come in, Doctor."

Marshall stepped back and I walked into the house. The air hung heavy with the fecund aroma of strong foreign tobacco. And as Marshall Latimer led me up the stairs I briefly examined the dirt, the art, the rouge of the curtains, the off-centre portraits on the walls of the staircase, the long drab dimness of the hallway.

"You know she has been in bed for several weeks," said Marshall. "We had hoped these things were in the past. But it appears such moods are forever waiting in the wings."

He opened a door at the far end of the hallway and stood to one side.

"Today she does not like to see me," he said, and pointed me inside.

The room had a ghastly smell of dead air and sweat and stale food. It was large, busily made up of darkness and orange shadow. Latimer, I could see, was in the four post bed in the corner, white as a sheet, her eyes fixed on me, bright as bells, a terrified hole of a mouth.

I started at seeing her.

She was gazing at me. She was still, like the stone relief of a corpse upon a tomb; a completely different entity to the one I had met at Sedgemoor's.

"What is it you want?" she said. Her voice was weak in tone but demanding in intent.

I stepped forward from the heavy shadows.

"I'm sorry for calling on you at home," I said. "Especially as you seem to be unwell."

Getting closer I could see the red edges of her eyes; they were like wounds in the silver shape of her face. She looked terrified, in danger, at the end.

"Why are you here?" she said.

"I am looking for my brother," I said.

"I cannot help you. Let them all die over there," she said.

"Who?"

Her eyes seemed to grow even more intense.

"Monroe stole her from me. And he has taken your brother captive also. But that happened long ago – you know that, don't you?"

I did know that. But I said nothing.

"Monroe always gets his way," she said.

"I need to know what you know," I said.

Latimer smacked her cracked, dry lips together.

145

"You're going to go get your brother, Mr Buren?" she said.

I could not answer. Latimer answered her own question:

"Yes," she said. "You'd do best to let them all rot out there in that god-awful country. That's what I intend to do."

Latimer carried on talking, but little of it made sense to me. She rambled, whispered, hissed. I sat with her for a few hours. I felt sorry for her. It was clear that the rumour Bess had suggested was true. Charlotte Latimer and Millie Monroe had been lovers. And now Latimer had fallen into madness. Madness takes many forms, and it may be that Piers had a form of his own.

After some time I leaned in and whispered to Latimer as she quietly wept: "I need to know where Piers has gone."

She wiped tears away, smacked her lips together once more.

"They would not tell me where they were going. They were running from *me*. That witch and her warlock. They would not tell me. But I know they were going to Barcelona. And your brother? He believes in the Divinity of poetry. He would follow that man to the fiery pit of Hell if he was promised Grace for it."

I sat back in my chair, looked across the room, at the clutter, the abandonment of routine.

"And they have a villa in Toledo," said Latimer, as if to no-one, nostalgically and weary. "Millie used to talk about the lemon groves on the hillside."

And she rolled over away from me.

I sat in silence, listening to the famous writer cry into her hands. I felt nothing for her but a twinge of disgust for her affair, and a lacing of ugly pity for her madness.

She cried herself to a broad silence – I could sense she was not asleep – and I quietly left the room.

Marshall Latimer came out of his study, cautious like a fox, his hands operating on a different piece of machinery now, and met me at the bottom of the stairs.

"What is your verdict, Doctor?" he said, drawing on a cigarette.

I placed my hat back on my head and donned my greatcoat.

"My verdict is that she may well write about all this one day," I said.

Marshall seemed relieved, as capable as he was of showing such a feeling. He looked at me over the top of his glasses and began nodding to himself. He offered me tea but I declined, and he nodded some more to himself. It was a lonely house, the Latimer house.

THE SIEGE

* * *

I had the information. So why, you may wonder, did I not act upon it?

I could excuse myself now, knowing what happened. But all I knew was that time was of no importance. Piers had prepared himself for this, and he had prepared me also. I knew that he had asked me to protect Bess because he had to go. Despite what Bess and Matilda may have thought, it was not my place to fetch him back; not this time.

In the years since all this, I have discovered the story of Piers in Spain. My investigators have been thorough – I do not deal in dime store gumshoes, but poets of the age of espionage and intrigue; with such men on my payroll the movements of a nervous poet, a pale foreigner, through a revolutionary country were easy to piece together. But there was for some time a lack of an ending. That came much later.

The story is pieced together thus.

Piers did go to Barcelona, just as Latimer said. Much of her supposition and sick bed ramblings in fact came to be verified. (Never discount the mad). Ki Monroe had taken his family in order to rescue his wife from Latimer, and from the scandal and depressive illnesses that would surely have come without his interjection. To achieve the reclamation of his beloved Millie, Monroe needed the focussed, compressed atmosphere of a claustrophobic inertia; he would squeeze her like a boil until she was rid of the puss of wrongful love and ugly lust.

Piers had no mind of this. He had refused even to admit to the obvious – that the affair between the two women was anything at all other than a malicious rumour to be dismissed if it was to be acknowledged at all. I don't know why he refused to treat it with the same gravity that Monroe did. All I can assume is that it interfered with his plans, and so, like a

151

child, he ignored it. Piers had a forceful myopia when it came to his own centrality. And so he went after them, to complete what many saw as his feeble, corrupting education in the search for worth to his writing, and in his writing, tragically, a definition of his own self. I put it simply, and it defiles his quest, I know. But simplest terms have their place, and tragedy, the ultimate human preoccupation, is a simple thing when it comes down to it. We have made it simple ourselves. As Spinoza said, to understand is to be free, and our attempts at being free from tragedy have been reckless if understandable. We have driven out the colour in tragedy, made it almost petulant, *wasteful. Oh but what a terrible shame*, we say. *There was so much to be done.* We must not waste our time here, and not have our time rendered unsatisfactory. That is the sadness most of us see: that tragedy is *wasteful*. Oh, but believe me, it is so much more than that.

Piers arrived in Barcelona the pale wide-eyed searcher that I knew. And as the story of Spain unfolded, so did the story of my poor brother, my heroic brother, the *warrior* poet who came and went; dry-throated, walking through the revolutionary streets, his knapsack on his back, his tongue dark with the pencil lead of his poetic sketches.

The sun was hissing, oppressive, flooding around the city like a tide. The Monroes had travelled to Bilbao in the north in order to come down through the country, via their villa in Toledo. Ki had said that he wanted to see some friends, check on the state of the interior.

Revolution was so close it was spoken of as fact in all the newspapers in London, and by the time Piers walked slowly and keenly through the Barcelona streets, his bag of clothes and books over his shoulder, all the talk was of General Franco's actions in Morocco. And that dead-eyed firebrand General Mola was trouble, too. The army was turning in on its own ungrateful people and blood would inevitably flow. *What else does a soldier know than how to lash out?* Monroe had said as much before they left.

"To you and I running a sword through a man is as alien and mythological as the antics of the *Iliad*, but to them it is like buttering toast, pouring coffee. You understand that is what the people will be up against? The Republicans will not stand a chance if the army comes back from Morocco."

And yet Monroe took his family to this. He would never have admitted it, but he saw the cleanliness of blood in everything. *Limpieza de Sangre.*

"Spain has a history of swaying this way and that; it is their tried and tested survival mechanism. Let's see if it works this time."

He spoke this way often, but most often to Piers, his keenest audience. In the last days at the Latimer cottage, the poet was drinking heavily; he was often distracted, leonine, probing the air around him with his snout, looking for the sources of his own paranoia. Of course, his suspicions were correct about his wife and Charlotte Latimer. His anger came out in speeches about the situation in Europe. The dangers of Stalin. The plight of the kulaks. The Spanish landowners. The persecution of the clergy by the communists and Republicans. They stayed up late drinking and talking about Dostoevsky, Maxim Gorky, Zinoviev and Trotsky. Piers' head swirled with the names, the places, the evils and the good.

According to Bess the talk became more focussed on Spain as the summer went on. Although it was never said in front of her, she was sure the two men were planning on going there to witness a revolution. Monroe, she said, for all of his bravado and experience, talked like a fantasist, and Piers fell for it entirely. There was never any talk of fighting, but Monroe knew exactly what he was doing by encouraging Piers to crave the truth that makes up great poetry. He made him *believe*, she said, that his greatness was on that horizon. He was dangling the revolution before him. So Monroe could only have expected Piers to go after him. He had manipulated it so. And Piers fell for it.

Barcelona was a city on edge. The market stalls and their vendors on Las Ramblas were muted – even Piers, a newcomer, could sense the reticence in them as he passed. They had seen other foreigners. They looked at him kindly. The International Brigade was forming and English, Yanks, Canadians, Welsh and others were making their way to Barcelona and to havens in the north offering their services to fight for the workers. The city was a serious place, it seemed. The tall grand buildings stood like generals with puffed-out chests, they were draped – every one of them – in the great red flags of the socialist cause, like exhausted tongues flapped out of windows. If there was a bare wall then the hammer and sickle had been scratched or painted on to it. The city as pantomime; the city as statement, as bellowing from the rooftops.

Piers had telegrammed Monroe from the boat, and Monroe had responded that they would be some days yet. Moving around the country was becoming difficult.

Piers walked for many hours before checking the name of the building which Monroe had left him, written on a piece of notepaper in his jacket pocket. He was to wait for the family there.

From the warm shadows of doorways and the white sun-hit walkways Piers could feel the tension of the city hanging in the air like the London smog. He took a glass of wine in a tavern just off Las Ramblas with the hope of trying out his Spanish, but the waiter was sullen, his eyes were bowed, he offered no way-in. Piers sat on the veranda looking across a small square to a cramped-looking church poking out from between two government buildings, red flags across them, the black and red of the Anarchists unfurling from the pock-marked bell tower of the church. It looked embarrassed, shimmying, coy, something inspired with the drab terracotta of the government offices at each shoulder.

A man sitting at the table opposite reading a newspaper and drinking a short clear spirit looked across at Piers and folded his paper closed. He wore large leather boots, a linen jacket and a grey cloth cap.

"Don't worry too much about the mood of people today," he said in English.

Piers smiled unsurely at the stranger.

"The news of Franco has everyone on edge," said the man.

"I understand," said Piers.

The man was Spanish, middle-aged, he had a pencil moustache. He removed his cap and slapped it onto his table, revealing a large smooth brow that seemed more shell than skull that stretched half-way across his scalp. There was discolouration to his head because of the exposure. Piers fixated on this for a moment.

"You are visiting?" said the man.

"I am," said Piers.

"English?"

Piers nodded – it was easier than the truth.

"You are here to join the fight?"

"No," said Piers.

"You are a journalist."

"A poet." Piers said this without thinking.

The man smiled, nodded, sipped his spirit, did not take his eyes from Piers.

"You have come to give some support to comrade Lorca?"

Piers did not like the man's tone; he did not like the city or its people so far and he was wondering for how long he would have to endure it without Monroe. He had been there for just a few hours and the revolution was airy, desultory, in fact. Piers had been expecting love and compassion, not this quiet, this paranoia, and the thin moustaches with their prying. The banners, roll after roll of all-encompassing banners, were garish, hostile, airless, not triumphal or celebratory. He looked out across the square, squinted at the church, crouched between the government buildings like a child at its mother's skirt.

"I do not mean to offend you," the man carried on.

"You have not, sir," said Piers. "I have had a long journey and I was just gathering myself."

Piers picked up his things, left some coins for the drink and went on his way, touching the brim of his hat to the man as he did so.

"Comrade," said the man, nodding his head to the coins Piers had left on the table. "That is too much."

Piers stopped, looked the man up and down, at his tatty attire, his cotton shirt and his grey threadbare jacket.

"Not that it is your concern, senor, but consider it a tip," said Piers.

The man smiled knowingly, placed his fingertips upon his newspaper so his arched fist looked like a predatory spider.

"There is no tipping," said the man. "It is an insult and it is illegal. And I would stop with the 'Senors'. You are in Barcelona now, comrade; everybody is equal."

Piers waited for the joke to set in, but the man's unkind smile faded. He was proud, sharp and forceful – his features were this way, too; glaring eyes and thin strong teeth.

The man gestured toward the coins with his head.

Piers picked up a few and checked with the man that he was now leaving enough. The man nodded. Nervously Piers placed the coins into his jacket pocket and went on. The man said something in Spanish as he walked off, something about solidarity, something about pain.

Piers walked some more, through the winding backstreets, passed shops and bars and taverns and food stalls, more banners and socialist graffiti, passed curious and non-curious faces, passed young lovers that made him think of Bess for a moment. He would send for her as soon as he could find the truth of this place, he thought. He knew she would be angry with him for leaving, and that she would take some convincing, but as soon as he returned to London and handed her the truth of a revolution as soaked into his skin, she would believe him as she always believed him and they could live in the hills, just as they had done through the summer with Ki and Millie and the girls. So far, however, since disembarking, he had not liked the truth he had seen.

Piers had always exhibited this impatience. It was petulant, but also endearing. He often blinked quickly and reprimanded himself for it. *Give the place a chance*, Bess would have said. He knew that to be the case. And he reminded himself that he knew very little of war, and *that* was the reality of the situation now Franco had made his move: war. I imagine Piers to have taken some time to align his expectations with the reality; but that was why he was there: to learn.

Piers asked directions to the apartment Monroe had told him to head toward. It was a long walk, a nice place on the south east side of the city Monroe was using with the permission of a politician friend of his. *Some socialist with property contracts*, Monroe had said. All very murky. *Do not try and fathom Spain*, Monroe had said; *it will spin you around*.

The apartment itself was large and without much furniture, with cold tiled floors and high ceilings. So this is a politician's house in Spain, thought Piers. He opened the shutters and looked out over rooftops toward the sea. He threw his bag

157

onto an armchair and slept for close to a full day on top of the made bed.

Fresh and focussed he walked down to the harbour-side and watched the ships coming and going for several hours the next morning. The sun beat down like a heavy hot pulse.

That evening he wrote a poem about the breathing coast line of a mythical city, a city without a face, with more corners than straight lines. He played around with the image of a man made from the parts of a city, his organs being the functioning members of the boroughs. It was simple. Cities can die. They died all the time. That was how mythologies were born – out of the embers of dead cities. What would be the legacy of this twilight? Barcelona was depressed, it was in hiding.

Monroe had told him how the workers, looking for decent pay and to be treated like humans, had installed a government to bring about change. *Intelligent belligerence,* as someone may have put it. But Franco was a sentinel of conservatism. Perhaps few could have predicted he would have had the intellectual rigour to mount a rebellion the way he was, but he did, like a robot finding it has a way outside of its programme, and that way is to be used to regress back inside the confines of its own servility. That Franco was a curious psychotic. And Mola, that other general, on the move in the Catholic centres of the north, was a fierier revolutionary. There were strong suspicions with Mola that his motives were in line with the soldier who, when not killing, is simply looking for something to kill. These men were *slaughterers!* Years of campaigns in North Africa had done something to these people. It was no secret. They had been rewired and now it was all coming back to the front door. It was a social exhortation, in fact; an *Africanista* was to be avoided on the mainland. Something had cracked in a man of these colours.

I hope you have never known a man home from facing war,

and I hope you never will. That is a brutal exchange of your innocence and his despair at innocence. But a man who has been forced to live in death and mud; that is another thing. And these men, these *Africanistas*, lived in death as in a medieval painting of hell, trudging their feet through the skulls and intestines of the fallen as the red smoke of burning villages upsurged behind them in the black sky. They came to call it home, and call it natural. Who does not loose themselves here? And now they were to bring that home to mainland Spain. Anyone who returns from Hell brings something of it back with them stained into their soul.

Where else would you want to be? Piers recalled Monroe's words as he looked out over the streets from the balcony of the apartment.

You can only know war if you have been surrounded by the lovers of war. And it *is* addictive. Of course it is. In the Great War, the average soldier saw four days of action in a cycle of 365. War is largely this, what Piers was greeted with in Barcelona: the quiet mixture of dread and excitement. The lovers of war slowly circling those who know nothing. And the lovers of war pick the flesh from the others. Sometimes the flayed do not even know they've been stripped.

As the night turned into the freshest reds of morning Piers tore up his poem into bits and flung it into the unlit fireplace and went to bed.

If he had been thinking of Bess it was out of both loyalty and compassion rather than natural yearning – there were more urgent things afoot than the hand of his wife – and as the days went on he began to think less and less of Bess. He had meant to write to her, and to me, and perhaps to Matilda. But each time he put it off it seemed more correct that this truth of Spain that he was looking for was something coming out of his own silence.

He spent a few days visiting the empty churches, gutted by anarchists, and spent some time writing a poem about a priest with no insides, just the garb and the speeches. Stolen innards, guts. He burned that poem with a candle light.

But more and more he spent his time watching the ships coming and going from the window of the politician's apartment. And then, in loneliness and drifting time, he began to realise that he could not be sure how long he had been in that apartment in Barcelona.

Piers went to a bar on Las Ramblas, a busy place, drank some wine, smoked the strong Spanish cigarettes he enjoyed, practised his Spanish with a young couple who liked T.S. Eliot, and walked up to the Park Guell in the north of the city, and snoozed on a bench for an hour or so underneath the shade of a tree. He woke drowsy and beaten by the heat and took some hours to walk all the way back to the east side of the city. On returning to the apartment, mid-evening, he discovered that the Monroes had arrived.

The first thing he saw was Millie lying on the sofa – like an arrangement of discarded clothes spread across the cushions, her pale listless face not registering Piers' entrance nor his attempts to say hello. It was as if she was a ghost, tripping in another place. Monroe was smoking at the window, a half-silhouette in the red downing of the sunset.

"She will not answer you," he said.

Piers smiled nervously at him. He was boyishly happy to see the poet, but everything was wrong at the same time. Monroe seemed rigid, tired, defensive. And Millie lay staring into space like the lunatic Piers had read about in Sartre.

"What's wrong with her?" he said.

"I am not sure of this place," said Monroe, coldly.

Piers, concerned for the doll-like figure of Millie, clad in black, approached Monroe.

"What has happened?" he said.

"To her?" said Monroe, dismissively. "She is intent on tormenting me." And he repeated the last two words loudly for Millie's benefit. "*Tormenting me!*"

"I give her everything she could need," he went on. "A roof, food, children; and what do I get in return? This crude, cosseted drama."

"But she does not look well," said Piers.

"And the sea air will do her good. If I can force her to *breathe*." Monroe turned to her again and raised his voice. "*Would you at least do that for me?*"

Piers suddenly noticed the quiet of the place.

Monroe's eyes sunk to half-closed and he said softly to Piers: "Forgive me: it has been a long journey from Toledo."

"Where are the girls?" Piers said.

"In Toledo. They are being looked after by a friend of mine, a priest."

Piers examined Monroe's exhausted features; every line in his face was a downturn.

"I have work to do," said Monroe. "And Millie needs to get well."

"I will do whatever I can to help."

Monroe carefully removed the cigarette from between his teeth.

"When I was in the north we spent some time with an old friend, Miguel de Unamuno; do you know of him?" said Monroe.

"No," said Piers.

"A great man. He predicts harsh times ahead. He has given me the keys to a farmhouse he owns in the hills above a small fishing village named Setubal on the coast of Portugal."

"Portugal?" said Piers.

"Spain may not be safe even for us soon, Buren."

"This Unamuno is to be trusted?"

"What do you know of untrustworthiness?" said Monroe, looking down at Piers for the first time.

"It's just you said to be careful," said Piers.

"Unamuno is as worthy of trust as I am. He is one of the finest poets of our time. And he says that we should step aside and let Franco do what needs be done: *cleanse* Spain."

Piers looked out across the rooftops, the hundreds of red banners flapping in the delicious cool seaside breeze. The word "cleanse" fell to the floor with a thud.

"I want you to be safe," said Monroe.

Piers was touched, but confused also. Spain was an alien chaos to him so far – those banners like Roman standards, giant legionary posits; or were they more like the fallen napkins of the Titans?

"You want me to go to Portugal?" Piers said.

"As soon as Millie is better we will follow," said Monroe.

Piers turned away from the poet, the powerful man in his creased seriousness. He could not remember why he had come, but he could neither remember what he had left behind. This golden burning heat of Barcelona – the now! – was all there was. It was myth and it was solid, a cataract on the mind and the memory. It was myth that was going to satiate that emptiness, wasn't it? The repetition of myth – the seven plots – repetition, repetition. We are serpents eating our tails.

"I would prefer to stay with you," Piers said.

"Well, that cannot happen," said Monroe.

Piers held himself steady. He was so tired, buzzing with frustrated energy at odds with the body.

"Go to Setubal," said Monroe, his lips terse with an unerring finality.

Piers could refuse Monroe nothing, but in silence he threw his belongings into his bag, took a glance to Millie who had not moved so much as her gaze on the sofa, and was out the building. Monroe had given him directions to the farmhouse from the train station at Setubal, and given him a folded sheet of paper on which was written a poem of friendship.

Piers, for the first time in his life, decided to drink alcohol to numb an internal pain, and walked across to a bar just off the west side of Las Ramblas, a dark basement bar with orange lights and whispered conversations – some things did not abate even in times of great equality; some people can only truly *live* in the air of subterfuge. But Piers had been there before and knew that he would not be disturbed. He drank sweet wine quickly, staring at the shadows in the corners of the bar. He felt light-headed quite soon, and even some tapas failed to bring him back to his sober senses. It was very late when a hand came to his shoulder.

"Comrade; you look a little drunk."

Piers remembered the man from his first day in Barcelona, the cloth cap, the heavy boots, the pencil-thin moustache. He was surprised the man remembered *him*.

"You still in Barcelona," said the man. "I did not think you would be sticking around."

And the man laughed, slapped his side and rocked his head back. He, also, was quite drunk.

"I am leaving now; finally," said Piers, his eyelids beginning to droop.

"Do I offend you? You are always leaving."

"I have outstayed my welcome," said Piers and unsteadily got up from the barstool.

"Wait, wait, wait," said the man, a bright moist grin across his face. "I cannot bear to see a man out of love with Barcelona." And he threw his arms wide. "You come with me," he said. "I will bring you love."

The man picked up Piers' half full glass and downed it in

front of him, grabbed Piers' hat, his arm and led him toward the steps up and out of the bar.

"Wait," said Piers. "Where are we going?"

"To find love, comrade," laughed the man, and they were out into the street.

They walked a short way – shortcuts through alleys and even through a café at one point, in the front and out the kitchen at the rear – and came to another bar with a rooftop veranda. The man – Piers, held so close to his face now, could see that he was young, good looking, but weathered – a half-smoked cigarette hanging from his bottom lip, pointed Piers to a large group sitting around several tables in the corner – men, women, a guitarist earnestly strumming a progression of major chords, smoke swirling around them all.

"I'll get drinks," said the man.

Piers approached the group slowly – he was sobering up from the walk but he was still unsure of himself. He looked up to the black sky specked with brilliant stars – they looked just out of reach. The air was both warm and chilled, someone grabbed his wrist – the soft touch of a woman – and a roar of approval went up as the man with the pencil-thin moustache joined them, put a wine glass in Piers' hand, and he was sat amidst them all, all the men in their cloth caps and blue shirts and rough faces and self-rolled cigarettes, the girls in their crepe-like dresses and tatty flowers in their hair, red lips and dark eyes.

The girl who had taken his wrist was close to him, smiling at him. The guitar robustly went up a gear and a cheer plumed coarsely into the air. The man with the pencil-thin moustache was next to Piers and he began introducing everyone, pointing at each person around the table and reeling off names: "That is Miguel, Xavier, Honore, Carmen, Federico, Antonio, Pio, Ramon, Ramiro, Angel, Angelina, Angela." The names went on, some people nodded at Piers, grinned, some of them paid no attention such was the intensity of their own conversations; the names went on and finally the girl holding on to Piers' wrist was named as Sabina, and Piers looked at her, smiled, she smiled back, her dark eyes alluring, and from somewhere one of the party pulled a trumpet horn from under the table and began to accompany the guitar with shrill melodic squawks, and Sabina kissed Piers passionately on the mouth, holding his cheeks in the palms of her hands, as if trapping him. She pulled away, licked her lips, the trumpet blew, another cheer went up and Piers, without thought, began to laugh uncontrollably, and necked his wine, held up his glass and shouted, "*Por avour; mas, por avour.*" Another cheer, and now Piers cheered with them, and he kissed Sabina again, a happy, thankful, sexual connection, and from somewhere in the throng an arm leaned in and poured more wine into Piers' glass.

***

Ki and Millie Monroe remained in the politician's apartment for only a few days after Piers left. Millie came and stood next to Monroe's chair at the veranda and said in her under-used voice, "I cannot get better without my children."

Monroe did not look at her, but he knew she was right and that coming to Barcelona at all had been misguided. He had wanted to see the city in its socialist glory, test the fervour on its own terms – see it for himself. It had nothing to do with Millie.

He rubbed his hands over his face and nodded. She returned to her position on the sofa, and a weight lifted from the room, from them both.

They took the train back to Toledo, through the quiet countryside, the yellow grass and blue skies. Millie, all in black, spoke very little, and Monroe, gentle, stayed close to her. The citadel of Toledo's Alcazar bright and brilliant in the centre of the skyline, they took a carriage from the train station to their villa, at the west side of the city beneath the monastery on the hill, next to the lemon grove.

Millie stopped Monroe from disembarking the carriage by putting her hand on his forearm. She was so small next to him, like a child, thin, pale, her pink eyes giving up a trembling gaze. Monroe smiled warmly to her. She wanted to thank him, to be sorry to him, to open up her regret and sorrow and let the dungeon-bleak stale air out of her. But Monroe leant his large dappled forehead against hers and kissed her gently on the lips. Toledo was a home to them, these nomads, and things would be better now.

At the doors of the villa the children waited with Father Eusebio, Monroe's old friend. They ran to Millie with permission, she took them in her arms with delicate joy.

Monroe raised a grateful hand to the priest who nodded in response.

"You came back," said Eusebio with a burdened smile.

Monroe put his hand on the priest's shoulder and squeezed it.

The rest of the day the girls would not leave the side of their mother who sat in the parlour by the unlit fireplace. They brought Millie great comfort in those days.

Father Eusebio and Monroe stood in the garden of the villa looking up to the monastery on the hill.

"I'm not sure if it was such a good idea to come back right now," said Eusebio.

"It was right for Millie," said Monroe.

He drew into a sigh through his cigarette.

"I mean you may have been safer in Barcelona."

"My concern is for my wife right now."

Father Eusebio nodded and breathed deeply.

"We go back a long way, my friend," he said.

"We do," said Monroe.

The two men did indeed go back a long way. It was Father Eusebio who baptised Monroe and christened the children, it was Father Eusebio who had found Monroe drunk and delirious in the village of La Dama de las Colinas all those years before. It was the first time Millie had left him. She had refused to leave London after the scandal of his Bloomsbury satire. He had dragged her to Spain, to this villa in Toledo but almost immediately she had vanished from him. Millie was as much the dark-eyed mystic as any of them were, and hiding, making do, surviving, was in her nature. Monroe had searched for her and found nothing. In despair he had started drinking one night and several months later he was in the whitewashed chapel on the hilltop of La Dama de las Colinas, his face dry as hard clay, and Father Eusebio's crisp blue eyes looking down at him. And it was Father Eusebio who had helped him find Millie. It was Eusebio who had helped them build a home.

"The news is that Franco marches from the north," said the priest. "The garrison at the Alcazar is preparing for an onslaught."

"They are?"

"Rumours are they will swear allegiance to Franco as soon as he gets here. So Madrid will send militia to relieve the garrison of its command. Blood will spill."

"And the people?" Monroe now aired concern.

"You are a foreigner; you will not be harmed," said the priest. He sucked his teeth and sighed, his clipped pointed beard overgrowing with grey in recent times. "But who knows what barbarity will overflow in the moment when the eyes fill with fire."

Eusebio had spent time in Morocco as a young cleric. He had told Monroe of the butchery he had seen there – not in details, but the pallid fall of his face spoke a thousand words in the telling. He knew the nature of the *Afrikanista*.

As the days wore on the sun grew hotter, Millie began to regain something of her former zest. She began to tend to the garden with the help of the children, and helping their housekeeper with dinner. Monroe was silently enjoying the peace in Millie's eyes, in her poses. Although they did not make love – Millie was just too delicate in the wake of her illness – they held each other close in bed at night, Millie rarely sleeping for more than a few forced hours. The girls were happy to be at the centre of a family once more. That was how Father Eusebio put it.

There was no drunkenness to this home, not like at the Latimer cottage. Indeed Monroe had not touched a drop since London. Eusebio gave him peace, his family as one gave him peace.

Father Eusebio, the soft mouth behind that greying beard

and beneath his sharp blue sapient eyes, would ride into Toledo on horseback most afternoons with Monroe. They would meet up with a rowdy bunch of Europeans at a favoured cantina where they would discuss the problems of the continent, the degradation of art, and, sometimes, the futility of all such topics of conversation. They all met at around two in the afternoon. Some of them ate and got drunk, some of them just ate, some of them just got drunk.

"I am perfectly happy watching the rest of you get sozzled," Darabont would say, and he would sip cautiously at his mineral water. Darabont, an English art dealer and travel writer, often sat at the head of the table. Next to him would be Schinkler the poet, then another poet, Gordon Marmaduke; and there would be several journalists – "here for the sport of shooting priests", Darabont would say; and Monroe would cast a look to Eusebio who would smile disapprovingly and shake his head.

"You don't seem concerned about Franco," Monroe said once to Darabont.

Darabont was lean, rakishly good-looking, his swish of blonde hair coming down his temple, but he was damp looking, as if he would never get used to the climate.

"I'll be concerned when he gets here, old boy," was Darabont's reply.

"I'm more concerned with the trigger fingers of the anarchists right now," said the poet Schinkler.

"It's all chaos," said Darabont. "Chaos, chaos, chaos."

"So there's no point in trying to second guess any of it, you mean?" said Father Eusebio.

"Precisely," said Darabont.

"Which is why you're running away?" said Schinkler, dusting cigarette ash from the lapel of his Italian linen suit.

"You're *going*, Ernest?" said Monroe.

"Pay no attention to Herr Schinkler," said Darabont. "I have been summoned to look at a long lost Durer in Stuttgart. I am running away from nothing."

But Monroe let this play on his mind. Ernest Darabont was one of the smartest men he knew, a shrewd dealer who took his laziness extremely seriously and put all of his efforts into making the most money with the minimal amount of effort, and when he gave his story of a forgotten Durer, he held Monroe's gaze steadily so there could be no misunderstanding as to the flimsiness of this excuse.

Within two weeks Monroe and Father Eusebio were alone in that cantina. Even the journalists had gone to cover the fighting in Old Castile, leaving the trembling ugly uncertainties of Toledo to its natives. The anarchists with their itchy trigger fingers had been harassing the monks on the hill. It always took place in the dead of night, and as yet nobody had been hurt, but the rumours were spreading darkness across the intellectuals of the city, and the devout feared the worst.

"Have you thought about what you're going to do if the fighting breaks out here?" Monroe asked Eusebio.

"What do you think I'm going to do? I will stay with the people who need me."

"But you have heard the stories."

"Of Catholics being shot in the streets of Madrid? They are not true."

"But stories tell us *something*," said Monroe.

The cantina was quieter than it had ever been that afternoon. And that was when the first gunshot was heard.

It rattled through the air. Neither Monroe nor Father Eusebio immediately reacted. They sat opposite each other in a cosmic pause that was only broken by a short puissant scream from the waitress. She began crying out in Spanish. Monroe got to his feet.

"That was a gunshot," said the priest.

Monroe was looking over in the direction of the waitress whose scream had suggested injury, but she just stood perfectly still in the middle of the cantina, her face a frozen caption of horror.

"Are you okay?" Monroe called to her.

But she said nothing, the climax of weeks of tension, rigid within her.

Another shot was fired, as if to confirm the first, and then an untidy barrage of gunfire clattered through the street. Monroe and Eusebio ran up to the window of the cantina and watched as a small loose collection of men with the red armbands of the anarchists advanced down the street firing their rifles toward a small crowd of civilians who were running for cover.

"Are they firing on unarmed civilians?" said Monroe.

"This could be the beginning of the true war in Toledo, my friend," said Eusebio from over his shoulder.

Another rally of gunfire, this time closer to the cantina, and a window on the far side of the building shattered. This brought further cries from the waitress, and this time she ran into a back room, and Monroe and Eusebio crouched into the corner where they could still see the street.

"What do these anarchists *want*? They are in control. There is no resistance here," said Monroe.

"The resistance is coming," said Eusebio. "They're clearing out the bad apples before it gets here."

The anarchist gunmen were hitting none of their targets. Monroe recognised the aged inadequacy of their rifles. The town men watched them pass down the street, firing freely into emptiness. And then a thing happened in a hot blur of a second. A figure darted from a doorway, seemingly heading for the cantina, and in a beat, one of the gunmen lifted his rifle, took aim, and fired a fatal shot. It all happened so quickly it was unlikely the gunman had seen it was a young girl in a man's coat. Monroe exhaled loudly, but it was Father Eusebio who made for the door. Monroe called after him but he was out into the street. Guns turned onto the priest. Monroe ran out after him.

"Put down your weapons, no good can come from this," the priest called to the men, all of whom were now walking slowly toward him with their rifles raised.

Monroe stopped at the edge of the pavement twenty yards from his friend. A few of the guns turned on him. He dare not move.

"We are *not* your enemies. This young girl is *not* your enemy. Spain is *not* your enemy," said the priest, and a gunshot cracked into the air. Father Eusebio, hit in the side of the head, fell heavily into the dirt, a cough of dust going up into the air as he hit the floor, a light puff of red mist seemed to hang where he had just stood.

Monroe cried out and ran toward his friend, sliding to a crunch into the gravel. The gunmen called out to Monroe to be still, and they gathered around him, their eyes glistening down the sights of their rifles. They shouted, screamed at him to get away from the priest.

"I am a South African," he shouted at them, his face shaking with rage, his voice degenerating into a growl. "I am not one of your *animal* Spaniards."

The gunmen called back at him, a din of voices, approaching closer.

Monroe's rage began to turn to tears as he held the lifeless, bloody, splintered head of Father Eusebio in his arms. A man of dignity and wisdom and deep intelligence, a man of learned godliness and compassion; here the one minute and now gone, wasted. What *waste*. Monroe began to say it. *What waste*. He

172

began to shout in Afrikaans, but it fell away from him and he looked down in silence at his friend. The gunmen soon stopped shouting as well, and the fervour and adrenaline seemed to pass. They lowered their guns, and a few of them began to shuffle their feet in the dirt. Some even now walked off slowly, their rifles at their side like fishing poles. There was a feeling of enough for one day amongst Eusebio's killers. Perhaps even a little of embarrassment.

* * *

Piers awoke slowly, as he did every morning, perched himself on the edge of the mattress, rubbed his face, scratched his beard, lit a cigarette and squinted to the brightness of the day outside. He looked over the smooth curved body of Sabina asleep in the bed with her face to the wall, pulled on his trousers and hooked the braces over his shoulders. It had taken just a few months for him to adopt the ways of the anarchists, with their heavy cotton clothes, cloth caps and hand-rolled cigarettes. His chin was charcoaled with stubble, and his eyes were dark patches in a ruddy plain. His pallor had taken the sun quickly, and a stranger could not immediately identify him as a foreigner, not now, not with the company he kept. He had, as they say, gone native.

He could remember little of the previous night, a pattern that had become the norm. He walked over to the roller desk in the corner and searched for his pocket watch amongst the leaves of poem sketches he had been working on the last few weeks. It was close to midday and the deep blue shadows on the tiled floor were made all the more low by the singeing blast of daylight at the balcony doors. Piers had the nagging feeling that he was supposed to be somewhere.

As he tried to gather his thoughts the front door to the apartment opened – a small open plan abode with paint peeling in the cornices, it looked out to a busy dirty market square on the edge of the Badalona region of the city. Ramon came in, his head bowed with the intensity of a lithe hunting dog. He had a bundle of posters and leaflets under his arm, another string-tied file under the other. Sabina stirred in the bed in the corner, pulled the cotton sheet over her naked breasts and returned to her heavy sleep. Ramon, saying nothing, planted his baggage on the kitchen table and turned

174

to Piers who was still rubbing his face and drawing hard on his cigarette.

They stared at each other for a moment.

"Sorry I'm late," said Ramon.

Piers shrugged, non-the-wiser.

Ramon was the secretary for the neighbourhood anarchist group; a wiry young Catalonian who was always serious, always in a rush, often late; his eyes were alert, darker and ruddier than Piers', longer in the gestation of edgy politics. He was sickly, Piers thought, until he met with the rest of the group in the cold light of day. They were all sickly, coughing, rugged, starving, poor, waning, wheezing. Every one of them – apart from Sabina – was a philosopher or a painter or a poet, but each had a trade, too; they came from good families with sensible parents, but thoughtful parents who could see in the spirit of the next generation a fluent need for goodness.

All of them were on edge and had been for weeks. Franco was coming up from the south west and apparently rounding on Toledo. Madrid would be next. The first conversation Piers and Ramon had had was through the tears of mourning for the death of Lorca. Not the left's first martyr, Piers had said, but the most stunning.

A few days later Ramon had tried to cut Piers' throat, lurching across the table with the knife he had been using to slice an apple. Piers had mentioned his acquaintance with Unamuno – an acquaintance that did not even exist – and the men around the table had gone silent before Ramon's outburst. Piers pulled him to the floor before others got in the way. Ramon spat up at Piers, "*Your* Unamuno, *Franco's* poet."

Unamuno, poet, playwright, philosopher, from Bilbao, had recently given a speech supporting Franco's charge of returning Spain to its traditions. The left had recoiled at the defection.

Betrayal was something just now making its way into the fabric of the Spanish war.

Each day something of similar middle-brow drama happened. Piers was tiring of the whirlwind passions and brash outbursts. Piers, athletic now and carved from his summer on the farm, was stronger than most of the powdery anarchists. Outwardly he feared no-one. Also, he found it difficult to believe any of his new friends. They all had a penchant for high-drama, every sniff was plague, every cough a gunshot. Europe was the one-nation under a banner of revolution, thought Piers; and it was little wonder now he had spent some time with the revolutionaries. It was a collective edginess; even while in power the Left had been waiting for the fight to erupt.

Generations had dug pitch-forks into hay bales and it all added up down the decades to a bursting psyche in the middle and lower classes. Was it education that released murderousness? Was it money? Of course not. Education was a tool in the industry of death, just as much as the preying on the naïve was. So what *was* it that made Europe so intent on turning itself inside out every fifty years or so?

There are the saved and those who want to be saved, Monroe had said. *That's where the tension comes in.*

Piers had been thinking this over. Did these anarchists want to "be saved"? Some of them indeed did just enjoy the drama, a reason to get up every day that could result in death or glory. Piers was seeing a great deal of that philosophy. But was it a matter of covetousness? If it was, it wasn't in the sense that Monroe meant. At the centre of all this was a genuine collision of celestial confusions and earthly needs. A man can be pushed only so far, thought Piers. And this accounted as much for the Right as it did for the Republicans. Tales of General Mola's inspired massacres in the Catholic north were inescapable on the streets of Barcelona. And it meant that young mongooses such as Ramon moved even quicker, looked even more intense than before.

"Have you made some notes for the speech?" said Ramon, pushing aside the poems on Piers' desk and spreading out his own paperwork.

Piers could not remember having agreed to write a speech. But he could imagine having done so. This was how the Left worked, Piers thought – the governing classes now; find a poet and get him to write the speeches that were to bind the country to this new age of equality.

"Well, not to worry," said Ramon when Piers did not answer. "I will have to give you pointers, after all."

What were speeches to do when Mola was executing women and children at the roadsides of Galicia, Navarre, Andalusia and Old Castile?

Piers looked Ramon up and down. More and more Piers felt he was being dragged closer to the core of someone else's fight, and a core that had no roads out. More importantly, his poetry was going nowhere.

"I can't remember anything about what speech I am supposed to be writing," he said.

Ramon shrugged.

"I will tell you what to write, you make it sound like Lorca," he said.

Piers rubbed his face again. He felt flabby, coarse, overwhelmed by a dedication to nothingness. *Make it sound like Lorca.* He shuffled to the desk, lit a cigarette, and slowly took the seat. Ramon, fidgety, edgy, pulled up another and handed Piers a pen.

"Just like that?" said Piers.

Ramon fidgeted some more and nodded toward the blank piece of paper.

"Now is the time we need to fight as one," said Ramon.

Piers looked at him.

Ramon pointed at the blank sheet of paper.

"This is it," he said.

Piers began to write, his shoulders high, his head low.

"Now is the time that we drive out these murderous minorities, these demons, these devils," continued Ramon.

Piers stopped writing.

"What is the matter?" said Ramon.

"I just remembered I have to be somewhere," said Piers, and stood, pulled on his boots and his jacket.

He needed to be anywhere but this terrible anteroom to the world. He felt wretched, physically greasy on the inside, he wanted to unfold his skin and scrape away the mucous. Where had it all come from? He had been cheated on, hadn't he? Piers knew the difference between the heart and the ass, and he was being spoken to through the ass. Monroe had kicked him out and he had spent the last few months fucking Sabina in the hope that he might die in his sleep one night. The alternative was returning to his wife, to beautiful Bess and that astute mind that would read everything of him immediately. His damned foolishness. It would be the death of him, he thought. What did he have left? The cocoon of anarchism.

Ramon called after him as he stumbled quickly down the stairwell and out into the street – he could then hear Sabina shouting his name from the window as he dipped into the bustle of the market that wrapped around their building.

Piers walked headstrong through the bannered streets, the clear blue sky sheen above him, his large boots clumping onto the cobbles. He was feeling ill, weak, and he pulled his jacket closed across his chest as a chilled sweat began to build upon his brow and down the centre of his back. He could not be sure where he was going or what he was going to do. He needed to find Monroe, he needed to realign himself with the poetry in him. That stuff on that desk, lyrics about revolution and Sabina's golden skin; it made his stomach turn as he swiftly, heavily, moved through the streets.

Why had he come to Spain? To find the revolution, to find in the dirt and the grime of the people fighting for their freedom a song of his own meaning? Did he come to taste the dirt of the heroes? He had followed Monroe and his stories. But why had Monroe come to Spain? That was the question. My god, thought Piers; Monroe had come to save his marriage. It was as simple as that, and no less noble. And where was he now? Piers had been abducted by flights of fancy, by seductive Spanish women and their seductive brethren. Even the dirty words of the street sounded like poetry when glazed with revolution.

Piers reached the Monroe apartment but a government man told them that they had been gone for almost two months. Piers realised he had very little money – his new friends had found him a supple resource in that sense. He sat on the steps outside the building. He was tired – months of crushing, pressing, swirling at the hands of the anarchists. What made him think that it was *he* who deserved to be above the usual existence of man?

His life had been unusual. Perhaps his expectations had undermined his happiness. Was his existence a myth of his own making or the charade of others? Bess had given him the chance to indulge in the glories of simplicity, the realness of usualness, but surely now she would give up on him. What would returning to London achieve? And the revolution? He would have to play a part. Bess could accept him as a warrior poet, not as a fool. He had rejected her offer of normalcy. That was all that was left. Why had he come to Spain if he returned to Bess without the poetry to prove his greatness? Be a child, play in the dirt, go to university, write some verse and marry Bess and father some children, make love, drink some wine, retire and become irritable, play with grandchildren in a big summer hat, drink too much wine and on to whisky and die. That was the life he could have happily had. What would the poetry do for anyone? He could be no Ki Monroe. There was no room for another. There was no space for human progress to house another poet, another swashbuckler.

He walked down to the harbour and, with the only money he had left went to find a ship that would take him to England. Bess would forgive him. She could not love him as he was, but she would forgive him. His heart had never been so heavy. And there, as he looked for some passage back to his wife, he saw Ramon, Miguel, and Sabina, and they saw him, and waved – Sabina smiled, the two men looked urgent – and they ran toward him through the crowds. And his heart lifted. He had not expected that but it did lift.

"We have been looking for you, our friend," said Miguel, and grabbed him around the shoulders in a warm brotherly embrace. "We cannot lose you now. You are part of us. And when the fighting comes, my friend, we will need a great poet."

✳ ✳ ✳

Monroe did not remember the beating.

He had been drunk and fighting with his fists for over a week since Father Eusebio had been killed. First he had been seeking his friend's killers, but soon the drink blurred everything, and he was fighting anyone who looked at him. Millie had barely seen him since Eusebio's death. And then one morning Monroe awoke in his own bed at the villa, his jaw bound and broken, his torso bruised, his ribs cracked; Millie – that poor pretty dark spectre at his side – looking down into his eyes. The first thing he did was try to say Father Eusebio's name, but Millie, tearful, smoothed his hair down and shook her head.

Despite the power of his will, Monroe lay in the bed for some days more. Before he was ready he began to sit up, and through the pain he mouthed certain words, saliva wetting the bandages all around his chops. *The girls?* He wanted to know. They came in, happy to see him, grateful, but frightened of his state also.

When they were alone, Millie, her knees together, her hands fidgeting in her lap, said, "The anarchists have been ransacking the churches all through Toledo. Word of what General Mola is doing in the countryside of Castile has driven people wild here, Ki. Nobody trusts anybody."

Monroe could not speak. He looked down at his bruised chest, and all he could think of was the bloodied face of Eusebio in his hands. It seemed to be the last thing he remembered at all.

"I have been praying for us," said Millie.

Monroe looked over to her, his eyes dark like those of a bird.

"You have been going to church?" he said through the pain of his broken jaw.

Millie nodded, sensing the tone of her husband's voice.

Monroe, angered by his own invalidity, shut his eyes and waved her from his presence. He could not be sure of what was going on outside of the room, outside of the house. He could not know the dangers of the streets of Toledo now, no more than he could know the truths or the lies of the rumours of what Mola and Franco were doing in the north. He was locked away, unable to defend his family, unable to avenge the murder of Father Eusebio. He could not hear the bells from the monastery on the hill. He could not hear his children playing in the lemon groves.

He pulled himself from the bed, every inch of him aching radiantly to a different degree, and took some time to pull on his trousers and a shirt. His head hung as if in a bubble, as if he was pressed and pushed and tugged at all at once. But he stood tall when he was able and looked at his sorry state in the full-length mirror on the wardrobe door. A wounded soldier indeed.

In the corner of the room, against the wall, was a wooden crutch – like that of Long John Silver – that Millie had brought for when he would able to get about. Monroe installed it under his arm and steadied himself. He went out into the parlour where Millie was drawing on scrap paper with the children. They all stopped in silence and looked at him, unsure of what was to happen next.

"Today I will come to church with you," he said.

Millie, with a sad face, nodded, stood from her kneeling position on the floor with the children, walked over to her damaged husband and kissed him gently on the cheek.

The family slowly walked into the city, Monroe leaning heavily on the crutch, his little girls watchful and quiet. They moved in a column down the dusty streets. Few people passed them, and when someone did they stared at the odd procession. Millie had dressed her husband as best she could in his church suit, but his head was still embalmed in bandages, his jaw blue and ballooned with bruises, and his eyes pink with pain and rage. The women of the family were all in black.

It took them an hour or so to walk to the street that Father Eusebio's church was on, St Botolph's. As they walked past a roadside cantina, a group of men who were talking and drinking at a table turned and stared at them. Monroe noticed how Millie ushered the girls to shield themselves from the men's glances. Monroe stared back at them. He stopped in his tracks.

Millie put her arm around Monroe and said, her voice trembling and weak, "Please, Ki; let's keep moving."

But Monroe did not move. He was trying to remember the faces of the men who shot Eusebio. But he could not see their faces in his mind; they were all a craggy ruin of gremlin heads, demons and harbingers.

And then one of the men said in Spanish, "Listen to your wife, Senor; we know who you are. We will come find you when we want you." And he laughed; and all the men at the table laughed.

But one of the men, a grizzled, bearded man in a long coat stood and began to approach the Monroes. The other men at the table did not look so sure that this was where they wanted the moment to go.

Millie began to pull her husband away but Monroe turned and puffed out his chest as best he could. As the man came closer he pulled back his coat – Monroe expected a gun and moved in front of his family – but the man pulled out a long thick piece of wood, tied to which was a grim regiment of pathetic dead frogs, bloated and loose-limbed, hanging like condemned men.

"You see these frogs, my friend," the man said in English, still walking slowly toward them, his voice like boiling tar. "You see them? When the war comes I will string your family up like these frogs I caught. And all the Catholics will hang like this."

Monroe pushed at his girls to get closer behind him.

The grizzled man began to cackle a wheezy laugh. The other men at the table were quieter now, waiting to see the outcome of this encounter.

"Your precious little daughters will be strung up like frogs, they will be fucked and killed, my friend; what do you think of that?"

As the man opened his mouth to carry on his talk, Monroe took one step toward him and with all the strength he had brought his crutch up into the man's face. It was quick, and the man fell several feet backward into the road, his cheekbone cracked wide open like a cardboard box – the crack echoed through the empty street.

The other men at the table grimaced at the sight and sound and although Monroe had turned to them, drool falling from his damaged jaw, with just his crutch for a weapon, they did not draw their guns on him. The man on the floor was groaning on his back. One of the men at the table got up and, watching Monroe carefully, went over to his injured comrade. The others followed. Monroe could see now that these were not men at all, but boys, teenagers – farmers or shopkeeper's sons. One of them, as he lifted the deadweight frogman to his feet, said under his breath in Spanish, "Do you always have to be such a cunt, Alfonse. You make us no better than them."

But the eyes of these men were still filled more with hate than with regret, and as Monroe moved his girls away he knew that this ugly scene was a sign of things to come. Monroe knew that he did not have much more fight in him. If the frogman had withstood that blow, he might not have been able to deal out a second.

They made it to St Botolph's, bedecked with notices of mourning for the Father Eusebio from members of his congregation. Inside the hall had been disembowelled of its icons and its treasures. Monroe sat upon the sill of a window and held his family close. They prayed together for some time before returning slowly to their villa.

Monroe sat up all night thinking of ways to stay and protect his family. His daughters slept in each other's arms in the master bed. Millie, knelt at Monroe's feet in front of the fireplace, rested her head on his knee.

"We must leave," she said.

"So that Eusebio died for nothing?" said Monroe.

"It is not for us to decide whether or not he died for nothing. This is Spain's war. All you can decide is whether your family is safe. Let us go to Unamuno's cottage until all of this terrible business is over with."

She slept with her head in his lap. Monroe could not sleep.

The next day word came that a Republican militia from Madrid had entered the north of the city and was headed for the garrison at the Alcazar. To combat the march the army sent troops out to meet the Republicans and fighting began in the streets of Toledo. Monroe kept his family in the villa. They had to go, he knew that now, and every moment he stalled it became more difficult for them to escape.

As night drew in the sky burned orange with the death cries of torched churches as the Republicans made their way through the city, pushing the troops back toward the Alcazar. Bombs began to fall on the citadel from the few government planes that had been sent from Madrid, and from the window of the Monroe villa Toledo was soon lit like medieval murals of hell – the orange, reds and yellows of damnation against the thick black backdrop of endless sunken night.

Still Monroe did not want to leave the memory of Father Eusebio in a gutter along with the rest of Toledo for these bastard communists. In a dazed rage – with Millie begging him to stay – he took his crutch and went out into the warm swirling night. Immediately he saw the monastery on the hill beyond the lemon groves was filled with fire. Gunshots rattled, explosions crashed their cymbals – the full orchestral works of war. Within just twenty four hours Toledo had fallen to impoverished knees.

As Monroe stumbled into the heart of the city, his face still bandaged at the jaw, his eyes filled with tears at the death that he saw, the destruction. One narrow street was lined with soldiers' scattered bodies where some fierce fighting had driven a platoon back to the Alcazar by a difficult route. They had bottlenecked and been cut down mercilessly.

Further on, a building had lost its side, rubble spilled across the road, an iron bathtub hanging precariously from a dilapidated upstairs washroom. Shots rang out close by. A group of men ran across Monroe's path. They paid him no attention, this mummified wanderer.

He came upon a square where a band of soldiers were wheeling a small canon into a strong defensive position. Monroe was now in the shadow of the Alcazar; his pain and aches had evaporated in the dense blackness of the night, supped up by the inky darkness. Still he stumbled through streets and alleys. He could not even remember why he had left the villa. *It is my duty to protect my family*, he said to himself, as he kicked his feet through the charred and scattered remains of the city.

He was closer to explosions now; the Alcazar had become the focal point of the fighting. He had been away from the villa for several hours and all he could smell was death. He gathered himself; figured out where he was and the best route back to his family. But he stopped still as he came to the end of the next alleyway. In a small square at the foot of a wall at the other side of a fountain, were the heaped bodies of the Carmelite monks from the monastery on the hill. At first he did not recognise what they were, and then the orange flashes came down the narrow alley to light up the scene. The blood against the walls, the bodies hunched on the floor in their robes like soiled laundry. They had all been executed, that much was clear. Thirty men or so. This was the world at its end, thought Monroe. These anarchists are not trying to quash a rebellion, he thought; they're trying to kill God.

Monroe stumbled through his numbed pain, back into the main streets where great bonfires burned the relics being looted from the churches. The night was black, heated by burning crosses.

He made it back to the villa in a blur – there was a moment when it seemed as though the house was empty, but Millie and the girls were in the loft space watching the sky light up through the window. Monroe appeared to them like a war-weary angel, tattered and dejected in the frame of the door.

"Grab what you need," he said. "We're going now."

* * *

The orders came down to the militia that it was time to move out.

Piers had spent some hours in silence sitting at the foot of the hillside watching Miguel take target practice, shooting at tin plates on a dry stone wall next to the old abandoned dry stone barn. The column had been there for several weeks. It had been a time of plentiful food, but of no hot water; all the men had grown beards, and Piers had not taken his shirt off for days. And the days were hot, but there was a merciful breeze that came down from the hills. The nights were bitterly cold. They had left Barcelona singing through hangovers, heading north on the back of a truck. The songs had gone, replaced by boredom and a suspicion that the war was going on without them somewhere across the dusted wastelands of Old Castille.

Piers had good days and bad days. There were days when he replaced his alienation with souped-up fervour, the like of which went down very well with his comrades. But there were days when he just sat alone in between training manoeuvres, and looked out across the rubble of the terrain, back toward Barcelona and the road that could take him to the sea.

He had told Ramon about Bess one night, after much wine. Ramon had held him tightly by the shoulders and given a speech about how victory here in Spain would reverberate across the globe.

"That is fine," Piers had said back to him. "But how often will we have to fight for this universal freedom?"

Ramon did not like his tone. He did not know that these words were Monroe's sentiments coming through him.

Piers had been thinking a great deal about Bess, about his decisions, about the loneliness he had taken from her. He had been reading Yeats from a pocket book he was given by Sabina before he left the city. *I heard the old, old men say, 'Everything alters, and one by one we drop away'*. He turned this phrase over in his mind. He thought of Bess in her ball gown, walking steadily amongst the tables of the restaurant. She smiles on catching her husband's eye and she stops for a pace in her tracks. He thought of her that day at Sedgemoor's when they first met Monroe. He thought of what she said to Monroe. What *was* it she said? The words would not come, but he was proud of her, in love with her. Did she ever know how much he loved her? She would be doubting it now, now he was gone. In the days he sweated in his cloying linen shirt, and he thought of Bess, and in the nights the sweat iced and his shirt stuck to him in the cold, and he thought of Bess. One evening Miguel told him he looked miserable.

"Wait until the fighting starts," he said to Piers with a lopsided, mischievous grin.

Captain Fonseca, the column CO, gave a speech every morning, a variation on the grim and necessary joys of killing fascists. He liked to stoke the fires with reports of mass executions of anarchists in towns all across the north. The armies of the *Afrikanistas* were moving in a horseshoe shape – like a devil's cloven foot – from the southern tip around to the north and down again. And, as Fonseca told it, they left death in their wake. They were like the locusts of the Inquisition, all over again. The war had immediately become a struggle against annihilation.

Piers did not always believe Fonseca's bulletins; he found Spaniards – Europeans, in fact – more susceptible to rhetoric than he was used to back in London. They cheered every morning, and the stories intensified as Fonseca judged the boredom of his men. Piers watched in silence, waiting for the moment when his gaze met with Fonseca's suspicious and narrow eyes. Miguel told Piers that Fonseca was unimpressed with his credentials, his attitude, or his talent.

"I told Fonseca you were a writer."

"Isn't everybody here a writer?" Piers said.

"That's exactly what the captain said. He asked to see your work."

There was nothing to show. Piers had not written a word since Barcelona. He could feel the poetry corroding within him, clogging up his arteries as it crumbled, fattening and dying, wheezing to nothing.

"You'd better learn how to shoot if you don't want to end up being a water carrier," said Miguel.

"Somebody needs to carry the water," Piers said. "Why not me?"

He knew how to shoot. Monroe had taught him at the Latimer farm. He was a natural. And watching Miguel trying to hit plates in the coarse sunshine of the Spanish hills, he could see that such natural flair was less common than he might have thought. Piers stood heavily, stiffly, and walked slowly over to Miguel.

"You need to calm your breathing," he said as he approached.

Miguel looked at him over his shoulder without lowering the rifle.

"What do you mean?" he said.

"You're all over the place because you need to steady your breathing. I've been watching you for hours. Every time you squeeze the trigger you exhale."

"I do?"

"You do."

Piers took the rifle from Miguel's hands and took aim at the plate, some forty paces away. Without much fanfare, he straightened his shoulders and steadied his stance, levelled his breathing and fired. The plate pinged, spun into the air and disappeared behind the wall.

"You can *shoot*," said Miguel.

"I'll fetch some water," said Piers, and handed the rifle back to his friend.

He was only a few steps off when Ramon came running over the hill waving his cap at them both and calling instructions that the column was to move out immediately.

"Fonseca says we are heading for Toledo," he said when he was closer.

Miguel slung the rifle over his shoulder and pulled the brim of his cap over his brow in a serious gesture. He made for the hill Ramon had just run down, patting Piers firmly on the shoulder as he passed him and saying, "We go fight."

Ramon looked flustered. Not like Miguel who had seemed to tighten at the news, he seemed to condense into a natural firmness. Ramon had a smile on his face, but his eyes were nervous, they gave him away. Piers rubbed the back of his neck and looked down into the dirt. The dirt is the last thing all heroes see, all they taste, he thought. He looked up to the beating sun and wiped his brow. It is the dust we feel, he thought.

Ramon ran after Miguel in his heavy boots, pulling his cap back onto his head. Piers did not hurry. If they go without me, he thought, so be it.

But they did not go without him. In fact they were nowhere near ready when he finally made it over the hill and caught up with them at the camp. The column set off several hours later, when everything was in order and the ragtail collection of anarchists had finally grown tired of Captain Fonseca's badgering and name calling. Fonseca was young and no soldier. The militias were often made-up soldiers at the head, and amateurs throughout the file. But here Piers could not see a soldier anywhere.

"Where are we going?" he said to Fonseca.

"Support our comrades in Toledo," Fonseca said without turning to face him.

The Toledo that had been the stage for some of the fiercest fighting anybody had talked about. Priests wielding machetes, they had heard. Children burned at the stake. Mola's men had descended and turned the place into a hell on earth. Piers looked around the column as they prepared to set off and saw only prey for the *Afrikanistas*. He was tired, and dirty, and sick of the same conversations, empty and platitudinous. All around him he saw only his own errors, and his cowardliness: not to fight, but to fail. To return home with nothing would have been worse than death. He was sure it would have meant the end of Bess' love for him.

After two days' march north, Fonseca received word that all militias were to make haste to Toledo as Mola's army were on the verge of complete control of the city. The Republicans, who had fought so heartily and patiently, were about to be out-numbered and bettered by the brutal *Afrikanistas*. The message from high command was unusually gushing, overflowing as the prosody of fatal glory. Fonseca's hands shook as he delivered the message.

✴ ✴ ✴

The Unamuno place sat secluded from an off-road that itself eventually found a main road that wound down into Setubal. The cottage was small but homely, wood and dry stone, and had retained a clearing in front of the porch as the rest of the surrounding area had become overgrown from neglect. It was a place for the girls to play, said Millie, and for them to stay from under the feet of their father.

Millie was strong now; she had replenished – she had been forced to in the way that mother's do when they have to look out for their children. It is the fathers who concern themselves with the wider pictures. And Monroe, back to the drink, had his mind only on what had happened in Toledo. His eyes were dark and his shoulders broad and low. He ignored Millie's attempts at comfort along the journey, ignored her pleadings, her love, and then her sullenness and reprimands.

But Monroe was not choosing to dig himself deeper into a dark place – he was trying to restrain himself from madness. He knew a thing or two about madness, after all. He had held his wife on the precipice, and he was not ignorant of Latimer's demise. He did not want to forsake his girls by going insane. And so he focussed intensely upon what he had seen in Toledo. And the lifeless face of Father Eusebio was the most frequent image. Again and again those eyes looked up into him. And now it was framed in the burning orange hazes of the Alcazar.

Whenever he looked at his daughters he saw their deaths – the world he was leaving them, the place in which he was allowing them to live was a realm of death and immorality, an unstoppable slaughter. Monroe believed in the rituals of righteousness, and in the rituals of evil, too. It was action that created freedom, even if it meant destruction. Things are born from the ashes.

These were thoughts and debates that would have fired the foundries of his verse in times past. But not now. It ate away at him, poisoned his muscles. He sat on the porch, in the same clothes he had travelled in, for days after the family's arrival, his one hand with a bottle of brandy and the other just a clenched fist. He watched his girls play, which they did uncomfortably as a parade for their gargoyle father, a grim display. He watched them sometimes and it broke his heart, and other times he looked out into the overgrowth, a thicket as meshed and tangled as his own insides.

His condition, his depression as it seems to have been, was further confounded at the dashing of his hopes that Piers would be in Setubal on their arrival. Monroe longed for male conversation, and he had things that he needed to say that were not for the ears of women. It was not the political situation, you understand. He and Millie talked politics frequently – it was just he saw the pain when talking with his wife about these things; to her his every argument and opinion was a great burden that she wished expunged. Moreover, Millie could see the darkness brewing within him, and she wanted nothing to do with it. Monroe was as much a danger as he was a patriarch. Latimer was gone. All that mattered was her girls.

Millie too was deeply disappointed to see Piers had not made it to the cottage. She saw a chink of light in the possibility of his presence, a chink that would let the darkness out of her husband, perhaps. She had faith in Piers; she loved him as much as Monroe did, if with difficulty. But she could not help but feel a curious mixture of remorse, resentment, and relief that Piers had not made it to see what had happened to her family. *Her* family. That's right, it was hers again now. It was her husband who had twisted himself into an absence, just as she had done.

She had tried talking to her husband, against her better judgement.

"Your family needs you. They need your help."

"I brought you here, didn't I?" said Monroe. He did not even look up at her from his seat on the porch.

Millie and the girls worked over the next few weeks to get the vegetable patch in order, and to clean out the inside of the cottage; force the damp away and make a healthy room for the girls to sleep in. They bought some chickens and a goat from Setubal and soon, with Monroe watching on, it was beginning to resemble something as solid and functional as the Latimer farm had been.

And one afternoon, the eldest daughter, Katherine, was struggling to press splints into the dry earth for the tomato plants at the far end of the now half-cleared thicket. She pushed and dug and struggled and bent and even cursed under her breath, and the skin on her hands grew hard and her dress began to come torn at the shoulder, and then she felt something near, as if something was watching her from the thicket a few yards away. She stopped. There was no noise, but there was *something*. She could hear only the soft sound of her own worried breathing. Was it a bear? Were there bears in Setubal? A wolf? Her heart began to pound. She held the splint up nervously, like a dagger, and took a step back, but she came up against something sturdy and hard. She yelped and spun and fell on her back facing the thing. It was her father, an enormous silhouette over her against the clear blue sky. He stepped forward and took the splint from her hand and, with a gentleness that belied his size, he pushed it into the patch she had been fighting with for so long.

"Sorry I frightened you," he said.

Katherine said nothing.

"It looked like you needed a hand."

"Thank you, daddy," she said.

Monroe straightened and turned to walk back to the porch, but he stopped and picked Katherine up from the ground. His face came close to hers and he said, "You shouldn't curse," and he kissed her quickly on the forehead.

Monroe began taking afternoon walks down to the village where he would read the foreign newspapers that came with from passing sailors. He would read the articles on the Spanish war, and the drama of the "Siege of the Alcazar", as the international press were calling it. And then, after many weeks Monroe read that as the Alcazar was about to fall – the soldiers within were rationing water and had eaten all of their horses – when a column of fresh Nationalist troops – Mola's men – came down into Toledo from the north. The Republicans had fled back to Madrid.

Monroe wrote a poem that afternoon and sent it to *The Times* in London. It compared the citadel to his 'rock of faith', the fleeing besiegers to the eternal mists of doubt. He read it to his family on completion. At the end they all cried and embraced in a huddle. If there was hope for Spain there was hope for God, there was hope for poetry and the human soul, said Monroe.

A few weeks later the poem was published, and Monroe sat on the boards at the dock and looked over it again and again. He had not had a drink since he wrote it, and he had shaved and dressed in fresh linen and a wide-brimmed hat to protect his balding head from the pulsating sun. He tucked the newspaper under his arm and began the slow steep ascent back to the cottage. He had made his mind up to go back to Spain and fight.

***

Twelve men came out from Toledo from the column that went in.

Fonseca had been the first to die, trapped in a doorway during a street skirmish just an hour after they had entered the city, bullets and bayonet in his chest. Many more fell in the hours after. The *Afrikanistas* moved down the streets in waves, from pillar to post to doorway to portico, like a creeping illness. Piers' comrades leapt and yelled and fired indiscriminately down the way, often with their eyes closed or shielded from the gun flashes by their free arm. Piers was one of the few to fire straight and true, and he was one of the first to kill enemy soldiers and make a breakthrough closer to the centre of the city.

Those who made it through the first day spent the next two weeks barricaded in a residential house, rarely being able to stand straight for fear of being spotted, crawling below window level from place to place as the fighting went on outside. It was Miguel who was the first to suggest they leave and head for the east of the city where he believed the Republican army to be. Half of the column agreed, half did not. Piers felt that he would fare better alone than with any of them.

Eventually half of them left and were cut down at the end of the street as they had the misfortune to come upon a passing regiment of Mola's at the crossroads. Miguel had stayed, as had Ramon, both of them putting greater faith in Piers' shooting than in their own rhetoric. Miguel died the next day when *Afrikanistas* besieged the house. He was cut to pieces by the first volley that came in from the street out front. The column returned fire with a new form of meagreness in their hearts, and Piers, for the first time, took control and led the survivors out the back and down an alleyway. These were not fighting men. It was slaughter, the type the *Afrikanistas* most enjoyed.

Somehow, as the city rattled with gunfire and cannon fire and the waspish whirr of fighter planes, the remainders of the column made it back the way they came, out of the city. They crawled alongside a minor road for miles until they could see the edge of the mountains. They crawled through mud and faeces and corpses to get away from Toledo, a hell fire of a burning world. With no water and no food, they huddled in the cold night air in a clearing at the foothills. It was the first time Piers could see that only twelve of them had made it out. They had contributed nothing to the battle, other than to the accumulation of dead.

Piers looked around the group. They were shocked, glass-eyed, phantasmal. Ramon was without his energy. It was in this silence of the hills, Toledo burning in the horizon sky, that Piers began to think of the wounded who had been left behind in the streets as they fled, how, as a group, they had moved as individuals, merely in the same unsure direction. To leave wounded to the *Afrikanistas* was most likely to leave them to torture and terrible death.

Piers swallowed these thoughts, and put his fatigue, his aches and cuts out of his mind, and he said: "We need to find shelter. Who knows anything of these parts?"

There was silence.

"Anything at all," he repeated.

One young man leaned forward, the edges of his eyes burning red, his face black with dirt.

"My father was a wealthy man," he said. "We used to come here as a family in the autumn. If we are where I think we are – to the west of the city – there is a village over these first hills. La Damas de las Colinas. It is small. A church and some houses, a few farms. It is on no map. Nobody would find it unless they stumbled upon it."

Piers felt the cold thud of hope within him for the first time in a long time, pushed as far from its understanding as he had been.

"Then we will sit here for an hour. Sleep if you can. And then we head to this village."

La Damas de las Colinas was indeed a small village – a focal point for some of the farms and hermitages that took up spots in the surrounding hills and countryside. A small square with some buildings and a well, a cantina and goods store, a small open-fronted shack that seemed to be a school, and on a knoll at the end of the square was a whitewashed church, not grand, but proud for this place.

There was nothing within a few scattered miles of it that suggested war, that even hinted at the otherworldliness of what was happening within the walls of Toledo. Piers had not slept in several days. He was still on edge from the fighting. The snipping noises his eyelids made as they closed sounded like gunfire in his head, and so he could not blink, his eyes were wide and burned.

As the twelve men, rugged, broken, filthy, ruined, arms hanging, rifles slung over shoulders or used as walking sticks, heads hanging, faces enceinte of despair behind wiry beards, came upon the main drag of the village, what people that were around ran inside. A mother took her child and averted his face as she quickly escorted him from the street.

Piers was at point, and they walked in the vague formation of a column on patrol, as Fonseca had drilled them. Piers knew at the time they had been drilled for a war of toy soldiers. But the two days walk, at a lowly pace, through the dust and the hills, from their spot outside Toledo to this village, was not a time to think of things like that. Piers could see the others dipping, their lives coming out of them like sweat, their beliefs leaving them in an odour. Piers wrote poems in his head as they walked, and he recited them to the men when they were done. He even tried to make some of them humorous.

He had never given his work up to strangers before. Only Ki Monroe had ever seen his writing. It made him burn inside for Bess, for her cool hands to rest upon his face, and with every poem he recited, freshly composed in his mind, he imagined reciting it to her within the walls of a world of their own design. And when tears came to his eyes, they came also to the eyes of the men, and clean streaks came down their cheeks through the dirt. If only he could have been at home. If only he had never left. It was now, at this moment, that he loved Bess stronger, more acutely, than he had ever done. It was now, and only now, that he fully understood his love for her.

As soon as the villagers could see and sense that the twelve men were of such a state as to be of little or no threat, and after some astute words from Piers, they took pity, and the ragtag troupe was taken in.

They were housed in a barn at the far end of the main street, along with a few head of cattle and a goat with an unsettling grin. They each took a patch of floor and slept, apart from Piers who decided his priority was to wash at the well. The women of the village were very kind. The men had gone, Piers discovered. The war had come, even if it had not stayed, and it had taken their men, who no doubt left for Toledo with heavy boots and cloth caps, just as Piers and Miguel and Ramon had left Barcelona.

Piers also washed his shirt, trousers and his jacket, wrung them out next to the well and lay them on the wall in the sun to dry. He then sat beneath the shade of a tree to the far end of the square and slept. It was some hours later when he was awoken by a young boy prodding his shoulder. The boy pointed at a group of young girls across the way who were giggling behind their hands at the man sleeping in the street in nothing but his underwear. Piers smiled along with their joke and waved at them and they ran off. He got to his feet and, still smiling, he ruffled his hand through the young boy's hair and thanked him for waking him.

It is these moments, perhaps, that make life a level place. The innocence of children can bring everything down to the barest details. They will forget the war by the time they are old, Piers thought. And even if they have not, their children will do. And all of these terrible things will be left for those who read the books and care about the grey unreal matters of the past. He felt sad for them, that they would not know the truth about human endeavour, and for the same reasons he felt happy for them. The sun on his face was real, and was as pleasant today as it was cruel the day before. These children would pass under this sun long after he was gone, Piers knew. And their children would do so. *You* will, as will your children. The same sun, all the scenes acted out beneath it whether it is to us the past, present or future.

And when the little boy too ran off, his little boots kicking up scuffs of dust from the main drag as he did so, Piers' smile dropped and his thoughts moved away and he wondered if he would ever get back to Bess, and if Bess would love him, and if he would give Bess children in the way that she deserved.

The column, such as it was, stayed several days at the village, and Piers was beginning to see in the twelve of them that such was the ignorance of war in La Damas de las Colinas, and now that they were clean and fed and shaved and their thirsts were gone, some of them did not want to leave. They all knew they had homes to get back to, but also there was a war to get back to. It could not be ignored just because they had suffered a brutal defeat. They would all be expected to return to the fighting in one way or another.

One afternoon he heard one of the men refer to the place under his breath as a Garden of Eden. Even Piers thought it somewhat of an oasis. He had taken to teaching the young boy who had awoken him how to play chess. The boy said his father had been teaching him before he left to fight in the city. They took to sitting for hours in the shade in silence, occasionally the boy would make a naïve move and Piers would tut, and the boy would look him in the eye and they would both smile slightly, and before the boy had removed his finger from the piece he would move it elsewhere, a place where Piers would not tut.

Others would just sit in the sun, as if its rays would burn away the memories of what had happened to them in Toledo. Ramon did not look as though he would regain his energy; not ever. What quickness that had been in him may have gone for good. That energy – it is a certain kind of life force – is not something that can be replaced once it is gone. Ramon had become an old man in all but physique. He had been unable to get across the room to hold Miguel as he died, bullets flew between them, and instead he had to watch him from yards away. He was the last man to leave the portico before it was overrun and Fonseca was bayonetted. The captain's cries were close and clear as Ramon found himself crouched and hiding in fear beneath an abandoned fruit wagon. Many things can expunge that life force that Ramon had, and the realisation that powerlessness is not always inevitable, but sometimes comes from manifest cowardice, or manifest fear – paralysing fear – can be too much for the human soul to take. And it is the human soul that controls the limbs, not the muscles and blood-flow.

Ramon now moved slowly, heavily, achingly, his downcast

eyes like those of some foraging animal. And had Piers not instructed that the men take it in turns to keep watch over the north road, for a sign of *Afrikanistas*, then Ramon would not have been the man on guard when they came.

Another of the men, one of the men who had much less energy to lose, and so less far to fall, would have spotted them when they were a blip on the horizon, and so the twelve could have quickly gathered their things and been gone safe and unseen. But Ramon was lost in his thoughts, lost in his depression and his chilled innards and he did not spot them until they were close enough to spot him up on his perch in the church tower.

A shot was fired toward his position, and something akin to his old urgency hurtled him down the steps and out into the square, where the others of the column were already gathering and deciding the best route of escape. Nobody spoke of fighting, only running.

"They know we are here," said Piers. "But they don't know how many. So if we split some of us will make it."

The men swallowed and patted their heads, knowing the gamble was the only chance they had. Piers pointed in directions, splitting the twelve of them into groups, they said their swift and firm farewells, grave farewells, and taking their arms, they ran.

* * *

The soldiers quick-marched down the main drag of the village, their rifles in both hands held out on bent arms, ready to use if needed. They were not *Afrikanistas*, but Nationalist militia, assembled, for the most part, from the ashes of Mola's slaughter in the north. They were the Catholics who had been waiting patiently for the holy warriors to emancipate them from the Socialist oppressors. They marched gingerly, even though they had already seen death, already seen the edges of hell in the burning orange fires of Toledo. Scour the countryside, they had been ordered, and wipe out the scraps of godless dissent.

They moved down the hillside road like a twisting snake. Captain Jimenez was a few yards ahead with his pistol in his hand, the brass buttons of his tunic glistening in the midday sun. The rest of the men were tired, rotten dirty, the dust had got into every groove. The shale cracked and spat under their heavy boots. The main street deserted as they came down the hillside into the village.

Jimenez instructed his men to go into every building and bring those inside out into the street. They threw the most reluctant villagers to the floor, across the dirt. And soon villagers began to come out of their own accord. A gun went off in one of the buildings. Shouting could be heard. A few soldiers ran in to support those already in there. There was more shouting. Another gunshot. The soldiers came back out, their uniforms just a little darker than the beige dirt of the street. A few villagers ran from the building. The soldiers carried one corpse of a young boy, a teenager, and threw him to the side of the road.

Jimenez began shouting at the villagers who had been roughly arranged to sit in groups along the main street. He demanded the name of this village that was on no map, and the directions to Cantabria.

"This is La Damas de las Colinas," a little boy said.

"Go north," pleaded one of the women.

Jimenez pulled a tattered map from inside of his tunic, the one he had been consulting more and more as the journey went on, and began going over it with his tense glare. He muttered something to himself, and a few of his men standing closest to him looked at each other with concerned faces. It had been suspected for some time that Jimenez had got them lost.

The Captain confirmed the name of the village with another woman at the roadside.

La Damas de las Colinas.

"Why can I not see it on the map?" said the young Captain.

The woman looked back at him blankly, unfamiliar with the workings of maps.

Jimenez cursed and began to walk away from his men.

He stopped, as if something had occurred to him and he came back down the way to the platoon. He was looking back and fore, back and fore, amongst the gathered villagers.

"Where are your men?" he shouted. "Where are your men?"

He came up to the platoon.

"Where are the men? – there are only women and children here."

"Most likely in Toledo, already dead," said one of the soldiers.

Jimenez cursed again. His eyes were huge round sparking globes, pink with worry and fatigue. He rubbed his jaw with his fist, looked nervously down at his map again and then looked over the platoon.

"Fucking pig cowards," he said. "Bring the women."

And he marched with great purpose down the main drag of the village.

The platoon moved sluggishly into action, not sure what was going to happen, gathering the women to their feet and pushing them forward after the Captain.

Ki Monroe did not move with them. He had done many things in that uniform, in the hell of Toledo, and he was unsure if the cramps in his stomach were from the dirty water he had drunk the previous day, or if it was his will giving out, his insides objecting to the outer world. Regardless, he could not move forward with his fellow soldiers to round up the women.

He looked at the faces of the children sitting by the roadside. They were empty, dirty, swollen, the saddest sights in the whole war. Monroe felt his gut sink.

Gunfire rang out and up ahead the platoon began returning shots to one of the stables at the end of the village. Monroe, shaken into life by the familiar sound, had his rifle butt to his cheek before he even noticed what was going on. More shots. Two, three soldiers were killed, they smacked into the dirt, a volley was returned into the stable and the shooting stopped. Some soldiers ran in, a few more gunshots sounded and the soldiers came out. Jimenez, who had lost his hat in the chaos picked it up from the dirt and began screaming obscenities at the women. He was lifting from the floor with rage. Two Republicans had been hiding in the barn.

Jimenez bellowed in his youthful reedy tone, his hair now greasy strands over his face and brow, that he wanted to know where the others were. He put his pistol to the forehead of an old woman and repeated his question several times, his heels lifting from the floor in rage. Without tears the old lady said they had gone, that they had passed through, and that they would be long gone by now.

"Long gone? Like those fucks in the barn?" screamed

Jimenez, and he fired his gun. The old woman fell slowly, almost serenely, like a wave, backward into the dirt, a specked spray of crimson dashed across the earth behind her. Others began to scream and cry, but it all came out as a profound silence to Monroe, who watched from several yards away at the other side of the road.

Jimenez turned to the others lined in the street and began screaming more questions, more obscenities.

Monroe's mouth was dry, his body ached, and the execution of the old woman thudded against him like just another crippling blow – he was a prizefighter of hellishness now, he had seen more than should have been seen. He closed his eyes tight, and when he opened them he expected to see the next execution, the next body fall silently into the dirt. But it seems Jimenez's gun had jammed, and he stormed off in a fury over the failings of his tool.

The platoon marched the women on and up the foot of the knoll at the far exit from the village. At the top of the knoll was the old whitewashed chapel with the tall narrow wooden doors. From a distance Monroe felt it was familiar to him; but he was hollow now, and he thought that the sight of a chapel was what had brought him a speck of spirit. He did not remember that this strange little village was where Father Eusebio had first found him all those years ago, drunk and broken in the street, looking for Millie. He did not recognise the chapel, and he had no recollection of this village as the anterior parish of his old friend.

Monroe stayed at the foot of the hill. He would not go any further. Instead he turned away from the church and looked back down to the village. He would not watch. He only listened to the gunshots.

Soon, minutes went by in silence. Monroe began to feel a breeze come from behind him and he turned to feel it upon his face. As he did so he could see a group of soldiers coming down the knoll. Their faces were blank, white, dry, like mannequin's faces, featureless and taught.

"The Captain wants the children," said one of them as they passed.

Monroe looked up to the hilltop and could see bodies on the ground. Not one of the women remained standing. He thought briefly about raising his rifle, of killing Jimenez. His shoulders quivered at the idea, his eyes parched. But he didn't have it in him to do it. He didn't have the blood in his veins any longer. This – *this* – was insanity. He had walked into it. This was the life of the *Afrikanista* that Eusebio had talked to him about. The ultimate degradation of the human soul.

At the border Monroe had explained himself to the sergeant. He was a Catholic and he was here to join the cause of the Church. The sergeant, with the clear eyes of a bureaucrat, had admired Monroe's physique. The Nationalist militias were short of strong men. For the first few weeks he had been treated with respect, given extra rations at the first outpost to which he was billeted. All around him was the relaxed confidence of a conquering army, not the nerves of a militia yet to fight. After a few weeks the militia were joined by a column of *Afrikanistas* and trained up. That was when the mood changed. Here was an insight to a Spain ruled by the army.

These men were veneered with an otherworldly calmness. They were the ones who had seen it all before. They were the ones who were in their element – war was their mode – these men could breathe under water, walk through fire, they were the serpents who passed through the bowels of Bosch's damned. *This* was their calling. Monroe had never been around people whose first language was violence. They hummed with unordnariness, with an alien countenance that had much to do with an entanglement of their gaze, and something else to do with the aura of them when grouped together. This, Monroe knew, was an unknowable proximity to Hell. These were the men who were fighting for God.

And then the one day, a bright and dry afternoon, a small dusty motorcade came through the outpost, and in the centre car, an open top jeep, Monroe saw Mola. He was a small man, expressionless, rigid, high-nosed, his wire framed spectacles catching the sun, his face was soft around the edges. He had large unpleasant eyes, dismissive eyes, and thin lips set on a slight muzzle of a mouth. What did Monroe think of him? Mola didn't look like his idea of a revolutionary general; he looked like a secretary, a clerk, somebody encased in formalities and rituals, from his clipped lips to the brass buttons of his tunic. But this was the man to put things right and avenge the massacre of the clergy. This was God's messenger.

Monroe tried to forget everything, sitting at the foot of the knoll. He thought of Mille and the girls. Toledo had been carnage, had been the fires of damnation made real. But he had known he had made the wrong decision to come and fight the moment he had seen Mola in that motorcade.

Monroe's head sunk into his hands as the soldiers who had passed returned with the children.

∗ ∗ ∗

The sun was swamp-heavy upon the soldiers' backs as they reached the dry stone barn on the hillside. They began unpacking their equipment and passing round cantinas of water. The dust and dirt of the loose beige shale floated around them in the deep golden air.

Captain Jimenez, his uniform tightly buttoned, his cap pulled taught to his brow, walked among the men, his hand rounded on the hilt of his sword at his side. He looked intently across the long incline of the hillside, across to the valley and to the dead trees and the distant mountains. They were just half a day's march on from La Damas de las Colinas, in the direction of Cantabria. This would be the way the Socialists had gone. They would catch them up and kill them and head to Cantabria themselves in time for Mola's attack there.

Jimenez told the men to stand down for ten minutes, and he walked over to a stone wall at the far side of the barn and began to study the map he had been tightly grasping in his free hand.

"Where are we?" said one of the young soldiers slumping down onto the hard ground and sipping mercifully from his cantina.

Monroe remained standing and gazed long after the Captain.

"He's got us lost," said a sergeant with resignation.

"Shouldn't we be with the regiment heading to Cantabria by now?" said the young soldier.

Monroe said, "Everything will be fine."

Monroe was older than the rest, now they had become somewhat depleted from skirmishes and the bad decisions of their Captain. Monroe had fought ferociously in Toledo, and he was looked up to. Most of the others were reserve men, or

Catholics like Monroe. They were Spanish mainly, a few Moroccan converts who had swayed as the *Afrikanisas* moved through their regions. *Limpieza de sangre*. The pendulum of faith.

Captain Jimenez, the only real army man, was young, perhaps Piers' age, and Monroe had noticed that for the last two days of marching through the dust of the hills of Old Castile he had not taken his hand from his sword hilt for fear of betraying his tremble to his men. Monroe had met many Falangists in the last few months and Jimenez was the only one who had betrayed the nerves of a human in the wake of his actions.

"Do you think we're headed in the right direction?" said the young soldier, squinting up at Monroe who still watched with a straight, steady gaze to the far side of the valley.

"Unless the regiment has moved on," said Monroe.

"Might they have done that?"

Monroe placed himself next to the young soldier in the shale and took the cantina from his hand.

"You really want to know?"

The young soldier nodded unsurely.

"Who knows in this almighty fucking mess," Monroe said.

He took a swig and handed the cantina back.

Monroe watched Jimenez hunched over the map, his hand shaking in its black leather glove as it traced unsure lines across the crumpled paper. Millie seemed a thousand years travel from him at that moment. He had fought his hardest, with his heart as a club, to get his family out of Spain, and then he had abandoned them to return to it, to the spilled blood and the fire. His regret hung heavy in him, it pulled his shoulders downward and left a sharp taste in the back of his throat. He knew that from Cantabria he could desert, he could hit the road north to the coast, and as a foreigner he could fool the authorities into letting him aboard a ship away from this godforsaken place. With each blink of the eyes into the coarse sun he saw the sad faces of his girls on the porch of the Unamuno farm, and he saw those faces brighten and brighten further as they saw their daddy come down the pathway.

The sun was at its hottest. Monroe stood with a straight back. He watched Jimenez closely.

"What's the matter?" said one of the younger soldiers.

"If I was Jimenez I would be less worried about where we are and more worried about who we are following."

"What do you mean?"

"If we are lost, and they are not lost, then it is *they* who have the advantage," said Monroe.

The young soldier's head dropped to between his raised knees. Another soldier stood and said to Monroe, "You think they know we're here."

"I think there's every chance the hunters could become the hunted," said Monroe. The wilderness had never been so quiet, and they all noticed it.

Captain Jimenez folded the map and pressed it inside his tunic and walked up toward the men.

"Okay," he said. "Gather round."

As the tired ramshackle bunch got to their feet, amidst a few short grumbles, a long low fluted scream could be heard – the unmistakable sound of a rifle shot ringing through the acoustics of the hills – and the young soldier who had been asking the questions juddered and his eyes went pale and from a small grizzled cut in the side of his throat blood began to stream like ribbons, narrow at first and then a torrent. He grabbed his neck with his hands as he fell stiffly into the shale rolling a few feet down the hillside.

More bullet-screams followed and Monroe could see down the east side of the valley there were men running forward in a loose formation firing rifles, diving behind rocks, firing again, coming forward. He could not count how many – ten, maybe. Perhaps more. Monroe squatted as another of their platoon took a fatal shot to the chest.

Monroe began to head toward the protection of the barn, calling to others to follow, and he took his revolver and began firing back down the hill. The others in the platoon began to scatter, more of them fell. Jimenez was pinned in a shallow ditch, bullets pinging off the shale all around him. His platoon was being cut down at every side, and the enemy, coming up toward the barn, seemed to be increasing in number, in energy and in fearsomeness.

On getting inside the barn Monroe took stock. Of those who had made it, all had been wounded apart from him. Regardless, they began to prop themselves up at intervals to return fire to the enemy coming up the hill through the glassless windows.

Monroe wondered how long this could last. They were all physically drained, but ammunition was running low too. He looked around the dank dusty interior of the barn and could only think of a last stand. One soldier fired out of a window, holding his stomach in with his other hand, blood coughing from his mouth. Another, less gravely injured, stood to reload and took a bullet to the side of the face, his cheek and eye opening up like a mussel shell. The volleys of fire seemed to grow louder, closer, as if the enemy were now banging huge drums, creating a wall of sound.

Through one window Monroe could see Jimenez running down the hill to the barn. Another soldier was killed next to him, and then another. Monroe returned fire one shot after another, just firing into the void through the window. He could not see the enemy, only hear their gunfire, the deafening drum chants of gunfire.

Jimenez was getting closer, he was screeching like an Apache, his face black and his eyes carnal in their gore, his uniform torn and burnt. Monroe looked around and saw that all of his fellow soldiers were dead, scattered through the barn in various demonic poses. He reloaded his pistol and a silence fell – a split second perhaps, but it felt like it lingered and hovered and sucked up the air. And then the door was kicked open and the shooting began again. Monroe fired at the first man, and the second, and they fell quickly one on top of the other, and the third man was shot too, but he had time to fire back and Monroe was hit twice in the shoulder – he felt the bone crack and splinter, and he was pushed back against the wall and to the floor.

The shooting stopped again and the gunsmoke cleared and there he was, sitting against the wall, opposite the slumped figure of Piers. It was a frozen silence between them and around them, as if they had met at the very moment of heavenliness. There was no confusion, no questions, no shock; just the two of them as it had meant to be. Piers was holding his stomach, and he looked at Monroe with the white greying in his eyes. There was a little blood around Piers' mouth, and he coughed up more.

Monroe was about to say his name when the door opened again and Jimenez came in, looking like a demon stepped out of the black fire, his eyes wild and furious, a grin on his face. He looked at Monroe and then down at Piers who was nearest. And he calmly, luxuriantly, lifted his pistol to Piers' head. Before the Captain could fire, Monroe shot him twice in the heart, and Jimenez hit with a crack against the dry stone wall.

But Piers had already expired, perhaps even before Jimenez had burst in the door, perhaps even before the gunsmoke had cleared, perhaps even before he had hit the ground.

It was then as quiet as hell, as quiet as the graveyard it would remain, and Monroe immediately knew the crushing devastation of silence.

After a time he got to his knees. The pain of his shoulder numbed, and he crawled across the room over to the body. How could it be Piers? He went close to his face, an inch away, and could see it could be nobody else. The man was older, bearded, grizzled, war-worn – just like Monroe had become – but it was him alright. It was my brother. Piers Buren.

THE COTTAGE

* * *

I read Monroe's book in Piers' study.

The room was light, empty but for a desk and several low piles of books about the floor. No notes, no drafts of Piers' own work. A regiment of pencils and a clean pad on the desk. I sat at it, picked up the book and began to read. It was bespattered in pencil annotations, easily twice the scrawl of the original print. On the inside cover was an inscription:

> *For Piers, the truth inside the stone,*
> *the comprehension inside the truth.*
> *Forever in poetry,*
>   *your friend,*
>   *Ki Monroe.*

I examined the straightness of this handwriting, the rejection of any calligraphic posturing. It was markedly different to Piers' which came after in such abundance. The signature was that of a man balanced between the rough terrain of his soul and the unravelling dissonance of his own calling; the calling of *poetry*, the calling of attempting to dilate mortality through the power of words.

The poetry in *The Master of the River* that followed amounted to a battle between the earth and the city, the flat soil of the veldt and the mystical ponderings of the heavens. It was poetry populated by gods and shepherds, heroes and goats. It was viciously good in places, exciting, soulfully diluvian but disciplined, also. That nobody reads Monroe now is, simply, a testament to the coarseness of our civilisation. That we have no time to linger on minds like his is a sad thing indeed. He spoke as many truths as the Old Testament. What does it take to become ingrained? Is *that* the elusive definition of genius? To be constitutional, innate. What a tedious, lowly apex – to be everywhere, when thinkers like Monroe die away to dust.

To compare him to those you may have read? Monroe was chest-out, bold, cunning, unlike Eliot and Pound with their truculent hives of esoterism. I had found Eliot dynamic but pressured. He seemed to find it difficult to breathe, to *enjoy* – Eliot was buried in concrete up to his neck. Wordsworth would not have liked him; I doubt he would have understood him. And I didn't like Pound. *Usura keeps the stonecutter from the stone*. I had thought about that line a great deal. When I was in Germany, and the walls were closing in – not on me, but on my ideas of how a society should operate, and of course on the Jews – this was something that rung around those walls.

What *was* the thing that was going on across Europe? It wasn't my continent; I was not even allowed to believe it was. But of course in a way it was – *white* Africa was all about the drippings, the shavings of the Europeans, wasn't it? I don't mind admitting I was nervous about fascism. I just could not be convinced it was good business, first and foremost. But I did not really understand the developing nature of war. I didn't build the tanks, and I know nothing of genocide. *Usura kills the baby in the womb*. Did fascism become capitalism? Capitalism was born out of the death of fascism. The death of understanding humanity. What was Pounds *Usura*? Who was it? Not the Jews. It was us all.

I saw similar subtleties in the work of Monroe, similar big ideas pushed and pressed into short sentences – acres of expanse under the one glance. He was good at that; knowing what poetry was for.

I was brought from these tangled ideas that Monroe's book presented by Bess at the door of Piers' study. She looked as if she had just woken from a rare sleep. I turned in the seat and stood on seeing her.

"I didn't hear you come in," she said.

"It is very early."

"You have some news?"

I gave the slightest shake of the head. Bess had dark sunken eyes, her skin was ghostly pale. In her loosely bound night gown she glided on the balls of her feet across the floor and into the study, her fingers trailing across the tops of books, through the thin layer of dust, and she stopped by the window that looked out over the main street.

"We haven't seen you here for over a week," she said to me. It wasn't an accusation – at least not primarily.

"And I'm sorry about that."

Bess looked at me with a steady glare. And then she looked down to the book that was in my hand.

"You're reading Monroe?"

She stepped forward and took it, looked closely at the cover.

"Out of curiosity," I said.

"Not for clues?"

"You give me too much credit," I said.

Bess smiled, weakened.

"I don't think I give you enough," she said.

"He's good," I said, taking the book back from Bess. "Would you mind if I borrowed it?"

Bess shrugged and said, "Please yourself."

I motioned to leave but then stopped and said to her, "If Piers has any intention of being found then I will find him."

Bess said nothing in response, just sat softly at Piers' desk.

A few days later Bess appeared at my apartment. It was early; I was still in my dressing gown. This time Bess was bright, flitting about the parlour once she was in, distracted and light of touch.

"I'm afraid I have nothing further to report than I did the other day, Bess," I said in lieu of a suspected speech from her.

She looked out of the window down into the street.

"That's okay," she said. "I just didn't want you to think you had to keep coming across to the house to give us reports on how things are. This is difficult for you, too, obviously."

Sometimes she sounded like Matilda. When she was being forthright, boorish, I could see her adopted mother in her eyes. She was replicating the only form of female bravado she knew and it was not feminine. Matilda was not feminine, Latimer was not. Millie, as far as I could tell, would have been the perfect role model for any young girl until scandal and the behaviour of her husband was factored in. Madeleine? That was too far in the other direction. Bess was to be a woman like no other once fully formed; she would find a way to create balance between her forceful streak and the natural sways of female beauty.

"I went to the police," she said.

"Would you like some tea," I said, approaching my breakfast table and pouring some for the both of us.

"Did you not hear what I said? I said I went to the police."

"And?"

"I pleaded with them."

"And?"

"They said there is nothing more they can do."

"Then we'll wait."

"That's *it*?"

I handed her the tea.

"Oh, Hal; you could buy the entire police force if you wanted to. You could buy them and put them all to work on looking for Piers."

I gave some careful consideration to what I was going to say next.

"I wrote to Monroe."

Bess' soft eyes looked sharply at me.

"You did? How did you find out where he is?"

"That's not important."

"It *is* important."

I went over to the bureau in the corner of the room and rolled back the lid. I took from an envelope a note and walked it over to Bess.

"Monroe said that he has not seen Piers since the night of his leaving party. And that he hopes for his safe return."

"What is this?"

"It is Monroe's response."

Bess unfolded the note carefully, as if it might have contained a blinding light, and looked it over. I watched closely as she read, examined the paper, turned it in her hands.

"What's wrong?" I said.

"For all we know this could be a lie," she said.

"I don't think that it is."

"But what if Piers had written it himself? Copied Monroe's hand. Or if Monroe had written it under Piers' request to remain unfollowed?"

I remained straight, lean, unemotional. She suspected fraud but she did not suspect me.

"I think we should take it for what it is," I said.

She looked up at me curiously.

"You trust him?" she said.

"I trust *my* feelings on the matter," I said.

She looked back down at the letter and examined it again.

I had spent much of the previous afternoon mimicking Monroe's considered style from the verso cover of Piers' copy of *The Master of the River*. I had written several drafts of the note before deeming it close enough to Monroe's penmanship to pass in front of Bess and Matilda's emotional but astute eyes.

"What of Russia?" she said after a moment, resignedly.

"If he has gone to Russia he may as well have gone into space," I said. "But I have put out some feelers in that direction."

"If he doesn't want to be found," said Bess, her head dipping sadly, her voice imitating what was becoming a frequent line of my own.

My inaction was unjust. I know that now and I knew it then. But there was something of the artlessness of the disciplinarian to me back then, and I felt that Piers should go and find out the trials of the world without me coming to rescue him. It was, after all, what Piers himself had asked of me at the Surrealists exhibition.

I knew very well that Monroe was no good for him, that following him to wherever it was he would follow him was not going to end with fanfare and that meaning of life he seemed so intent on chasing. But now I see that he chased it vigorously for the same reason that I avoided it, because truth is as sharp as a dagger and we all react differently to such threats. "I want to make the truth sing!" he would say to me, his mouth quivering with excitement; "But I cannot find the notes."

Please don't think me disingenuous; I am not trying to excuse the role I played in my brother's death. I failed him. I did not elevate him to sainthood by allowing him to go and die in that barn amidst darkness and the fear. I do not think that of myself. I was two things: sick of his embarrassing insistence on freedom, and forgiving of his powerful curiosity. My god, it was the most fatherly thing I ever did, letting him compel himself toward his own destruction. I am guilty and free because Piers deserved his death and the freedom he met at its point. Because people like Piers *are* special. Because people like Piers *never* find what they are looking for. They are always expecting dispensations from the rest of us. I was not willing to give it, not on that day, not when he left, and not for the time afterwards.

I had put out no "feelers" toward Russia. It seems absurd now for me to even have intimated that I had. Bess did not remain this naïve for long. Or this trusting. I assumed, quite correctly, that Bess knew little of the details of the Buren business, apart from the fact that it was vast, had many arms, and stretched into distracting complexities. She had asked me where else I thought Piers could have gone and I had answered without thinking that he perhaps may have gone to follow his Russian heroes, the Kulaks, into the Urals. "Then you should look for him there," she had said. I immediately saw another blind avenue, another cloaked route where Bess and Matilda's questions could be led.

I looked down to Bess. She was still and silent, but her mind was recharging; I knew the look. I had not asked Bess to depend upon me. These things were crude, and they were real, and I had done nothing to make Bess vulnerable and I was doing nothing to pull her closer to me. I was sure of that. To Bess I was simply performing a brotherly duty. Piers had asked me to look after her. And she deserved to be protected from a world that could treat her like Piers had treated her. *Piers was better off gone*. He was better off learning and searching away from her. And I was sure he would return better for it, and they would both be better for it then.

I looked down at Bess' black hair, the thin line across her scalp at the parting, like a burning white cross. Yes, I suppose it was at that moment, in the sitting room of my apartment that I decided he was better off gone, we were all better off with him gone.

＊ ＊ ＊

Bess' visits increased from every few days to every day.

Some days she was preoccupied, pleasant, unwilling to be drawn on the subject of Piers. Other days she was held in the bleakest grip. The days she did not make it, I knew, were the bleakest of all. But most days she needed to see me, needed to be around someone who was simultaneously near to Piers and yet so far from him. I was like his shadow, his mirror image, or perhaps I was the black backing to his mirror. It is something to do with that strange investment that blood trickles throughout a family line. I am entirely myself and partly him. Like trying to understand the truth of a poem, it is apparent and yet just out of sight, just off stage.

But Bess also came to me because she needed to get away from Matilda, who had become a mere memory of sanity and reality.

"That woman haunts that house," she said.

Matilda had been decreasing as the years went on. First her husband left her by dying in the marsh. Then Algie Radnor had spinelessly run from her. And now Piers had gone. Abandonment after abandonment, slowly the iris of the camera closes until completely shut. Of course she could not see the bigger picture: that fate had taken our father (albeit cruel fate), that she was better off without Algie, and that she had had a part to play in the wanderings of her youngest son by squeezing on to him so tightly he had catapulted away from her.

"She is strong," I said.

"Her strength is what fuels her madness," said Bess.

Bess' routine by now was to stand at the door of Matilda's house and wait for the post to arrive each morning, check it for any sign of Piers' hand, and then dash to my apartment and wait for the post there, which arrived a little later. Any word from Piers? Any word from your spies?

"I don't understand with all of your money how you cannot make anything happen – *anything* you want to make happen?" Bess said.

"That is not what that money is there for," I said.

"It's not there for the purpose of good?"

"And neither is it there for the purpose of evil."

"So it just *is*?"

"It just *is*."

People often think money is a magic potion. It is not. It is the cement within the walls of all modern structures. Cement is not magic; it has attributes very much rooted in the physical world. Money cannot vault walls, cannot pass through them. It cannot perform miracles. And back then, politics was the currency of fate, palms were greased with rhetoric. That has changed. The smaller the mind the bigger the wallet, as someone once said to me. Hitler had been a tramp, a vagabond. It was his charisma, as dark and dubious as that may seem, that took him across Germany, across Europe. And Hitler knew that war was the only way to pay for his promises of power. He had to pay for those things. That seems less a fact of life now. Money was a tactile thing back then. Old women hiding bank notes in mattresses when the crash came in 'twenty eight. And what now? There is a company in California that owns the oxygen in the air. And they own it with dashes and dots in ledgers. I tried explaining the nature of money to Bess. But she did not understand. She equated me to JD Rockefeller. "If he can build skyscrapers why can't you move mountains?" That was her connection when at her most dourly playful. But she was not like that too often. She moved through stages of grief. She must have felt it appropriate to act as a normal person, to follow the script. But I knew her better than that; I knew that she was not normal. One afternoon she proved it by saying, "You may be interested to know that I looked in to traveling to Spain."

She said this sleepily, her head dropping into the bend of her elbow, her arm stretched across the back of the armchair.

"I thought we'd talked about this," I said.

"I thought we were still talking about it," she said.

"What do you hope to achieve?"

"I'm going to talk to Monroe."

"How will you find him?"

"You have his address. You wrote him a letter."

"Spain is at war, Bess. You cannot go into a war zone and tell people you are looking for someone. You will be laughed at."

"Laughed at?"

She looked genuinely hurt by the suggestion that she could humiliate herself, as if it was one slight that seemed to strike deeper than any other.

"*Everybody* is looking for someone in a war zone," I said.

I watched in silence as a tear built and then spilled down her cheek.

I leaned forward in my chair and said, "You know, everything is going to be okay."

She looked me in the eye and smiled, wiping the tears from her face.

"Could I stay here tonight?" she said.

Often Bess appeared to me no different to the little girl I knew at the Radnor cottage in those distant summers. She had an intense innocence about her sometimes. She was small, pale, easily-distracted. She was stubborn and strong to a point. She sometimes liked to approach a subject head-on, sometimes from around and about. But her glances were sweet, pure, un-sexual, undiluted, uncorrupted.

"Matilda will worry," I said.

"Matilda will not notice I'm gone," said Bess.

And so Bess began to stay over some nights. Two or three times a week. She had begun buying newspapers and pamphlets on the war in Spain and reading them over and over at my apartment. I did not ask, but I knew she was avoiding giving up too much of her theories to Matilda.

"She asks me a great many questions," said Bess. "She has these moments of clarity."

I looked at her.

"She doesn't ask about you," Bess said.

"I hadn't wondered," I said.

"Well, she has these moments of clarity – between the drinking and the catatonia."

"The catatonia?"

"The first time I called the doctor and he said it would pass. It was just that she was grieving and sometimes those in grief can build a wall around themselves."

"And it comes and goes?"

"Yes. As does the drinking. As does the clarity."

I moved an unlit cigarette around my fingers as I thought this over. It was the first I was hearing of it, although it did not surprise me; the energy Matilda put into her theatre of the mad would be enough to draw the blood out of anyone from time to time.

"Perhaps I should go see her," I said.

"I wouldn't have thought it would help."

Bess looked at me out of the corner of her eye.

"No. But I am her son."

"Her *other* son," said Bess.

Bess had taken to talking of Matilda more and more of late. The topic of Piers was burning through her. And she could see in me a drifting soul, I think. Both of us given up by our mothers! I don't think she really held her father responsible for her estrangement. There is something about girls and their fathers; they are too close, and so waiting for the moment to get at their mother over it. Did Freud go over this? I didn't get very far with his stodgy prose. And I have always been suspicious of people who spend all of their time talking about the problems of strangers.

Bess did not know how to talk about her family. That is a cruel inversion. In the years after the schism she had replied to letters from her brothers and the occasional pleading from her father that would perhaps come at the tumult of a particularly lonely period for him. She could see his loneliness in the bending of the ink. Having been forced to remember her family, forced to create them as memorable symbols, Bess knew very much the workings of her father. She knew them starkly, they were stripped bare in a way they would not have been had she seen him every day, been present to his dilutions – any of their dilutions!

She had her brothers as a couple; she only remembered having known them in each other's company, so now they were like a lean Tweedle Dum and Tweedle Dee. Some days this amused her, some days it made her sad at herself. Algie was a shadow sometimes, sometimes a broken man haunting everywhere he went. But his head hung low, his eyes were sorrowful, longing. It did not help that his occasional letters were full of sadness, regret. He missed her, he said; he had been wrong, he said. But there was never any word of reconciliation. Sarah Radnor did not write, she was rarely mentioned, she wanted away with all Buren filth and betrayal, Bess surmised.

"Piers told me that Matilda and my father had an affair," said Bess.

I was a little surprised to hear this, to hear her announce it.

"We talked frankly about such things," she said. "He said that he told me because he felt partly responsible, as a Buren. He said that he loved me beyond all rationality and that that was the only thing that could make it justifiable; to be beyond the rational, to make up one's own rules."

"You deserve to be happy," I said.

"That's what Piers is doing now, isn't it? Living by his own rules? A desertion like this is made of the same stuff that allowed us to be together in the first place. So I should be grateful for his absence, to the part of him that drives him away from me."

Bess was tearful once more.

"No," I said. "You have every right to be angry."

"But not mad? Not like Matilda?"

"You're strong," I said.

"Nobody is stronger than Matilda," said Bess.

"Matilda's strength was acquired by giving something up, I fear," I said. "There is a tipping point to strength just as is there is to power. And you have not done that."

"But how hard do I have to hold on?"

I leaned forward and rested my hand on Bess' hand. We sat in silence for some time, some hours perhaps. When Bess went to bed, I stayed up for the rest of the night smoking cigarettes and going over her in my mind. She was more brittle than I had imagined, there was more to lose for her, and she was close to it.

After that night Bess seemed less herself. Her weak, nimble days became more frequent; her clear days, her positive days soon were a thing of the past. She stopped buying the newspapers, and then, after a few weeks she ceased turning up at my apartment.

As we move through life we are needed to always think on our feet when it comes to our confidences. I thought that I had positioned myself to be Bess' crutch, and so take care of her, as Piers had asked. But she was drifting away the whole time. A ship passing a lighthouse.

And so I went to the Claypole, reluctantly. There was no answer to the doorbell. Bess had said that the servants had stopped coming, having found employment elsewhere in more stable environments. I used my key for the first time in many years, sitting as it had been, like an old bone, in my pocket. I stepped in to a close imitation of a mausoleum. The silence permeated the walls and the floors, it hung heavy in the air, the grey and white shadings folded throughout dusty shards of light from the high narrow windows.

Just a few steps in, I heard the first scream.

It came from upstairs, somewhere deep within the twists of the white corridors. Unsure at first at what exactly I had heard, I placed one foot upon the bottom stair, my hand carefully on the bannister, and I looked up to the direction of the noise. Then came the frozen sparks of unintelligible words, aggressively delivered, then another scream, the smash of porcelain, another scream. I bounded up the stairs and onto the first floor. I ran down the first corridor but on hearing another crash realised it was coming from higher up. I went up again, the smashing and screaming went on, and I followed it to the end of a hallway.

As I approached the open room at the hilt of the corridor Bess fell out of the door. She was in exhausted tears, her hair came down matted over her face, and her white lace nightgown was stained with blood across the shoulder. She collapsed to her knees, and as I ran toward her she looked up and saw me. She held out her arm as if she was falling, her face blindly crying out, her arm grasping. I crouched and held her, kissed her forehead, patted her hair from out of her face, looked for the source of the blood and saw it was from a small cut across Bess' upper arm.

Another crash came from inside the room, and I whispered into Bess' ear, "What is happening?" but Bess could not respond, she just cried and held onto me with clawing desperation. I stood, gently unravelling myself from her hold and stepped cautiously into Matilda's parlour; the room in which I now write.

In the room I first saw the debris: broken furniture, tipped up tables and torn down curtains, and then, by the fireplace, the shards of smashed ornaments around her feet like jagged rose petals, was Matilda. She stood crooked, this mother of mine, in a white lace dress, torn and filthy grey, her back to me. She held on to the mantle shelf with one hand, seemingly catching her breath. As she turned her head to face me, I could see the glazed terror in her eyes; they were twitchy, like birds' eyes, set deep in the grey shrivelled skin of her long drawn face. Her hair stood tall, serpentine, like the branches of a dead tree, and her teeth, set out on rescinded gums, came out in a muzzle from her mouth as she spoke.

"Where is that *cunt*?" she spat in thick Afrikaans.

I said nothing; I could not take my eyes from the woman.

"You've come to collect the *whore*?" she said, moving her body awkwardly to face me as if she was shifting a great mass, slowly, muscle by muscle.

"What have you done?" I did not know what else to say.

"You knew about *this*?"

Matilda, in long hands, held up a pile of envelopes, torn and scrunched in her spidery fingers.

"I don't know what *this* is," I said as calmly as I could.

"You know what they are," Matilda growled, her eyes narrowed. And then she screamed, a guttural inhuman scream, something that had been building within her for a time forgotten. She screamed and screamed, picked a vase from the mantle shelf and threw it onto the floor, and then another, and then picked up the poker from the stand next to the fireplace.

233

"I don't know anything about what you're holding," I said, my eyes firmly fixed on the poker in Matilda's grasp at her side.

"She is *your* whore now, is that it? You fuck her so she can fuck me?" She waved the papers once more.

"There is nothing going on between Elisabeth and I," I said.

"I should kill us all."

She turned from me for a moment, distracted, her rage burnt into tears.

"This is how it is to be?" she said faintly. "Piers took away my husband. She takes away Piers. And you take away her. You take away Algie. You take away Piers. You take away my John. But *you* always come back." And she turned back to face me.

Again she let out a scream.

Unable to see an end, I exited the room quickly and in almost one movement, closed the door and picked Bess from the floor with a strong hand under her tiny arm. I picked her up as I strode down the hallway to the stairs and held her close like a sleeping child. More muffled crashes and screams from behind the closed door; Matilda did not follow. It was as if a wild animal was trapped in the room.

I folded Bess into the great lapels of my overcoat and took her away from the house, to my apartment, as a man might protect a kitten from the rain.

Bess was silent the whole way, and silent back in the apartment. She stared into space, doll-like. I drew a hot bath but she would not move. So, a little bashfully I must admit, I undressed her from her blood-stained nightgown, sanitised the mild wound in her upper arm and bathed her. I knelt at the side of the bathtub with my sleeves rolled up; Bess sat upright with her knees up to her small breasts. I poured the hot water through her hair, pressed my hands through it, gently pressed a sponge down her spine, over her shoulders. Not once did she even blink.

I picked her out of the bath as the water began to cool, dried her, rubbed her hair between my towelled hands, dressed her in a pair of my own crisp pyjamas, far too big for her so I rolled up the sleeves and the trouser legs, her small round shoulder still protruded from the neck line on the one side. I walked her slowly to the room she usually slept in when she stayed over but she stopped still in the hallway.

I gave it a moment and then said, "I'm going to have a nightcap. Would you like one?"

For the first time since we'd been back in the apartment Bess showed signs of responding, and she nodded slowly.

We sat opposite each other in the parlour, a whiskey each in large heavy-bottomed glasses.

"I am sorry," she said.

"I am sorry, too," I said. "Would you like to tell me what happened?"

Bess' eyelids flickered, as if she was focussing for the first time on the room she was in.

"Everything has gone wrong," she said.

"Bess; I am here for you. But you need to tell me about Matilda."

Bess' eyelids flickered a second time at the mention of Matilda's name.

"She found the letters," Bess said.

"What letters?"

"My father wrote."

"Your father writes you, I know that. Did Matilda not know that?"

"My father wrote her. He wrote to Matilda."

I said nothing.

"I have been first to the post every morning, waiting for word from Piers," Bess went on. "And one morning, a month ago I saw a letter in my father's hand. I didn't even notice it had Matilda's name on the envelope. I was distracted. So I took it and opened it and saw it was not for me, but for her. I read it. I shouldn't have, but I did. It said that my mother had died. She had been taken ill; the doctors thought it was an infection and would work its way out but she was dead within the fortnight."

"I am so sorry, Bess."

"He did not write to *me*, he wrote to *her*. He wrote to tell her they could be together now."

"And Matilda found the letter."

"She found my response that I signed with her name."

Bess looked at me with empty eyes and sipped her whiskey.

"You pretended to be Matilda?"

"Yes. I wanted to hurt him, you see? I wrote that he was nobody to me, to Matilda. I said our affair was a sham. I said that he had made his choice and he should go to the grave with his wife for all I cared. But he wrote back. I intercepted it. He said he was heartbroken from the moment he left. He said he had made the wrong choice and he would give up everything for her. For Matilda. And I wrote back. I said his soul was black. That he was not a man. How could I love anything so black? And this went on. I told him he was the devil and he wrote telling me how much he loved me. Matilda. There are many letters. He took to writing two, three times a day. And every time I went to buy newspapers on the way to here I would post my responses, filled with hatred. And he would send my letters back with his own. And then Matilda found them. This day she found them. I have never seen her like that before. She was like Satan himself."

She sipped her whiskey.

"You can't go back there," I said. "You can stay with me for now."

But Bess didn't seem to be listening; she was staring in to the spit and crackle of the fireplace.

"I don't know why I didn't burn them," she said. "I don't know why I didn't burn the letters."

* * *

So, there was a time when it was just the two of us.

War came. Chamberlain waved his begging letter on the tarmac with that unconvincing and unconvinced half-smile behind his moustache. History has not treated him well, but history itself is subject to the treatment of those who are unsympathetic to many contextual shades. He was working hard for the will, not the benefit, of the people. And in the end the war was about the threat to British trade and oil fields in the Middle East. Hitler could hoover up the whole of Eastern Europe as long as he kept to confiscating cabbages and syphilis. War is never about people, never about love or faith. It is sometimes about politics and always about money. Remember that.

I didn't need to do anything other than be with Bess. I tried to look after her by being another living soul in the room, for sometimes she did not seem to live, or want to live. I held her by a strand of hair from the ravages of a fiery pit. And Piers stayed alive within her.

It was becoming normal for us to spend several hours in the same room and not acknowledge each other. We were like an old married couple who had said all there was to say. For me sometimes it was enough that I could see she was breathing, that her life was an irrefutable fact if nothing else. She would sit at the window and look out over the street, and I would read, or look over business documents. But I was always attuned to the slightest fluctuation in her mood. Her feminine swank was becoming brittle, deathly. And yet I was beginning to see another, purer beauty in her new-found fragility. It was a beauty attached coldly to an acceptance of death, I think. I cannot wholly explain it. She had become another form of existence, bypassing distress and torment. There was a new found poetry to the way she moved about the place. I did not enjoy seeing it, don't misunderstand me. She had become this creature through turmoil and internal havoc. But she was unassailable now, beyond the pale, a god, if you like. Her earthly body was becoming unhealthily thin and nimble, and her skin pale and shadowy. But her soul had left the human world behind.

She had moments of clarity, moments when the light got in and she tried to shake a life out of it. The topic of Matilda came up only once.

"When I am ready to apologise for what I did I will go and see her," she said. "And then I will be better placed to accept *her* apology."

But I had called on Rasmussen to find someone to look after Matilda. I now had daily reports from a nurse down the telephone. Matilda spent most days sedate and in bed. She spent a few of the days also letting the light in, and she had recently begun supervised walks in the park. I asked if anybody recognised her. The nurse said that if they did they did not make themselves known.

In the apartment, Bess drifting about the place, spells were being cast in the dim-light of the room, spells upon memory, spells upon reality. It was a world of its own accord, a mystical box in which we dreamed and moved. Live within a dream without consequence or the barrage of human thought. Do not accept the beauty of horror. I considered these things with a thick chest. The nausea would often turn to a burn at the back of my throat, as if I was holding down acid tears. A blackness deeper than black. We could survive in perpetuity within these walls, I thought some days. We could draw out the very meaning of life. But silence is no existence, is it? Not this kind of silence. The silence of plant life. Time had become inconceivable to us both. It was when Bess would sleep that I would allow myself to pace the floor, drink gutsily from the decanted whiskey, and worry about the nature of our lives.

I cannot be sure where the idea came from to move out of the city, but London over the next eighteen months became infused with memories of Piers; rather than them fading they became clearer.

When the war came I bought a modest cottage in the country. And when the bombs began to drop from the black bellies of the Luftwaffe planes I decided we should go.

With a growling, roaring, beastly war across Europe, we both knew, deep down, that it would keep Piers away. I said that Piers was likely to find a spot on the planet where the war could not reach him. He could become that *woodgod* – Bess had spoken of this often after reading Emerson recently. She was the reader now. It was the part of Piers' soul that she could absorb up into her own, she could touch him through the vastness of his mystery, run her fingers along the lines of the page as she had once done with the small of his back, the curve of his neck, lightly touched her fingertips to his lips. And the thoughts she read, were the thoughts he had read. And with war burning down the world, would we not all soon become Emerson's woodgod? And Piers would have been there already. He would be king and king-maker "who solicits the wandering poet and draws him into antres vast and deserts idle". Piers was soon to be the New World god, born of the wood. And would she not now be closer to him in her own wilderness? I knew that Bess' decision to go with me to the cottage was not from the threat of German bombs on the capital, but was of a need to believe that Piers had found his bit of earth, and she would find hers, and through that, when the world came to an end, they would find each other again.

The village was a one-street divergence of escapees from the city, mixed with functional locals. A post office, a greengrocer's, a pub, all at the meeting point of green valley walls, and most of the cottages spread without reason up the sides of the shallow valley. It was as green, living there, as it was grey in London.

There was a closeness to life in the village. Bess breathed softly, she turned with some of her old grace very soon after we got there. I think even the short journey to the place did her good.

"So what do you think?" I said as I led her through the hallway, luggage under my arms. She looked about the place curiously, slowly, and although she did not nod or smile, I could see she was not frightened by the change life in this cottage brought with it. I had bought it not only because I wanted her to be away from London, but to remember faintly the Latimer cottage where she had spent the summer with Piers and the Monroes; faint enough for it to be an indiscernible taste, a compound in her air.

We had bedrooms opposite each other. The ceilings were low to me, but not to her. Bess still spent much time sitting in silence, reading or just looking out to the greenery of the valley from the parlour window, or she would walk around the small, blossom-filled garden, do slow bare-footed laps of the small lily pond until dinner was ready.

There were times when I could be gone for several days, tending to some matters of business in London, returning to a bright smile and a prepared meal, Bess in a floral dress, like the dutiful wife. But her dresses were hanging from her now she was so thin, she failed to fill them as a child would fail – even her shoes were clattering around her bony feet when she walked. She would never dine with me; she would always say she had already eaten. I did not believe her, of course. It was obvious to the eye that she was lying to me. She would ask how the war was going, as if the war was a parade. As if the war was my work. I would say it was all going to plan; she

241

would take my coat and hat from me and sit me down to my meal. I would not bring any newspapers into the house. And the conversation would never go further.

"You would tell me if you had any word from Piers, wouldn't you?" she said once, as she watched me eat.

"Of course," I said.

After a while it was evident that Bess never left the cottage in my absence. She would not go for the walks she seemed to enjoy when I was there, and it became obvious she likely did not eat. She was fading away, her skin so pale it was hardly there, her dissolving weight beginning to draw the moisture from her eyes and lips. And she was drinking. I would come home and she would be in the sitting room in silence, in her evening dress, her gaze frosty, her head unsteady. I did not bring it up. The meals were not prepared anymore.

At the grocer's one morning – I had decided to make something hearty and delicious for us both for dinner – I encountered a young woman. I was examining the lettuces – not really sure what embellishments I was guarding against – when I felt the gentle, prying tap to my arm.

"Mr Buren, isn't it?" she said with a wide, irregular smile.

I smiled as coldly as I could in return.

"We haven't met, but I wanted to welcome you to the village. I am Desdemona Wright."

And she held out her hand. I shook it lightly.

"You've been here some time now and we haven't had a chance make our acquaintance," she said.

"Is there something wrong?" I said, replacing a lettuce and picking up another, examining it as intently but as clueless as the first.

"No, nothing wrong," said Desdemona – I had wanted to laugh at her name, how unfitting it was, how lacking in allure she was, how lacking in poetry.

"Then how can I help?"

"We are a close community here, and we all like to get along."

"Are we not getting along right now?" I said.

"I certainly hope we are," she said, finding it difficult to locate a way in. "We were hoping to see you and your lovely young wife at church, perhaps, this Sunday. It would be nice to get to know you both."

"Do you know anything about vegetables?" I said.

Desdemona Wright offered a toothy, confused grin. "In what regard?"

I looked down to her.

"Bess is my brother's widow," I said. "We are here for the good of her health, not to attend church."

I put the lettuce back, tipped my hat, and passed her in the aisle, leaving the store.

I mentioned the encounter later that evening. We were both reading in the garden, drinking wine and nestling in the gentle tweets and rustling of the country air as it turned dim and hazy.

"I encountered a local today," I said.

Bess often did very little of the talking in these conversations.

"I was at the greengrocer's and this young woman approached me." There was a pause. I looked up from my book and across to Bess who was still reading, her legs tucked up under her. "She invited us to church."

"What on earth did you say to that?" said Bess, not looking up from her book.

"I politely declined," I said.

Silence resumed and when I realised the conversation was over I said: "Would you have preferred I accepted?"

"To go to church?"

243

"Yes."

"I don't know," she said, and turned the page of her book. "But you've declined. So there it is."

The next day Bess did not get up from bed. I took her meals to her room, but they all went untouched. She was under the duvet as I brought them in. She did not answer my questions and I did not persist, in case she was asleep.

About a week later I returned to the cottage from London – four or five days I had been gone this time – to find Bess in hat and overcoat at the dinner table, her packed bags at her feet, the solidity of sobriety all around her. I saw her from behind and entered the dining room still in hat and coat. I trod slowly and softly upon the bare boards.

"Bess? Is there something wrong?"

As I faced her front she looked up to me; her pale pretty face, those once full cheeks now low and hard, the dark rings about her eyes tinged with redness.

"I am going back to London," she said.

I took a seat.

"London is not safe," I said.

"That does not interest me," she said.

"Bess, what is wrong?"

She began to cry again, turned her head, held it back.

"A woman came to the house," she said.

"Yes?"

"From the village. She brought a basket of gifts. She said she hoped to see me at church on Sunday."

"Oh, yes; I bumped into her at the greengrocer's last week. I mentioned it, do you remember? I told her to leave you be."

"She said the church would help me come to terms with the death of my husband."

I dipped my head and placed my hand gently on Bess' forearm.

"Did you tell her Piers was dead?" said Bess.

I took a moment and looked Bess in the eyes.

"I told her a simple story for her simple ways."

"Why would you say he was dead?"

"Mainly so that I could end the conversation as quickly as possible," I said.

"Is he dead?"

I squeezed Bess' forearm lightly.

"I truly do not believe he is dead," I said.

"And yet you lie so easily to a stranger," said Bess. "So freely."

"You know, I don't even know if I said he was dead. She may have just come to the wrong conclusion. I don't remember what I said exactly."

"She said I was here to recover from his death. Did she make that up?"

I said nothing.

"I am going back to London," said Bess.

"I don't think you should."

"I don't really care to hear your opinion about it right now," she said. "Enough to say I think you have brought me here to die."

I removed my hand from Bess' arm and sat against the back of the chair.

"I need to be where Piers can find me when he returns. I need to be exactly where he can find me."

I looked out of the window. A robin seemed to be watching us from a naked branch. It flew off.

"I have put some things in motion to visit Monroe in Spain," I said.

I had done no such thing.

Bess sucked up the sharpness of her tears and looked at me.

I continued to look at the trembling branch from which the Robin Redbreast had just launched.

"It may not be possible, you understand," I went on. "Travelling to Spain may not be possible. But I'm looking into it."

"Why now?"

I would not look at her as I lied.

"As time has gone on I have begun to feel uneasy about how readily I accepted the poet's line of things in that letter."

"But you said he could not be found."

"The war in Spain is over," I said. "If I can get to Spain I think I can find him."

Bess dried her tears and straightened herself in the chair. She did not go back to London that day.

* * *

The days in that village were long and shapeless.

I suppose they were as grey in Bess' mind as the ideas of the city were in mine. I had been infused with such hope in the first weeks of life there. Bess seemed to brighten, seemed to be on the verge of a flourishing. But she drew back, like a hand at a hot plate. I would speak to her, I would ask her things, simple things – *would you like a cup of tea?* – but I realised she could not hear me; she would not have realised there was any question at all until I had left the room and a smattering of bleak silence was left in my place. She could sometimes feel herself reaching out to that silence, to me, to come back to be with her, but she would look down and her arms were at her side. She was haunting her own body.

She spent much of the time at the window sitting on the red velvet cushions of the sill and looking over the white-grey street, a few people coming and going, up and down, insects with human business to attend. At times the street leading from the cottage to the village high street was empty and she would stare at the turf and the cobbles until the world before her would evaporate into something else altogether. It was then she could have been anywhere. Mars, the battlefields of Europe, ancient Troy, heaven. I tried to allow her these static wanderings. Perhaps I thought she would come out the other end, as through a crack in the mountain. Let the thing run its course, I thought. In truth, I did not know what else to do.

Whilst back in London, I had been going to Claypole. Matilda was committed to her bed now. "Insanity will pass," the doctor said. But she needs to remain still in order to allow it to do so. My mother goes insane and the doctors treat it like weather, I thought. I have learned since then, in all the years since I was young, that madness is *exactly* like weather.

During this time we received a letter. Algie Radnor addressed it to the Buren family, informing us of Michael's death at Dunkirk. I kept the information from Matilda. After the first hour of my first visit, I had not been up the stairs to see her; instead I sat at the fireplace and watched the flames tickle the air. But I did take the information back to the cottage to tell Bess.

I was standing, she was seated, and I said that I had some very bad news, and that her brother had perished in a very large and serious confrontation in France. I had not been able to confidently predict how she would react.

"That is such sad news," she said after a moment, in a tender, reflective voice.

"Would you like me to get you anything?"

"My poor brother," she said. "And poor Matthew, also. They were inseparable."

She showed no sorrow for herself. And I think she felt none. Piers had, perhaps, taken up all the use of that facility. She was immune to its supplicatory demands.

Bess' tight state of sadness was something I spent much time reflecting on, so intriguing was it to me, so decisive and uncompromising was it. I watched her often, as if she was a work of art, and in many ways she was: a sculpture of sorrow. I'm sure she could feel my eyes over her. And I think it was comforting to her, my gaze, like the rays of an electric fireplace, my eyes throbbed over her. I'm sure in her clearer moments – and they were there – she wondered how much I could see, how much I could understand that she felt as if she was wrapped in tight swaddling, like a caterpillar with no hope of emancipation into bold colours. And like the tri-stage existence of such an insect, she felt as if this world now, the one in which she was held, bore nothing for her like the one previous had done. Her life was new, separated by thick black lines from the life before *his* disappearance. Her brain functioned differently; it was closed, heavy, as if sodden. She moved through a bog. Her limbs needed convincing every step of the way. That was the most notable strand of her new self: no more reaction, no natural haste, no occupation of herself, as if the electricity had been turned off and she was creaking like a wooden tower wheeled to the battlements of a besieged city. And so the death of a brother did not seem at all real, not of her experience, because Michael had been the brother of that other Bess, the one who moved freely and did not have to think her hand to her mouth, instruct the tears to her eyes.

And in those moments of clarity I know she looked at me sometimes and wondered. Did I care about her? Everything I did must have seemed little more than dutiful. I was, perhaps, frustratingly dutiful. She must have wondered of my intentions. Piers had been gone for several years now, and we had lived as two actors playing husband and wife. When would I realise there was no stage, no audience, that the props were as real as real could be. She must have thought this.

"I am worried about your health," I said. "I never see you eat. I never see you drink anything that does not have a dram in it."

Ah, the booze. It was stuck between us. I had no objections to sinking martinis before dinner, wine with the meal and then scotches until bed time, but a female drinking alone is unseemly. It was not of her class. Even a washerwoman has too much purchase of herself to be drunk by lunch – only whores drink throughout the day. And men, of course. But Bess resented the delineation of the antidotes to despair. It was a flicker of life in her that I recognised from the old version. But the truth is important: Men, repulsed by the grey hard steel of the ugly world they created and perpetuated could drink that despondency, that guilt, out of themselves all day. But poor Bess, whisked out of the city, could not even become a souse in the hideaway. She resented me for it. She added it to the list. But still she tried not to take it out on me. She didn't obey me, after all. She drank all day. But her resentment usurped her guilt and I was hated as the voice of conscience.

When I was in London she would drink the moment I was out the door; she would poor a tumbler of gin and swallow it, tilt her head back like a sword-swallower and glug. And then another and then another. She could spend two or three days straight under the bed sheets, waiting to fall asleep, hoping that the burning to her eyes was the beginning of a fatal brain illness eating into her head from the edges. Why didn't she kill herself? Why didn't she take pills or poison – the feminine ways – why didn't she jump from the railway bridge that crossed the far end of the village? She did not because she believed Piers would one day return.

So she was being tested. (It is easy to see where Biblical fallacy comes from – the transcribing of hardship as a test). She had not been a practicing Christian since she left her family. But those painful lessons were coming back to her now. She spent fewer days in bed; she even took to sitting in the garden occasionally. The countryside birdlife tweeted something akin to airy therapy; it was the purest soothing music. This test – if that's what it was – did have moments of relinquishment. This despair was old hat now, she had to admit. She had lived inside of it for three or four years – she had no concept of real time – and it had levelled out. She found herself playing with gnostic ideas. She would mumble things under her breath. How could Jesus love us without knowing about loss, and he would need to be human to know about loss. Joseph must have died at some point – he does not appear in the later parts of the Gospels, whereas Mary does. So Jesus would have mourned him and were he not a man he would have marvelled at the expectations of that grief. But he could not have indulged it. He simply could not. It was Piers who had taught her the difference between the Bible and Jesus, the difference between the Church and morality. Piers read her *Thomas Jefferson's Bible*, the one he wrote with all of the religious nonsense taken out, the one with only the lessons. Now these things were blank phrases for her. Bess was in the coffin of despair – the Church meant nothing, morality felt like a triviality meant for children and for the wealthy.

I noticed this change in her, how her despair emerged into a journey. I came home one day and saw her in the garden – "Who are you talking to?" I said.

But as usual Bess did not summon a response. The birds sang at different distances.

She went into the cottage and I was sitting in silence having poured myself a drink. The light was dim; I had neither taken off my hat nor coat.

"I don't want to stay here," Bess said.

I said nothing, just looked at her. I held her hand as she stood next to the armchair and looked as though admiring her floral dress.

"Hopefully we can go back to London, soon," I said.

But I always said that. I would not tell her about the war or that the Germans had ceased bombing London some time ago. And she had no real money with which to escape.

We sat opposite each other in silence and drank scotch for the rest of the evening. There was nothing to say.

The days went on formless, fluid. Bess was floating, now; not sinking. Jesus must have seen something like this during his forty days and nights in the wilderness. She had heard his time out there was a battle, but what if it was just like this, a timeless curious forever? The devil tempted out there? Well, she had a tougher time than that, then. Nothing happened at all. What she would have given for a fight. Her strength was returning – to her mind if not her body; she could not swallow, the food would stick in her throat.

Before we returned to London she had begun reading again: Browning, Ford Maddox Ford, Mallory, Homer, GK Chesterton, whatever she could find in the cottage. Paperbacks as well as real books – that was what Piers used to say. She wanted to be prepared for the people.

She began to watch the people about the village from the window sill of her room no longer with blank disinterest, but now with a tinge of covetousness for their range, their confidence, their trickery. She walked down to the village store – she had never been in it before and the eyes of the shopkeeper were on her. She realised immediately that her hermitic relationship with the village had been a topic of conversation about the place at one time or another. She bought a newspaper and some boiled sweets.

"You're Miss Buren, aren't you?" said the shopkeeper. He had a kind face, bright red cheeks and dark hairs coming from the corners of his nostril.

"I am," said Bess, cautiously.

"What a pleasure it is to meet you," said the shopkeeper.

His wide smile hit Bess right in the centre of her soul, and she carried that feeling with her back to the cottage.

She read there, whilst sucking on the boiled sweets one after another, that the Germans were on the run, being pushed further and further back across Europe after being held in the snowy forests of the Ardennes. It looked as though the entire war had passed her by. How much else had done, she did not know.

I was due back that afternoon. She bathed, put on some make-up, and dressed herself with care. She wanted to look like a person again, not a ghost. As she kept saying to herself: my despair is to be incubated. The war would be over soon, it seemed. Piers would return and she needed to be something like her old self.

When I returned later, she was stood in the hallway. She

252

looked beautiful, purposeful, made beautiful by the life within her found anew.

"I hear the war will be over soon," she said.

I glanced over at the newspaper on the dining table.

I nodded.

"Then I am ready to go back to London. I am ready." And she forced the widest, most confident smile she could.

I put my briefcase down, took off my hat.

"Very well," I said.

The news that we were to return to London seemed to release something in Bess. It was exhausting, as if living with a small child. She was eager, keen; she cooked and ate, and she drank less, and we went for a long walk through the countryside – up along the valley and over into the next and through woodland and fields – the day before we left.

I suggested that she take the spare room at my apartment, and the situation could go on very much as it had done before the war. She could list her official residence as being with Matilda at Claypole to avoid any awkward questions or Soho gossip.

"That's if you intend to start going out again," I said. "I assume eventually you will want to get some fresh air and it may lead to linking with some old faces."

"If I do I will tell them I am living with my husband's brother," she said. Her voice was no longer a whisper, but it was something like the voice of her previous being. "I will tell them that you took me in and that I don't know what I would do without you."

And when she did eventually turn an afternoon stroll through the park into an afternoon coffee in one of the old haunts it was not painful or sorrowful, but rather it was warm and she felt close to Piers, not bereft of him as she had always feared – and as she knew I had wished.

She did not hate me now – I am sure she did in the depths of her illness. If it was a symptom of the despair, or whether it was genuine, did not matter. It was past. Even she could see how it had been a phase, a colour of grief as it matured into cholera, like a nicotine stain. I had, after all, done everything I could to find Piers, hadn't I? She did not have the energy to disbelieve me. And even if she had, her disbelief had nowhere to go. In an unintentional way I had become her world.

What did she think of me during those recuperative days? She began to look at me. I would catch her examining me from the window sill, looking over me as if I was a puzzle. She found me odd, I think. My motives were a mystery to her, I think. So she found my mannerisms odd. Charming at times; but odd. Perhaps even handsome. I think she was discovering that my core silence was awkwardness, amongst other things. A little sadness, but mainly, as far as I allowed her to see, it was fortitude. Fortitude is most often silent. She said to me once that I did not know how to act around people so I tended not to act at all. She said I knew the worth of action when called upon – Bess and Piers would not have been together or married if it was not for my interventions, after all. I was like one of those deep sea fishes she had read about; waiting reluctantly to strike and do something of significance. She said she thought my inner soul was inert; and every movement I made – and I was graceful, it had to be said, on the outside – was against my will. I was sharp, crisp, well-presented in my Saville Row suits, my black-framed spectacles, my expensive haircut, my glistening, absorbent eyes. Was she attracted to me, then? She looked at the world differently now, and what she had thought she understood she realised she did not. I was one of those things. She said she felt I could be cruel. She had never seen it, but sometimes she felt uneasy near me, like when stood near an unfamiliar animal. She was no less uneasy for my retracted claws.

* * *

We settled. It was a quiet life.

We both lied to ourselves that we would walk around breathing oxygen until it ended, and life would be little more than that. We were wrong of course. I found that out. Perhaps some people don't appreciate how things are learned. I have had to teach myself the solution to all of life's problems. Of course, yes; that means mistakes can happen. How easy it is to live life by adopting the tried and tested. What made me decide that I needed to find Piers? Was it an outcome from the failure of my efforts to let him be? I don't think that was the case. I think it was because, one way or the other, he would not leave us be. One way or the other, he was always loitering at the window, like Peter Quint.

I was on my way to a meeting one morning in late October when I saw Charlotte Latimer as she waited to cross the street on High Holborn. I had not seen her since I had visited her in her house. It is strange but I remember myself as very young that morning. I remember going through the encounter as Piers might have done. I wore my passions on the outside. I called out, without knowing why, raised an arm and waved. It was not like me to shout in the street. It *is* not like me. She turned to see me, and took a moment to focus. She tentatively waved back. I jogged toward her – again, I remember *running* – as she hung there on the side of the street, her heavy shoulders, her lean frame and that tired equinity to her face, the sad eyes. She was so much bigger than those around her on the busy pavement; she towered over people and her greatcoat billowed.

"Mrs Latimer," I said.

"You're Hal Buren," she said, with a tired, hollow voice.

"I'm sorry to call across the street to you like that."

"It is rather demoralising that nobody else recognised my name," she said.

It was a dull morning, grey and on the verge of rain.

"How are you?" I said.

"I am on a rare solo excursion through the human rubble of the city, Mr Buren; what is it I can do for you?"

"*Do* for me, Mrs Latimer?"

The last time I had seen her she was in the darkest recesses of her despair. But now she seemed to not remember that afternoon.

"You have prevented me from crossing the street," she said, peering to the other side with a touch of melodrama.

"Could I buy you a drink, Mrs Latimer?"

"No, Mr Buren. I need to be getting home. My husband does not know I'm out of the house."

She seemed vulnerable now. I looked at the sadness of her face, her unsure eyes, the downturn to the corners of her mouth.

"Does he worry?" I said.

The rain began to spit down, big gaps between the drops slowly narrowing. Latimer looked slowly up to the sky.

"You mean does he have reason to worry?" she said looking back to me.

"Well, can I walk you to your car, or the train?"

"I am not really much company, I'm afraid. I am a little under the weather."

"All the more reason for me to accompany you," I said.

Latimer shrugged languorously.

I placed my hand gently on her shoulder blade and we crossed the road. She was distant, cold, slow-motion, drugged-almost. She felt jagged to touch.

"Are you still looking for your brother, Mr Buren?" she said.

I looked at her. She said it matter-of-fact, as if remembering an occasion we spent together, an anecdote.

"It's been a long time," I said. "I always thought he would come home when he was ready."

"He was a poet, wasn't he?" she said.

"Yes," I said. The rain began to come down harder as we made our way between the vegetable stalls and shoe-shine stands.

"Yes, I remember him," said Latimer. "Seems such a long time ago now."

"Are you sure everything is okay, Mrs Latimer?" I said. She was ashen, becoming greyer as the dark clouds closed in overhead.

She smiled blankly.

"And you don't know what happened to him?" she said.

"No," I said.

"I don't know anything about Piers Buren," she said. "Except that he followed Monroe to Spain." The rain came down a little harder and Charlotte Latimer stood getting wet, oblivious to it. "And Millie, of course," she said, stabbing the words into the air.

"Mrs Latimer," I said, now hunching as the rain hit down; "Do you not remember my visiting you when you were ill some years ago? It was the last time we saw each other?"

"I remember nothing of the sort, Mr Buren," she said with a bite.

"And you told me then that Piers was with Monroe in Toledo."

"I could hardly remember telling you that if it never happened," she said.

"Is there something else you want to tell me?"

I could feel her playing around with something in her mind.

"Monroe is here," she said. "I've been told he's back to talk to his publisher."

"Monroe is in London?"

Latimer held up her long arm and pointed to an office building at the other side of the street.

"He's in there. Or at least his publisher is."

I looked across the road at the grey building, inconspicuous, hunched, in the row amidst granite financial buildings.

"I came to find him. To confront him," Latimer said. "But I need to get home. Millie isn't with him, anyway."

Her voice trailed away and even her attention seemed to drift. And she walked off into the rain, her head and shoulders above the heads of all the other people crowding the sodden streets.

I wanted to follow her, but I stayed opposite Monroe's publishers, the building taking on a strange glowing quality, hemmed between two others, wider, cleaner but less clear. I began to feel my heart beating faster, my throat was drying. I didn't understand my perturbatious state. I spent a minute pacing the pavement, rubbing my jaw. I had seen Piers do this when nervous about something. I walked swiftly, sturdily, across the road winding in and out of the busy traffic, and I clattered through the main door of the office building. In the smoky lobby I went up to the reception. A young girl, making marks on leaves of papers with a red pencil looked up from behind the counter, and from behind horn-rimmed glasses that were too big and old for her.

"Can I help, sir?" she said.

"I need to see Ki Monroe," I said without thinking.

"There is no Ki Monroe in this building, sir," said the girl.

"I need to see him."

"Sir, there is no Ki Monroe situated in this building."

"No – he doesn't work here. He's a writer. He's in to see his publisher. His editor, most likely. He's here to see his editor and I urgently need to speak with him."

"Well, sir; if there was a Ki Monroe here to see a member of the editorial staff today I wouldn't be able to let you see him."

"So he's here, then."

"No, sir; he is not. But if he were, it would make very little difference."

I stared into the girl's eyes. She held me firmly in her stubborn grip from behind those horn-rimmed glasses. My throat was dry, and my heart was jiggling in its cage. I began to count in my head back from ten, counting my breaths. I was controlled on the outside, more controlled than I was on the inside. What was going on inside me I did not know. I felt too small for my soul, I felt ready to pop. I had been staring at the girl, and she was unmovable – round features, pink and soft, round cheeks and a small pursed mouth.

"I don't believe you," I said.

The girl exhaled loudly.

"It is extremely important that I see him," I said.

"I wish I could help you, sir."

"Can you tell me who his editor is? I will speak with them."

"I most certainly cannot do that."

"I think you can."

My voice rose through my frustrations. It sounded young, childish, panicky.

A man at the far end of the lobby in a brown woollen suit entered the reception and noticed my agitated state and approached.

"Miss Jenkins: is everything okay?" he said.

"Mr Fuller," said the girl. "This gentleman is adamant that he wants to talk to someone who is not here."

Realising I was being unreasonable, and unable to fix a reason on my irrational outburst, on my crazed being, I turned to the man.

"I believe Ki Monroe is here and I need to speak with him," I said. "Can you help with that?"

The man folded his hands across himself and leaned back slightly.

"Well as a matter of fact I think I can," he said.

"Good," I said. And I felt a slight coolness come over me.

"Mr Monroe is not here. I believe he had a meeting with one of my colleagues this morning but it was cancelled."

"You're not lying to me," I said.

The man looked puzzled and smiled.

"Why on earth would I do that? I have no idea who you are."

I gathered myself. More clearly now it was dawning on me how crazy I must have seemed. I was sweating, and I felt as if my skull was pushing itself out of my skin. I thanked them both, apologised, and left, back into the heavy rain of the city street, the cooling rain, and sunk into an alleyway for a moment where I could gather my thoughts. I looked down at my wet shaking hands. They began to steady. Just the thought of Monroe back in London had sent me into a spin. But a spin like nothing I had ever experienced. I spent the rest of the day walking the streets before returning to my apartment. It may seem absurd, but I had always known Piers was dead. I had felt a thud. And I believe that day he came to me, possessed me, drove me to find Monroe, because it could not be allowed that the poet would tell Bess the truth. Piers came to me, possessed me, to protect her. That is what I decided had happened. There was no other explanation for it. I am a careful man, a serious man, some might say; but I know I could feel my brother that day. Protect Bess. *Protect Bess*. That was the day I decided to find Monroe.

THE BROKEN FOUNTAIN

✷ ✷ ✷

I wake some mornings and think: I am the guardian of this century.

Do I really believe I was possessed by the spirit of my brother, dead, unbeknownst to me, in the Spanish dust? I do believe I was possessed by something. The whole of Europe – the people, I mean – did not know what to do with itself in the immediate aftermath of the death of Hitler. Was I made sick and trembling by the spirit of renewal? I may have been hopeful in the days and months after the end of the war. And then the thought of Monroe being back in London, the idea that Bess could be presented with the truth – he had written no letter because there was no letter to which he could reply. The hope, the renewal, was blackened on that street that morning. I could only think of Sartre's words: *Everything is going to begin again – the shame, the wretchedness and the madness.*

I had to act, I had to put one foot in front of the other. I had always meant that to be my way. It's strange how intentions get lost between the brain and the limbs, what I've heard called the "most important journey". I decided very quickly that any future or further uncertainty would simply not do. I could not allow the prevailing winds to threaten us on a whim.

It took me several days to get to Toledo. Not wanting to exploit the avenues of my wealth, I took an American government train through the bleak, shamed landscape of the former Vichy state and a boat from Marseille to Barcelona.

Barcelona was sedate. But I did not stay to explore, I ventured northwards to Madrid, to the robotic triumphalism of Franco's capital. In white linen suit, a few days without shaving, my Boer skin reacting redolently of the veldt in the heavy Spanish sun, I almost began to look a Spaniard myself.

As I went deeper and deeper into Spain the police guards on every corner stopped looking at me, their well-nurtured suspicions fraying. I was still too tall, and not incognito. If anything, at more than a glance, I looked eccentric, in a banal sort of way. Perhaps they assumed I was some damaged *hombre gentil* – there was enough of them about in those years after the revolution, wandering the land, muttering, broken, lost to the thick gas of war's legacy. The rich had won, but some had seen the cost for what it was: another chapter in the Decline of Man. (Not enough saw it this way. Many saw it as the will of God. You will find God to be the most common character in the theatre of war. You could be forgiven for coming to the conclusion He is in fact a Soldier of Fortune.)

But I could have been seen as one of these eccentrics (who saw the war for what it was), with my furrowed brow and foreign outfits. Regardless, it fitted my means.

It was important that I was inconspicuous without trying to hide. This was a private journey, one I could not assign to any of my "agents" – I call them this because it is a title you might best understand. My network of contacts was complex, and largely unimportant to this story, an army of traditional governmental rogues who saw money as the key to every door, as the answer to every question. A militia. This century of which I was guardian was the Golden Age for such weasels. The Century of Weasels.

But for this they would have been no good. It was a delicate presence I needed, one that was seen and not seen, one that was below the sight of the authorities and yet known to those who likewise sought no publicity with the authorities. I had no fear of persecution or incarceration. Franco was still in the process of cleaning up the stables of the losing left. He did this mainly in the form of summary executions. But there is only one form of society more corrupt and corruptible than a revolutionary one, and that is a post-revolutionary one. There was not a scrape I knew I could not pay my way out of. (Has there been a century when money has been as powerful as this? Pound's warning of the *usurer* turned out to be perhaps poetry's greatest moment).

At Toledo the sky burned blue and clear like the kernel of a flame. The streets were peopled, but hushed, as if the memory of the war put its finger to their lips. Downcast eyes mostly, and the ones that cast level were suspicious, aggressively so, and muddy in thought. I preferred the simple insinuations of the ones that would not look at you – the one that confirmed we were all a part of this shame.

There were marks of the bloody siege all around the city – Franco could be as lackadaisical in his oppression of the people as he could be pro-active. So little time and so many to kill. You will remember the bloodshed; it was how he governed the rest of his days, even after he had exterminated the defeated. Murder is a difficult habit to kick. It is said Franco liked to sign the death warrants of at least fifty civilians before bed. It was a routine, like sit ups. If he had been Asian and dressed in a collarless tunic, they would have called him an animal. He was almost certainly a psychopath. And his country grew in his image. I could see it in the fabric of Toledo. It was muted, weary, uncaring, uninterested in care – it had been beaten down and abused, just as a child is who grows up to be rotten. That first day there I felt myself beginning to fear for the future generations of that country, of that city. This was no place to be a person.

I asked the receptionist at my hotel if there was an area where writers traditionally gathered. Every city has one, of course; the bohemian hub. And I knew that one way or the other, for all of his opprobrium in London, Monroe would not be able to keep away from the debate, the back-slapping, the puffed-out chests, the narrow eyes and cynical jousting of the literary elites. I recognised Monroe as a transient force. A transeunt one, also. Now that the figures of *his* London had dispersed – to other forms of madness in some cases – he would put his energies elsewhere. Here. And after this? Another touchstone in another sphere. There were always places for such a man to dock.

On the second afternoon, with guidance from locals, I came upon a small cantina on the east side of the city, outside the shadow of the Alcazar. The place was moderately busy. At the bar, having ordered a beer, I noticed the cut-glass English of a man speaking in a group languorously gathered around a table in the corner. I turned to get a better look at him. He was dashing, lean, an angelic blonde curl to his thick hair. He had energetic lips, and held the group tightly in the grasp of his oratory.

"I was in Portugal," the man was saying, leaning back on the wooden chair, his cigarette held to the side of his smooth face. "I came upon a small community of cork farmers. And I stayed with them for several weeks, working labour in return for food and lodgings. Now, my Portuguese is not without its flaws but we managed to all get along. A farmer's vocabulary is not at all extensive, after all. While I was at this farm I received word that there was a Durer in Stuttgart that I really needed to focus my attention on. These things do not come along every day. So, I bade farewell to my new friends, stating that I had to get to Germany as quickly as I could, and I thanked them for their generosity. Well, they looked at me blankly to the point where I thought I may have insulted them – perhaps I had not worked off the food I had eaten or the wine I had drunk; which, obviously, would have been deeply embarrassing. But then it became clear that their blankness was out of a sort of confusion. You see; they didn't know what

266

Germany was. One of the men had heard of it; but didn't know what it *was* so couldn't really explain to the others. I said that Germany is a country, just like Portugal, not all that far away. But, you see, they didn't really know what *Portugal* was, either, except that they knew it bore some kind of relation to powers above them. Not God, but something in between them and God. A greyness that lurked around the edges of the Church. The concept of a country meant nothing to these people. Anything beyond their community and the people in the town who bought and distributed their cork was an abstract to them. You see; every generation looks down upon the last as being yesterday's step in the onward march of righteous progression. 'I have heard of Germany,' said the one man, 'but I do not know what it is.' Do you think that when I explained to him what a nation state is the price of his cork went up?"

I listened, watched, as the others around the table held their poses in the theatre of the speech. And I knew that this was the place where Monroe would have ended up, with these people.

"We have to realise that progression is a myth propagated by the ignorant," the man went on. "What were the Dark Ages? An epoch of unimaginable ignorance? A time when not even God's light could break the cloud cover? Well, no. What have the working-classes got now? All across Europe the working-classes are illiterate, depoliticised; perhaps some community members can read the Bible. But some do not even know what *Germany* is. And yet the medieval peasant had a literacy all of his own in the understanding of complex religious symbolism. It informed him, as a kind of literature, a kind of poetry, the motivations and implications of myriad philosophical ideals. Does the peasant-class have more understanding than that now? or less? A medieval peasant

267

would garner more information from one stained-glass window than an Italian nickel miner would from the alien etchings and scratchings on a page of the Old Testament. So, how is it we think we have righteously progressed? The Enlightenment? *A sham*!"

"So, now Newton is not even good enough for the English," laughed one of the party; a German to whom the main story had obviously been aimed. The laughter spread around the table.

"Senorita," I lowered my voice to the passing waitress. "What is that man's name?"

"Senor Darabont," she said, hurriedly, and moved on with her tray of drinks.

I sat at the bar for a few more drinks, listening to the conversation, listening for clues. I did not want to alert my presence to more people than was necessary for the time being, and so, as the party began to disperse, I said nothing. But I returned early the next day and there was Darabont, alone at the same table, reading a week-old copy of the *Financial Times*, his round spectacles perched at the very edge of his nose. Later the previous night I had talked further with the accommodating waitress. She told me Darabont was a writer and art dealer. And if you're looking for someone in particular, she smiled cheekily, senor Darabont knew all the *hombres extranjeros* in the whole of Spain.

"Mr Darabont," I said, approaching the table. "I am a friend of Ki Monroe's."

Darabont looked up over the top of his spectacles and examined me entirely in two sharp movements of his eyeballs.

"Are you really?" he said, slowly and incredulously. He looked me up and down once more and kicked out a chair smoothly. "I haven't heard that name in some time."

I took the seat. Darabont closed his book and straightened

himself toward his guest. His lips were moist, his skin looked extremely smooth, well-looked-after in the heat and the swirling lingering golden mid-air dust. He had brilliant blue eyes, the only thing of startling colour about him; his blonde hair, his peachy skin, sandy teeth, his white shirt and lank beige suit.

Darabont smiled at me, a charming, warm, lopsided smile.

"You know him, then," I said.

"Yes, I know him. Or should I say I *knew* him. I haven't seen him since before the war."

"You mean the Spanish war."

"Yes; I mean the Spanish war," Darabont grinned. "Why on Earth would an Englishman be looking here for Ki Monroe?"

"I'm South African," I said.

"Even more intriguing," said Darabont. "As far as I know he hasn't been here for ten years. Not since the siege. You're a decade off the warm trail."

"But nonetheless I'm here."

"Yes you are," said Darabont and that grin emerged once more. "What's your name, traveller?"

I looked over Darabont's handsome face, the blonde lick to his hair, the blue eyes. I had planned to lie if asked that question. I had planned to use Rasmussen's name, claim to be pursuing some kind of legal matter from Durban. But Darabont was looking at me side-on, the deep golden sunlight shone through the dust in the air. He drew a long drag on his cigarette, his lips pursing wonderfully.

"I am Hal Buren."

"And what is it you want with an old rascal like Ki Monroe?"

"He knows where my brother is."

"Does he indeed?"

269

Darabont continued to move in and out of a moist smile.

"I'd appreciate it if you could tell me whatever you know, Mr Darabont."

"Please," Darabont leaned forward and offered me a cigarette from his silver case. "Call me Ernest. We're all foreigners here together, after all."

Darabont ordered some drinks and we talked a while, a little about Monroe, a little about Spain. Darabont needed minimal prompting. He was confident in most topics. He was a travel writer, after all, and had, it seemed, intellectualised almost every experience he had been fortunate to have. I had to admit sheepishly that I had not heard of or read any of his books. I felt unusually coy in front of him. This was Darabont's adopted territory and he patrolled it with aplomb.

"I travel half of the year going around the world buying and selling art and the rest of the year writing up my travels. I seem to have found the most unlikely of systems by which to live my life. How do you live yours?"

"Me?"

"We all have a system. Are you married?"

"No."

"I see. A bachelor."

"Of sorts."

"Is it complicated? Of course it is."

Ernest seemed to have little interest in playing games – something I had found commonplace in London with his sort. You must understand that the hours for an artist, be that artist wealthy or in penury, are largely open and empty. Life is *so* long, so boring for them, that such meaningless games become part of the fabric of the day to day. But Ernest was not like that. He enjoyed his silences as much as he did his speeches.

"I understand Ki had a hard time of it in the early days of the rebellion," said Darabont. "Priests were executed in retaliation for Mola's executions in Castile. Monroe was beaten and left to die on the roadside at one point. I think that's how the story goes. Turbulent times. I was gone by then. And the wise take their wisdom with them."

Darabont had missed the war in Spain – he was in Dresden following up word of a Bellotto at the time the Siege of the Alcazar broke out, he said; and so by the time he returned to Toledo Monroe was gone, all the writers were gone, and the region was under Falangist control.

"Did any of the others come back after the war?"

"The others?"

"The poets and painters and the like."

Another round of drinks arrived at the table.

"Most of us. You saw some of them at this table yesterday, didn't you?"

I couldn't help but half-smile. Darabont was sharp. I was momentarily caught-out at having been noticed, but this melted into a strange feeling of flattery.

"You saw me here?"

"I most certainly did," said Darabont, and raised his glass in a silent toast.

We talked further, less and less about Monroe, not at all about Piers. Darabont asked no more questions about my life. We even broached the subject of literature: Ernest clearly was steeped in the arts. He quoted Tolstoy, Baudelaire frequently, Flaubert, Goethe. He mixed not only metaphors but, with a mischievous glint to his eye, mixed the metaphors of different writers.

"I am an amateur in such conversations," I said. "It was my brother who was the poet."

Darabont noticed the use of the past tense even before I did. Ties were loosed by this point, the heat of the midday sun pouring into every nook and cranny. But, preparing to explain my misspeak, I was relieved to see Darabont stand and gather his things.

"Come on," he said; "I'll show you around."

The two of us walked the back streets of Toledo like old friends for the rest of the afternoon, stopping occasionally to top up on liqueurs and tapas. As the sun began to dip behind the thrusting towers of the Alcazar and the sky dimmed to a burnt orange, Darabont pushed his hat to the back of his head and turned to me, his feet taking a moment to find purchase on the cobbles of the alley.

"We seem to be just around the corner from my apartment," he said, his hands in his pockets as he walked backwards, facing me.

"You live here?"

I was quite drunk, but level, well-paced. I felt young, dizzy, punchy, ready for anything. The day had been a swirling poem all of its own.

"I live just up there, through those gates. My veranda looks down over that rather pathetic-looking fountain. I've kept this apartment for over a decade and the thing has never once spat out a droplet of water."

We both laughed, I more awkwardly than he, and we stumbled toward the enclosed square.

"Would you like to come up?" said Darabont.

I straightened. I was sure that he knew what this meant. The meeting of minds, of bodies, and even on the verge of acts there are still some things that cannot be said aloud. We're clever, my type; clever enough to fashion the most primal and important of acts from mere glances and, most importantly, the lingering silences between banal words.

The day and evening had been one of remarkable openness; there were times when we were like lion cubs prattling with each other in the shade. Drink helped, of course; and the ability for us both to fold into and out of our 'Britishness'. Spain helped. The way the locals ignored us. They had their own problems – they couldn't care less about two foreigners getting drunk in their white flannels. We were like ghosts wandering amongst the living. It made me wonder if ghosts are ever happy. Or is it only the trapped and morose who are left behind? Those trapped in the control of a punitive bureaucratic God who has boxes left unticked in his heavenly entrance policy, and so leaves you to wander the hall of gothic castles to think about what you've done. It is a mechanical afterlife, this trapping. I felt even more ghostly with this thought, trapped as I was, in the living reality walking toward Ernest's apartment overlooking that courtyard.

Darabont had walked ahead of me and was on his veranda looking down as I examined the broken fountain.

"Hey," he called down.

I looked up, unsteadily. Again I felt young. I felt disconnected from all of those dark terrible truths of life. And of death, I suppose. I had not felt that way since the last summer in Norfolk with Douglass. And I decided I would let everything go, at least for that night, and stop weighing things up, and stop thinking of Bess, and Matilda, and Piers most of all.

I watched Darabont up on the veranda take off his shirt and walk backwards slowly into the apartment. And as I walked up the spiral staircase to Darabont I felt happy.

* * *

I don't wish to sentimentalise the relationship that developed between Darabont and I.

We were men with several lives between us, and those lives allowed a No Man's Land where we both met. He was sensual as well as arrogant, and I found the heady combination of the two things enlivening, emboldening – I was just as infuriated by him as I was intrigued. If I allowed myself to become distracted from my mission – such as it was – whilst with him, I do not castigate myself for it. And Monroe, lost into the Spanish dust, was perhaps less of a problem than I had convinced myself when I was back in London.

And Piers? I imagined reading about his death. That was a nightmare I regularly had. I did not want to have to understand that in ink, in a newspaper or even a telegram. There was something defunct about the message process when it came to Piers. Either that or he would turn up at the apartment one day, one day when I was not there, and Bess would be alone to answer the door. They would rekindle their intense childish love for one another, and the universe would slip away.

It was a long time now since Piers had been gone. Since Monroe had snatched him from his own journey – the one where he got to make his *own* mistakes. I could not forgive him for that thievery. Taking him away from his family was secondary, and besides, the loss of family members was now Europe's natural colouring, it was the way of things. Bereavement before the war was a different animal. It was more a part of life than anything else. That is where the systems come from, the ways we interact formally. I remember those who came to the farm after my father's death. They came to put their pennies into the process, to help it move along, achieve its subsequent stages. Getting on with things was a respected phase of grief, just before the final phase when an old photo is put in a prominent place of the mantle shelf, or a locket is donned in memory of the departed. But now, with such all-encompassing wars, such losses were pandemics. The Great War should have been the war to end all wars. But twenty years later we put everyone through it all over again, with no apology, just Churchill's earnestness and tea-stains for stockings. Nostalgia was on tap within months of VE day.

And now Toledo was a bubble. The courtyard was a bubble. We looked down upon that broken fountain and nothing moved. The dead and the living were held tightly in amber, away around the world in unknowable places. Do you understand now? We are all insane in our obsessions with time. I hope you can break free from this. See the eternity of what has gone before, and be sure of what you see in front of you.

I know now that I was considering this during those days with Darabont. I could not formulate it. I could not verbalise it. Not then. But I was beginning to understand.

It seemed something about the past that was drifting around us there and then.

I asked Ernest of Monroe: "Was he your lover?"

It was a beautifully cool morning, the heat was just stirring up and a breeze came in through the open window. I was naked on the bed, Ernest smoking on a chair near the veranda reading a book on local flora.

He had awoken me that morning with coffee, whispering Baudelaire into my ear; "'Your eyes are tired, poor lover – close them, then; lie still, just as you are, in that casual pose where pleasure found you, took you, let you go! Down in the courtyard the fountain whispers on, never falling silent, day or night – an echo of ecstasy that was this evening's overwhelming gift of love'."

The place, my thoughts, was flooded with sun – the bustle of Toledo had been awake for some time. Across the rooftops could be seen the towers of the Alcazar. A church bell tolled in the dusty sky.

Ernest laughed to himself.

"Were Monroe and I lovers? No," he said. "Monroe is not queer. Not in the slightest. Unusual for one with such machismo, but some people won't even give it a shot."

I wondered if Ernest had tried to seduce Monroe, been rejected; there seemed to be some story there.

"And Millie?" I said.

"Ah yes, poor Millie."

"You knew of the rumours?"

"Rumours? Yes, I heard the rumours," said Darabont.

"They were true, you know," I said.

"I don't doubt it," said Darabont, drawing on a cigarette with those small pursed lips.

Later that day we went for a walk, sober, hungover.

"So, what did you think of Monroe?" I said.

"Now that is *some* question," Darabont said, gathering himself. "Well, you have the myth to deal with first. Irascible. Impossible. Dangerous. Genius. He's the real thing. I'd stake my life on that. People don't like him because he is not only completely lacking in pose, but he is deeply suspicious of anyone who possesses a pose of their own. You know, he used to live in Provence – he took his family there – they completely integrated with the local community. He became a fisherman. An excellent fisherman. His colloquial French was the stuff that a travel writer such as I could only dream of. Within months you'd think he was a native. Well, in Provence they have an ancient sport that you won't find in any other place. It is essentially water jousting. Yes, *water jousting*. So, the competitors are standing on a raised platform at the rear of a boat, with a wooden aegis for body protection and a large, heavy lance for their aggression. The boats charge towards each other and the winner is the man left standing. Of course, Ki, being athletic, being a powerful man, excelled at this test of courage, strength and daring. He became so accomplished at this feat that he joined the local team, who were the most successful team in their region. He won a substantial amount of prize money. And he put all of the money back into the local community."

"So, that is *some* of the myth," I said.

"Not at all," said Darabont. "This is all true. I am a journalist; you can trust me."

I leaned forward and lit Ernest's cigarette. The day was bright, oppressive; the streets were high, shadowed at the corners, dusty.

"You asked me what I think of Ki Monroe?" said Darabont. "I think he is very special. But not, perhaps, of *our* time."

Not of our time? Piers, it had to be said, had a flourish of classicism to his conversation after he became associated with Monroe. And it was a characteristic of Monroe's poetry that it was very traditional in metre, and iconoclastic in content.

"And Millie? She has been stolen from her life," Darabont said. "If we're speaking frankly; Millie Monroe was bowled-over in love with Latimer. That deep corrosive love that extinguishes all other light. Not many people experience this love. It is power beyond power. It can turn a flesh and blood human to mere solid stone. And in Millie's case it could not *be*. She loves Ki – I don't doubt that – but this was different. Like finding a missing piece of yourself, really."

Darabont stopped in the street and casually began examining a pair of canvas shoes in the window of a shop.

"We should go sailing," he said.

"We are a long way from the coast," I said.

"That we are," said Darabont, and he moved on.

"She didn't strike me as an adulteress, the few times I met her," I said.

"Millie is not an adulteress," said Darabont morosely. "Latimer was not an affair; it was her rightful place on this earth. If anything she was having the affair with Ki. And still is. And always will be. It is a matter of the heart, not of a marriage certificate. But the ties of our civilisation are made of stern stuff, Hal. They're getting sterner if anything. Ha! But Millie? She was so delicate by the time I met her, and yet one was of the feeling it was not her natural demeanour; that something had been spent of her."

Darabont marked the end of the conversation by ducking into a basement bar. I followed and soon we were several rounds in, lost in a sudoric smoky corner of clammy walls and stained sticky tables.

"What will you say you did during the war?" I asked.

Darabont laughed – his head rocked back.

"I have seen those posters," he said. "Kill Nazis or your children will be ashamed of you."

"It's a serious question."

"What a generation we're bringing up," said Darabont, and blew a long thin plume of smoke into the air.

"A generation who believe in action," I said. "I don't see what's so wrong with that. A generation who will make fun of Chamberlain."

"I'll say I did nothing in the war," Darabont said. His foot was up on the edge of the wooden bench, his hat pushed to the back of his head.

"Nothing?" I said.

"I'll say I went to America as a journalist. I'll say I saved some Jews. I'll say I hid in the Spanish hills. Hal, who the fuck is going to ask me a question like that?"

I felt sad all of a sudden.

"Anyway," Darabont went on. "It is my full intention to get to America."

"Intention? Why not just go? You have the money and the contacts."

"I just need a reason," Darabont said, and he and I looked at each other until we both began to laugh and Darabont slapped me across the back.

I stayed with Darabont again that night and the next day we spent in bed and half naked on the veranda.

"It is beautiful here," I said looking out to the courtyard, the broken fountain, and the rooftops and the deep blue sky.

"It is what it is," shrugged Darabont; "as is everywhere, I've found."

"I don't get to just relax very often," I said, closing my eyes, tilting my head, absorbing the morning sun.

"What is it you do, again?" said Darabont.

I looked at him.

"Why would you ask that now?"

"It just occurred to me I don't really know what you do. You've never told me the details."

I thought this over for a moment, our eyes locked.

"I teach," I said.

"Such an honourable profession," said Darabont, with an apparent lack of irony.

"What is it you teach?"

"Whatever needs to be learned," I said.

He laughed. I don't think he believed me, but he lived his life in a swirl of stories and counter stories. He saw no real harm in lies.

I expected him to grow tired of me within days, but we settled into a peculiar routine over the next few weeks where we would take breakfast together and then go for a walk around the city, pushing our way through its hush. We would drink in the afternoon, and then go back to the apartment to read and sleep before more drinks in the evening. It was easy, lucid, otherworldly. I began to forget to ask about Monroe, and Darabont never once asked about my brother, or the intentions I might have had on finding either of them. A city after a massacre is a peculiar place; it holds everything at arms-length. Things become flat; what once was beauteous now only hovers in the middle distance, unable to bring itself into focus. This was how Darabont talked about Toledo. And I had to be reminded of the history of the place. I was, dare I say it, *happy* with him. I did not love him, and he did not love me, but there was an equilibrium mirrored in the quiet opposites of the city of blood and fire in which we found each other.

But still I was there less than a month. I had my taste of another life, and I could feel Bess back in London, as if she had been sleeping in an adjacent room and now awoke. It is easy to understand the present, if you put your mind to it. And it is easy to understand the past, such is our arrogance in judgement. But it is not easy to understand the understanding of the present when looking back on it. I know now why I had such dedication to Bess. And I know I was sure of it at the time. But I do not know how I knew, or how I came to know. I am trying to explain my truth to you but there is a chance that I blind myself during the unveiling. An irony I'm sure you appreciate. It seems it is myself I understand least of all.

These faces that come back to me. Ernest Darabont. I almost fell off the edge of the earth because of him. God, I was almost relieved to discover a man like that. I considered staying in Toledo. I considered the eternity of truth. I considered the damnation of lies. It was possible that I could sink into another existence.

I told Darabont I had to leave, that I had family matters to attend to back in London.

"You have a family?" he said.

"Doesn't everybody?"

"No, not everybody."

"You don't even remember why I came here in the first place," I said.

Ernest lit a cigarette and dragged on it deeply. His eyes narrowed.

"I remember. I just didn't believe you," he said.

He got up and took his hat from the stand by the front door, gesturing me to follow him.

The cantina never altered, not a dusty glass out of place from one day to the next. The warmth was always the same; a dry pressing heat that only beer could upheave. Darabont introduced me to the others around the table, the regular faces, the ones I recognised from my first evening in Toledo.

"I have been telling these young boys what a unique place they find themselves in right now," Darabont said. "Spain, Nineteen Forty-Six. We have the burning buildings all around us, and beneath us, also."

I lit a cigarette and seated myself a little back from the table. The others, two young poets, a German, and a chubby English journalist acknowledged me with respect and looked at me attentively awaiting some reaction to Darabont's proclamation. But I said nothing, just crossed my legs and put my hat over my knee.

"You think Franco is here to protect the Church for the people?" Ernest said. "There was a time when religion was true. But not now. Religion *was* free and it *was* freedom. But not now."

For Darabont the medieval peasant, a creature built to work and worship, had been turned into a slave over the centuries. I was already becoming familiar with the current preoccupations of Ernest's intellect.

"Slavery," Darabont said, "was only truly exploited *after* the Enlightenment. It was an Enlightenment for those with the ability to exploit, and only those. The Fear of God became the fear of the Cloth. Why did Franco fight for the Church? Because his head is a graveyard of ideas. He is a symbol-reader like all of those anti-progressives. And there is no greater symbol for brutality and power than the shining gilt of Catholic unity. Do you think the Nationalists would have won if its ranks had been filled with poets? You need regressive intellects to win such wars. Which, of course, is no intellect at all."

They could speak this way here. The cantina was friendly to subversives. Not that these around the table were particularly subversive. They were artists, list-makers rather than trouble-makers. They dealt in abstracts not revolutions.

"You think art lost?" said one of the poets.

Darabont rolled a thought around in his mind and turned his glance in my direction. I huffed and looked over to the bar.

"They still serve beer here I take it?" I said. I was annoyed that Darabont was leading me on, and he knew that.

"Mr Buren," said Ernest, "this young poet is asking us a question."

"Me? I don't think he was asking me."

"I can ask *you*," said the poet, "if you like?"

I looked at each of the company in turn; the two poets young, pale, beaten by the light, the journo was stupefying in the heat, and Ernest was simply Ernest.

"Very well: I think art should pick its battles more carefully," I said. I looked at the blank faces, at Darabont's barely concealed wry smile, and he got up and went over to the bar.

I had already put my finger on the gross imperfections in

this picture. The two poets were laudanum addicts, and smiled gormlessly at me as they groped each other. I did not like the German with his permanent grin on his thick Prussian lips. And the overweight journalist never spoke, he just belched and sweated and folded tobacco clumsily into paper. The comfort I felt when lying in Darabont's bed was flipped over when I was in this place with these people. And my thoughts turned to Bess once more.

I leaned to Darabont and from behind my hand I said to him, "What are we doing here?"

"Refreshments," said Darabont. He always called them *refreshments*.

"You gave me the impression..." he cut me off with a glance.

"I gave no impressions," he said sharply. His eyes went hard and he straightened his back.

"Anybody know anything of Ki Monroe?" he said to the group. The mood changed.

"A sad story," said the English journalist. And he told me a largely accurate story of how Monroe fled with his family but returned for revenge. He knew nothing of Piers.

"Where is he now?"

"I've heard America," said one of the poets.

"I heard France," said the German.

"But he's not here," said Darabont. "And neither is your brother."

I had one beer and went for a walk. I liked to walk around the walls of the Alcazar; I liked to look closely at the brittle clay of the fortress, chipping away as the centuries faded before it.

I walked for hours that day. This was not happiness, after all; it was a filthy dream, complete with sweat and dirt and semen and the inevitable onrush of guilt. Oh, yes; I could feel *that* waiting around the corner.

"I haven't been completely straight with you," I said to Ernest the next morning. I was drinking burnt coffee, leaning by the veranda doorway. Darabont was still in bed, his eyes tight in the grip of a mild hangover.

"No?" Ernest smiled sarcastically. "I meet a man in a bar and it turns out all is not as it seems; now, *there* is a turn-up for the books. You're still leaving, I take it?"

"I'm not sure how I managed to be here," I said.

"You've been following me around for a couple of weeks now. I can see when the interest lags."

"I have to find Monroe," I said.

"You're not looking for anyone, Hal," said Darabont, sitting up, putting his long feet onto the cold tiles. "First you blamed the war. A man of your means and you pretended there was nothing you could do." He looked over to me. "Oh, don't look so surprised. You think I haven't heard of Harold Buren? Your wealth precedes you. You got as far as my charming smile and stopped dead in your tracks."

"I admit I've been distracted."

Darabont looked me up and down and smiled sarcastically. He nodded as he rubbed his forehead.

"Well, you're not the only one for whom the war was an excuse to sit back," he said.

I sipped my coffee. I wanted to argue, to stand up for myself, but with Darabont it was never really an option. The man could overpower with a glance – and on this occasion he had the added armoury of being pretty close to right.

"Would I know your brother?" said Darabont carefully walking over to the stove and pouring himself a coffee, lighting a cigarette along the way.

"If I'm honest, that doesn't interest me at the moment. I want Monroe."

Darabont looked cautiously at me.

I was beginning to see him for what he was; weak. But this realisation was on the edge of a blade. My feelings had not evaporated; but old ones had returned.

"I could tell you whether it's worth tracking him or not," he said.

"What do you mean by that?"

"There won't be much point in chasing all around Europe if I already know he's dead."

The sentence brought with it a crushing silence – even the muffled noise from outside seemed to subside.

Darabont looked at me straight. He could see he had said something hurtful. Darabont the elusive, the lost; if ever there was a man to warn against the life of the wanderer it would be Ernest Darabont.

"He's been missing for ten years," I said.

Whenever I admitted this to anyone the figure was hard to believe.

"The English are slow to worry," said Ernest.

I felt my face harden and I went out on to the veranda.

"I'm sorry," he called, and followed out after me into the lush morning sun. He put his hand gently on my shoulder.

"If you know where Monroe is, Ernest, you're going to have to tell me."

"I don't know where he is. But I'll do what I can to find out. It's been a long time, Hal."

I looked him in the eye. I knew how this was going to work out. Darabont knew exactly where Monroe was.

"I'm going back to London tonight. When you have information for me, call me on this number." I placed a small card on the veranda table. "Speak only to me." My voice was straight and subtle and cut through the morning heat. "This is very important, Ernest."

"Of course."

Darabont's voice was soft, vulnerable. I had not seen him look the way he looked at that moment. He looked old, worn-out.

Our eyes lingered on each other for a moment, a cool breeze coming between us both in the hot air of the courtyard.

"Come to America with me," said Darabont.

It surprised me this vulnerable rounded edge to him. I said nothing. I held a steady gaze.

"I'm sorry," he said.

I looked him over. He was a different creature, this Ernest. He was slight, submissive. This was a nuance of love, I thought; the different sides to people, getting into the skin of a lover. I did not care for it. It was too much, too close, too dark.

But it was now that I also saw my moment; the weighting in our connection had changed.

"The war is over," I said. "There are no more excuses. Find Monroe."

"Can't we talk about this?" he said.

"I have not said no to you, Ernest. But I need to do this."

Darabont nodded, smiled distantly, sadly.

The first thing I heard on arriving back to London was the news of Charlotte Latimer's suicide, overheard from two young women as I waited in a doorway for the rain to pass. She had stepped in front of a train in Richmond.

* * *

I remember Bess' face when I returned from Spain that time. She had her suspicions about my recent absence. I could see it in her eyes. But she did not ask.

"How was your business trip?" she said. She did not even look up from the book in her lap. That was an unusual welcome home. As if she was trapping my deceit in the stagnation of the pages before her. And for some time I put effort into not revealing what I had done, and what Darabont was now doing: searching for Monroe. But Bess continued to mourn in hope. And I continued to watch her.

And so began a further period of quiet domestic stasis. Bess said very little about Piers, but I could feel her preoccupied thoughts fill the air in the rooms she occupied. Darabont and I wrote back and fore to each other for the next few years. It seemed to calm me to know that Ernest was out there somewhere, looking for Monroe, waiting for him to show his face. I would some mornings go and stand in the rain on High Holborn opposite the offices of Monroe's publisher. At first I saw him in every shadow. As time went by it just became a habit to stand there. I had been afraid. But fear, when fed for long enough, becomes a comfort.

Darabont wrote eloquently, concisely, mixing his lack of information into anecdotes of his recent travels. He would relay amusing stories about characters in Toledo whom we had laughed about when we were together. He would inform me of the changes under Franco, the street subtleties, the calmness of the day and the silent terrors of the night. Darabont, of course, was wise and kept out of the struggles, kept his rhetoric toned down.

He wrote about the art he was collecting, his travels around Europe to the crushed cities and the relieved cities. Darabont,

287

like many art-dealers, was picking up valuable scraps from the abandoned Nazi table – neurotically gutsy for their great art as they were. He could pick up a Durer here, a Gierymski there, following the brutal path of the *Kunstschutz* officers, Hitler's private collators, his official thieves. *These people have been quite unrelenting in their requisitioning of the continent's art*, Darabont wrote. *What exactly they planned on doing with it all I could not guess, but from the Nazis I have met in the last few years they would probably use it all for kindling. A more roguish race of philistines you could never hope to meet.*

Darabont was no conservationist, of course. He could not help but inform me that he had made his fortune. *I have always found money quite easy to come by*, he wrote, *but from now on it can be a plaything*. I surmised that he had privately sold some Nazi plunder.

And then there was the letter about his visit to Mauthausen-Gusen. Like the rest of the world, I had observed the revelations of the Nazi war crimes with detached, confused, theatrical horror. Darabont had travelled to Gusen to verify a painting that had been found in the study of SS *Standartenführer* Franz Ziereis, the commandant of Mauthausen. Darabont described the painting in detail, with all the catchy superiority of his most popular books. But then he questioned. How did Ziereis look at this painting – not an original but a very good copy of Franz Ludwig Catel's *View from Ariccia Against the Sea* – as he sat at his desk going over the figures of cruelty on balance sheets? Did he look up at the landscape and wish he was there? What was the functioning of the man? Unutterable horrors under his command, and there was a subtle landscape above his desk. Of course, Hitler had been a painter – a failed one. Perhaps Ziereis was researching the starting point of a friendship with the *Fuhrer*. Darabont shuddered at the thought of it, and it came through his letter, through the ink. *Art used by evil*, he wrote.

Art; the only thing on God's great earth that cannot be evil. The only creation that cannot be used for murder or corruption. How can I go on after seeing the remnants of the human experience that I saw in the dirt of Mauthausen-Gusen? I suppose I go on because there is no alternative.

I replied to the letter: *and no news of Monroe?*

I was beginning to wonder if Monroe could be forgotten about, and then soon after him Piers could be mourned. I was drifting, just as Bess was. And then one day – it was a Tuesday – in *The Times* was published a poem titled 'To P____'. Monroe was the author. It came up from the page like a rising tide, with me bound to the immovable rocks.

I wrote a frantic telegram to Darabont in Toledo. But I did not know where he was. I ran to the store on the corner where I know Bess bought her newspapers and I bought them all and burned them in the park. Over and over in my mind kept turning the words: *she cannot see what I have seen.*

I went to Monroe's publishers and paced back and fore for some time on the opposite pavement, the rain dripping in strings from the brim of my hat. All the time I muttered to myself how Bess must not see that poem, must not be allowed to know that Monroe was still connected to Piers. What if he returned?

The day dragged on. I returned home. It was very late. Bess was asleep in the parlour with the gin bottle half empty at her elbow.

That night I did not sleep, but I went to see Matilda. I sat at her bedside in the blackness of the night as she slept. She seemed so small. The nurse, Maria, who lived in the house now as permanent care, assured me that she was medicated and would not wake. I watched her sleep, her chest rising and depressing, a slight wheeze to her breathing. Around her neck still was that Dragon's Eye pendant my father had given her. Our origins in one pip of diamond. She looked peaceful.

289

"She is quite content most of the time," Maria said when I asked. "She spends as much time as she can sitting in the garden looking over the chrysanthemum bushes. She loves those bushes."

"Please, don't mention to her that I came by," I said.

At some point that evening, sitting in the dark listening to Matilda's breathing, I had decided to go back to Spain. I knew that every morning from now on I would agonise over whether that would be the day that Monroe returned to our lives. His poem in *The Times*, it was the finger grab on the rim of his own tomb. I could sense his resurrection.

And then one morning a letter came from Darabont.

He had been in the United States and was planning on moving there. I could sense the tones of an altered affection. Darabont had fallen in love with someone else. Ernest had often spoken about America, and now he had substantial money he could live there in the comfort to which he aspired. *That* was the "reason" he had been looking for. He needed to be able not just to relax, but to relax with the elite. That was a straight delivery of ambitions; but something lay beneath the beautiful prose of his letter. America, it seemed, had *opened up for him*, *delighted* him, and *persuaded* him. I recognised the innuendo. I wrote back to him the same day instructing him to find Monroe. Darabont's response came from Harley, Massachusetts. He said that Monroe would be found now only by accident and that he himself was tired of putting his own body and mind in the pathway of such coincidences. It was upsetting to the balance of the cosmos. It was distracting. And he was sorry that he could not help.

And here, the only suitable symbol of the space that followed would be a blank page, the beautiful crisp whiteness of the waiting for the end of the world.

✳ ✳ ✳

God, how those years went by; with Bess and me living in the silence of that apartment.

And then two things happened on the same day. It was a wet April in 1950. I remember it so well as all of those days were as one up until that point, when everything changed. On the same morning I saw in a shop window near Russell Square, a new collection of poetry from Ki Monroe. It was titled *The Siege of the Alcazar*. And on getting home, I opened the mail to find a letter from Ernest. He had found the poet. The stasis of our lives ended that morning.

Ki Monroe was living on a small farm just outside of Setubal, on the coast of Portugal. The Unamuno villa. Darabont had returned there to research his opus on the peasants of Europe and to spend some time with those old cork farmers. They had remembered him, Darabont said in the letter, and they had fed him and put him up, just as they had all those years before. The decade had treated the farmers well, it seemed. And then one weekend Darabont drove to the coast to sleep in a hotel room with a real mattress and electricity, eat fish and drink wine, and he arrived in Setubal. He said he was in the town less than an hour, checked into a hotel and went for a walk along the quay and he could not believe his eyes to see a man who looked remarkably like Ki Monroe dragging netting in from a boat.

I approached the man, the letter went on, *with trepidation, I must admit. But in my life I have grown to embrace coincidence, not to be suspicious of it. I always wondered if one day you would find your target. I cannot be sure of the use of this information; but found him I have. He is a fisherman, a farmer, a family man, who wants nothing from anybody but to be left in peace. I saw no sign of your brother,*

291

*no sign of the ghost of your brother. I saw Monroe, I spoke
with him, I sat on the stone wall of the quay and ate mussels
with him for an hour. He has warm eyes now, Hal; I don't
know if you remember his eyes but they were never warm.
Part of me hopes that he can help you find your brother. Part
of me wishes you well. Part of me worries for him, Hal, as I
know that the kind of determination you possess is not the
kind that dies out with a whimper. If it is Monroe you still
want, in Setubal you will find him.*

I considered the letter. I considered Darabont's fears. I
considered the letter and I thought Darabont was wrong about
Monroe. He was a devil.

The night before I left for Portugal I dined as usual with Bess.

She moved more freely nowadays. She could be erratic but
her character was solid. She was clear of insanity. She was
clear of being pathetic. I had no idea of the effort she put into
the part she was playing. Her days were spent reading. I
believed her to be searching for Piers in the emerging poetry
of the world as it adjusted after the reality of war. Reading a
new poet in her search could lead to several months of reading
other writers suggested along the way, who had no connection
to her mythical Piers whatsoever. She drank too much, but she
knew it, and as long as she knew it she was confident it would
not kill her. And she was writing a little of her own poetry. It
was bad, and she recognised that too, but it was flexing
muscles she did not previously know she had. I noticed she
had been writing, and sometimes she mentioned a poem she
had been working on. I said nothing, dug no deeper, allowed
the moment its rarity of air. In her verse she was speaking to
Piers across the sadness of space.

I leaned across the dinner table and took her hand. She
smiled warmly at me with her full, delicate lips. I would find
Monroe. I would protect her.

✳ ✳ ✳

I remember so clearly the image of Ki Monroe in that tavern in that Portuguese village. He sat with two locals, their threadbare straw hats pulled close down to their glazed eyes, one picking at a stone in his boot with a fishing knife, the other hunched forward with his eyes fixed on his glass. Monroe too was drunk, and seemed to not care that his small audience was uninspired by his speeches.

"War, violence, cruelty," he said; "is nothing without language."

He slammed his drink down onto the table for emphasis, his eyes wide and glassy. "Without language pain is nothing. How much would it hurt if I pushed a dagger through the palm of your hand?" He pushed his fist to his chest and gave a mock grimace. "But how much would it hurt if I nailed your little Catholic body to a cross?" he took another large swig from his beer, and stood unsurely, his arms winding, his face glistening in the humidity.

The tavern was busy with conversation, with games of draughts and backgammon, with beer sloshing from mugs. It was late in the evening, much had been eaten and drunk, and the sinking sun across the veranda had turned a burnt golden. Everything in Setubal smelled of the sea, of fish and seaweed, of salt and grit. I had been there less than a day and I could feel my skin hardening on my face, building a crust of defence against the salt in the air.

"We're all fucked!" Monroe said in an exasperated tone, and puffing out his cheeks, he collapsed back into his chair. His company seemed to pay no attention. "I give up," he mouthed, and, pointing to the man digging at his boot, he said, "And you, my friend, are *beyond* help."

Since Monroe had made his home in Setubal he had become

a local notary, the eccentric foreigner who lived on the hill. The villagers had known Unamuno, and so knew the presence of a philosopher, knew the other-worldliness of the breed. They treated Unamuno like a Lord, and then Monroe, his adjutant as they would have it, as the regent. He was indulged, enjoyed, without suspicion. Melded with his adeptness at mixing with any culture, it made him something best described as a local celebrity, in the same way Euripides would have been to the Shepherds around his cave.

Bess had told me how they had walked down to the local pub near the Latimer cottage, the four of them, and Piers and Monroe had told stories, recited the classics, to an enraptured clientele of farmers, shop owners and alcoholics, the open fire crackling long into the night, pipe smoke spiralling, beer flowing. And he had jousted in the rivers of Provence. The man had no roots but the dirt beneath his feet.

"I am not making an argument – this is the way things are." Monroe sat forward, leaned across the table on his elbows. "Look at the madmen," he said. "Pound, Holderlin. Their sanity buried beneath the weight of their own poetic visions. Language has a connection to our pain that cannot be denied. Why is the ultimate so dark to us? Because we cannot understand God – it is our nature to be ignorant of him. So being closer to him is true agony. You write that first great poem and it's like the breaching of a hymen. *Bah!* Language is agony."

He growled that last line as if it was a call to arms.

Language is agony!

Monroe repeated the line and stood again, keeping his balance by pushing down on the table top. A few of the other locals looked at him as he growled and spat and bellowed – a few nodded sleepily – but they quickly returned to their drinks and games.

It was then, during this pause in the symposium, that I

noticed Monroe's eyes had set on me, the shadow-hidden figure at the far corner of the veranda, leaning against the banister, smoking slowly. The big man squinted into the dimness, waved smoke out his face.

"Who is that in the corner with those Saville Row slacks?" he called. "Who is it?" he called again, angrily. "Fucking spies. See how I go mad like Holderlin? Seeing spies like angels out of the corners of my eyes."

I stood, stepped on my cigarette butt and moved forward out of the shadow. I watched Monroe's face alter. His squint relaxed, and he straightened his pose. The big man looked smaller, tighter; his leathery features had become kiln-burnt, his hair was now just a horse-shoe crown of wet white wisp, his scalp was smooth and speckled.

I took a few more steps forward –the two of us now were but ten paces apart, one with loose shoulders, the other, Monroe, his shirt open, his brown skin flecked with silver hair. His eyes were pink, he stood with a slight inebriated stoop – at one point he even raised his hand to his eyebrows as if glaring into the far distance.

"*You?*" he said.

I lit another cigarette, straightened the brim of my hat.

"I expected something a little more profound from a bearer of the Divine language," I said, relaxed. I had waited a long time to play this role.

Monroe looked back to the spot where he had made the speech. He then looked me up and down. He laughed, and when he stopped, his mouth remained open.

"I don't know what to say," he said.

"You look well," I said, my tone making it clear I was lying.

"It's been a long hot day," said Monroe.

"Yes."

Monroe was still coming to terms with my appearance.

"You'll join us?" he said, gesturing to the table of empty tankards, carafes and well-fingered petiscos. His two companions looked at me and both offered the slightest gestures of welcome with their eyes.

Monroe had aged definitively. I examined him surreptitiously. He had been a heavy-set, brutish, powerful man, his athleticism a fluid aspect of his build. Now he looked wooden, as if he had crawled out of woodland; he was brittle, sinewy, oaky. He looked rough, hard-edged, but on the downward turn. He looked as though his vulnerability was closer to the surface than it had ever previously been.

"I have been looking for my brother," I said after we sat.

"I know why you're here," said Monroe, his face softening.

He found an empty tumbler, rubbed the rim of it with his sleeve, poured generously from a carafe of wine and pushed it in front of me.

"Drink," he said. "You're staying in Setubal?"

"I have a room in the hotel on the edge of town."

"Beira-mar? I know it very well." Monroe waved his hand wildly. "But that will not do. You will stay with us. I will hear of nothing else. Millie will be overjoyed. She misses the old London faces."

The old London faces. A sentence delivered with a weight that pulled down at Monroe's jaw.

"So tell me about the coincidences that brought you here," Monroe said.

"I've been looking for you," I said.

"Yes; but for all your strategies there were coincidences, right?"

I took a pause, took a light sip of wine. There had been a thousand nights where I acted out this scene where we finally met and discussed Piers – and it had always been this straight, this unclouded.

"I happened upon Ernest Darabont," I said.

"Of course you did," Monroe said with a wry smile. "And he happened upon me." He lit a cigarette. "It is a small world."

Monroe was a fighter – that much of him was not just myth; I had seen the fire in his eyes in the past. It was that moment the punch that had connected with Quimby came back to me. And the big man was currently sizing up the situation, gauging the levels of hostility, the avenues for untruths.

"I want to know where Piers is," I said.

The idea was to cut him short, not allow him time to regroup and dazzle. And this was a man made up of less than he once was, perhaps created solidly from scar-tissue and a fraught ability to hold on.

"I haven't seen Piers in many years, Hal."

"So you can't tell me where he is?"

"No."

"Can you tell me where you last saw him?"

Monroe's eyes softened, his face sunk.

"We should talk about this tomorrow – it's not a conversation for here," said Monroe.

Music started off somewhere, a fiddle, a guitar, some gypsy jazz, and people began to stand and clap and beer sloshed again and wine was knocked over. A young girl danced passed. Monroe poured more wine into both of our glasses.

"What you were saying earlier," I said. "It interests me."

He leaned in to me, his eyes heavy.

"You want to know about language? It won't make you rich," he said.

"I'm already rich," I said.

"You don't have to worry about reaching God in that case; he'll come to *you*."

I could see that this old, tired Monroe was a man with vast

battle-lines; deep battle-lines. And he knew how to pick his enemies.

We sat for a short while saying nothing; the dancing, the cheering, the playing circling us. After a while, and a few more measures of wine, Monroe stood.

"You should come see Millie. She's always awake, so it's not too late," he said, and began the long search for his hat.

Millie Monroe had changed also. She was extremely beautiful; dark, intense eyes, sometimes a drooping, shy way about her, almost as if the weight of her thoughts, behind those dark eyes, was too much for her skeleton. Now, framed by the craggy doorway of their Unamuno place out in the hills above Setubal, she seemed weak, tempered, surrendered perhaps. Someone else not of her own time. I pondered as we approached, hit by the booze, kicking our feet through the dust of the long dirt road swathed in the black of the night.

"It is so nice to see a face from those days," she said, wrapping her arms around my arm and leading me into the cottage. It was peculiar how quiescent she was at my turning up, but I noticed the glances she was giving her husband – glances Monroe was too drunk to register. They were quietly nervous, they were questioning, abrupt, secretive. What is *he* doing here? But her affection was genuine, I thought. She sat me down at the large kitchen table and cut me some bread.

"Soak up some of that awful booze," she said. She spoke softly but with that warm straight familiar language.

Monroe was outside pissing into a bush.

"I feel I should apologise for turning up like this," I said. "I am booked into a hotel in town. But Ki insisted I come and see you, and stay here."

"Don't worry, Hal; it's not unusual for my husband to come home with a surprise."

Millie smiled coldly.

Monroe stumbled in through the kitchen door, his shoes clodding along the floorboards. A heavy silence came with him.

He sat next to me and helped himself to a fistful of bread.

"It's not exactly the Ritz," said Monroe. "Please, accept my apologies."

I looked around the kitchen; grey, dark, damp. This was more austere than I had even imagined the Latimer farmhouse those many years before. And here I realised that Monroe was not penniless – or at least that was not the reason for the style in which he forced his family to exist – but rather he was compelled by something grave within him to be as naked as possible. If I lived beneath my wealth, Monroe lived in squalor because it was what he stood for: the beauty of human thought in the midst of the degradation of the physical existence. He was forcing it. He was forcing everything.

"How long have you been here?" I said.

Monroe and Millie looked at each other.

"Hal is looking for his brother," said Monroe.

Millie said nothing, she did not move from her standing spot by the stove.

"I've been looking for you both," I said.

"I said we haven't seen him," said Monroe.

"But he followed you to Spain, didn't he?" I said.

Millie's eyes began to betray the edge of fear and she looked away from me. Monroe stopped chewing the bread in his mouth, took it out with his fingers and threw it on the floor. I looked at his burned, leathery face, watched it soften and lighten, watched the big man's eyes tingle with moisture.

"I loved your brother, Hal, as if he was my own," said Monroe.

Millie left the room.

"I want to know what happened," I said.

"Tomorrow," said Monroe, and he stood steadily.

"Now," I said.

Millie and Ki looked at each.

Something seemed to return to him in light of my forcefulness; his ruddiness washed out, much of the drunkenness went with it.

And in that dank joyless kitchen the Monroes revealed everything. They revealed truth through a fog of lies. The poet told me that Piers had died, but he would not tell me that it was he who killed him. In my description in these pages I gave the poet the benefit of the doubt. But there is a version where he takes aim at my brother while my brother tries to understand the cruel coincidence of the two of them coming across each other in the way that they did, divided and in opposition. In this version Monroe takes but a second to see his cosmic redemption in the slaying of my brother, and he takes the chance offered him. Everything is straightened out with this sacrifice and at the same instant God is insulted. How very poetic.

But they could have lied entirely – I could not blame Millie for this; she was allowed to defend her husband, and possibly to only believe his story in the first place. But they did not seem like a couple who could lie to each other. Not after everything they had been through together. The truth must have been the bond through all that. They simply must have promised the truth.

When they told me the story of Toledo, Millie looked ashen and regretful. When Monroe told me how Piers had met his end, Millie cried and dabbed at her nose and eyes with a kerchief. It was a brutal skirmish with few survivors, was how Monroe told it. How did they end up on opposing sides? It was God's will. I knew Monroe had killed my brother. I knew Monroe regretted only that he felt he was forced to.

I asked Monroe if Piers suffered. It was a question for the judges in heaven to hold on to. I did not care if Monroe *thought* he suffered. Of course he suffered. Monroe *needed* him to suffer.

"Everybody suffered that day," he said.

I gave him credit for sticking to his philosophy in that instance. If he had been cowardly with a gun in his hand and my brother before him, he was being recklessly brave now.

As for me, what had my reaction been to confirmation that Piers was dead? The active part of me was engaged with his killer. An inactive part was holding Bess close to me and absorbing her tears. What an almighty flood would that have been. The unloading of many years' grief; a torrent, an avalanche fluming and rolling. The human body can only push out so much without exploding. The full collapse, the unbridled giving up.

"Why did you not come to me?" I said. "If not to me, to his wife? I thought Bess was your friend?"

Monroe said nothing because I suppose he could not answer. He could not say he was a coward.

"This has not been easy," said Millie.

"Is it easier now?" I said, the first click of anger to my voice.

"We were – *are* – ashamed," said Monroe. "We are ashamed of what happened, and ashamed of our inaction. Our inaction is a terrible thing."

Monroe had lost his oaky, earthen colourings when he told the story; he was white, perspiring, chain-smoking, only occasionally glancing up from his coffee cup.

"He died in your arms?" I said.

Monroe nodded and dropped his head into his hand, dragging onto the cigarette in his other.

"We are both so sorry, Hal," said Millie.

I said nothing.

"I didn't know what to say," said Monroe.

"*We* didn't know what to say," said Millie.

"We had our own grief to deal with," said Monroe. "You don't know what war is like. You don't know what we went through as a family back then."

I didn't like the waves of pleading that came from the poet. I was more comfortable with him as a foe, not as a victim.

"It seems there is much I do not know," I said. "About very many things."

How do I try and understand the blankness in this situation? If I felt nothing it was a profound rattling of nothingness. It was the precise nothingness one associates with the darkest recesses of space. Unimaginable nothingness.

I was calm to my viewers. It may have been beginning to unsettle the two of them. I had had time to prepare for this moment, I suppose.

"Where is he buried?" I asked.

"He was buried on that hillside, with another twenty or so. They were unmarked," said Monroe.

I thought of Bess; poor beautiful Bess. The reality of Piers' death could destroy her. Or it could set her free. Would that be the worst outcome of all? She would be initially burned to the ground and then she would emerge anew, stronger and brighter than before.

"Not a day has gone by when I haven't written a letter only to tear it up," said Monroe.

"You've been back to London since the war."

Monroe looked surprised at the suggestion. He looked at Millie and then back to me.

"No," he said. "Not once."

"Your book?"

"The manuscript was sent from here. I have not even been out of Portugal in maybe ten years." Monroe looked at Millie for confirmation of the date.

I took a mouthful of coffee and rolled it around my mouth. The Monroes seemed uneasy at my lack of response.

"How *is* Bess?" said Millie. "I miss her."

I felt a dark thud to my centre at the mention of her name.

"As far as I know she has gotten on with her life," I said. "She moved back up north to be with her family when the war began." I stood. "You should forget about Bess."

I motioned to leave, but Millie began to weep.

"How can we just forget?" she said.

"I've heard what I came for. Leave it at that," I said and I picked up my hat and steadily walked out the door.

＊ ＊ ＊

By the time I returned to the Biera-Mar on the far edge of Setubal the sun had come up. I spent some time watching the white-crested waves overrun each other up to the rocks like serpents. Something felt complete, but, also, something did not. My preoccupation with Ki Monroe was over, but there was an edge to that thought – a sharp edge – that prevented me from leaving the Portuguese town immediately. Something lingered. Had I made myself clear when I told the Monroes to stay clear of Bess? It was very important that they understood.

There was a coldness to my core, one that continued to echo that Bess could not know the truth about what happened to Piers, that he died in the dirt. She could not know that he went to Spain to find his poetry and ended up fighting someone else's war. He found the dirt of the Homeric heroes and he suffered in it.

Bess was built up by the sum of her memories of Piers and the promise of his return. As the years passed the memories rewrote themselves to fit her current poise, the promise became a part of her make-up; internal rather than external. But in that morning at the hotel, I could only know that giving this news to Bess would take her away from me. I would have failed in my duty to protect her.

I thought of my father a great deal that morning. The anger of Matilda that should have been sorrow. I could not see her lie to the world again about someone I loved. Piers deserved better than her bile. But in there somewhere also – I could feel it now – was my own anger. Perhaps it had filtered down from Matilda, a figure burned black amidst the dust of the veldt in her mourning dress, but it was there. Matilda must have truly loved those people who turned her mad.

In that golden morning light I became, for the first time,

angry at my father's death. Was my anger a pose? Mimicry? Was I even angry or was I convincing myself of it years later? So I did not love my father, is that it? I was playing at sorrow. And the sorrow, if it was there at all, was for my own loneliness; not for the tragedy of my father's demise. How horrible it must have been to feel that tight fist grip the heart, to fall all that way from the saddle into the puddle and the dirt. How terrible it must have been to be so alone in the vast burnt browns of the veldt, to try and hold on to each breath, to use up vital energy in lifting the nose and mouth out of the few inches of dirty water.

Matilda did not cry when John Buren died. She went out into the veldt with Belky and returned without a tear. The next day she emerged and she was all in black, and her face was raw. And she would not speak.

This was my introduction to grief. The dead were hated. Or, like Douglass Karlchild, something to be ashamed of, something to be kept hidden and never spoken about. I did not want that for Piers. I did not want that for Bess. The living became crippled by hatred. I did not want to live in that world.

At around lunchtime I took a drink in a tavern and then went for a walk along the quayside, the salt air bristling in my nostrils. The place was busy with life; men, grizzled, roll-ups between rough lips, fishing nets tossed between large rough hands. The sun was high, heavy, but the ocean gave an openness to what in La Mancha would have been a closed killer of a heat.

Although conspicuous in my hat and white flannels, few of the locals paid me any attention, some tilting their heads from bending over to tend their nets, squinting at me and then returning to their chores.

At the far end of the harbour I could see Monroe, tossing heavy bags into a small engine-powered fishing boat. He looked lively, athletic, in cut-off denim shorts, a tatty straw hat covering his balding head, his naked torso easily carved, deep mahogany, the white wisps of hair like strands of wire-wool on his chest. I watched him for a moment, this impressive man – this devil manipulator – in his middle years, powerful still in the daylight, moving like a machine, muscles moving under the brown skin like cogs and pistons as he moved his paraphernalia from the quayside to the boat.

I walked toward him. As I got closer, Monroe straightened up, saw me and waited, slanted, for my arrival.

"Going fishing?" I said.

Monroe's chin lowered, he rolled his shoulders.

"Every day," he said.

He squinted into the sun, moved his hat and scratched his head with the same hand, replaced the hat.

"You have a lot of equipment," I said.

"It all has a purpose."

"Do you have much success?"

"A man cannot live on vegetables alone," said Monroe. He gave a disarmed smile. "Jump in," he said.

I looked down at the boat. It looked uncertain, uneven angles and depressed wood. At the head was a somewhat dilapidated wheelhouse, coloured in red, white and blue hoops, the paint peeling from the door. The masthead appeared to have once had a purpose, but now it was naked, and stunted. And I could see no buoys or rubber rings.

"It's perfectly safe," said Monroe, obviously recognising the look in my pose. "You swim, don't you?"

"I'm not really dressed for it."

Monroe laughed a coarse free laugh and climbed in, arranging his gear.

"There is no uniform for this."

I stepped awkwardly on.

306

I could not judge Monroe's tone, his mood. He seemed relaxed, open, but there was also something embarrassed about him. He was coy, shamed – I could understand this. He was feeling relieved of the burden of his secret. People react differently to the release of pressures. Monroe was filling his lungs, presenting his face to the life-giving sunshine.

But I could still see Mephistopheles where he stood, also.

Monroe the trickster, like the devil liar. Piers had been killed, yes. But struck down on a hillside? I only had Monroe's word for that. And what could have happened to make Monroe fire that fatal shot himself? Piers was a brother to them all, was he? Only a brother to Millie the adulteress? Only a brother to Monroe? You have to understand the coruscation of these ideas as they came to me that day. If I had gone to Setubal with a dark purpose, it was vague, unformed – but it was lingering enough to have its moment in that boat. My mouth was drying, my shoulders tightening. I was there, and Monroe was there, where we stood, but there was something inter-dimensional about it, too; as if we could leave the realm of the Real at any moment and continue our talk in a mythological realm, where only the Oversouls existed, where only destiny reacted to actions. We were both at the tip of a curtain, and we were both now prepared to step behind.

As the engine rattled and choked into life, a black cough of smoke coming from the hull-hatch where the dragon-like engine lay, Monroe leaned his head out of the rickety door of the wheelhouse and said, "I hope you don't have any plans this afternoon; I go quite far out and don't come back until late. Now is your last chance to jump ship."

I took a beat and calmly replied, "No, that's quite all right. This feels quite right to me."

Monroe nodded – solemnly, I thought – and within a minute the boat had set off.

I was surprised how quickly the boat pushed through the water – it did not glide but pushed through the ocean; I could feel the wheezing effort of the machinery as it moved the boat forward.

The traffic in the bay was quite heavy, Monroe waved to other fishermen from behind the wheel, some of them shouted calls in Portuguese at him, smiles on their rough faces, waving back.

I leaned on the door frame of the wheelhouse.

"You say you go quite far out," I said over the grumble of the engine-noise.

"Well, these others do this for a living. I do it simply to put food on the table. I don't like to fish their waters. There is beer in one of those duffle bags I brought on board. I made it myself. Fetch us a couple, would you?"

The sun was intense but the breeze of movement made the conditions perfect, the light reflecting off the glass panes of the ocean. I sat on the bench at the rear of the boat, my hat pulled down, the beer sharp and unpleasant but cold. After several hours I felt the boat slow down to a stop, the engine cut out and Monroe emerged from the wheelhouse, a large grin on his face.

"We're here," he said, and set about busying himself with equipment.

"What is it I can do?" I said.

"Have you come to fish?" said Monroe.

"I don't know why I've come."

Monroe stopped what he was doing, straightened, a net between his fists, his physique silhouetted by the sun.

"I thought we could make peace," I said.

"We are not at war," said Monroe.

I put down the beer.

Monroe began to run the net through his hands, feeding it swiftly from one through the other.

"I have to live on with my brother's foolishness confirmed," I said, but Monroe could detect the disloyalty in my voice.

"He was not a fool, Hal," said Monroe. "His death was a tragedy, yes, but not foolish."

He began to arrange some equipment on the side of the boat. He tossed the net, unravelled, over the side into the water; and he laid out the components of an old rusted rod, a diver's knife, some line, other tools that I could not identify. I felt easier when Monroe's attention was on the fishing.

"Is that how you feel, Hal? You feel he was foolish?"

"I am sorry he is dead," I said, without emotion.

"You are sorry he is dead."

Monroe repeated the words slowly, kneeling now, with his back to me as he sawed the line with the diver's knife.

He stopped.

"I have to tell you, Hal; that I am going to go and see Bess."

I let the words soak in like blood into fabric, a dot of sound spreading outwards throughout me.

"I asked you not to do that," I said.

"And Millie has been talking me out of it for some years now. But seeing you I realise that this is never going to go away. It all needs to end. I have been a coward."

"Bess needs to be safe."

"Do you not think she's safe?" said Monroe, half turning his head to me.

"I think she *can* be kept from danger," I said.

Monroe sawed heftily at the cord.

"And you're the one to protect her, I suppose?"

Monroe was looking for an ending. And there lay his redemption, no matter what the ending looked like. It was his opening to God. His heroic climax. This quest for meaning in life would go on for him – through his grievous errors and his attempt at recompense – it would go on for him until everything was destroyed.

"Is it true your mother used to call you the Stonecutter?"

he said, turned away from me once more. "Piers told me she used to call you the Stonecutter."

"He told you that?"

"We laughed about it. That's quite a title for a child." Monroe crouched down onto his knees and began to unravel more fishing line from a large metal box. "We were not laughing *at* you, you understand; but the notion of being unkind enough to give that label to a child. It is from the Brothers Grimm, of course; but it has its origins in the East. Did you know that? The lowly Stonecutter who tries to rise above his station and become something he is not. Always on the outside looking in, covetous and plotting. It doesn't work out well for the Stonecutter, needless to say."

Monroe cut the line, held it in both hands and looked out to the endless desert of the ocean.

"I don't think Matilda meant it quite like that," I said.

"That doesn't mean it wasn't cruel," said Monroe.

"I can't tell you how disappointed I would be if you sought out Bess," I said, but it must have been under my breath because Monroe said, "What?"

I stood and slowly approached Monroe. I stood over him. Monroe looked up to me. I felt clean now, open and as honest as the wind.

"I can't have you telling Bess that Piers is dead," I said.

"I know, Hal," said Monroe.

Calmly, silently, I picked the diver's knife from the bench and held it in front of Monroe's face as if trying to decide what to do with it. Monroe showed nothing in his eyes. He did not move. And, putting one hand on Monroe's shoulder, I pushed the knife into the poet's neck, once, twice, three, four times. The blood, as if released from a tap, came down and out in scarlet ribbons. Monroe made no noise, his eyes did not change, and I followed him as he fell onto his back, his one hand trying to stop the flow of blood, the other reaching out, reaching, reaching. I kneeled at his side – his eyes were bright with fear now – and I watched him die – as Monroe had watched Piers die.

The boat bobbed, the water lapped at the hull, I sat on the floor looking at the blood, the body. He lay there like a fallen Titan. There was a soft serenity in the air, like a thousand years had passed away in my arms. I drank another beer and stayed there for a couple of hours, maybe more.

The sun flooded down upon the deck. I was crimson from my chest down to the lap of my flannel trousers. I looked down at myself and tutted, I remember – a lulled domestic tut.

I stripped naked and, looking around for any sign of other boats, wrapped the garments around a full bottle of beer with fishing line for weight and threw them overboard. There were spare clothes of Monroe's in one of the bags. I then wrapped the drained corpse in yards of plastic sheeting that I found in the hull, tied the ends with fishing line, weighted it with various heavy paraphernalia at hand, and lifted Monroe over the side and into the sea. I watched him disappear into the swallowing blueness.

I then spent hours naked on my knees scrubbing everything I could get at; my chest pounding, the sweat streaming from my brow. When I was done I packed everything up just as Monroe would have done, dressed myself in the poet's spare clothes, and sat back on the deck. I dried quickly in daylight, and drank another beer waiting for the sun to go down.

After sunset, I waited a little longer, estimating it to be around one a.m. before turning on the wheelhouse light and starting up the boat. I could not figure the controls, and could only operate it as I basically understood an automobile to operate and so the journey back to land was perilously slow – perhaps even suspiciously slow had anyone come across me that night.

On arrival – the harbour was deserted – I slowly and silently unloaded the equipment into the back of Monroe's truck. I hoped it would have the look of peace and normalcy. I wanted Monroe to have vanished, just as Piers had done.

I made it back to the Beira-Mar hours later after many detours through backstreets and alleyways to avoid running into anyone. I undressed, poured myself a whiskey and took a seat by the bed. I could see the sun was poking over the horizon through the window of my room. My hands were shaking, I noticed for the first time. And now I was safe, now I was still, I began to weep. I wept for Piers and for Bess, and for sad Matilda, for Millie and her fatherless girls. But I did not weep for Monroe, and I did not weep for myself.

What is one murder in this Century of Blood?

You may be shocked at this point, to have read of my sin. But there is a context to all of this, a tapestry of which it is a part. It is now a hidden legend, swamped in the age of massacre. Statistics do no shed tears. And I have lived my penance, so it's best not to read on expecting line after line of regret and guilt and the begging for forgiveness. My life has been a wasted opportunity by most measurements. This testament, if it is anything, is an attempt to assist you in not wasting yours.

The worst of my actions on that boat seems to be that it was all so long ago it has proved to really not have mattered at all. You could even argue it did some good. If it protected Bess, it protected me also. But I know that Monroe's family were set free, if you'd be happy putting it in such dramatic terms. I kept a close eye on them. His daughters have done well for themselves. Lord knows what would have become of them had they remained dragged around by the shadows of their cruel and nomadic father. I set them free. Yes.

But we must not forget the blood. I slept in it for decades, a soaking blanket of sin. I thought about the flat nature of my century, and now I realise the peaked landscape of yours to come. It all comes down to death, and the way that death enters a room – with a flourish or with modesty.

Modesty, of course, is functional – the Victorians knew this better than anyone, that great epoch of achievement through poise. *Application* was the byword for that century. See how the sciences unfolded, how they inflated. What an exciting time. They taught us, in many ways, how to mythologise, how to create poise as an addendum to achievement. This is so very important if achievement is to last. As Lytton Strachey said of

Florence Nightingale: *fact was not as facile fancy painted her*. You see, *thought*, an *idea*, is not enough. It needs to be delivered dressed for maximum impact. And in there too we need our heroes. It was not propaganda – although it may have well become that by the time I was walking the earth. I am saying that my century had been in preparation for some time. It was a signed contract that blood would flow, signed by the ancestors of us all. But I believe it was the breaking of the back, and your time, your era, will be one of relief, of goodness and virtue. But you have the wasteland to build upon. We? We had the megalith, the monstrosity of Victorian achievement to unpick. And we did it with bombs and gas chambers.

It was the simplifying of genius that bedevilled the following era, of course. The last great age of monarchical overrule in Europe, and when it crumbled it brought with it two things that bypassed the age of the sword – industrial death and the coldness of it. The Germans developed the gas chamber because they did not want to waste bullets. Cardinal Manning wrote that when he was a child his brother told him that God had a book and in it He wrote down everything everybody did wrong. Well, now Manning was a medieval romantic planted into the exact span of the Victorian era, and in the era after him, my time, it was the Devil who had the book, and in it were the tattooed numbers of the innocent. Genocide had happened before – it was common. But not in the wake of such enlightenment. That is what we could not understand, what we still cannot understand. The Germans gave up on the bloodlust; there were greater goals. The goal was the annihilation of enlightenment.

Bombs – they are the other things. Of course bombs cause bloodiness, but they also deny humanity. People become offal when a bomb does its best work. There is no face or fingers to hold on to. And the gas chamber dead could have been sleeping. My century decided to bypass the vital brutality of death, and turn it into a process. And not like religion had done – making it a doorway to a further phase. Death was now vast, and the people went with the flick of a switch. When I killed Monroe at least I gave it my all, I gave it my mind, and I allowed it to affect me. I looked into his eyes and I saw the blood spill out. It was the death of a human, not the crossing out of a digit. And there was no metaphor – it was *not* the dimming of a light. It was the most human of actions. I gave a soul to this soulless age. I honoured him with this execution. He deserved the deed in all its form.

But for this, my reasoning took time. I returned to London slowly, and from there returned to life with a similar distrusting pace. I needed time to figure out exactly what it was I had done and why I had done it. I needed to align the deed with the wayward nature of the road ahead. It was now I began to understand history, now that I began to understand my time, my era, and yours too. I realised what Nazism was. It was to replace the Devil, who so many – probably you among them – no longer believe in. The Nazis could not and cannot be disputed. In England, Napoleon Bonaparte is still regarded as a villain, but in France he is a complex and championed figure. I suppose I am trying to say that one man's enemy is another man's friend. The Nazis swept all of that aside. We had evil back in our lives, and it has been a gift to every generation since. Knowing evil is an imperative human facet, a part of the DNA. We *must* in order to live. What did Bess know when she looked at me?

When I finally did return to her, I must have looked a different man.

She was sitting by the fireplace with a book in her lap. She smiled quietly at my appearance, before the smile dropped and her eyes became concerned. I was pale, and unshaven, and my eyes had sunk and darkened. She was about to stand and greet me but she said, "Are you okay; you look unwell?"

I looked down at her, walked directly to the drinks cabinet and poured myself a large scotch.

She stood, slowly, unfolding herself from the seat.

"What has happened?" she said.

I turned to her.

"What has happened?" she repeated.

Where to start? The flippancy of the thought, swimming through Bess' most generous gaze, relaxed me a little.

"Why don't you sit down and I'll run you a hot bath?"

I swallowed the whiskey like it was water. I had been back in England a week, at Claypole, in an attic room, without the knowledge of anyone in the house. I looked down at Bess; she was like a child, her eyes moist and longing.

"I feel rotten," I said.

I wanted to explain the truth to her. The pressure to unveil everything to Bess had never been so strong. And had I had more energy I may have done so. I may have melted like candlewax to a hot puddle at her feet.

"I will call a doctor," she said.

"No."

Bess waited, said nothing.

"I do not need a doctor," I said. "I need a rest."

"You work too hard."

"It is not work."

"Then what is it?"

The silence hung between us in the air.

"Tell me," Bess said.

She stepped closer and put her cold soft fingers against my cheek. I closed my eyes at the touch. So gentle, so innocent. It was worth everything.

"What is it that troubles you?"

I looked at her, her clear blue eyes, the lightest of freckles across the bridge of her nose and under her eyes.

"How about you run me that bath?" I said.

She smiled up to me. The air seemed to lighten.

"You do *too* much for me," she said.

She placed her small pale palm on my breast.

I wanted to tell her. I wanted to unleash the flood of lies. You have to believe me when I write that. But I knew I would never see her again if I told her the truth now.

She made to walk away.

"Wait," I said. "There is something."

Bess turned at the doorway.

"What is it?" she said.

"I am leaving," I said. I had thought about little else in the week I had been back.

"What do you mean?"

"I want you to have this apartment. But we should have our space."

Having her near was fuel to my sedate ways, but I could see a time when I would crack and it would all come forward from me. I needed to be prepared to see her; I needed to be packed, solid, rehearsed. At least for the time being.

Bess looked wounded.

"I don't know if we're going to ever find Piers," I said. "He has made a good job of covering his tracks. And I think we should begin, slowly, to restart our lives."

I had practised the speech but it remained worthless, even to the lips that uttered it.

Bess moved back into the room a few steps.

"What has brought this on?" she said.

"I have been thinking about it for some time."

"And you have just made the decision. You didn't think it may be worth talking to me about?"

317

"I didn't want to fight."

"Is that what we do?"

"I mean I've made my decision."

Bess said nothing, gathered her thoughts.

"Where will you go?" she said.

"Near," I said, and offered a conciliatory smile.

I needed to be alone to allow the lies to eat into me, for them to make their carnivorous home, without danger of being witnessed. Where did I go? To my *penance*, of course: to Claypole.

THE STONECUTTER

✷ ✷ ✷

June the twelfth. 'Fifty-six or 'fifty-seven. It's not important to be specific. Bess Buren's birthday. That is the scene.

I held the note, written in Bess' hand, picked from the pile of bills and notices on the bureau in the hallway. I had been in the States on business for several weeks. And I was between housekeepers, between routines, between many things. The note said simply, BIRTHDAY CELEBRATION, MY CASTLE, OF COURSE, 8pm, BRING GIN.

The taxi driver, who had brought in my bags and placed them in the hallway, was paid and walked out into the heavy dark rain. Still holding the note, I placed my attaché case on the floor at the bottom of the stairs, and hung up my hat and overcoat. I looked at myself in the mirror on the wall, the brass frame making me look like a tired, aging and wet portrait. It was not a confident face, the one I saw; it was the face of an animal that had survived an encounter. Weeks of conferences and meetings in New York, dallying with a mixture of the swashbuckling and the pragmatic – the new breed of American money man. If I was beginning to like their style it was markedly down to their progressive understanding of the bold possibilities of capitalism. This was before the outer-reaches of this philosophy – the greenery of greed – corrupted everything and started their decline. But I had been spending much time there in recent years, and yes, I was considering leaving Claypole and relocating to a property not too far from Darabont, whose friendship I had regained, as well as that of his lover, a Hyannis Port trust funder with a striking sense of both humour and money. Life, to get to the point, had not ceased. It had kept involving me in its chapters.

I heard footsteps and from the top of the stairs I saw Matilda's nurse, Maria. She had been a loyal servant to

Matilda's needs during these years. And her skin had hardened much like her heart must have done. She was attractive, had a curved warm way about her. And she emanated simplicity, dutiful, relaxed control. She was as rare a woman to me as she was quietly valued.

"Mr Buren, we weren't expecting you back quite so soon."

"How is she?" I said. "Can I see her?"

"She is sleeping but I don't see why not."

Matilda always looked at perfect peace when she slept. She lay on her back, her chest rising and falling.

"Don't you envy her that dream world?" Maria said at my arm in the doorway.

"Could you run me a bath?" I said.

I did not want to think about dream worlds at that moment.

I sat with Matilda for a while. She stirred and looked at me, a smile emerged on her face.

"You're home," she said.

"I'm sorry I was away for so long."

She slowly raised her thin arm up to my face and ran her thumb across my cheek, gently, with a wide warm grin.

"My darling, Piers," she said. "You have grown up to be such a handsome man."

I said nothing. She often drifted into a delirium. I stood slowly and pulled the blanket up to her throat and she went back to sleep.

As I walked up the next flight of stairs to take my bath I met Maria at the top.

"Could I ask something of you?" I said.

"Of course."

"I have a party to go to. I'll need a fresh bottle of Tanqueray and some flowers. Some very expensive flowers."

"I'll go and get some."

I took the bath and then dressed in a tuxedo. When Maria

returned with the wares I was walking around the garden under the protection of an umbrella, inspecting my drowning chrysanthemums. I saw Maria at the patio doors holding the bags up for my inspection and approval, like a weightlifter with dumbbells.

"You didn't have any plans for tonight, did you?" I asked her on stepping inside, shaking the umbrella out the door.

"No, Mr Buren."

"Good. I wouldn't want to inconvenience you."

"Not to worry on that front, Mr Buren."

I inspected the bouquet of flowers. Dragon lilies.

"Very good," I said.

"It is Mrs Buren's birthday?" said Maria.

"It is," I said.

"Wish her many happy returns from me," said Maria.

I looked her over. I noticed the change in Maria's stance; it drew back from informalities.

"She hasn't been here during my absence has she?"

"Bess? No, sir."

"You're certain of that?"

"Absolutely."

I straightened.

"Good. That is good. For everyone."

I brushed my hand through the greenery of the stems of the dragon lilies.

"May I say you look the perfect gentleman," said Maria, but there was a nervous edge to the delivery now.

"Thank you," I said. "I want you to relax tonight. Regard it as a night off. But I need you here."

Maria nodded, her eyes wide and round.

"Maybe this weekend we'll go somewhere nice," I said. "To the beach, perhaps."

Maria nodded again, gave me that awkward smile of hers,

and her shoulders relaxed. She was a good person, Maria. It was through her, as a matter of fact, that I was introduced to Claus. I suppose she recommended him. "I figured on a German doing you good," I remember her saying.

With gin in one hand and dragon lilies in the other, I knocked on Bess' door at eight on the dot. She opened it with a lavish swipe of her arms – that Hollywood swish – and looked at me with dark, seductive eyes for a moment, a smile emerging over her face. She was also in evening dress, her hair was glistening, soft, buoyant, twisted up into a nest of tendrils, her cheeks red. She had some colour to her, some meat to her, although she was still slight, still youthful. Her youth was in her eyes, in her garrulous intensity – this is what had replaced her naivety, and it had replaced it in clods.

"What brings you here, Harold Buren?" she said with a smile.

I allowed myself a lopsided half smile and held out the gifts.

"Happy birthday, Bess," I said.

Her knees bent, she laughed, and hugged me tightly.

"I am so excited you're here," she said, and kissed me on the mouth. "The finest birthday present a girl could possibly hope for. Come in, come in." And she backed into the apartment – my old apartment – down the corridor, spinning halfway to lead me into the lounge. "Gin, gin, gin," she said as she headed straight for the drinks table. "I haven't had a drink all day. I've been waiting for you."

I didn't believe that for a moment. But she *was* sober.

"So what *is* for dinner?" I said as I examined the room for any significant changes in the time I had been gone. "You've decorated."

"I have to keep myself busy," she said. "And I have to keep up with the latest fashions."

"Is that right?"

The room was overwhelmingly white, powerfully so; it was like a surgical theatre. The dining table had white chairs and there were some white cushions on the white sofa.

"Is the latest fashion *heaven*, by any chance?" I said.

Bess turned and handed me a gibson.

"Ha! Celestial Chic! How did you guess?" she smiled, and rolled her eyes.

I took a sip of the drink. She had been abstaining that day no more than I had.

"When did you get back?" she said, and positioned herself, relaxed, onto the sofa, patting the seat next to her with the palm of her hand.

"Today," I said, taking the seat.

Bess put her feet up under her and faced me.

"And how was New York?"

"New York?"

"I spoke to that nurse you're so obviously sleeping with."

"She said she hadn't seen you. And I'm *not* sleeping with her."

"So you asked her if she'd seen me?"

"I ask everyone if they've seen you."

"Looking *out* for me or looking *after* me?"

I took two cigarettes from their case, lit them both with one light and handed one to Bess. She took a long drag.

"Both," I said.

She was watching me closely, examining my face, looking for changes in it.

"So, come on; what did you get up to? I haven't seen you in weeks."

I knew she had counted the days.

"It was business. Very tedious."

I took another sip of my drink and flicked ash into the tray at my elbow.

"It can't be much more tedious than my life," she said.

"Have you been working on your book?"

Bess looked across the room to a stack of bound papers by the fireplace.

"If by that you mean burning it," she said.

"I would like to read it one day before you burn the whole thing."

Bess looked at me. She took a breath, as if changing gear, took a drag of her cigarette, finished her drink. "I thought you might have gone after him," she said.

She stood and went back over to the drinks table.

"It was just business," I said.

She looked at me over her shoulder, her smooth white jawline resting on her collar bone.

"Looking for Piers is your business, too," she said.

I looked into my glass, swished the remnants in a circle with a flick of the wrist and necked it. I stood.

"It was the other business," I said. "The one that pays for everything."

"I know," said Bess, with the tender soft voice of a child.

She turned and took the empty glass out of my hand.

"You didn't say what we were having for dinner," I said.

Bess handed me a fresh drink.

"Chicken," she said.

"I don't smell anything," I said.

"It's being delivered. A friend of mine. The chef from Chez Francoise. It *is* my birthday."

I nodded and retook my seat.

"You have everything under control," I said.

"Is that so unusual for me to have everything under control?" Bess said, a mischievous, catty look in her eye.

"I didn't say that."

"You didn't have to," she said.

I sighed.

"I was hoping we could enjoy this evening," I said.

"I have every intention of enjoying this evening," she said.

"Maybe without Piers being here," I said.

Bess' eyes narrowed.

"Can you not help being a shit?" she said.

I looked at her. What was I supposed to say to her? It always came back to this; to Piers. The subject was tireless to her. Bess saw no-one, did nothing. She lived within the walls I had donated to her. She pretended to write a book. The book about Piers. That was all she said it was. She never went any further. It was her way of trapping us all in the past.

"I thought about Piers, yes," I said. "Of course I did."

"And?"

"I still think he could come back one day."

Bess softened. I offered myself up as an ally of passion when it came to Piers. I lied to Bess every day. Some days I could see she believed me, other days I could see she simply preferred to believe me. Piers, it seemed, was both the enemy outside and the sustenance within. I had spent so long, after what I did in Setubal, on the edge of reason, on the very edge of a new understanding. Those lies I did not know I could live with; they became a new skin to me. Lies could be powerful tools. Piers was dead, but Bess did not know – and even better: she *would not* believe it. Every molecule of her being was dedicated to his existence. In this way lies could become a truth all of their own.

I patted the seat next to me with the palm of my hand. Bess broke a half-smile and sat down.

"I have been working on my book, you know," she said.

I put my arm around her and she nestled into my shoulder, holding her drink steady.

"I've been thinking a lot about Monroe recently," she said.

I held still.

"I haven't thought of him in a long time," I said.

"It doesn't bring me much joy to think of him, I have to say."

"An unpleasant man," I said.

"Did they ever find him?" Bess said.

For a short time, Bess had been quietly obsessed with the small notice in The Times that declared the search for Ki Monroe. Local Portuguese police had been careful to note he was very much the kind of man one might expect to run off, to live freely. Millie, it seemed, had been unable to convince anyone that the opposite was true. Monroe was misunderstood, she testified. He always came back.

I knew that Bess' suspicion was that Monroe had gone off to be with Piers. All I could do was profess, without giving up any reasoning other than 'instinct', that she was very wrong about this.

"If you ask me Monroe has come to no good walking home drunk one night."

"I wouldn't wish that on him."

Bess had nothing to add. Yet again it was hope getting the better of her.

Bess reclined and gazed into the middle distance.

"We would spend weekends at the Monroe farm; you remember?" she said. "Millie and I would go walking, or take their children outside to play – Millie was a warm soul, a mother through and through; how she put up with that man I do not know. They – Piers and Monroe – would sit up into the night talking – those two African voices punching and spitting into the candlelight." Bess moved her drink and cigarette through the air matching the rhythms of her speech. "You could hear them through the walls. Dostoevsky – that name always meant the volume would go up; they were both becoming obsessed with Dostoevsky." She giggled. "You know, they talked of him so loud and so often that Monroe's youngest daughter named their cat Doctor Efsky?" She took a long drag on her cigarette as she reflected on the joke. "Millie and I just rolled our eyes at the sound of it. And the debates would turn to politics. Monroe would lecture Piers on the Kulaks in Russia and what had happened to them. Communism was fierce, was a beast. They would shout, drink. The whole farmhouse would stink of pipe smoke and sweat and candle wax."

Piers had never been political. This was his education. The damn Latimer cottage. He was perhaps an aesthete – or an aesthete-in-the-making – but his devotion to poetry meant there was very little time to dedicate to too much else. His intelligence meant that he was aware of the wider world, clear about who was doing what and to whom; but I would never have seen him as a crusader, a burning vigilante on the international stage. This was the only truth I had to come to terms with in the years since finding out how Piers had died. My brother, the poet, died in battle. Would knowing that have helped Bess? I am sure it would have dragged her down, confused her to death.

"I never thought of Piers as a political animal," I said.

"He only ever was when he was with *that* bastard."

It was heart-breaking that this was not true, that this was the man she thought she knew, that she had manufactured for the sake of her own grief.

Bess scowled and greedily finished her drink. She held her empty glass out to me. "Your turn," she said.

"G's and T from now on or you won't make dinner," I said, and took it from her dainty grasp.

"I'm just over-excited. I haven't seen you in so long."

"I'm flattered," I said, standing. I looked back to her small, pretty, girlish face, the big eyes, the quaint jaw-line. "And I missed you, too, of course."

Bess grinned.

"Oh, you don't mind me talking about Piers do you?" she said, happily.

With my back to her I said nothing.

"I know exactly how pathetic I can sound."

"He was your husband," I said.

"And he was *your* brother," she called, sounding a little drunk – the solidarity was her angle now.

I said nothing; just mixed the drinks, dropping an equal amount of tonic into each gin – ice, gin, tonic, lemon; always in that order.

"Nostalgia can be corrosive in some instances," I said, handing her the drink and sitting on the sofa. Bess stretched her legs over my lap and transferred her cigarette to my mouth, taking a fresh one from her case and lighting it. I tilted my head back and took a deep drag, placed my drink on a coaster on the table next to the sofa and unbuttoned my tie.

"Oh, don't be like that," said Bess in a baby voice.

"It's not like I haven't told you a thousand times," I said.

"But I like your speaking voice."

"Then perhaps I'll record it on a reel to reel for you."

"You would do that?"

"What is technology for if not to relieve some of the burden of our daily lives?"

"Who was it who said that?"

Bess laughed; a cool easy laugh.

I stubbed out my cigarette and began to massage her foot.

"You look tired," she said. "All that traveling. You know you didn't have to come over. We could have done this another night."

We paused for a moment and looked at each other. Bess had

330

a composed look to her – her outdoor look; her party look – the make-up that kept her emptiness hidden from the outside world. Her eyelids were low, her lips were pursed, her chin delicate.

"I'm sorry," she said. "We can just sit in silence if you like? I forget sometimes that you have a life away from me."

She meant this with an edge of sarcasm that on darker days would have been more forthright. I ignored it.

"I don't have a life away from you, Bess; I have this life and then I have some other things I have to do."

"O," she gasped, and slung her head back. "Don't stop rubbing my feet," she said.

After a moment she said, as if from nowhere, her head still away from me and her eyes still closed: "Tell me about Africa. Tell me about where you and Piers are from."

She had never really mentioned Africa before. There had been times when I had wondered if this omission from our constant raking of the past had had some significance.

"You really want to know about Africa?" I said.

The softness in Bess' face subsided. Her eyes drifted off to the side. I resumed the foot-massage.

"I've never been, you know?" she said.

"I know," I said.

"You should take me to all the places Piers would have loved to see!"

"To Africa?"

We may even find him, I imagined her saying next. But we would not find him away from the hillside where he died. I closed my eyes and saw Monroe's blood-soaked body supine on the deck of the boat.

"I may not be your best guide for that," I said, calmly.

Bess fell silent once again.

"I was hoping you'd say yes," she said after a moment.

I opened my eyes.

"You're serious?"

"I've been meaning to bring it up for some time," she said.

Bess removed her feet from my working hands, bent her legs from off my lap and placed her feet firmly on the rug. She sat up and put her elbow on her knee, her forehead in her hand. Her hair fell about her face.

I realised then that a rehearsed approach had gone off-plan.

"Of course we could go to Africa," I said.

She stood and took her glass over to the drinks table.

"Forget I said anything," she said.

"I thought you were joking." I straightened myself, crossed my legs formally.

"Maybe I was," she said.

"We could take a trip later in the summer," I said. "I haven't been there for a long time. I haven't even thought about the place in decades. It would be nice to go back and see the old farm."

"The summer is no good to me," Bess said, turning back to me, composed once more.

"I can't go now, Bess."

"Well, it's now or never; I may not want to go by the end of the summer. The summer is not usually kind to me."

She returned to the sofa. I looked at my empty glass and then at her full one.

"Sometimes I feel like I could kill," she said, coolly. "Just to let some air out of me, that black thick air – like it would release a tap."

Perhaps it was the talk of Dostoevsky seeping through the walls of the Monroe farmhouse that had put such thoughts in Bess' brain. Monroe had morphed into Raskolnikov before her eyes, stooping in doorways in his bushman's hat, smoke spiralling up and out from his quellazaire. But Raskolnikov could never have been a poet. Wasn't the truth that they were all Alexei Ivanovich in those days, the roving gambler? And they all emerged from the 'thirties in the same why that Dostoevky's gambler emerged from his own light-heartedness; broken, corrupted. At the beginning of Dostoevsky's book, *The Gambler* (I read it once on the train to Berlin in the mid-thirties), Ivanovich asks of his European counterparts, all bloated moneyed wanderers, all idle in their repose, "So everyone here is in expectation?" I could see them all – Monroe, Latimer, Bess, Madeleine, Matilda, Piers, myself – every damn one of us – waiting, ignorant of our own desire for some drama. And Monroe was a man of action; there was, no doubt, a central truth to the myth of the man. Monroe had not seemed a brute to me in those days, and even less of a dim plotter, a conniving slave to the bright promises of ordeal. No, he was more than that. Mephistopheles and Robin Goodfellow combined. He was a man grown of the dust.

There was a knock at the door and Bess threw her arms in the air.

"Ah, my chef-in-shining-armour," she said, and darted out of the room.

She returned with three young men trailing behind her, each dressed in black tie and waistcoat, each with two dishes. She ushered them to the dining table, where they prepared the delivery as if it was a restaurant table.

"That is a lot of food," I said, standing back admiring the waiters' fastidiousness.

"It is a birthday feast," said Bess.

As the waiters arranged the table, Bess put some music on the dansette – that cloudy French jazz she had a liking for. I remember so clearly the way she moved in time with the saxophone to the table, her dress swaying, her hips swaying.

She lifted her fork and circled it above the plate. "You may think I should have ordered the steak," she said. "But he does something to the chicken – I'm not entirely sure what, but ginger is involved."

"Shouldn't we eat the first course first?" I said.

"I suggest we concentrate on the best food and work our way outwards," Bess smiled, and dug her fork into the moist golden back of the chicken breast.

I lightly shrugged and followed.

Bess was able to live a life of miniscule indulgence. The trust-fund I had set up for her was modest by her own demand, and it was spent on gin and dresses. Little else interested her. Her books came from the library, her pampering was limited in need due to her natural beauty. She simply had moments when she realised that having no faith in money, having no love for it, meant that she could treat it with no respect.

"One day I'd like to sit in one of your meetings," she said.

"You would?"

Bess rocked back and laughed in her chair.

"You're the richest man in the world, Harold Buren; everyone must sit in those meetings completely terrified of you."

I offered a gesture; a dipping of the corners of my mouth, the eyebrows inched upward.

"I'm just saying it's odd," she went on; "Piers used to say how scary you were. I've never seen it."

"He did?"

I spoke slowly. After a few mouths of chicken, and a few forks of vegetables, Bess had leaned back in her chair and lit a cigarette, now she was sitting side-on to the dining table, her smoking-arm arched in a triangle along the line of the chair back and up to her mouth, her jawline was straight and sharp. The night was drifting onward, I noticed, timeless, as it did on those evenings at Bess' place.

"What is it Piers said about me?" I said.

"I think he always imagined you as a shadow, actually," Bess said, her body rigid in her smoking pose.

"And what does that mean?"

"You know what it means."

I returned to my food.

"The stonecutter," I said under my breath.

"That's a crude way of putting it," said Bess.

"He never brought that up with me."

"Oh, Hal; when did you ever talk about anything with him? He had to infer everything about you. We *all* did. We all *do*."

Bess dropped the pose, her thin eyebrows raised, as if she had been sitting for a painting, and she rolled her bottom around in her seat.

"I'm just saying he would have been proud of you," she said. "For the way you have looked after us all. He probably *is* proud of you; wherever he is."

Bess liked to do that – drop in a reference to Piers' *animam iam absentibus*. She looked for a change of expression in my face.

"I just cannot imagine how impressive you would look standing at the head of a conference table talking about whatever it is you talk about."

"Money?"

She laughed a short sharp yelp. "Exactly!"

"I am the great all-knowing," I said, smiling, indulging Bess in her mischievous mood.

"So, what is it you talk about?" she said.

I put down my knife and fork.

"You really want to know?"

Bess looked into my eyes with a brash intensity.

"What were you doing in New York?" she said.

I returned the gaze, or tried to. I dabbed the corners of my

335

mouth with my napkin. On the tip of my tongue I was about to tell her the truth. I sat back and looked over to the far side of the room. Monroe came back to me, the blood, the eyes.

"I told you," I said.

"I think you were looking for Piers," she said.

"It's been twenty years, Bess," I said; "I think he does not want to be found."

"But you cannot let it go. Just like I cannot let it go."

"You cannot let it go, Bess? Then what has been stopping *you* going to find him all these years?"

Bess had never had that question thrown back at her before. She had no response. We both knew that the next phase of this limbo was unknowable and that there was a chance Hell was the other realm.

I took a cigarette from its case and lit it. I looked around the room, at the whiteness of it, like a lunatic asylum, not heaven at all. Bess had tried to bleach everything pure in Piers' absence, and now in my absence, too.

"I am back now, Bess; you don't have to do this," I said.

"Do what?"

I lingered on the tapping of my cigarette into the ashtray.

"Punish me," I said, slowly.

I could see a tear come to her eyes.

We have all made our sacrifices, and we have all said our goodbyes, I thought but did not say. All accept Bess. The world had sunk into a vast plain of dirt and rot all around her and she had gone on regardless. Wars raged and she said nothing. Death was on hold while Piers was missing. Some days I admired her for it, some days I found myself just as frozen in a state of nothingness. How different things could have been – that was almost a mantra during some periods. Bess the frozen. Bess the godly, unforgiving of mankind's pettiness. The truth was, I feared, she had learned this from my brother.

Things might have been no different at all had Piers lived and remained with his wife. Piers had missed out on all of this mess by going and getting himself killed, sure; but who would my brother be now?

How the dead benefit from never having to answer questions that age asks. I have never known a single young radical who did not end up either dead or a conservative. To spend years building wealth, comfort, stability, only to argue oneself out of it all for the benefit of ungrateful strangers.

I had been nothing but an observer, I always told myself. I was lucky I had never had to change my own position on anything. Piers was lucky in this respect also, never having to explain to his unborn children how poetry failed to save the world. Was that what Bess was doing now? Keeping poetry in a zoo? Tie it to a post. Piers was alive as long as the lie of poetry was breathing in her house. Those walls of lies, those barricades, battlements of lies. Neither Bess nor Piers had had to make decisions like I had; never had to do terrible things for the greater good. All Piers had was the golden robes of youth to colour people's memory of him. What did I have? That silence. Poetry versus silence.

"It's not true that I never talked to him about anything," I said, feeling like giving something up to quieten the tension.

"Everything about you extolls the power of suggestion," said Bess.

I said nothing to that.

"You can't even tell me what your business trip involved," she said. "You weren't working the whole time while you were there, were you? Did you meet anyone? Any holiday romance?"

I smiled slightly.

"You see," said Bess. "This is you and me. Not everything has to be so dark."

I lit a cigarette.

"There is always someone," Bess went on. "That's what holidays are for. You know I know of at least three of my lady friends who go abroad just to fuck the waiters. Foreign waiters, apparently, make up in the cock department what they lack in personal hygiene."

I wanted to tell her that something had happened on my business trip. But nothing had. Life was quiet. That was the truth. And every time I came back from a trip we would go through these motions. If I had told her the truth when I murdered Monroe everything would be clear now, everything would be clean. Instead we were destined to live the pantomime.

"Let me clear this all up and we'll get properly drunk," I said, and stood to collect the plates.

And I left her at the table, the air swirling around her.

I took the plates into the kitchen and stacked them, food still on them, into the sink. The music became louder in the other room and I heard Bess call something.

"I've been reading the Bible," she was saying.

I thought of Bess' birthday the previous year. We had driven to Winchester to see Jane Austen's grave. At the time Bess was going through a period of morbid literary fascinations. She had spent quite some time travelling to see the resting places of writers she admired. She had felt uneasy about leering at the Austen plaque in the cathedral – "Once you're buried, one clump of dirt is very much like any other," she had said, the both of us stood before the marble memorial; "but to be entombed below a church. There is something sinister about that; as if they *finally* have you."

"And why does the House of God need a tourist attraction, anyway?" she said, her head tilting back as her eye-line followed the ornamental carvings up to the ceiling. "Is the lure of God *only* not enough?"

338

"Maybe you shouldn't shout such things," I had said, keeping an eye out for clergy.

"Why do you care?" she said.

"It's just a matter of respect," I said.

Bess shrugged.

"What would you have done if you'd been born in a time when religion went unquestioned," she asked.

"Has it ever gone unquestioned?"

"I mean when nobody was an atheist."

"Is that how you see me? An atheist?"

"Well, you are godless, aren't you?"

"Damn, Bess, if you haven't just condemned me for eternity."

She laughed, but I wasn't entirely joking, and her laughter echoed throughout the vastness of the cathedral. Many years ago, when we were children, she had come into a room at the Radnor cottage and asked me why I told Piers stories about ancient myths. A precocious question, of course, but one I felt she wanted to ask again and again at regular intervals of our existence together.

She called from the lounge once more, "I said, I've been reading the Bible recently."

I leaned against the doorframe and sucked slowly on my cigarette. Bess was sitting on the floor, her skirts about her like petals, flipping through jazz records.

"You've been looking for God?" I said.

"More seeing if he's left me any messages," she smiled.

"And has he?"

"I don't think it was written for me."

"You know the Bible makes you morbid, Bess," I said, walking slowly into the room and lowering myself onto the floor opposite her.

"Well, I don't see why everybody else is entitled to salvation and I'm not," she said.

"And who said you weren't entitled to salvation?"

The music on the record player burst into life, a saxophone gurgled and emerged into a stream, a beam, of light. Bess began to bob her head in time with the wooden, hollow, thudding bass-line. She swayed and rose, levitated it seemed, to her feet, gazing at me. She held out her arms.

"Dance with me," she said. "Let's see if the Devil holds anything for me."

"I don't dance," I said, not getting up. "You know that."

Bess shrugged and began to move around the room regardless, at first not taking her gaze from me but then losing herself in the smooth, rolling, hollering of the music. Her arms began to swing – she was the woodland nymph called to the duty of the modern world; awkward, pleasing, innocent, lost, found, glorious, lurching, discovering. I began to laugh but she paid no attention and my laughter faded, and I just watched her move. It was a devilish dance indeed; her hips moving, her thin pale thighs jutting out, her toes pointing. The music throbbed, stabbed into the air, the golden saxophone line glistening, flying.

I stood and backed up to the wall, leaned, watched her move, this child in a woman's body. That's what she was, wasn't it? She had been given no time to grow, she had halted when she met Piers, and had prepared herself to move through life with him, and then she had lost him and she had stopped altogether. Her body had not. Or rather the truths of her skin and flesh had not stopped. With her had I stopped, also? I watched her move, spin, fling herself around the room. What had happened in Setubal meant nothing now, not when with Bess. I had done it for her.

Bess twisted and turned and flew around the room and music huffed and blew and glided and shuddered and just as it stopped Bess came toward me and when the music halted she threw herself at my feet with all the drama, one bent leg, one straight, her hair over her face, her lips at my shoe. The music ended, the stylus tripped upon the centre of the record. I looked down at her. She was perfectly still. I bent my knees, lowered myself, took her by the shoulders. She looked into my eyes, tears filling hers, and she leaned in and kissed me on the lips, hard but sensually. I pulled back. Bess looked over my face.

"Wouldn't we be happy together?" she said.

I stood and lifted her with me.

"We are happy," I said.

I walked her over to the sofa. She was drunk, exhausted – exhausted with life and with the evening.

"Take me to Spain," she said as she fell into the sofa.

I looked her up and down, her eyes half closed.

"First it's South Africa then it's Spain. You need to make up your mind."

"I want to go to Piers," she said, sleepily. "Why won't you help me?"

I took the white blanket that was folded on the arm rest of the sofa and spread it over her.

"I am helping you," I said.

"I don't trust you," she said, almost asleep.

I looked at her for a moment, watched her disappear into dream, her little mouth muttering something, her pale pretty face turning to the side. What's done is done, I decided. No-one would ever know, and no-one need ever know. Piers and Monroe were the past.

I stubbed out my cigarette and then hers, took my hat and coat and left her sleeping soundly on the sofa.

* * *

If ever I have been happy it was in those years when we lived away from the real world, as if we were protected by glass from the very molecules that made up the births, deaths and tragedies of the actual universe. It was as if we lived inside a radio wireless and we were the drama played out every afternoon. Bess held on to the hope of Piers' return like a child talks to a doll. And I held on to her like the mother of that child, happy to allow the doll to contain all of the childish pleasures that one day should belong to the adult version, and should be real and perilous. But no peril for us. No peril.

But there was a time when all that changed. Bess was feeling easier. She had been making friends. She had been working on her book and it was beginning to actually resemble a book. She went for walks in the park and she had coffee each morning in Sedgemoor's, just like in the old days. Business there seemed to be doing well off the back of a lick of paint. People were now well and truly out of the habits of rationing. A new decade hung in the air like a cloud about to burst. Bess smoked cigarettes whilst thinking about things like the curiosity of artificial milestones. Why should the end of a decade seem any more apt-a-time to readjust than any other day of the week? Why should she feel more at ease in nineteen-sixty than she did in 'fifty-nine? She had long ago shied away from those most likely to keep telling her to move on. She had moved on in a way, hadn't she? She was clear, full again; her healthy beauty returned, her drinking subdued, the heavy losses of battles and such behaviour lifted. She still drank too much, but she drank less than many of her friends, less than me, and she had survived her unbalance. Many had not.

"Nice to see you, Mrs Buren," said the waitress. "It's my favourite type of weather this morning."

Bess looked out of the window. It was cold, frosty, but the sun beat down upon the narrow Soho streets in icy waves.

"Mine too," said Bess.

"I was just saying this morning that we haven't seen Mr Buren with you for a while," said the waitress, referring to me.

"Well, he's meeting me this morning," said Bess. "He's found time for me in his busy schedule."

They smiled at each other

"Oh, good; it's always nice to see him," said the waitress, and moved on.

Bess smiled to herself.

It was then, in her contented state of mind, that she noticed the table next to her had a reserve sign on it.

"Shelagh?"

"Yes, ma'am?"

"Are you expecting some dignitaries in today?"

"Ma'am?"

"In all my years I have never seen a reserved table here."

"Well, you wouldn't have done unless you were in on this date of any year," said the waitress, not desisting from her duties. "A Mr Latimer comes in every year on this date and has one coffee and a cigarette. It's the anniversary of his wife's death, I'm told. He marks it here in the quietest of ways. She was a writer, if memory serves."

And Shelagh was gone into the back room.

Bess felt a strange tightness come to mind, a drawn out memory. It was not unpleasant, as such, but it felt dangerous; it came from a place built upon unsure foundations. Marshall Latimer would walk through that door at any moment and the links to the past would be reformed, and they would blind anyone unprepared.

She sat there for some time, drank more coffee, and when Marshall Latimer came in she said nothing. He was an old man now, and he walked with the stoop of a man ready for his last days – drearily comfortable with the natural cycle of things. He hung up his overcoat and took a seat at the reserved table. He sat opposite Bess, did not look at her, did not look up. The waitress went over to him.

"So good to see you, Mr Latimer," she said.

Latimer was grey-skinned and his gestures were slow. He had a long sad face, lined copiously, and even when he offered a genuine smile it hung loosely on his jaw.

"Thank you," he said.

"Will you be having your usual?"

"Yes, please – I'm sorry I've forgotten your name."

"Shelagh."

"Shelagh. That's right. A nice name."

He tapped his forehead with his fingertips. Bess felt strangely joyful at the presence of such a dear old man. He was very different to his late wife, she thought. But even now, in his gentle old age, he showed his dedication to her.

Bess decided to approach him.

"Excuse me, sir?" she said,

He looked up to her.

"My name is Bess Buren."

He smiled up to her.

"I'm so sorry to disturb you, but I knew your wife."

His face changed slightly, like a man realising his duty was not yet done.

Bess suddenly thought differently about taking the conversation further. How would she clarify their connection? Mentioning the Monroes, as the old man tried to remember his wife on the anniversary of her death, would be a cruel interjection.

"I just wanted to say how much I admired her, and how nice it is to meet you," she said, and went to move away.

"Wait," said Latimer.

Bess stopped.

"How did you know her?" he said.

"My husband was a poet," said Bess. "And she showed him great encouragement. We used to come here often."

Wistfully the old man said, "Yes; she had great affection for this place."

This, as fate would have it, was when I came in. I was in a rush and apologising for being late, taking my overcoat off mid-stride, and I only half-heard Bess when she said, "I'm so glad you made it, Hal; this is Charlotte Latimer's husband." And she held out an upturned palm toward the old man sitting at the table. I turned to face him as the introduction began to make sense to me.

"The doctor?" said Marshall Latimer.

I felt my face drop, I felt the blood drain away, as my hand continued to outstretch to the old man. Marshall did not take it.

"You're that doctor," he said again.

I was perfectly still, my mouth, which was about to smile, remained half-open.

"No," said Bess. "Hal is not a doctor."

She spoke down as if the old man was confused from senility.

"I know that now," said Latimer. "But I didn't at the time."

Bess looked at me and then at Latimer, and could see that the confusion was hers and hers alone.

"What is going on?" she said.

"This man came to my house many years ago to see my wife," Latimer said, his face very serious, but not angry. "She was very sick, and he pretended to be a doctor so he could see her."

"What is he talking about, Hal?" said Bess, and she nervously smiled at me.

I said nothing. I closed my eyes as the old man finished.

"I did not know until afterwards that he was an imposter. You were looking for your brother, if I remember rightly, Mr Buren. You came to ask my sick wife where your brother had gone."

The reality of the moment was bubbling up inside of Bess from somewhere it had always lain dormant. The truth was foaming up to her edges.

"And where was he?" she asked the old man, tears lining her eyes, she was shaking.

"Spain," said Latimer. "With Ki Monroe."

I felt a drop in my gut at the sound and on opening my eyes I just caught Bess running out the door. I looked down at the old man who leaned back with a broad look of satisfaction on his face as he sucked on his cigarette.

"I think that today I may have cake," he said.

I caught up to Bess in the park between the coffee shop and her apartment. She was in tears and would not stop walking. I called after her but she would not turn. I ran in front of her and stopped her in her tracks. The rain was falling now. Bess had left her coat in the coffee shop, and her hair stuck to her face.

"We need to talk," I said.

"No, we do not," said Bess. "We have done all the talking, Hal. You do the talking and I believe you; that's how it's worked up until now."

She moved to go past me but I grabbed her, and her face changed from taught sadness to a loose rage.

"You take your hands off me. You lied to me. You lied about everything."

"I only lied to protect you."

"I don't believe you."

"I went to Latimer, but I did not find Piers."

"I don't believe you."

"I did not find Piers."

"You wanted me for yourself?" she was as disgusted at the words coming out of her mouth as she was surprised at them.

"That is not it," I pleaded.

"Leave me alone, Hal. Just leave me alone."

And this time I allowed her to walk off across the park in the rain.

I did not see Bess again for a few months. I thought I would never see her again. But she knew I was not cruel enough to have lied to her so abruptly. I always had faith that in giving her the time she needed to forgive me I would see her again. I sat in that house with poor Matilda and waited.

It was difficult not to go to her. Some nights I had to all but lock myself in the house, have Maria hide the keys. But eventually Bess came to me.

I invited her in without a word. The house was silent, dark and cavernous.

"I came to tell you I've finished my book," she said.

I tried to hide my surprise but my eyebrows arched anyway.

"And a publisher wants it," she went on. "They're going to print twenty thousand copies and see what happens."

I invited her in to the parlour, but she did not take off her coat or hat and stood in the centre of the room with her gloves folded over her upturned palm.

"Can I fix you a drink?" I said. "We really should celebrate."

But my heart was not in the invitation; that much was obvious to the both of us.

"I cannot, I'm afraid. My editor is taking me out."

"I see."

"Don't you want to ask me if you're in it?"

I put my hands in my pockets.

"Am I?"

Bess smiled warmly but awkwardly. She looked a whole person, fresh, full, her lips glistened when she spoke and her teeth were a clean white, her eyes were luscious and quick.

"You are an important character," she said.

"And Piers?"

She looked down at her hands, her handbag draped over her forearm; she tapped her gloves twice in the palm of her hand.

"Oh," she said, "well, he's in it."

We stood in silence for a moment looking at each other.

"I have to go. I have a taxi waiting," she said. "I just thought I'd pop by and let you know the news."

I nodded my appreciation.

"How is Matilda?" she said.

"Fine."

I walked her to the door and as she stepped out into the cold evening air I said, "I forgot to ask what the book is called – I'll need to know in order to buy a copy."

Bess turned to me at the gate.

"It's called *The Stonecutter*," she said, and smiled.

I did not smile back.

✳ ✳ ✳

My health began to deteriorate.

I thought I was closing down, bit by bit. I thought I was going to be one of those men who died too young, in middle age, an abrupt ending just at the time when all those lessons begin to come in handy. Headaches; nausea, days on end spent in bed, in silence, staring into space. It felt as if my spirit had left and just my mind and body remained, abandoned on this dreaded mortal coil.

I thought of Bess constantly. I did not know what she thought of me, or what she had in store for me, or what she knew about Monroe or Piers. Every waking hour she was there and every waking hour it covered me like a cloud.

But my illnesses seemed to pass. Who does not go through life without some kind of physical setback? What had caused it? What had cured it? It had never seemed to matter.

I had seen a doctor who prescribed some migraine tablets which I didn't take. I do not believe in medication. So why go to the doctor? I wanted confirmation of the pain. I wanted a man with a deep voice of solace to tell me that chemicals were playing havoc inside of me, not that the Eumenides were prodding at me for my pagan sins. I had taken to sleeping on a cot in the corner of Matilda's room. She was better nowadays than she had been in years, leaving me to wonder if I had not gotten closer to her state than she had to sanity.

Bess' book came out and was a success. I wonder if you know of her writing? I cannot pretend the success of her book was not a surprise to me. I began to carry a copy around with me in my pocket and yet I could not bring myself to read it. I started to spend entire nights stood in the doorway of the building opposite Bess' apartment – still *my* apartment. It had come to that. I would look up at the window waiting for the

349

light to go off. I would walk the streets; sit in the park until the sun came up. I had stopped eating. I just drank steadily throughout the day.

And then one evening, Maria having gone home for the night, Matilda Buren died. Her wheezed breathing just ceased. I knelt at her bedside, leaned in to her. I had no memory of ever being so physically close to Matilda before that moment; I could have pursed my lips and kissed her neck – my breath moved her light, thin hair, the stale air, the shadows, her eyelids like crepe paper, her mouth open like a sand dune. The silence burst out of the room and migrated back to the veldt like a scream when she died.

I knelt at the bedside for an hour – two, was it? – running my eyes up and down her body, along her face – not touching her once. I looked down at the dragon's eye pendant around her neck; that jewel taken from the earth, cut from stone, a symbol of the Burens' journey, a reminder that we had come from the earth and that is where we would end up. I bent over, unclipped it and put it in my pocket.

I had been expecting something to blast me from my seat when this happened. I had been expecting the planets to shake. But I sat in the same silence I had been sitting in all my life. It was just me and Bess now, I thought. And I could not allow her to drift away.

I made my way across the city. Rain crashed down into the night, but it did not hurry me – I walked steadily, and knocked on Bess' door. She opened it and looked at me. Neither of us spoke – we both knew something was different. She stepped back – she was in an evening dress, just returned home from dinner – and I stepped in after her; my face was hard, sturdy. Her eyes were moist, her cheeks were full, her lips red upon that misty complexion of hers. I put my hands on her shoulders, protectively, warmly, and she looked up to me. My hands moved inwards toward her smooth throat, she looked nervous, frightened, my fingers touched behind her neck, my eyes were burning, her eyes were dark at the edges, bright at the centre, and just as I felt I would press her throat with my thumbs she moved forward and kissed me hard on the mouth. My loose grip loosened further still and she kissed me with more force, as if authority had passed between us through our lips, and then I responded kissing her and walked her slowly backwards, the two of us connected, up against the wall where we slowly slid down to the thick carpet of the parlour entrance. The kissing went on, Bess searching, her hands undoing my tie, pulling at it, scratching at it, and I pushed my hands along her stockings and in one reach tore off her panties, tore down her stockings – Bess moaned, breath untied – she pushed my shirt off my shoulders, the buttons shredded off, and she reached down to undo my belt. We connected with unerring naturalness – a beautiful, rugged, sombre tension in our limbs. I remember her lipstick faint from her lips across her cheek; I remember how she bit down on her bottom lip, and how her eyes rolled to their whites. And somehow I was behind her, then; her dress was torn, her hair flung about, and she held on with white knuckles to the doorframe and as I climaxed Bess pushed back, pushed back so hard that I lost my footing and I tumbled down, slid back onto the cold tiles of the hallway floor with a thud, and Bess turned and fell sideways propped up against the wall, her dress down, her hair across her face, and she was trying to catch her breath.

That fall, that ending, has stayed with me. Clumsy, comic, but something telling about the act between us.

We both stayed in our landed positions for a minute, catching our breath, not looking at each other. Bess then pushed her hair from her face and looked at me, sitting on the cold tiles of the hallway floor with my shirt buttons gone and my shirt down and hanging by the cuffs, my trousers around my ankles. I pulled my shirt on and tugged up my trousers. I looked at Bess, her face was plain, ruddy, but her eyes were blank. I stood up and pressed my damp hair back over my head. Bess watched me stand. She sat up, adjusted her torn and twisted dress and put her elbows on her knees, her spine up against the doorframe.

"I'm sorry I pushed you over," she said in a soft voice.

There was silence and then she smiled, and then I smiled also, and we both laughed freely, briefly; and then sadness came to both of our faces.

I said nothing. I tucked in my shirt and did up my trousers. I got to my feet, stepped forward, and stood over her.

"I got you a gift," I said.

Bess would not look up, her hair fallen over her face once more, the paleness of her skin white like scattered pins between her strands of hair.

I put my hand in my pocket and pulled out Matilda's dragon's eye pendant and held it up to Bess, the pendant hanging from my fist on the silver chain. Bess looked at it.

"It's your mother's," she said.

A tear tripped down Bess' cheek. She did not look at me.

"I want you to have it. A Buren should always carry it."

"What has happened, Hal?"

"Matilda died."

I knelt down in front of Bess and held the pendant up to the light. She looked at me, her pretty pale face, soft, warm, her cheeks glowing, her lips full.

"When?" she said through tears.

"This evening. In her sleep."

Bess wiped her eyes. She kissed me on the mouth and said, "I am so sorry."

352

I kissed her back.

"I failed her," I whispered. "I failed you both."

Bess held me by the head and we spoke closely into one another's ears.

"Did you go and look for him?" she said.

"Yes," I said.

Now was the time to unburden myself.

"Did you find him?"

"No."

"Did you follow the Monroes to Barcelona?"

I had to think. No, that wasn't right.

"No; they went to Toledo. They had a place in Toledo."

And Bess sighed, she even smiled, her eyes closed, and she kissed me on the neck, on the cheek.

Had she asked me any other questions, I would have answered, the two of us crumpled on the floor in the doorway. But she did not ask any more questions. She took me to bed where I slept as if I had not slept in years.

I awoke late the next day and Bess was gone. And her things were gone.

That was the last time I saw her. I sold the apartment soon after I realised she was gone for good. There was a danger it would have turned into a museum. I was, of course, tempted to track her. I even wrote to Darabont.

I drew up large plans and systems to track her. I was always certain that the moment she discovered I had killed Monroe I would have a knock on the door. But it never came. And months became years became decades and life goes on. Life goes on.

QUIXOTE COUNTRY

✳ ✳ ✳

When I met you I was preparing to die.

My things were in order; I had made peace with Eumenides who refused to make peace with me. I had nothing to live for but the slow decline. What a strange thing the past is, the way we design it for ourselves, the way we use it for our own means. But it is a snake, a many-headed snake. A man of seventy, as I was when I first met you, has things in place. The regrets, the pride, the myths and the truths; they all sit in counsel on their designated thrones. And then you came into my life. Let me explain how everything changed at the very tip of my failed existence, like the glowing hurt at the hilt of a dagger.

Bess used to say things to me – she liked to talk about the make-up of the people in her story. "You have a devilish goodness," she said to me once. "You view the world as a non-participant," she said another time. "Your money, Hal; it has closed you off. And yet you don't use it, you just make it. It means nothing. What do you do? I mean what do you *do*? Have you set up a charity? You could set up a Utopia with all your money. Hitler needed the support of the desperate and cruel masses to build his hell on earth. All you needed was the investment of his kind. It could be invitation only. Raise Atlantis. I know how you sit on it all. It must be more money than the Bank of England shifts around. You're a miser, but not a precious one. It's a compulsive disinterest in the thing you're best at, I think; shaking hands, money-filled hands. That is the extent of your actions. Unless you get up to things I don't know about." I remember this speech so well. There were so many others.

Of Piers she once said: "If he were here now I would be repulsed by his divisions, and love him for them, too. He could not keep quiet, could not keep still, and yet essentially he was the same as you, Hal; a spirit, not a flesh and blood human. The both of you have haunted the lives of others. I hate you both for it, but that otherworldliness keeps me in the game, too. I am obsessed with the two of you. I fell in love with Piers, but my God, I need you no less. You are branches of the same tree. I always knew that. You have poetry, Hal; but Piers became englobed it, it became his bloodflow. I thought it was exciting to watch. Didn't we all? Those were heady times. We all had a part to play in that Soho pantomime. But this meaning-of-life bullshit, Hal; I have no time for it. I just wanted him to hold my hand forever. He wanted to discover the difference between myth and life. It ruined him. Where do I think he is? Part of me thinks he found his answers and is king of some tribe somewhere, blessing marriages and waging wars. Part of me thinks he's still looking, drunk in an isolated cabin having conversations with ghosts. What if he can't find his way home? He could be lost. Part of me thinks he's ashamed of his foolishness, of his betrayal. All of these parts. If I really knew him I'd know exactly what had happened to him. I could look up to the sky and see the messages he left for me there. Twenty years he's been gone. I know you better, Hal; and I don't know you at all, do I?"

On Matilda she noted it was the witchcraft that killed her. "She thought she cast a spell over people, but the spell was over herself. She'll be lucky to die in a bed and not tied to a stake; or, as she would have liked, nailed to a cross." She hated her? I think Bess could be bitter in those days, but she could not hate. It was that witchcraft which made her talk the way she did. "Matilda could not love. She was incapable of it. Some people are. And yet all around her was the necessity to love. That's what was so unbearable to her. That's what drove her mad."

Monroe was not the same type of creature was he? "I don't think Monroe ever wanted to hurt anybody, you know? I think he was trapped in his own circumstances. We don't always make our own circumstances. I liken him to the Minotaur. His labyrinth was his life. People would be sent in to confront him and he would swallow them up and spit out their bones. But if he could have made it out, what is there to suggest the Minotaur would have been a killer had he lived in the fields or the woods. I think Monroe is the most tragic of us all. He had to destroy the soul of his wife in order to keep his family. No man should be asked to do that."

In the middle-years she took to swishing her hair out of her face like Gloria Swanson did with cigarette smoke. "I am just the foothills of you all," she once declared to me across the dinner table. She laughed miserably. "It's you everybody looks to."

I don't know if she truly believed this or if it was a manifestation of her lingering despair. When she left she seemed close to a whole person. It was I who had taken to feeling lessened by events. What is the old monster who feeds on people's souls? Bess had that about her. That monster is tragic, is it not? Love makes us human, and the thing that stops that monster from being human is its curse of theft. The soul eater. I guess we'd all done it. Pass to the left. A curse, a myth, and a game. That sounds fitting.

Claus Julius came. Maria left when Matilda died and she sent the Bavarian. She did not want to watch me decline; Germans have no qualms about such things. He came and we locked ourselves into Claypole, into the labyrinth, as Bess might have it. Days turned to weeks, turned to months to years. I was waiting to die, only occasionally stopping to wonder why it was taking so long.

You know a part of what comes next. You know how you

and I met. You know now who I am and I know now who you are. We know about drama. You have your lessons tucked harshly into your belt. If I'm honest I can say I resent you the life you have to come. You are free. Free of all the people in this testament, but free of our century, too; free of the history that all this story weaves through.

✷ ✷ ✷

The ending here is where you come in, where you begin, really. You have your own story, one that perhaps you can tell me one day. But here I give you *my* ending, the one you know. It was 1977 when the letter arrived; the letter that took me back to Spain.

I stood motionless in the middle of the dirt-track street looking over the facade of the cantina I had come to find, the engine of the old battered taxi coughing and grunting behind me. The hollow breeze flapped through the heavy heat and lifted the dust down the long empty uneven thoroughfare that made up the main drag of the village. I took the crumpled letter from the pocket of my jacket and scanned it yet again. I looked to the door of the cantina, at the flaking blue pastel paint, and at the small smudged square windows in the face of the pock-marked whitewashed walls.

"Are you sure you have the right place? La Dama de las Colinas?" I said, bending down to the driver's open window. The driver grunted, rubbed his rough hands along the glistening silver bristles of his jaw, nodded, and pointed to the building.

The village was not what I had been expecting. It was derelict, a shanty town, a grubby regiment of decrepit stone buildings with corrugated tin hats. And the dry haze of dust throughout the air. I looked up and down the main drag again but still saw no sign of life. The village was sunk into the valley, the valley sunk between the hills.

I had changed since receiving the letter, like air had been breathed into me. I was sturdy again, my shoulders broad as they once had been, I had no stoop, no slowness; and even though the journey had been long and rough, and my bones were aching, my brow was matted in a cold sweat, I held my shape. The heat wheezed around me, the car engine grumbled.

361

"Money," the driver said sharply and lowered his arm out of the window like a drawer bridge.

The taxi pulled away scuffing dust into the air. The dry, wide silence of the Spanish desert returned.

It had been many years, but I could remember the Spanish sun, the way it bristled and shimmered and sunk into the dust. It seemed to reflect off nothing, but turned everything a murky golden.

The signatory of the letter in my pocket – the much studied behest – was Victoria Mancores. She had the soft steady hand of a careful correspondent. Every sentence had the crisp, cautious English of a second language, the taughtness of many painstaking drafts. I had doubted immediately that she was the solicitor she claimed to be. I have had a life of business with solicitors; I know their clotted forwardness. They do not write with such humanity, such pleading. No solicitor I have ever known has ever used a word in a letter that I have also seen in a poem. Lawyers use hard words. Victoria Mancores used soft ones, breathing ones.

You know the letter. *You* wrote it. Claiming to be the solicitor of Elisabeth Buren. She is dying, dying in the village of Las Dama de las Colinas. It means the "lady of the hills", you wrote. Located in the hills near Toledo. In the hot heart of La Mancha. Quixote country. *Spain and her dramas be damned*, I thought when I saw your letter.

I cupped my hands to the window of the cantina and peered in. Behind the counter I could see a girl in a blue cotton dress and white pinafore – a young woman, a teenager (eighteen I would find out later) – her black hair tied up in a bun, her long neck stretched out as she wiped down the worktops. She was pretty, but strong-looking, she had a straight mouth, and all the imperfections of a country girl; that type of beauty that had no knowledge of the trends of the encroaching cities; this girl had dark down in front of her ears, her teeth were neither straight nor particularly white, and she had creases in the skin between her eyebrows that faded up to her hair-line. That was the first time I laid eyes on you. Through the muted mistiness of the cantina window.

I tapped at the window and caught your attention. You came over, and bent to the smudged pane to get a better look at me; I thought you were preparing to shout at whoever was disturbing your routine – the dish rag in your hand was now clasped like a weapon, tight and slightly raised. But you lightened when you saw the unfamiliar face, the smartness, the foreigner. I even saw the beginnings of a surprised smile that came up and then faded. You disappeared out of sight for a moment before the pastel blue door opened and you stepped out onto the step.

"I am sorry to disturb you, senorita," I said, removing my hat. "I'm looking for someone."

This time you did smile. It was curious, with narrow eyes and a half-turn of the head, somewhat sad.

I scratched my neck and grinned incredulously at what I was about to say, my eyes glancing over the state of the cantina's façade. "I'm looking for a lawyer," I said.

You straightened, your brow creased as if you were translating what I had said in your mind.

"You are Harold Buren?" you said.

I feared on sight that you might have been the person who had written the letter. Lured by a child dabbling in adult games, I thought. I looked up and down the street once more. What was I doing here? Chasing after Bess still after all these years.

"You're Victoria Mancores?"

I inspected the name on the letter to ensure I had pronounced it correctly, but also to present the proof of your deception and the proof of my willing foolishness.

Your body language was interesting. You had strong shoulders, but they dipped and hung, and your long neck seemed stiff. You had not thought your game this far ahead, perhaps, I thought. Or if you had you had thought it out quite wrong; misunderstood the players.

"If you don't mind me saying you don't look much like a lawyer," I said.

"And you don't look much like a millionaire," you said.

Your English was good, but you delivered it after considerable thought. I was, and am, wary of such careful speakers, in any language. They have too much time to form their thoughts – they are more writers than speakers.

What was I thinking at that moment? That there was something you knew about me now; that the mention of Bess would be enough to drag me to any dead village on the planet without much question. I could see an evolution going on behind your eyes as you weighed up the situation to find that you had some control over it. You were not a natural at this, I figured. You were trying something out, dipping your toes. For some, I know, that first deception is born of desperation. It hadn't been the case with me, but it is with some. And there are those who get a taste for it and those who recoil at the experience. But even the negative can be euphoric. Getting what you want is the ultimate in value of any kind. Lying? Acting? Minor factors. But what was it you wanted? And what made you make that step to writing that letter? Had Bess put you up to it? That was the most likely scenario, I was thinking, stood in the street with the truth, I thought, in front of me – the young lady-in-waiting running errands for the queen of the desert dust. But there was no need for such enticements. The twenty-odd years since we had last seen each other marked nothing more than a pause in our story.

"You look tired," you said.

I *was* tired.

"Please come inside," you said.

"Are you going to explain all this?"

You smiled warmly and nodded.

The cantina was humid. The paint on the walls was fading, peeling, and the wooden chairs and tables were dotted around the room in strict formation in front of a small bar cluttered with cleaning paraphernalia.

You poured a glass of water from a jug on the bar and handed it to me.

"Here, drink this," you said with kindness.

I took it. My throat was dry, sharp, ridged. And, in the dimness of the cantina, I only noticed then that my head had been throbbing in the brightness of the day. I perched myself steadily onto the edge of a barstool and watched you move around the room.

"This is the hottest part of the day," you said, "You should be more careful."

"I'm fine," I said, unconvincingly.

I waited for some kind of explanation. What was this girl's connection to Bess? You were no con-artist after my money. There was nothing in place to elicit money from me. And besides, I didn't deal in money anymore. I was above all that, beyond it. So there was maybe something else to you.

I finished the glass of water and relaxed. You had me there. I could take the time to see what you were up to.

"You know Bess," I said.

"I know Bess," you said. "I have been taking her groceries since I was just a little girl."

"And you know me?" I said.

"We've been expecting you," you said.

I had nothing for that.

"Tell me," I said after a moment. "How is she? Is she here?"

You were very still. I wondered what you thought of me. A myth made real?

"She lives on the mountain," you said.

"You make a habit of tricking old men?"

"I have not tricked you," you said.

You looked offended, surprised.

"You're a lawyer?"

"I did not lie when I wrote that Bess is dying," you said.

It was a prick to the fabric of the air. Someone else saying her name. I had not heard it done in decades. It didn't seem to matter the context. *Bess is dying*. But the crux was the name not the decay. For a moment I thought only of Bess. The glorious Bess of her youth, the sad, forlorn Bess, the drunken Bess, the older Bess stood in her hat and coat in my parlour; it was all wrapped into a tight longing in my chest, a oneness of time made from the stretches of ages.

"I want to see her," I said.

"I didn't think you'd come," you said.

"Well, I'm here."

"It has been a long time since you two last talked."

"It does not feel quite so long now I'm here."

I had been trying to imagine what she looked like. A Greek princess, in robes and tiara, gliding along on a cloud. I laughed at that. I could not conjure up a real image.

"You are the brother of Piers," you said as if to confirm your thoughts out loud.

"Is that how Bess refers to me?" I said.

I had sounded bitter and your eyes dipped.

I took a slow breath.

"I am Piers' brother," I said.

"Her husband," you said.

"Yes; Piers was Bess' husband."

"He disappeared," you said, as if confirming further.

"A long time ago," I said, and took the last mouthful of water and swallowed it loudly. "It was very sad. Very sad indeed."

It seemed you did not know what else to say.

"Thank you for the water," I said.

"Would you like some more? It's important to keep hydrated – is that the word?"

"Senorita Mancores;" I stopped you; "I have paid you a fine compliment by going along with your games. Now I'd like some straight play."

I was leaning with my elbow on the bar, the cigarette turning to a curved ash baton between my fingers. The cold sweat to my brow had warmed, but I was feeling weak.

"We didn't think you'd come," you said again.

Your eyes moistened. You looked down at your feet.

"I am very sorry that I deceived you," you said. "But I felt I had to do what I must in order to get you here."

"You know some details of our friendship."

"I know that you looked after her when Piers went missing," you said, your voice full of verve, keen to establish yourself as my ally now. "I know what she owes you – what she feels she owes you."

This was new to me: *debt*. My eyes lingered on you. My mind had been preoccupied with lies, with deceits, with what Bess might know of my deceits. That had been the fill of years in her absence. Perhaps I was looking at you wrong. You had played a trick, yes; but for the good of an old woman? Extraordinary. I had come slightly out of fear. And now I was feeling overdressed, as if goodness was untouchable for a man of my station. Perhaps, at the time, that day when we met, you knew nothing of the details of the story; why Bess left, why Piers left. All those rusted memories of long dark years.

"I can take you to her," you said.

We took your jeep – more of a roofless truck. You drove with a masculine confidence. The truck jutted and growled as it made its way up the trail to Bess' house. You looked starched with energy out from the dull humid air of the cantina. Your hair, unfurled, pulled out behind you like the black tail of a dragon in flight. You were powerful-looking, had sturdy bones, a straight mouth and a firm round bosom.

"After the summer," you said, as I held on tightly to the frame of the truck, "I am going to Madrid to study."

"You are?"

"It was my father's dream," you said. "He passed away recently. Everything he did he did for me, for a better Spain. I owe it to him."

"Any chance you're going to study law?"

I thought I was being funny but the joke was lost in translation.

"I am going to become a journalist," you said, eyes on the road.

You had the fire to be a good one, I thought.

"Before he died my father said that soon Franco will be gone and Spain will be born again. So I should be there for the birth of the New Spain, ready and waiting. And Bess says all young women should live in a city."

"I can imagine Bess saying that," I said.

I looked out across the uneven rooftops of the village to the vast, beige plains of La Mancha beyond; flat, soft, velveteen. This, of course, I reminded myself, was Quixote country; stretching from the foothills of the Montes de Toledo to the western spurs of the Serrania de Cuenca. It was Quixote's playground of delusions; and there, in the distance, as the truck rattled up the hillside, I could see the black-hatted windmills of Molinos de Casuegra. Something about seeing them made Don Quixote's comical hallucination less humorous. The windmills were not so far from battle-hardened giants, after all. They were imposing, sentinel-like, lonely guards, waiting centuries. Had Quixote been the wise man after all? His ill-fitting old tin helmet, his nag, Sancho Panza loyally trotting alongside on his mule. The arms of the windmills were steady, motionless in the distance.

We pulled into the drive of Bess' house – a gravel entrance to a large, tiered garden that inclined with the gradient of the mountain side. The house itself was larger – grander – than it had looked from the foot of the mountain. It had a marble porch of Doric columns, and a veranda that formed an apron to the entire east-facing side. The porticos were overgrown – everything was overgrown; and I noticed your head bow a little as we sat in silence looking out to the sad smile of the building.

I opened the door of the car and stepped out, walking to the edge of the veranda. The sun hit down on me hard. The plains that stretched out from the foothills of the Monte de Toledo seemed to me like an ocean floor, sucked dry by the relentless sun. La Dama de las Colinas was small, an afterthought, a coral-like impermanence on the shoulder of the eternal Titan Earth – and the windmills lined along in the distance like a regiment of sharks waiting for the return of the waves. But it was so dry – a dryness that crackled in the air. It seemed curious, childish, but I could almost feel Bess was near. I took in a deep breath of the thin warm air and turned at the sound of your canvas shoes on the marble of the porch.

"Are you coming?" you said.

The warm air followed me into the opaque light of the villa like a mountain breath. The main hallway was stark, a Delacroix print was the only ornament – Bess liked the serious faces of his patriots, I was reminded. The interior of the villa was warm to the eye; terracotta walls and yellow tiles. You led the way, along the corridor into the lounge area. What the hallway boasted in minimalism, the lounge made up for in clutter. The room was large; a den of browns and shadow at the foot of three stone steps. To the right-hand side was an enormous bookcase that reached from floor to ceiling. The books were two-deep, and more were pressed into any available gap, books on their side, diagonally, uncomfortable-looking bends to spines and hardback covers. Books about the Renaissance, about Rome, about botany, sailing, the Karma Sutra – twenty, maybe thirty different editions in various languages – novels, modern, classic; shelves and shelves of poetry; cookbooks, religious essays, literary criticism. I scanned the titles, my eyes skipping around the collage of spines. Bess was not as alone as I had thought.

The rest of the room was given over to medleys of mismatching furniture; a heavy looking suite in deep ruby, and a large dining table up against the facing wall, decorated with a candelabra and stacks of old newspapers tied into bundles with twine. There was a large peacock armchair near a window, a small table next to it on which were a few volumes of poetry and an empty stained tea cup.

"She must be sleeping," you said, softly. "I will see if she is up to seeing you."

I took a moment to take in the atmosphere of the room; like a mausoleum, like a display in a gallery of the last hours of Dryden or some such glutinous poet. The shadows were thick, gloopy, dust covered everything in different depths.

You returned.

"I told her someone has come to see her," you said, reticently.

I stepped into the burgundy darkness of Bess' bedroom. The smell was heavy, stale, and the dust here also floated crumbling in the air. The room was cluttered: furniture – flea market stuff

– and books and newspapers, lamps, mirrors covered with scarfs, cups, a chamber pot, piles of clothes, coats, blankets. I did not even see the figure lying thin and motionless on the bed at first. She was still, her eyes were half-closed, her mouth half-open, her skin smooth and delicate-looking. This must be how you saw her every day. It was Bess, less bright and formidable than she had been, but still Bess; now old, tired, beautiful and grim in equal measure, both parts fighting for control of the inner and outer-her. Her hair was still dark and thick – the Spanish sun did not allow women to go thin up there – and for every inch of her face there was a youthfulness in it. But age had encased that youthfulness, strapped back that beauty. And her illness floated about her like the dust. Death lingered. O, my poor Bess; to fight this way.

"Bess," I said, hearing the age in my own voice. "It's me."

She focussed her green eyes, her lips patted together once, twice.

"Hal?" she said.

"Yes," I said.

The faintest of smiles emerged on her thin dry lips. And then it dropped.

She muttered something, mouthed it. She seemed confused, almost frightened. I knew then that she had played no part in Victoria's letter.

I took another step closer to her.

"Victoria, the girl from the cantina, sent for me," I said.

With a wave of youthful energy Bess rolled her eyes and said, "How am I to ever trust anyone?"

I smiled, sadly. Everything I had imagined her to be crumbled from me now. I could not remember a single thought in the lead up to this encounter, a single presumption, a single dashed painting of the Bess I expected, the one I had compiled from assumptions. She was this figure on the bed, had always been. She was the creature in this dark musty room, she had always been.

I moved a stack of books from a small velvet-covered chair and sat close to the bed.

"So, you didn't want to see me, then?" I said flatly.

Bess smiled weakly and turned her head away from me.

"Ha!" she said. "You must have had some ideas about me."

I said nothing; I held my hat in one hand and ran my fingers of the other around the brim.

"Of course," I said eventually.

Bess turned her face back to me. It was a hard look and seemed to take much from her to give it.

"Hal Buren," she said, thoughtfully. "I suppose this was bound to happen."

"I suppose so."

I looked at her lying still on the bed, and thought of her for a moment lying by the lakeside when we were very young – children – I was ten or eleven, she a toddler – at the Radnor cottage. It was something in her eye that was eternal; it had been there then and it was here now. A knowing. I wanted to ask her if she knew of my deceits; the ones I have explained to you. I wanted to ask her, it was clear to me now, if she had always known. And I could see in her lingering gaze, the one examining every millimetre of my face, that the answer was near her surface, and that she carried the answer with her everywhere. But I could say nothing. And she said nothing. And we sat in the darkness of that musty room for some time in silence, staring at each other, communicating as a painting does to a viewer.

"I'm not usually this pathetic," she said, finally. "I had a very late night. And I'm very old."

"Not that old," I said.

I smiled at her but she did not return it.

"Younger than you," she said. "Well, you were always destined to outlive everyone. Like a fucking cockroach."

I looked at her, like a doll with a human head, her arms out straight, thin and criss-crossed with creases.

"How long have you lived here?" I said.

"I came here soon after I left London," she said.

I looked around the room.

"Why here?"

"It seemed the end of the world," she said.

"And you just decided to stay?"

I rolled my bottom lip over my mouth.

"What have *you* been waiting for?" she said.

"I suppose I was frightened."

"You mean you suspect I'd discovered the truth?"

I nodded slightly.

Bess said nothing; she breathed deeply, heavily, as if a weight was on her chest.

The encounter was like a memory to me; the past, in its viscous globe of remembering, was a moment now to touch and explore. It was bleak and spasmodic, blurred in dimness, as if underwater, slow, creeping, effortful. There were silences that perhaps lasted for minutes upon minutes, some that snapped back into life. There were sentences which disappeared into smoke, exchanges that were gone before they had been completed. It was like a heavy hand crawling along the keys of a piano, from bass note to bass note, creeping, lumbering.

"I've been reading a great deal about forgiveness lately," Bess said. "The philosophy of it is riddled with disingenuousness, you know? There is always a reward for it – somewhere far off, like the Kingdom of Heaven. Piers would have wanted me to forgive you. He loved you without question, you know? So, if I was to offer you the hand of friendship, Hal, I would be doing nothing but hoping Piers was looking down on us and smiling. His wife and his brother finally reconciled."

"I realise I made mistakes, Bess," I said feebly.

"He's not looking down on us, Hal. He's dust and bones somewhere. If I could have buried him maybe I could have forgiven you."

I looked down at the floor and gave a short sharp nod.

"I can't ask you why you did what you did," she said.

I looked at her eyes, glistening, moist and bright.

"I don't know what you think you know," I said.

"Give me the honour of allowing me to forget you exist, Hal Buren," she said, and she closed her eyes once more.

"I went to look for Piers," I said, "and I discovered he had been killed, and I kept the truth from you. I lied to protect you. To protect you as I had promised Piers I would do."

Was this the truth? It is what I said.

More silence, as if the air had grown dead between us.

"Why did you come to see me?" she said after a while.

I sat back in the crooked chair.

"I didn't want to never see you again," I said.

"Liar," Bess croaked. "You thought you were coming for forgiveness, didn't you?"

She coughed.

I could not help but smile to myself; Bess was strong – the creep of death couldn't mute her. She pushed herself up onto her elbows, her face sagged, looked much older now, and her hair fell draped over her shoulders.

"You are a coward," she said. "You are a *coward*."

She slowly lowered herself back to the pillow, turned her head away from me once more.

I knew she was wrong. And then I knew that she had only the bones of the story of my deceit. I was no coward. Crooked maybe; a vagrant, a black arrow. But not a coward. The things

I had done in order to keep my secret. The things I had done in order to protect Bess from the reality. She had forgotten much of our time together. Memory is a fluctuating narrative, untrustworthy and in love with fiction. In it we see what we need, not what is true. I was no coward.

"I wanted to see you, Bess," I said, "Not for forgiveness."

"Then why?"

"I wanted you to know that I did not hate you, that I did not hide things from you out of cruelty."

She turned to face me, her eyes moist, and in a soft, fragile voice she said, "You know sometimes here I feel like I'm living in a cave, a dark and damp cave with moisture dripping from the walls and just one dimple of light in the far distance. I feel like I'm drowning in the darkness and that light is my air. I feel like I am alone in the damp and the dark. And then I remember that story you used to tell me of when you were a small child on your parents' farm and you fell down the well that was in the yard. And you were down there for hours – or was it days! – before one of the servants came to fetch water and you saw his face in the light and you called to him and he lowered the pail to lift you out. And you'd tell how you did not call for help until you saw his face in the small circle of light that looked up to the sky. You just sat in the water with your arms around your knees and looked up, waiting. And I remember you saying that as time went on you honestly couldn't remember whether you'd fallen down that well or whether you'd climbed down it, down those damp dark walls."

"I still don't remember," I said, my voice dry.

"I don't know how you ended up down there, Hal, but sometimes I question how you got out."

I thought of saying goodbye, but certain finalities go beyond such words. I looked down at her. Bess' speech had taken such delicate energies out of her. She looked vacated. And within that hollow skin I thought for a minute I could see a flickering light of truth coming out through her eyes, a moment when everything could be laid out bare, when all could be given a new realm in which to exist, one without all of the cumulative errors of the human world. We could tell each other everything, live untainted together for the first time, without heroes and without villains. So this is what the final act looks like, I thought. And I saw a *lie* within her, as decrepit as the one I had carried; a lie as solid as my own, glowing red in the moisture of her eyes.

Bess had over-reached, and she began to cough heartily, hacking, her pink tongue curling out from behind her lips. Hearing this from the other room, you entered in a hurry and comforted Bess, gave her some water, held a cloth to her face to catch the red-tinged sputum, as you had no doubt done a thousand times before; and eventually, as I watched with my back to the wall, Bess coughed until she passed out and you laid her head carefully back upon the pillow.

I followed the palpable trail of fresh air out to the veranda. You followed shortly after.

"Bess has always been like a mother to me," you said. You had been crying. "She and my father were very close when my mother died."

"They were together?" I asked.

You looked at me, your face hardening at my directness.

"It was when I was a little girl," you said. "It ended long before I ever met her. And it wasn't an affair. My mother was already in her grave. My father moved us here from Bilbao and that's how he met Bess. She was alone."

The sun was silently fierce now. My mouth was very dry, my forehead cold with sweat. My legs were tired, meagre; I sat on one of the rusting iron garden chairs. Dabbing my forehead once again with my handkerchief, I took some deep breaths.

"Do you know how Bess found out about all this?" I said.

You smiled sadly, pushed your long dark hair behind your ears and looked down to the floor. Your tears had stopped.

"Does it matter?" you said.

"At my age it is difficult to always tell."

You paused, looked back out over the vista.

"She had a letter from Millie Monroe."

The name was a thud inside of me.

"Bess used to read it often," you went on. "She would sometimes read it aloud to see if she had missed something. Millie Monroe said that many years previous, when her husband was alive, you had visited them and her husband had told you everything; how Piers had died in Castile. You had known all along."

Your eyes locked on me; not harshly, not cruelly, but openly and sympathetically. I felt sick, pale, burning from my core to the cold outer shell.

"I didn't know about any letter," I said.

But that didn't seem to matter.

"Mr Buren; you do not look good," you said. "Come inside out of the sun and I will get you a glass of water."

"Victoria; is there something I need to know?" I said.

"Like what?"

"Is there something Bess is not telling me?"

You stood.

"You mean is she keeping something from you?"

"Yes."

"Could you blame her if there was?" you said.

You were already walking back toward the entrance of the house.

I stood slowly and looked up at the sun.

You were gone inside.

I tingled, my fingertips were numb. Bess was dying in that villa. She was dying with something she wanted me to know – I could see it in her.

I remember my hands were unsteady. I remember examining them, front and back. The skin was tanned, tea-coloured, but translucent; the wrinkles across the back now so condensed that they formed a vast smoothness all of their own, like a mosaic.

After two steps toward the house the numbness in my fingertips turned to an electric rash, it spread upward, and then my shoulder banged into a heavy wide pain, my breath chugged, I bent over and vomited, fell to my knees, the ground became a spiral, and the heat of the sun became cold on me, my face hit the floor, and everything went dark.

✸ ✸ ✸

I awoke from what seemed a bottomless sleep, my body aching, stiff, old, got-at; my surroundings formless, off-white, like the insides of a cloud. What had I been dreaming of? My whole life in a confused bundle, the good and the bad and the never to be forgot. I did not know where I was, but that smell of hospital was the same the world over – unless it was a morgue.

I took a moment, kept still, and remembered being at Bess' house in the hills, and there was something of Spain as well as hospital to the smell of the place I was in now; something sweet, something warm. I tilted my head slightly. My eyes were frosted over. There was the outline of a window – a square filled with yellowed light – and I could see the mahogany of a bedside table. And the outline of a figure reclining in a seat. The figure stirred and came forward. I could see now it was you. And I remembered everything that got me into this blank white room. Leaning over, you padded my brow with a cold damp cloth; a low smile emerged on your face.

"You had us worried for a moment, Mr Buren," you said.

I tried to focus, my eyes fighting against the endless magnolia of the ceiling. The last thing I remembered was the dirt on my cheek, on my lips, as I coughed into the floor.

I felt angry, ended. Before then I had not spent a day in hospital in my life.

"You stay calm, Mr Buren," you said. "I'll go and get a nurse."

I searched for you with my hand. I wanted you to stay. I wanted you to stop calling me Mr Buren, and I wanted you to just sit with me.

"The doctors say it was just exhaustion," you said.

My mind crawled to a clearer place – I began to make out

the shapes of the room; flowers, the window, the door. My mouth was dry, as if lined with paper.

My vision was demisting; the white walls reforming.

After a short while you returned with a nurse; a slim, humourless young girl who patted about, took some notes from the machinery I was attached to, said some things in Spanish to you, and left the room once more.

"The nurse says you will be fine," you translated. "You need fluids and plenty of rest. You are a very lucky man."

You had added the last line yourself.

You looked casual, tired, relieved. I remember there was something about you there and then. Next to the nurse you did not look Spanish – *you* looked invested in Spain, not the other way around.

You brought your seat closer to the bedside and sat down. I could see clearer now – a private room, small but comfortable, and it looked out to a sheen blue sky.

"You've been out for a couple of days," you said. "It was very worrying."

I looked over your face; the darkness, the kind browns and charcoal rings around your eyes. You hair was tied back just as it was when I first saw you through the grimy mist of the cantina window. You looked like Bess; the jawline so sure and gentle, those eyes moist and alert. You were tall, yes, you had strong shoulders and a straight mouth; there was something masculine, powerful about you, something that Bess did not possess. But your core was deeply beautiful, sensual, kind and knowing. Something strange occurred to me, right then in the silence between us; one of those strange ideas that comes out of the fog of such a sleep, something that came from an unknowable place deep within, something known beyond knowledge. I looked you over and you noticed and you began to blush.

"What is it?"

"You remind me of your mother," I said. I remember the words being as unusual to me as they clearly were to you.

You frowned, lightly; obviously dismissing my words as those of a delirious old man.

We were close to each other now and spoke in whispers.

"You did not know my mother," you said, and you smiled kindly, condescendingly.

I was lucid, although would not have seemed it on the outside, my ashen skin and old wrinkled appearance. I caught myself; halted the progress of the idea I was contemplating: although I already had no need for contemplating. I knew what I knew, grown upwards and outwards from the deepest sleep. I had been visited in the dream. I had no recollection of the visitation, but I had been left with a revelation. I knew to the depths of my rotten soul that you were Bess' daughter, and she had never even told you.

"I mean I can imagine how beautiful your mother must have been from looking at you," I said. "She would have been so proud."

Still with a confused look, you smiled at me and pulled the edge of the blanket a few inches up my chest.

"What a kind thing to say," you said.

As the days went on you stayed close and looked after me, helped me regain my strength.

"I keep thinking of those two old battle-hardened friends, Adams and Jefferson," I said.

"Who are they?" you said.

"They were American presidents," I said. "They were the oldest of friends, bonded by experience – even though they'd fallen out numerous times. They'd even stood against each other in elections. They signed the Declaration of Independence together and they both died fifty years later to the day of

381

adding their signature to that document, miles apart, in different states; each talking of the other on their deathbeds. Like Bess and I."

"You shouldn't talk that way," you said.

"You don't think the symmetry is beautiful?"

"For historians, maybe," you said.

It kept with me, that overwhelming feeling in Bess' room on the hillside that she was positioning herself for the last laugh, the last great act of the play. I could see it in the old woman's eyes, and it was in the tone of her voice. Bess knew everything. And, unbeknownst to you, you were part of the scheme.

"I'm feeling much better," I said.

"You are looking on the mend," you said.

I looked up to you. Your eyes were sorry. You went to sit back in the chair, bending forward as you did so, and that's when I saw the pendant around your neck as it fell from the v-line of your blouse. Why had I not noticed it before? I went cold. It was the dragon's eye pendant I had taken from Matilda and given to Bess. It glistened.

"That pendant," I said.

Having not noticed it had slipped out of your top, you smiled at it and held it up to the light.

"It is pretty, isn't it?" you said.

Your smile was nostalgic, proud, warm.

"Where did you get it?"

"It was my father's," you said slowly.

"Your father gave you that?"

You smiled, still looking at the pendant.

"All I have of my parents is this pendant. It is a dragon's eye pendant, you see? It is meant to remind me where I came from, and what we all owe the earth."

You leaned in toward me and held it out on the end of its chain for me to see. But I already knew it was the very same pendant. I did not follow your admiring gaze to the stone, but I examined you close up. Bess' daughter; and mine also.

"It is your father's pendant," I said again, but lowly, almost whispered.

"Are you okay?" you said.

"I am fine," I said distantly. "I need a glass of water."

You lifted the empty jug from the bedside and took it to the sink by the door to refill.

"No," I said. "I need to rest, to sleep."

You could see something had changed, it was obvious, but you nodded and collected your things, said you would return tomorrow morning after you opened the cantina. You held the pendant that hung from around your neck, rubbed it between your thumb and forefinger, and your words fell out of your mouth in a sprig.

I sunk into the pillows, closed my eyes and rested my head. My mind would not rest, however.

✳ ✳ ✳

The next day – I had barely slept – you came in with fresh flowers and set about arranging them at the window sill as you had done the day before; methodical, tactful, inch by inch you aligned each deep green stem with the next, each fragrant bud with its neighbour. I watched you, watched the concentration on your face.

"You should be a florist," I said. "Or a horticulturalist."

"You're awake."

"I didn't sleep an awful lot," I said.

"Anything wrong? You are not in pain, are you?"

"No, I am not in pain."

You perched yourself on the corner of the bed pushing your long dark hair behind your shoulders.

"You have done a wonderful job with the flowers since I have been here," I said.

I spoke with a new found intimacy toward you, and you seemed to respond to it.

"I used to help Bess in her garden," you said.

"How is Bess?"

You shrugged.

"She spends most of her time sleeping. She is worried about you, though."

"What do you know of your mother?" I said.

You looked at me sharply. But this is what you had come back for, wasn't it? Something that had happened the previous day had run like ink on blotting paper deep inside of you.

"What has she got to do with this?" you said.

"Do you have pictures of her?"

"I have no picture."

You said this with sadness, yes, but something was taking over; a life-long curiosity awakening. Something had never

384

seemed quite right to you. The sadness could wait. Here something was happening.

"How did she die?" I said.

"She drowned."

You told me that your father had brought you to La Mancha as a baby after your mother had drowned in Bilbao. La Damas de las Colinas was his home town. He had left to fight during the war, but while he was away, fighting in Valencia, he had learned of the massacre in his village. When it was time to return, he could not do it. He could not have made real what he had imagined in his mind. It would have destroyed him. So he wandered, looked for a new life, and came to Bilboa where he learned to fish. He met your mother, a local girl, and when she died – you could never be sure of the details: had you ever asked? – your father realised that misery was not geographic, but it was human, and he came home to La Damas de las Colinas. Nobody had known your mother in the village.

"Bess had known her," you said, defensively, knowingly. "She told me she was beautiful and loving."

You were childlike when you said this, as if regressing to your indoctrination. But you recognised all of these things, didn't you? The game was up for us all by this point.

When you left that day, filled with the realisation that Bess was your mother, silently defiant to this truth, and refusing to accept that she had lied to you, created a backstory, created a tragic princess as your mother, a Dido of the crashing waves, I watched you from the window walking down the driveway of the hospital grounds toward the exit, through the delicate piles of leaves at the side of the path. I saw you stop, stand still and then place yourself on a bench where your head seemed to drop into your hands. My daughter? Could it be? The pendant was proof enough without the feeling I felt in my gut when I was with you.

My daughter. This knowledge, this full-stop to a life of pauses and errors, did not shock me, but rather it let me loose over my own past. Your existence, if I may examine myself for a moment, means that everything has been worth it, doesn't it? Surely it means *that* at the very least. I was enmeshed in my own time, and from my sins you have come. You told me you had planned on being a journalist: the new generation's freedom fighter. Information, and the truth of it, will be the greatest weapon of your era. It will not be gas chambers or bombs, but newspapers and cameras. Go to them, Victoria. You are to sculpt a beautiful century for your children, *My Victoria*; the battlefields of my own time have cleared the way for you.

I looked down at the drip in the back of my hand. It was coming soon, your opportunity. And you had benefitted from never knowing me. But maybe I could do something that would help you now. Maybe I could do some good. And perhaps that had been Bess' plan all along, to bring me in at the eleventh hour, and to poke and prod at my sense of fatality, and my sense of creation, and my sense of ecclesiastical revolutions. The water pours into the sea. We survive only for those who come after.

If you did come back to the hospital I was unaware of it because I checked out later that day and took a taxi back to my hotel. The air was thick and I couldn't get away from a feeling that everybody was watching me, as if my early departure from the house of well-being had left me with an unearthly glow, or a distinct powerful aroma. I kept thinking over in my mind how you could finally be the goodness that my life had always lacked. I had perhaps been robbed of it, but it had been an inside job, hadn't it? I had opened the door for the thieves.

I sat in the armchair by the window, looking out to the

Alcazar – a fortress impregnable to everything including time – and to the noises of the city outside. I began to doze.

Why had I not gone straight to Bess from leaving the hospital? I wanted to be sure that my far-fetched summation held together. If this story tells you anything it is that I am not a man to act rashly. You were my daughter. You knew this, somewhere down inside. We shared atomic structure after all; those atoms would recognise their relatives and shudder, just as mine had done when I first saw you. A recognition sparked that was some way beneath an understanding of the brain. It *was* atomic, wasn't it, this push to resolution, to finality, to a place beyond remorse, crime and punishment. Constant was the internal pressure to put some things in order, to strive for that ultimate clarity that I could see now had evaded me all my life. Why had you summoned me? Duty? You had called it that – bring resolution to a part of Bess' life that seemed repairable to you. A good deed. But what was it really? Ask yourself this. You suspected her lies, and you suspected my presence – the liar of liars – would open something up. When I realised this, I realised how brilliant you were, how unlike your parents you were. You were – *are* – bold and brave. To be sure of yourself and compassionate at the same time is a rare thing in this world.

A jazz band played in the bar down the street. I had slept most of the afternoon. My whiskey had gone unfinished, the ice melted, a beige circle had burned into the table top. The music reminded me of that French music Piers and Bess used to listen to. I thought about my brother with a clarity I had not enjoyed in decades. I thought about his sharp eyes and his energetic lips, always talking, always watching. I thought about Bess and her devotion, her beauty of the soul, her kindness. I thought about Matilda in her white lace, I thought of Monroe and his blood-red eyes. I thought of you, an unknowable light. I thought of Bess, seeing her own daughter every day and living in the shadow of the fictitious mother she gave you. And I thought of Victoria the New, Victoria the future of the whole rotten world.

I kept thinking of you as I dressed and freshened the next morning, slowly, and I kept thinking of you as my taxi rattled its way out of Toledo and onward along the track to La Damas de las Colinas until the village was coming into view at the foot of the mountains. The little rooftops, the houses on the hillside, flung up the ground like dice, and there was Bess' place in the far distance, a speck.

I considered this upcoming encounter. They were the thoughts of a man returning to the scene of his own death. And I had been sure I had died when I hit that dirt. It had not been a terrible experience, once I had calmed and realised that *this was it*. I had thought of people whilst trying to catch my breath. I had thought of the moment when I was happiest and it had been in Darabont's arms. Revelations never cease. *Lover, whom the darkness so becomes that I rejoice to lie upon your breast and listen to the never-ending plaint which murmurs to itself in marble pools among the trees dishevelled by the wind.* Those lines came to me from Baudelaire. It was Darabont whom I had forsaken, and it was Bess who had fooled me into a *purgatorio*. And all the while I thought that it was I who was the cruel maker-of-worlds.

I walked slowly through the dark and humid villa, through the shadows and still-unmoved turrets of newspapers and books. I stood in the doorway of Bess' bedroom for a moment, looking at her lying there, asleep, her small chest rising and falling, breathing through her mouth, her head tilted back into the pillow. She looked like a little bird waiting to be fed, blind and knowledge-less. A curtain was half-pulled back from the window beyond her head and a shard of yellow light ran across the silvery skin of her face. I stepped in and as I moved toward the bed she stirred, her eyes blinking blackly at me.

She smiled weakly.

"I heard you fainted," she said.

"Apparently my body and mind do not agree on my age," I said.

"I really didn't think I'd see you again," she said. "I had visions of us dying at the same time – like Adams and Jefferson."

I pulled up a chair and placed myself next to the bed.

I looked at her straight in the eye, did not shift my gaze. I did not know how to begin and I could see in her feeble eyes, her fragile lips, that all was being said between us; my presence explained so much.

"I see," she said.

"I'm sorry about Piers," I said plainly. "I'm sorry I kept things from you. I thought it was for the best and I was wrong. I am afraid I may have wasted our lives."

Bess' face was expressionless; perhaps accept for a deep idea of exhaustion and relief.

"But it seems we may be even," I went on.

Her eyes closed softly.

"Victoria is your daughter," I said.

Bess said nothing.

"And she is my daughter too," I said.

A single tear came from the corner of her eye. She nodded unsteadily and turned her face back to the ceiling.

There was a pause between us.

"That is quite a trick you have played on the girl," I said.

Bess turned back to me, her face had succumbed to tears now, her eyes were moist, young with wetness.

"Have you told her?" she said.

"No. But I don't think she's completely blind to it."

389

"How did you know?" said Bess.

"The pendant."

"Of course," Bess closed her eyes again, tightly this time, as if reprimanding herself for such a mistake. "I never intended for her to meet you. But I wanted her to not be alone when I was gone."

"So you gave her Matilda's pendant?"

"I thought it may do something for her – give her some of your steel."

Bess dried her tears and looked at me.

"Monroe," she said. "I could never believe it of you. But it was as plain as the nose on your face. I chose to ignore it. Millie's letter meant that I could no longer play that game. I was always ashamed of myself for it, anyway." She smiled again, from behind the tears, her face so pretty and pale. "You did it for me, didn't you? The goodness and the badness."

"I told myself I did it for you," I said. "I was convinced I was doing everything for you. But who can say?"

"Are you going to tell Victoria?"

"I don't know."

"Hal," said Bess, her eyes almost closed again now, her voice weak.

"Yes?"

"I don't want you to apologise for keeping what you kept from me. My life is not a regret. Victoria is a wonderful young woman and she came out of all of this. You should be proud of her."

I put my hand on Bess' forearm, so cold and thin.

She told me that she had learned of Piers' death from Millie, and she had been looking for La Damas de las Colinas when she was pointed toward Miguel Mancores, a fisherman, yes, but one time he had been a soldier and a poet and philosopher. She had inside her a baby, and she wanted the child to be born in the dust in which Piers had perished.

"It sounds foolish now, to have come here and to have wanted that," she said. "But she reminds me a little of Piers. She is forthright. But she is not doomed."

"She is going to be a journalist," I said.

Bess smiled widely and began to cry. She nodded and I leaned forward and kissed her softly on the forehead.

"Our daughter," she whispered.

They had come to the village and bought the cantina, where Miguel made his living, and the two of them set about paying homage to the massacred. While Franco still governed a plaque or monument would have been impossible. But time finds a way to pay its own tributes.

"You must do something for me," your mother said. "You must make it up to *her*. You must ensure she is given the time to become the person she is destined to become."

I stayed with Bess in silence for some time until she fell to sleep. Her breathing was laboured, her eyes flickering underneath their thin lids. I watched over her. There was much I wanted to say, much I wanted to hear; but we had touched, we had removed the need for words, almost. As the evening drew in I carefully lay next to her, put my arm around her and ran my eyes slowly over the cold translucence of her skin, her neck, her lips, her cheeks. *How* I loved her, your mother; *how* I adored her, *how* I believed she was the essence of everything. I know now, as I sit in the dimness of this room, writing these sheets, handing them to Claus Julius, that it was Bess who was in control all along. She controlled me, my will. And however much she had manipulated me through our lives she did so because she was pure and I was corrupt and the corrupt should always be the pawns of the pure. I know that now. This manuscript is my truth, but it is hers, and it is testament to her authority in matters of the soul. It is as if every moment of my

391

life with her was one more strand in a tapestry that was leading to your life. Bess was intent on saving the world.

I dreamed about her when I too fell asleep. I dreamed about her ducking and weaving through crowds in Sedgemoor's, a drink in one hand, dancing around, her hair flashing, her smile bright. The mother of my child.

"Where is Piers?" she said with a wide intoxicated smile.

"He has left," I said.

"Then it is just the two of us," she said.

"We have to deal with whatever life throws at us."

"One day you'll write about all this," she said.

"*Me*? *Write*? Why would you say that?"

"Because you can't keep fooling yourself into thinking you are the opposite of Piers your entire life," she said. "Eventually you'll do what you were put on this earth to do."

"You think I have a calling?"

There was playfulness in this, almost sarcasm.

"I think we both could do better," she said.

Was this a dream, or was it a memory? And what is the difference? What is symbolic, and what is documentary?

In the morning when I awoke, the shard of light stretching across my eyes from the gap in the curtain, I could only think of young Bess. I took a moment to gather myself. It is unusual for me to dream so lucidly. That has been the case all my life. And on this occasion I had been so close to Bess in the dreams, so close to Piers, so close to those wonderful days before the war in Spain, that I was sad to wake up. I looked across and saw Bess, pale and still. I knew immediately she had gone. And the last conversation I had had with her was in a dream; the young, vibrant, essential Bess.

Epilogue

Unlike her biological father, it was not difficult to find information on Victoria Mancores. She was an award-winning journalist and editor in New York, and she was the totemic figure of her own magazine, *Aeon*. *Aeon* had won three Pulitzers and she herself was bedecked with international awards for her writing, her vision and her editorships. She had saved lives, brought down dictators, averted genocides. I could read the details of her life from the desk in my office.

In the early eighties she graduated from Madrid and went to Harvard grad school, from where she got a job at the publishing house Darabont and Klein. While there she wrote an article for *Vanity Fair*, "The Edge of Civilisation", where she detailed the massacre of forty women and children in the village of La Damas de las Colinas during the Spanish Civil War. I read the article. A magnificent piece of narrative journalism. It was the reason I decided to not use Hal Buren's manuscript, but to take it to her in New York. She would do better with it than I could hope to do.

She had indeed used Hal's money for good. It had set up the magazine; and the trust fund that had put her through university and grad school was now under her charge, and the Buren estate no longer trades arms and diamonds, but it trains journalists in the developing world, and campaigns for freedom of speech. It campaigns in opposition to lies, myths and propaganda.

I explained to Claus Julius what was in the pages of his old master's memoir. I told him that Hal Buren's daughter was the rightful owner of it. The old man solemnly agreed, and he allowed me to have it, to give to her, to hand over to her in person. So I took it to New York and met with Victoria in her office in Manhattan.

"I never spoke to Hal Buren after that afternoon in the hospital," she said to my surprise. "Of course, I knew the trust fund was his money, and when he died I was passed control of it all, a bequeathment steeped in secrecy. But uncovering secrets is my business, and he knew that."

"So he never told you what he hoped from you?" I said.

"No, he did not."

"I suppose he suspected he might corrupt your natural instincts."

She looked at me quizzically.

"I mean, you seem to have surpassed his hopes without him having to guide you," I said. I gestured to her surroundings, to the awards on the wall behind her desk, to the view from her office window out to the Manhattan skyline – a cliché of American success in one panoramic vista.

She smiled distantly and looked down at the tattered manuscript that sat between us on her desk.

"I have always wanted to write about all that," she said. "Things get in the way."

"Perhaps now is the time," I said.

"Personally? I feel it might be time. A new century approaches. We have hope."

Victoria Mancores spoke with a measured gravity that I had rarely encountered in my life. She seemed to have an inner knowledge, a foresight, like she was the only one in the room who had read the script all the way to the end. It was not confidence, it was awareness, pure and simple. When she spoke I felt everything was going to work out, that as long as people like her had power, the world would pull itself out of the grim trenches of its past, and now was the time to move on. I felt strengthened as I sat in her office looking out to the

Manhattan skyline, a monument to human constancy, as if it were forged there in the dawns of time.

She thanked me for bringing her the book (and she offered me a job at her journalism school in London, which I said I would think about). She looked at her father's testament with trepidation, but with strength. Perhaps Hal Buren had been right in what he thought; that everything had been worth it in the end.

What happened to the manuscript in the hands of Victoria Mancores? Well, she wrote the book. *My Father's Century*. And it won her many awards.

Acknowledgements

Eternal gratitude for faith and love and the compulsion to redraft: Sian Cox, Alex Ferris, Craig Haywood, Rob Dinsdale, Samantha Harvey, Colin Edwards, Richard Davies, Claire Houguez, Rob Jones, the team at Wales Arts Review, my always supportive parents and family, and, of course, my Amelia.